REJECTED BY THE ALPHA KING

THE ALPHA KING'S BREEDER
BOOK THIRTEEN

BELLA MOONDRAGON

For Paulie

CONTENTS

1

HE'S NOT THE ONE

BRIE

I CAN'T GET OUT OF THIS GOWN FAST ENOUGH.

I lean against the door of my bedroom to close it, praying the butter-white walls give me some sense of peace, but my heart is absolutely racing.

I rip at my bodice, cursing under my breath as the satin fabric snags and squeals instead of just–of just coming off. I can't breathe. I can't force a breath past the painful squeezing sensation echoing through my lungs.

I gasp, tugging at the fabric until the bodice finally gives way. I grip my knees, gulping down air. The room spins for several more seconds before slowing, but I feel...

Totally, completely overcome.

"This isn't happening," I rasp, rising up and leaning my weight against the door. "This isn't happening." I close my eyes against the view of the mountains peeking through the white curtains currently dancing in the warm breeze.

Only when I find it easier to breathe do I move from the door, stepping out of my dress until I'm in nothing but the tight shape-wear I stuffed myself in beneath. I wad the dress into a ball and thrust it into the very back of my closet, kicking shoes and old pairs of jeans over it, then strip out of my undergarments and hastily pull on my usual outfit—a pair of loose fitting cream colored trousers and a white, flowy button-down top, rolling up the cuffs. I secure the pants with a belt and stomp back into my bedroom, looking around like the man is going to be standing here, waiting for me. Waiting to claim me, to take me as his mate.

But I'm alone.

I sink in front of my vanity and make my hands busy pulling pins from my thick, chestnut brown hair. It falls in bouncy, heat-manipulated curls against my shoulders, rolling down my mid-back. I brush it thoroughly, ignoring the tightness plaguing my chest, until it shines and feels like silk between my fingers. I don a headband and scrub my face with makeup wipes until my freckles come out to play, and the dark circles under my eyes stare back at me through the mirror.

I sniffle, shaking my head as I roughly open and shut drawers and spread an assortment of lotions, serums, and salves on the vanity, then I begin to piece myself back together.

But my hands shake. My fingers tremble as I brush blush over my cheekbones. My skin pebbles against a sudden chill I can't find a reason for other than the strange, overwhelming sensation of feeling utterly, completely empty.

This isn't what it's supposed to feel like, is it? People talk about finding their mates all the time. Hell, there are reality TV shows about it playing on an endless loop. How do they describe it? Tasting color. Feeling like you've never once felt whole until you see them for the first time?

I feel… terror. Dread. Worry. All bad things that tangle and yank at my chest until I find myself breathless once again.

This wasn't the plan. I'm supposed to find an Alpha—someone with a large, influential pack. Someone with power and sway that can stand at my side and pledge loyalty to my family, and my sister, when she ascends the throne, because she'll need all the support she can get when that time comes.

Not a… not a warrior.

I start to panic, clapping a hand over my chest to try to steady my thundering heart as the room starts to tilt to the side, spinning off its axis.

But the door to my room creeps open on a phantom wind.

"Go–go away, please," I murmur, swallowing back my feelings and burying them deep.

The faint clicking of a bell and tiny, soft footsteps trot in my direction. I glance at the pure white, exceedingly fluffy cat easing into the room, its sea-green eyes bright and swirling with magic. It wears a silver collar with a large moonstone around its neck, like usual.

I watch its reflection in the mirror as it prances across the room and hops on my bed without a care in the world and makes a show of getting comfortable.

"Please leave. I don't want company."

I fumble with a bottle of lotion and drop it on the ground. The cat yawns widely and rolls over onto its back, all four legs splayed in the air. I curse under my breath, bending down to fetch the bottle that has now rolled under the vanity, and when I sit up, the cat has been replaced by my sister, dressed in hot-pink pajamas made of velvet with her gorgeous dark hair pulled into a bun on the top of her head.

She toys with her collar–now a necklace–while smirking at my reflection.

"You don't get free rein of my room whenever you feel like it," I hiss.

"Don't get all pissy with me," she snorts, rolling her eyes as she flips to her stomach and props her chin on her fist. "You're the one who stormed out of that lovely little luncheon and got mom all in a tizzy. She called for a healer, you know, thinking you were having an aneurysm or something."

"I–I wasn't. It's just a migraine."

"Sure, sis," she sighs, kicking her legs. "What are you doing now?"

"I have a meeting this evening with the Beta's wife about the charity ball next month," I mumble, leaning toward the mirror to adjust my eyeliner.

"Well, I don't care about that–"

"Obviously–"

"Why are you up here picking at yourself instead of downstairs with Dad and Aris? You've been an absolute menace the past few days about how late they were returning, and now you've ghosted them completely."

"I needed a minute *alone*."

"Well, you missed Mom chewing out Captain Atrayis. Thankfully, his minions had already gotten their plates and went out on the veranda to enjoy the sun and their lunches–"

"Who?" I cut in, looking at her over her shoulder.

"*Captain Atrayis*," she sighs, her voice dripping with boredom. "I'm shocked you didn't recognize him, but I guess it has been years since–"

"Who are you talking about?"

"Logan, *duh*. The tall brute of a man that you took one look at and nearly fainted? Or was I just imagining that?"

It all comes back to me in a rush that leaves me breathless. She's right. I hadn't recognized him at first. He's no longer the gangly, incredibly serious and standoff-ish teenager who used to steer clear of us whenever we visited Silverhide when I was young.

He's sometimes referred to us as a cousin, but in reality, that couldn't be further from the truth. He's never made an effort to be a part of the family.

"Logan," I echo, swallowing hard. My chest aches again, worse than before, like my heart is trying to pull me from the room. "Why did Mom–why did she chew him out?"

"Why do you think?" she asks, shaking her head as I absently reach for my comb just to do something with my hands. "He's on leave for two weeks I guess and spending it here instead of visiting Aviva and Ryan in Silverhide. She told him he keeps breaking Aviva's heart and then turned to Dad and asked why he keeps Logan out in the field so often, knowing how Ryan and Aviva feel about it, and Dad told her to lay off, that they'd just returned from a six-week stint in Tarsian–" Maeve's words start to blur together as I needlessly comb my hair, unable to think past that... look he'd given me.

The way his pupils expanded at the same moment my entire body lurched in his direction against my will?

There's no way around this. There's nothing I can say to convince myself what I felt–what I'm feeling–wasn't the mate bond.

"And he just stood there and took it. He reminds me a lot of Dad, you know. Just... unfazeable."

"Mhmm." My comb clatters to the floor. I knock over several nail polish bottles in my haste to retrieve it.

"What is up with you?" Maeve laughs. "You're acting so weird–"

"I'm just–"

"It was that Alpha thing, wasn't it? That fucking prick–"

"Maeve–"

"He basically said he's not interested, and that his son wouldn't be interested, because you don't have powers. That's fucked up. Like, could they do better?"

I wince even though Maeve is in my corner. She doesn't understand. How could she?

"I mean, look at you!" She slides off the bed with cat-like grace, sauntering over to me. She runs her fingers through my hair, twisting the curls back in place before leaning down to rest her chin on the top of my head, staring at me through the mirror. "You're a fucking bombshell."

"You don't need to butter me up."

She sighs, frowning. "You know, you have the best rack in Eastonia. I wish you got more credit for that."

"Maeve!"

I swat her away, but now she's turning pink and giggling, "What? You know it's true. People journey to Crescent Falls to go under the knife for breasts like yours. I'm willing to bet people cut your pictures out of magazines and take them to the surgeons, saying, 'That's what I want!'"

"You're making my headache worse," I cut in, trying to glare, but my mouth ticks up into a smile.

"Meanwhile," she says dramatically, turning side to side in the mirror, "I have the body of a praying mantis."

"You're just very tall–"

"Anyway," she huffs, flopping back onto the bed. "Fuck these Alphas and their sons, and nephews, and uncles or whatever. I think you should just quit."

"You know I can't."

"Uh, yeah, you can. You're coming to Moonrise with me to serve as my second when the time comes, and when I'm queen, we won't need men. We'll… rule together–and eat chocolate and drink wine from sunup to sun down."

"You'll be very busy running a kingdom."

"Like it's hard?" She snorts a laugh, closing her eyes.

I watch her take a deep breath, smiling to myself. She has no idea I'm doing this for her. For all of them, actually.

It's just impossible to articulate why.

That horrible, twisting feeling of guilt settles in my belly, nearly erasing the pesky, throbbing ache in my chest. I feel suddenly torn in two different directions. My lips part as I slowly swivel in my stool to… tell her what happened, what I felt, how I found my mate but…

"Oh!" She yawns, stretching her arms above her head as she slumps into the mattress. "Dad wanted to talk to you."

"When?"

"Like, ten minutes ago. That's why I came up here."

"Ugh, Maeve," I grumble, rising and smoothing the wrinkles from my shirt. "Tell me these things, first, okay?" I hurry out of the room, skipping steps on my way down the winding stairs leading away from my bedroom in one of the many towers. I chose the room long ago, when I was a little girl and no longer afraid of the often dark hallways and the spooky spirit inhabiting our home. I have a view of the entire territory from up here. I get to watch the sun rise from one window and the sunset from another.

It's my own personal haven… when Maeve leaves me alone—which is rare.

Dad isn't in his office. I hurry through the hallways branching off the grand foyer, skidding to a halt when I notice a few of his Ghost warriors leaving through the front doors. They don't see me scanning their group, but my heart skips several beats before settling, and a feeling of relief washes over me.

Logan isn't here.

I should feel good about that, right?

I gather myself and race to my parents' dedicated wing of the castle, climbing another set of stairs, then another, until my legs burn, and my breath starts coming in short rasps.

I finally find Dad in a sitting room painted in dark blues, pouring himself a drink and running his fingers through his normally short cropped blond hair.

"You wanted to see me?" I gasp, bracing myself on the doorway.

He turns to me, scanning my face while furrowing his brow. "Did you run here?"

"Maeve failed to tell me you wanted to talk."

"It's not that serious." He motions to an armchair.

I hesitate, choosing to stay fixed to the doorframe. "What is it, then?"

"You haven't seen me in six weeks, and this is the welcome I get?" There's a teasing glint to his words, but his eyes remain serious.

I've always been close to Dad. He understands me. I'm drawn to his quiet, serious nature. It's a far cry from the drama of emotions in the castle when me, my sister, and my mom are left together without him as a buffer.

"What is it, Dad?"

"You're done with this… arranged marriage scheme you have going on."

I straighten, stealing my expression. "I'm not—It's not a scheme or an arrangement. No one's forcing me to do it. I need to find a husband—"

He shakes his head. "You don't."

"I do–"

"You're giving your mother heart palpitations, Brie. She won't admit it, but she's going insane trying to support you in this, and I can't take it anymore. I wasn't thrilled to begin with."

"I'm turning twenty-three this year."

"Does that matter?"

"I'm a princess and–"

"And a historian," he cuts in. "With a second degree in law–"

"To help Maeve–"

"You're smart and talented and have a future ahead of you–"

"I don't have powers," I cry out, then clasp my hand over my mouth.

It's rare for me to have emotional outbursts. I'm normally very good at keeping those feelings contained, but today has been anything but normal or routine. I feel completely out of it, like my brain has fallen from my skull and left the building with no plans to return.

Dad sighs heavily, looking at me with so much pity it makes me feel sick to my stomach.

"You're done, Brie. No more meetings with Alphas. No more sending your mom and grandma on escapades to match-make for you. In fact… I think you need a break."

"I already told Mom I'm not going to Crescent Falls this summer."

"You're right. You're not. You're going to Maatua, instead. A few weeks with your great-aunt Maddy will do you some good, I think. It's already been arranged. And," he says, sinking into a chair. "You'll have an escort to the island."

I grip the doorframe. *Please, Goddess, no…* "Who?"

2

A NEW ASSIGNMENT

I stare down at the words covering a single piece of pure-white paper. It's my evening ritual these days, especially when I'm closeted away in this room, in these barracks, instead of in a tent or curled up in a ball in my wolf form somewhere in the rural Roguelands or desert of Tarsian. I glance at the two other letters beside the paper, both neatly folded, Lexa and Nora's names written clearly, cleanly, just like Aviva expects.

She taught me how to read and write in the language of Eastonia and Crescent Falls. She was strict about it, forcing me to spend hours working on my penmanship, drilling the translations into my skull until I began to think and even dream in the language of my new home.

Even at nearly thirty, I still feel an obligation to check my work, to ensure the letters I send back to Silverhide are flawless, because Aviva still cares.

She's always cared about me.

I've failed her in so many ways.

9

I fold up the letter I intend to send out through the post to Silver-hide for Aviva, with a few lines for Ryan added toward the end, and put it in the stack.

The golden light of sunset filters through the blinds, casting shadows across my desk, across my fingers as I tap them on its surface.

I've spent my entire adult life training myself not to feel. Being a Ghost came naturally. I was made to do this–to be a warrior–to be merciless. But becoming a captain of this specialized army wasn't my intention.

I didn't mean to stay here this long.

I especially didn't intend to be here long enough to find my mate.

"Fuck," I murmur under my breath, running a down over my face. I scratch the stubble on my jaw, not used to it being there for this long. Three days of travel on patrol from Moonrise to Veiled Valley meant being in my wolf form for days on end, and stopping to keep myself groomed wasn't part of the plan.

Even Evander didn't care. We'd been in Tarsian for a month and a half, helping the Alpha King of Oasia deal with a rogue criminal enterprise that we believe has its fingers all over Eastonia.

I shouldn't be spending my days dealing with thieves. I should have gone back by now, to Emberfyll, if there's anything left of my homeland.

I grab the duffle bag that contains my entire life in its depths off the floor and toss it on the bed, reaching inside to find a change of clothes, when a knock sounds on the door.

"Come in," I grind out.

The door creaks as it opens, spilling fluorescent light across the worn, gray wood floorboards. Nothing about the barracks is luxurious, by any means. The rooms here are all the same. A bed, a dresser, a desk. Captains get better rooms. I have my own bathroom and don't have to sleep in a bunk bed, which is a blessing, I guess.

"Boss," Helion says with a smirk as he steps into the room.

"You're on leave," I remind him dryly. "You can drop the formalities."

Helion leans against the doorframe with his arms crossed over his white tank top. He's one of the young ones–twenty-five–full of spite and fire. I was like him once. Ready to burn the world at the slightest inconvenience.

That type of man is actually the kind of warrior I want in my ranks. They're the hardest to break but the best in situations that require immediate action, when the body must separate from the rational mind.

What kind of monster have I become?

"You doin' anything on your leave?" he asks.

I glance at him over my shoulder. "It's only two weeks. Didn't have much in mind."

"Not going to the Deadlands, then? I had it in mind to go with you, if so."

"Yeah, well… it would take four days to get there by car. Doesn't seem worth it." I walk to the closet and pull a towel off the shelf, draping it over my shoulder.

"I mean, let me know if you change your mind."

"What do you have to do in the Deadlands, Helion?" I ask, not necessarily curious. I'm willing to bet he's trying to go see some girl, like usual.

He purses his lips, his cheeks going a bit rosy. His dark brown hair and bright blue eyes make him look like some wealthy, privately educated Alpha or Beta's son from Crescent Falls… which is exactly what he is. His Wellington University sweatpants catch the light of the sunset as he props his thigh on the doorframe, smiling to himself. "Uh, there's a girl I've been trying to see."

I knew it. I smirk, shaking my head. "Good luck with that."

"I need more than luck on my side for this one. Her Dad's a patri-arch. I doubt I'll be able to get within a mile of her."

"Bring him a gift," I offer.

"What? Why?"

"Bring the man something valuable. He'll give you his daughter in return."

"Is that true?"

I smile to myself as I gather a change of clothes and my towel, and step past him through the door. "Yeah. It's how the Alpha King of the Deadlands ended up with his queen."

"Commander Aviva was given to him?"

"So the story goes."

I turn out of my room and walk steadily down the hallway toward the indoor gym, looking forward to a few hours of quiet where my mind will be focused on lifting weights instead of dragging me back to the luncheon a few hours ago.

Brie. I've known her since we were kids. I haven't seen her in many years, however. Of course, the family gathers once a year in Maatua for the Solstice, but I never went with Ryan, Aviva, and the girls. I kept everyone at arm's length, refusing to let myself get close. I loved them–still do. Ryan and Aviva are the closest thing I have to parents… and the thought of losing them like I lost my own flesh and blood family has made it impossible to give in.

Aviva inadvertently helped me find my purpose in life. Become a warrior. Learn to fight. Learn the history of this land. Make connections, climb the ranks.

Get a fucking boat and go home to take back what was stolen from my father.

I focus on that through deadlifts and squats, through bicep curls and intervals around the track. But when I sink to the floor two hours later, sweaty and exhausted, I catch my reflection in a mirror nearby and find my mind rushing back to the luncheon–and *her.*

Brie is *not* a little girl anymore. My memories of her from childhood are fractured and hazy. The full-bodied goddess in that satin dress that fit her so perfectly it could have been painted on was a stranger. Her thick, light brown hair and round, dark eyes drew me in, turning me inside out.

And when she looked at me, I felt it. That unearthly pull. That yanking of the threads binding us against my will.

The burying of roots to this kingdom, this continent, that I didn't need, nor want, to have.

She looked just as horrified as I felt.

I hang my head, panting as I try to catch my breath.

A few warriors come in and out of the gym. Life moves on around me as the sunset bleeds into full night. I eventually drag myself back to my room to shower. I ready a razor to shave my face but look at my reflection, deciding against it for some reason.

I'm sitting in the cafeteria finishing a late dinner when the main door to the room flies open, and everyone sitting nearby stands abruptly, all conversations coming to a screeching halt.

Evander walks in, alone, wearing a casual button up shirt and slacks. It's strange seeing our leader like this. Normally, he's dressed in all black with a sour, stern look on his face. Everyone stands at attention until he motions for them to sit, to relax, but no one is ever relaxed in his presence.

He walks in my direction. I sit, eyeing him wearily as he takes the seat across from mine and folds his hands on the table.

"Commander," I say, and I'm almost relieved he's here. Something must have happened. He must be sending me and my men out into the field again, thank the Goddess. I need the distraction. I need to put miles upon miles of distance between myself and Brie, his *daughter*.

The thought that he's here about the mate bond strikes me. I curl my hands into fists under the table, preparing for the worst.

"I understand you're on much needed leave," he says. "But I need your help with something. It's minor, but it will eat up the next two weeks of your time off."

"What is it?" I ask, relieved he didn't just ask if I'd given any thought to the *upcoming wedding*.

"My eldest daughter, Brie, is going to Maatua for a month. She can't handle the jump. It makes her violently ill and that would completely defeat the purpose of her vacation. So, she needs an escort, a guard, and I'd like you to be the one to take her there."

Fuck.

"Can I speak freely, sir?" I begin.

He searches my face, then nods.

"That's not a job for a captain."

"You're saying it's above your pay grade?" he jokes, which I'm not used to.

"I have two weeks to prepare my men for whatever field placement we have next."

"That can be taken care of otherwise, but right now, you're the only one I trust to get my daughter to Maatua safely, without incident."

"How?"

"Boat. A yacht, actually. She'll be the only guest, but it's manned by a crew of roughly twelve." He sighs, but his shoulders remain rigid. "As you know, this... rogue theft ring nonsense is all over Eastonia. We're no closer to finding the ringleader, and there have been a few incidents of wealthy young women being taken hostage for payment. I'm not dumb enough to think no one would try to do that to someone from our family."

Our family. He meant it, too. I'm part of this family, a fringe member, aren't I?

"You'll be paid handsomely, of course, on top of your salary as captain. And, you'll have another chance for leave when you return."

"You know I don't care about the leave aspect."

"Well, Aviva and Ryan do."

I drag my hands down my thighs. "When would she be leaving?"

"Tomorrow morning, before dawn. She'll need to be driven down to the river port. It's a day's travel up river to the oceanic port in Avalone where the yacht is waiting. It should be ready to disembark immediately once the two of you arrive."

I have no choice but to nod and accept the mission. But... "Is there any other reason you're asking me, personally, to do this?"

Evander purses his lips, thinking about it for a moment before replying, "Yes, actually. I could easily put a lower ranking warrior on this and not bat an eyelash, but Brie is... she's a little different. She needs a firmer hand."

A firmer hand to... what?

I don't ask aloud, but the comment sticks in my brain like glue for the rest of the night. I find myself staring out the window at the valley below, my gaze occasionally creeping toward the castle that hangs from the opposite mountainside, shimmering in the light of a full moon.

Spending a week at sea in a confined space with my mate was not in the cards.

This can't go on. I have to end it. For her sake—and mine.

I can't be tied down. Not now that I'm as close as ever to returning to Emberfyll to take back what was stolen from my father.

My title as Alpha King. My lands. My people.

But I can't force her away from hers.

3

REJECTION COMPLETE

BRIE

I LIKE TO THINK I'M A FAITHFUL BELIEVER IN THE MOON GODDESS. I never skip church. I celebrate Her holidays, say Her prayers, and dedicated at least ten years of my schooling to Her lore and scripture.

I squint at the sky through my window in the tower, frowning at the moon. She's up there laughing at me, isn't She? Is She entertained by my predicament? The mate bond She ordained to ruin my plans?

I sink onto the bench under the window and rest my arms on the windowsill, watching the clear, brilliant night sky slowly rotate over Veiled Valley. The buildings and bridges glisten in the moonlight, but across the lush, green valley, lights twinkle against a sea of emerald.

The Fortress, as my siblings and I have called it since we got a grasp on vocal vocabulary, is nothing more than a big, square, gray block built out of the far mountainside. I'm sure it was a foreboding, albeit lovely, sight to look at way back in the day, millennia ago, when it was built, but now I'm glaring at its twinkling lights and cursing the wolves who built it.

Within those gray walls rest the royal warriors of Veiled Valley–

those who are too young to have mates and family homes for themselves. Single men, mostly, I'm sure. I've never been inside.

But I know for a fact that Dad's little Ghost minions who don't go to visit family wherever they're from are being housed there this week while they're on leave.

That includes Logan.

I press my forehead against my arm and squeeze my eyes shut... but only for a moment. I'm pulled back to the view, taking it in, trying to force myself not to look at the barracks and ponder what room my stupid, unwanted mate is sleeping in tonight.

This is wildly unfair, in my humble opinion. Ever since I was a little girl, I've understood my true purpose in this family. I am here for Maeve. *She* is my purpose. Everything I've ever done is to make her ascension to her rightful throne easier on everyone.

I have a reputation to maintain, and that's grown harder over the past year with the tabloids running wild now that all of the royal cousins and siblings in my generation are coming of age.

I groan as I look down at the magazine on the far side of the bench. A picture of Blake, wearing sunglasses and a finely tailored button-up shirt, stares back at me. It's a paparazzi photo, of course. He was spotted leaving some exclusive nightclub with a random girl on his arm. He's the *It Boy* in Crescent Falls, every girl's celebrity crush.

I'm in the magazine, too, unfortunately. A picture of me in a sparkling gown last year at a gala held by my aunt Sarah, the Queen of Crescent Falls, takes up a corner section of a gossip article about what we're all up to–and with whom.

Maeve had raged when she brought it home, slamming it on the table so hard my lunch plate rattled as she furiously explained what had been written about me.

But I'm beyond being shocked. Having someone write that the dress was doing nothing for my exceedingly curvy body isn't anything new.

What was shocking, however, was the line about how it was rumored I'd been hunting for a husband, followed by a rumor that the crown princess of Veiled Valley was powerless, seemingly a plant to win public favor.

I tried to act unfazed, but the words stung.

It wasn't the writer's fault. Only a select few know I'm adopted. My parents and extended family want to keep it that way for my own sake… and this is why.

The older I get, the more my differences stand out when surrounded by powerful, magical family members.

I look up as the curtains swing closed on their own accord, followed by the soft squeal of the windows rolling shut. When I don't get up right away, the spirit of the castle gives me a little nudge by ripping the pillow I've been leaning against out from under me while simultaneously folding down the sheets and duvet on my bed, patting an imprint on my perfectly fluffed pillow.

"I'm not tired," I argue, but the magazine zips off the bench and roughly lands in the trash can next to my vanity. I smirk, rubbing my tired eyes. "I'll miss you, you know that? Maybe you should finally break free of these walls and come to Maatua with me. I think we both could use a vacation."

A soft rustling of air echoes around the room like a laugh.

I don't fall asleep until the early hours of morning, and even with only an hour of fitful, broken sleep, I'm up before the sun.

"It's only a month," Mom says, twirling one of the curls falling around my face around her finger. "You'll get a suntan and drink fruity drinks all day. Maddy has a wonderful library with all the books you could ever want. You'll come home feeling refreshed, and Maeve and I already have plans to come visit in two weeks."

I nod, giving my mom a smile I hope conveys excitement, but my entire body is starting to thrum to life. My cheeks heat, turning a bright red. Mom frowns, pressing her fingers beneath my chin and tilting my face upward.

"Brie, are you all right? You're warm to the touch–"

"I'm fine," I whisper, sniffing indignantly while stepping out of her way before she can lay a hand over my forehead, which I'm certain is on fire.

"Are you sure? You look flushed. Are you running a fever? I can fix that–"

"Just nervous for the journey is all." I grip the handle of my suitcase until my knuckles turn white. "You know I hate traveling."

Mom nods, relaxing a bit, but grips my shoulder and pulls me in for a hug.

I hug her back, but my eyes are locked on figures speaking just beyond the grand entrance of the castle where a black SUV is parked and idling in the warm, early morning air.

All I know is that Dad tasked Logan with escorting me to Maatua. I can't spirit like my family members can. I get incredibly sick when I do, something even the herbs Mom gives Dad can't help. My body simply rejects the magic. I nearly died the last time I tried.

So, I have to travel on foot... or by car or boat.

Which means I'll be on a boat with Logan for a week, at least.

He nods at something Dad says. I watch the way his shoulders stretch in his tight, long-sleeved Henley shirt–a very casual choice considering the Ghost armor I'd seen him in yesterday morning. He looks suddenly familiar again, his rough, brutal features bleeding back into the farm boy from Silverhide I remember from my childhood. He looks over his shoulder, his eyes meeting mine in the haze of morning sunlight. Green-hued hazel, like polished serpentinite. I remember that about him from a memory so distant it's hard to conjure the details.

I was... a child. He'd saved Maeve from that rogue witch. He'd kept her safe.

He holds my gaze while Mom continues to squeeze me. Only when she pulls away, murmuring assurances about my journey, does he turn his gaze back to Dad.

"You can return with the boat, and Ryatt has already signed off on three months of leave," Dad tells Logan as they step off the porch.

I follow with my suitcase, craning to hear the conversation.

"I don't need three months of leave."

"You take a month every summer to help Silverhide with their harvest. You have an extra two months now to spend with family while you're at it."

I watch Logan's eyes for any sliver of emotion I can find, but he's... cold. Utterly serious. His sharp jaw clenches, but that brief flicker of muscle could have easily been the sunlight playing over his dark stubble.

He didn't shave this morning, that's obvious. He looks slightly unkempt and tired as he nods, forgoing arguing against my dad's orders.

I tear my eyes from Logan at the last second before Dad could catch me staring. He braces his hand on my shoulder, looking down at me with a secret smile he only uses around his family. "Remember what we talked about."

"How could I forget?" I sigh, rolling my eyes. "You'll regret this," I tell him then turn to Mom. "Now Maeve has you all to herself. How do you think that's going to go?"

"That's why we're coming to visit you," Mom says with a knowing smile. "I love you, Brie."

Dad presses a kiss to my forehead before turning me toward the car.

Logan walks over, takes my suitcase, and puts it in the trunk. I slide into the passenger seat, inhaling rapidly through my nose to try to catch my breath without my parents noticing my obvious distress. I look out the tinted window as Logan talks with my parents for another moment before he turns to the car. His shoulders fall just a touch as he scans the passenger side. He can't see my pained expression through the tinted glass, thank the Goddess, but judging by his expression, I'm wondering if he shares in my misery over our situation.

My chest feels impossible tight. Prickles of misplaced anticipation fizzle through my body, threatening to ignite a fire in my blood as he climbs into the driver's seat.

He takes up most of the front seat. His elbow brushes my arm as he settles, gripping the steering wheel.

I don't even blink until he's driven away from the castle and past the gates. When the gates close behind us, I close my eyes, my lips parting to tell him what needs to happen now… but he beats me to it.

"You need to reject me," he says.

Relief momentarily blinds me before dissipating as quickly as it came. Thank the Goddess he feels the same way, and I wasn't going completely insane. "Will it hurt?"

"I've heard it will. It'll hurt less for you, I assume, if you initiate it."

I look out the window at the city blurring by as he drives us down into the depths of the valley, where a small river port will take us to an even larger port on the sea where a yacht from our family fleet is waiting for me. Apprehension coils through my veins like a snake, twisting and writhing. "What happens once we reject each other?"

Out of the corner of my eye, I notice the way his hands tighten on the steering wheel. He exhales, his gaze firmly fixed on the road ahead. "I assume nothing."

"We'd be breaking a bond destined by the Goddess."

"She probably has bigger things to worry about." His hazel eyes briefly flicker to mine. The only way I can describe the look he gives me is… smug disdain. "Plus, I'm not an Alpha, Princess."

I look out the window, biting down hard on my lower lip to stop from lashing out. Embarrassment creeps through my body like a heat wave, burning to life in the form of a deep blush. So, he's heard, hasn't he? That the Princess of Veiled Valley is on the prowl?

I'm not shocked. "Well, my desperation and repeated failures are obviously the talk of the town."

He says nothing as we reach the river port, which is nothing more than a row of bait and tackle shops, a ticket station, and a dock with a dozen or so boats the size of large SUVs. A ferry bobs in the water nearby, however, and the ticket station is teeming with passengers waiting for the ferry to make its early morning arrival.

Half an hour from now, I'll be sitting on the deck of that boat, far, far away from Logan. I sigh in relief.

"We share a family," he amends, roughly putting the car in park, but he doesn't make any moves to get out. In fact, he swiftly locks the car at the very second I yank on the handle. I whirl to throw him a glare, but his eyes... they're searching mine, going a shade darker than his usual polished, imperfect jade. "I only meant I've heard how they feel about it."

"That's a bold thing to say," I snap, pulling on the handle, "given that you've refused Ryan and Aviva's love at every turn."

Now, *that* struck a nerve.

Logan exhales deeply, nostrils flaring, before shifting his weight and turning to face me. His proximity is... too close. Far too close. His arm brushes my midsection as he reaches past me to physically uncoil my fingers from around the door handle. "I had no intention of ever settling down and having a mate. You had no intention of being mated to anyone lower than an Alpha. We're not suited. You don't want this, that was clear from the moment we saw each other again yesterday. We're going to reject each other, Princess Brie. It's what we both want."

He's so close that the words drift over my skin, igniting that fire driven by the bond that's practically begging me to change his mind.

But I'm not in my right mind. He's right. Neither of us want this.

Maybe it's easier to swallow knowing he doesn't want this, and I'm not going to break his heart... not that it mattered to me... right?

He doesn't pull away. He remains close, his chin only an inch from my forehead as he looks through the tinted passenger window, his eyes scanning the dock.

I can hear his heart beating. A gentle, thump, thump, thump. He's calm, totally unaffected by the conversation we just had. He smells like cedar and the salty breeze coming off a cold sea.

"I reject you as my mate," I rasp, and he looks down.

"I accept your rejection," he whispers, but he's still so close and I'm... I'm wondering if... maybe I haven't thought this through–

A snapping sensation erupts in my chest, stealing my breath. I arch against the seat, squeezing my eyes shut. Pain like I've never felt before surges through my body, turning to a dull ache that throbs and echoes through every muscle and bone.

I open my watering eyes when I hear the doors unlock and feel Logan moving away. I look at him, breathless, and notice the bright red mark on his wrist where I'd grabbed him, sinking my nails into his skin. I don't remember doing that.

He closes the door before I can say anything further.

4

THIS IS PERFECTION

I'm not sure if I'm experiencing sea sickness for the first time or if this horrible ache in my stomach is from the mutual rejection I just experienced. I should have been more prepared for this feeling, actually. I curse at myself while settled on a plastic bench, watching the startling green valley on either side of the wide river sprint by. Smaller towns and villages hug the river bank, everything nestled under the umbrella of control of Veiled Valley, forever protected by my family. One day, Aris will rule all of this. He's the new Shadowsynger of the family–the one with those creepy shadow powers passed down by my grandfather, Ryatt, and my mother.

I look down at my normal, powerless hands and curl them into fists, closing my eyes against the rolling nausea threatening to pull me to my hands and knees.

I didn't eat breakfast. I didn't have the stomach for it, knowing I'd be thrust into a week-long journey with Logan, my mate.

Not anymore.

I slouch on the bench, leaning my head against the window while fiddling with the flowy cotton pants and matching shirt I choose for the day. The pale gray does nothing for my warm tones, but again, I didn't have it in me this morning to dress up. In fact, my normally perfect hair is tossed in a lopsided ponytail now falling out of its scrunchy, and my normally made up face is bare, freckles on full display.

It's not like I have anyone to impress.

I glance at Logan, who's seated on the opposite side of the indoor upper deck with his neck bent as he looks down at the heavy-duty laptop resting on his thighs. He's wearing glasses with a dark rim that make him look… sophisticated.

He blends in with the crowd of passengers milling about with paper cups of coffee and tea, but we're the only two people not dropping into conversation with anyone. I continue watching him, watching the light of his laptop reflect off his glasses. I can't stop. To think I've known this man since I was a child but know nothing about him other than he's one of my dad's captains in the Ghost army.

That's a high ranking position. It takes years of dedicated service to reach the level of captain. Years of training and missions, in fact.

I briefly wonder what he's seen in the field, what he's gone through, and whether those experiences turned him cold and emotionally void, or if that's just who he's always been.

But then his eyes meet mine and hold.

I blink, then turn to the window.

Eventually I get up to move around and search for a snack. The coffee is stale and weak, but I welcome the rush of caffeine that unthaws my rejection-addled head. I wander the lean, unimpressive ferry, taking in the signs plastered on the wall that prohibit shifting, smiling at the irony as I notice several men grumbling on the outdoor deck, all of them itching to stretch their wolf legs the second we reach land again.

Hours pass like this—with me wandering, sometimes sitting, sometimes leaning against the railing and watching the water go by. I ignore the buzz of notifications coming from my purse, knowing it's likely Maeve blowing up my phone now that we're out of range to use the mind-link.

As the hours drift into late afternoon, we reach the mouth of the river, having ridden against its current for several hours, and the valley fades away behind us, replaced by mist that robs the air of the warmth of the sun.

Only then do I go inside.

But Logan isn't on his bench. I feel slightly relieved, but right as I sit down, he passes from behind me and settles back on the gray plastic surface of his old spot, legs splayed in a very male position.

I stare at him, my cheeks heating. He just… looks back at me, expressionless.

"Have you been following me around all day?" I ask, and not kindly.

No one nearby looks in our direction, but he leans forward, resting his elbows on his knees. His dark jeans fit him like a glove, much to my dismay. Thick, muscled thighs ripple underneath as he shifts his weight, glancing toward the inner sanctum of the ferry before meeting my eyes again. "I'm your bodyguard, remember?"

"I fear that's far below your rank, *Captain.*"

He smirks, and I feel my stomach twist. Goddess, he's nice to look at. The stubble on his jaw has only grown darker during the course of the day, and his normally brushed back dark hair is loose and curling wildly in the sudden surge of humidity brought on by the mist now hugging the boat.

He could be in the movies. He could be a contestant on one of those stupid reality dating shows Maeve's particularly obsessed with.

He would never be interested in someone like me, mate bond or not.

I reach up to pull out my scrunchy so I can fiddle with it, needing something to do with my hands. My hair bounces over my shoulders, and I make the mistake of glancing in his direction again.

His pupils are blown wide, watching my natural, unruly waves settle against my chest… my breasts.

I find it impossible to swallow past the lump in my throat. I toy with my scrunchy, winding it around my fingers.

"I–I don't need a bodyguard," I stammer.

"No one needs a bodyguard until they're in a situation where they actually do, in fact, need a bodyguard."

I frown, refusing to look at him. "The odds of me being assaulted on a private yacht owned by my parents is slim–"

"But not zero."

I chance throwing him a glare. He's still seated nearby but hasn't adjusted his position. He's entirely relaxed with the ghost of a smirk on his wide, full mouth.

"Are you messing with me?" I ask.

"No."

"Then why are they looking at me like that?"

"I don't know what you're talking about."

"You're–you're smirking at me."

"This is just my face, Princess–"

"Brie," I correct, swallowing hard. "Brie is fine. There's no need for formalities at this point."

I hear him sigh through the murmur of unrelated conversations whispering between us.

"Brie–"

The captain of the ferry's voice blares from the speakers, alerting everyone onboard that we've reached the port city of Avalone, otherwise known as the Gem of the Sea. It's a beautiful city, if anyone could see it through the mist. It's the second largest city in all of Veiled Valley, second to the capital, my home, of course.

I rise and shrug my purse over my shoulder. My luggage is locked away downstairs with the rest of the cargo. I start heading in that direction, sandwiched between passengers who don't recognize me or don't care that they're in the presence of one of their princesses.

It doesn't surprise me. I'm often overlooked, and I'm fine with that, honestly. The stares and whispers Maeve has to endure every time she leaves the castle...

I jump when I feel someone touching my lower back and turn my head, finding myself staring directly at Logan's chest.

He looks straight ahead, giving me a little nudge to keep moving through the narrow passageway leading to the stairs to the cargo hold.

When we reach the bottom of the stairs, he gently grabs me, his fingers wrapping fully around my soft upper arm and steers me in the direction of the luggage lockers. He lets me go to fetch my suitcase and the trunk I brought, and directs me with a nod of his head to move with the crowd now getting into vehicles or walking off the ramp onto the dock.

I can't see much through the fog hugging the massive commercial port. Trade ships and cruise liners surround the dock, which is full of local workers and tourists either leaving Eastonia to explore Crescent Falls and the northern territories or coming to Eastonia for the adventure of their lives.

I breathe in the coastal air, closing my eyes for a moment as I fill my lungs, but I'm rudely interrupted by the scraping of the trunk being dragged across the concrete floor of the ferry.

"The yacht is in bay six," Logan says to me, I think. He's not looking at me as he scans the crowded dock, narrowing his eyes. He's not wearing his glasses anymore and looks like himself again–the Logan I know. The warrior. The ruthless jerk in a tight Henley.

"I can carry my suitcase–"

"No," he says matter-of-factly, tilting his head in a motion to get a move on.

I hug my purse to my chest and step off the ramp, moving slowly through the crowd while Logan stays within three steps of me, occasionally tapping me on the waist to move me in one direction or the other. He has his hands full with my trunk and suitcase but carries them effortlessly while also silently bossing me around.

When I pause to stare longingly at a cafe settled on the outskirts of the dock, he gives me another nudge.

Past the cruise ships and cargo boats, a private area of the port comes into view. Yachts bob in the calm water, and I feel my shoulders slumping with relief when the sleek, black yacht owned by my parents comes into view through the fog.

It's not the biggest, but it's high-tech and totally, completely sea worthy, which is all that matters.

"Princess Brie!" Captain Louis beams, meeting me on the ramp. He bows, smiling broadly, his wide smile making his eyes crease. His silver hair is full and swept back over his head as he offers me his hand.

A few other crew members I don't recognize hurry to take the luggage from Logan while Captain Louis explains that we're fogged in and won't be leaving until later tonight but that my suite is ready for me.

Behind me, I hear Logan tell one of the crew members he'll be back in twenty minutes, and when I turn my head, he's gone.

Maybe he'll stay gone and leave me in peace.

Wishful thinking, of course. I have a feeling he's going to be watching my every move for the next week on the water.

The captain personally shows me to the main suite, normally inhabited by my parents when we take this exact route to Maatua. Now, the spacious room is mine. The modern finishes, the giant bathroom with a walk-in shower, the windows that overlook the water...

The quiet, nothingness when he closes the door.

I sink to the edge of the king-sized bed with a groan, hanging my head in my hands. A voice over the intercom tells me dinner will be served on the upper deck in two hours before shutting off, leaving me in silence once more.

I rise and take a long, hot shower. Hunger tightens my belly, reminding me I've only had half a dry bagel and three or four cups of weak ferry coffee today. Dressed in a robe with my hair gathered in a towel, I pad back into the bedroom to fetch a new pair of clothes when I notice the drink tray on my bed.

An iced vanilla latte sweats in the soft, warm light of the crystal chandelier above my head. Beside it, a small cardboard box rests on the sheets, cinnamon and chocolate spicing the air.

I stare at the latte. It's my order, exactly. I open the box and find a warm, double chocolate muffin and a flaky, buttery croissant stuffed with cinnamon cream.

It's from the cafe I saw. The same cafe Logan refused to stop at as he escorted me through the crowded port.

I swallow past the knot in my throat, plucking the drink from the tray, and sip.

It's perfect.

5

NOT A BODYGUARD

Logan

Captain Louis watches me as I lean against the wall in the cockpit, looking through the manifest I picked up from the port master. I scan the document, memorizing every ship scheduled to leave the port tonight along with this yacht.

The captain chuckles, turning back to the helm where he sits and begins pushing buttons that light up his control station. The second officer, Charlie, arrives, saying, "The crew's been briefed. We're just waiting for the green light from the port master."

"I doubt we'll be moving anytime soon in this fog. It'll be a long night." Louis swivels back to me, arching a brow. "Commander Evander said you have some naval experience."

I look up from the manifest. "A bit."

"I was told you served for a few years under the Alpha King of Oasia in Serpentia, captaining a naval cruiser along their coast."

I run my tongue along my lower lip and tuck the manifest under my arm. "That's correct."

Louis smirks, shaking his head as he turns to the controls again. "A man of few words, huh? Doesn't surprise me that you left the royal navy to become a Ghost."

Charlie eyes me for a moment before grabbing a few pieces of paper from the printer, scanning them instead of my face.

"I need a list of everyone on board, down to the deckhands and ETOs," I tell the men.

"Do you want their home addresses, too?" Charlie asks in a sarcastic tone that immediately grates on my nerves.

Louis sighs, punching a few more buttons. "That I can do, *Captain*," he says to me over the hum of the printer. "But I can assure you, we've been escorting the royal family, including the princess, back and forth from Veiled Valley to Maatua for decades. The princess is perfectly safe here."

"I have orders to ensure that safety," I reply sternly, and Charlie hands me the list of crew members aboard.

"We've got a few new faces this trip," Charlie says. "Just deckhands. Four of 'em."

I scan their names, but nothing feels familiar when checked against my mental list of criminals at large I've been hunting as a Ghost. I tuck the paper with the manifest and leave the cockpit, making my way down past the rooms dedicated to the captain and his second officer and into the private, luxurious lodgings now inhabited by Brie.

I pass a stewardess with fiery red hair and a face plastered with makeup. She gives me a sly smile but disappears around a corner.

Brie's soft voice drifts toward me as I move toward the outer deck. The smell of food and a hint of wine hits me as she comes into view, sitting at a long table while a second stewardess pours her a glass of red wine.

"Just the salad, please," Brie says. She doesn't notice I'm walking toward the table until the stewardess leaves. Brie has her wine glass pressed to her full, plush lower lip, and her cheeks go a rosy pink when I close in on her, looking down at the sparse spread of food she hasn't touched.

I've spent the day getting to know her at arm's length. She's quiet but not shy. Her brain is constantly whirling, taking in little details most people miss. It's like a light is always on upstairs, so to speak.

In fact, she would have made a brilliant warrior if she hadn't been destined to become a princess instead—the kind of soldier that rises up the ranks. The kind that not only commands in the field but strategizes, making moves that determine who lives and who dies.

She's self-conscious, however. That became startlingly clear as I followed her around the ferry today, watching her stare longingly at the meager food spread and checking her reflection in every mirror or shiny service she passed.

She moves like prey, always scanning her surroundings before getting comfortable. She turns away from conversation and rarely looks anyone in the eyes if she doesn't know them.

Right now, however, she's looking right at me.

She lowers her glass, her dark brown eyes wide and concerned as I come to a stop a few feet from where she's sitting.

"We're not leaving port for another few hours. There's a delay because of the fog, and we're behind several cargo ships with priority on the manifest."

"Oh," she says under her breath, reaching for her wine glass again.

"After you finish eating, you need to return to your room immediately for the night. No wandering around."

She furrows her brows. "Excuse me?"

The stewardess returns, placing a plate of nothing but dark greens in front of her and hurries away again.

"No wandering," I repeat, but I frown at the plate of what looks like plain spinach. "Is that all you're eating? Spinach?"

She bristles, rolling her eyes to her plate, and mumbles, "Are you here to criticize what I eat now, too? Or just to boss me around and tell me I can't use the facilities of my family's private yacht?"

I grip the top of a chair. "You need to eat more than that."

"I don't," she snaps, her cheeks going from a rosy pink to a crimson red. "In fact, *someone* left two pastries in my room this afternoon. I'm not particularly hungry this evening."

I scan her face, unable to tell if she took that as an affront or not. I saw her eyeing the cafe like someone who hadn't eaten in weeks, and while I picked up the manifest, I made a stop. "That was a snack. You need protein. Carbohydrates–"

"Are you my personal trainer now, too?" She grips her fork until her knuckles turn white.

Brie is the definition of rigid, classical elegance. She looks like she walked out of one of the ancient murals that sweep across the ceilings of the dozens of Firestone castles littered across Eastonia. Beneath that pale blue, satin sundress, I know her figure is full and supple, that her fair skin is soft to the touch. Even when glaring at me, she's beautiful.

I honestly doubt she realizes it.

Watching her take her hair down today on the ferry had filled me with a momentary sense of regret that we'd rejected each other–but I beat that feeling into submission within seconds. She is, unfortunately, exactly my type. Softly beautiful. Elegant. Her hair and dark brown eyes the color of polished mahogany draw me in and spit me out–and those lips?

I sink into the seat opposite hers, pressing my elbows against the surface of the table.

She stares at me for what feels like an eternity but might have been only a few seconds before the stewardess, who was probably lingering in the hallway nearby, sweeps in with a dinner menu.

"Steak, rare, with the potatoes," I tell her, keeping my eyes locked on Brie's face as she goes even more red in the cheeks. I lean back in the chair, adding, "A basket of bread, as well. With butter."

"Do you want anything to drink?"

"Scotch."

"Dinner salad?"

"I'll be finishing hers." I motion to the plate of spinach.

The stewardess leaves again, and all around us the yacht rocks gently against the dock, the entire skyline alive with lights blinking through the mist.

"What do you want from me?" she asks testily, setting her fork down and reaching for her wine, sipping deeply. "I didn't invite you to dine with me."

"I didn't need an invitation."

"You're a prick."

"I've been called much, much worse."

The tension between us crackles.

She takes another drink of wine without breaking her gaze. "Just because we were mates–key word *were*–doesn't mean you need to follow me around or feel obligated to give me any kind of attention."

"I'm not following you around."

"You're here, aren't you? Interrupting my dinner?"

"I wouldn't consider a plate of greens dinner unless you're some type of forest dwelling rodent."

She scoffs. I smirk.

"I do not want you here, Logan. I have no use for your bodyguard services at the present. Go. Away. Go… lift weights or stare at yourself in the mirror, whatever men like you do in your free time."

"I'll leave once I've eaten dinner."

She picks up her plate and wine and moves to the far end of the table, sitting down with a huff.

I expect that to be the end of the conversation and consider it a win, but she says, "I'm going to be on the upper deck using the hot tub tonight whether you like it or not."

I turn toward her as the stewardess practically tosses my glass of scotch on the table and hurries out, likely sensing the tension. I murmur my thanks while Brie stabs at her spinach.

"You're not going to be using the hot tub," I counter, sipping deeply. "You're going to be in your room with the door locked until we're in open water."

She mumbles a rather colorful curse under her breath, shaking her head. "I could have you fired, you know. I could have you strung up on the gates outside the castle in Moonrise if I really felt like it."

"I have a feeling your father and grandfather are familiar with your games, Princess."

She shoots daggers with her eyes as she glares at me. "My *games*?"

"Your insistence to bend everyone to your will," I amend.

"I'm not bending you to my will. I'm telling you how it's going to be. You might have been tasked by my father to keep me safe, but controlling what I do and where I go–"

"There's a ring of criminals operating in Eastonia," I cut in, swirling my drink. "Thieves. Gamblers. Murderers." She pales, but I continue, "Men who've only known hard times but refused to dig themselves out of the debts they owe to a man named Hannibal Arachnis, otherwise known as the *Spider,* for obvious reasons."

She drains her wine. The name apparently rings a bell.

"You've likely heard about the murders across the packlands, both in Eastonia and Crescent Falls. Even a few Alphas have fallen to his assassin."

"Who is his assassin?"

"We have no idea," I answer honestly, smoothing my finger over the rim of my glass. "But the Ghosts have been tasked by the Allied Kings to track these men down and deal with them, hoping one of them leads us back to Hannibal himself."

"What does that have to do with me?"

I lean forward, watching her from across the table. "You are a princess. A granddaughter of the Queen of Eastonia and the Alpha King of the Roguelands. What makes you think, if those criminals were desperate enough, they wouldn't see this journey as an opportunity to take you and hurt you in some way? Perhaps using you as ransom to pay their debts? It's happened before. Recently, too."

Her eyes lock on mine, heavy with sudden emotion. "No one wants me, Captain Logan. I think you forget which princess you're referring to. I'm... nobody in their eyes." She rises, abandoning her salad, and tries to hurry away.

I catch her wrist, pulling her to a stop. "I don't like this either, Princess Brie." I don't mean the thought of criminals trying to take her and ruin her vacation. I mean the cruel twist of fate that thrust us together as unwilling mates now trapped in close quarters for a week straight.

She exhales deeply, looking down at me but not making any

moves to run off. "I understand why you were tasked with escorting me to Maatua. I know that you couldn't say no. I also understand quite clearly that you didn't want a mate, and honestly, it was a relief, because neither did I."

I let go of her wrist. She remains standing by the table but crosses her arms over her midsection like she's trying to hide herself.

I *hate* that.

"But I don't expect you to be at my beck and call. I am safe. If thieves wanted something from my father, they could easily go after Maeve. She'd probably go with them willingly just for the sake of an adventure. In fact, I'm shocked she hasn't been hired by the Ghosts to be willingly used as bait. It would be a great training exercise for her powers, I'm sure."

I blink up at her, watching a myriad of emotions wash over her face like a rogue wave.

My food is delivered and laid out on the table by both stewardesses, and the red-haired one makes a point of throwing me another sly smile that Brie definitely notices. She frowns at the woman as the duo disappears around the corner again but doesn't make any moves to leave the table yet.

"Will you sit down and eat something?" I ask.

"Why does it matter?"

"Because you had four cups of coffee and half a bagel today. That's not enough."

"I had the pastries you bought," she argues, meeting my eyes.

I hold her gaze while I kick the chair opposite mine out from under the table, tilting my head in that direction. She sits down in surrender. I rise, reaching toward the far end of the table for her useless salad and drag it toward us, then begin divvying up the steak.

"Are you really from an island somewhere?" she asks after several minutes of silence.

I hesitate. It's been so incredibly long since I've talked to anyone about Emberfyll. I'm not even sure how to begin.

"Yes," I tell her, pushing a plate in her direction piled with meat, bread, and potatoes. "And it's a very long story."

6

BARING IT ALL

BRIE

"HE'S BRASH AND… BOSSY." I PACE TO THE OTHER SIDE OF MY SUITE AS warm morning air drifts through the windows, washing the room in tropical light.

Maeve chuckles through the phone. I imagine her sprawled out in her bed, hanging her head over the mattress while flipping through a magazine on the floor, kicking her legs. "Wow. That sounds like someone else I know."

"Who?" I ask, running my fingertips along the wall. It's morning, and we're finally out in the open water, leagues from shore. I was asleep when the yacht finally left the port and woke up to waves all around me and no other vessel in sight.

"You, duh." Her bed creaks like she just rolled over to her back. "It sounds like you've met your match, my dear."

"Don't '*my dear*' me," I grumble into the receiver, perching on the couch across from the windows. "You sound like Mom."

"Oh, Brie, she's so worried about you. Promise me you're dropping this whole Alpha husband hunting scheme, please? Mom's

41

considering shipping you off to some Moon Goddess convent in Celestoria and has Dad half convinced it's a good idea."

I pale, rubbing my temples. "I–you have to understand why–"

"Why not just wait until you find your mate, Brie? I mean, Goddess, what if you marry an Alpha and meet your mate later on? What are you going to do then?"

I'm speechless. Not a single word materializes on the tip of my tongue. I stare at the endless waves, trying to come up with something to pacify my sister, and all I can say in the end is, "You're right. It was a stupid idea."

"And if you don't find your mate," she says excitedly, "that just means the two of us can be together forever, ruling Eastonia like it's meant to be."

"Sure, Maeve," I smile, but my heart aches.

I hear Aris's voice nearby, followed by Maeve grumbling about having to help him get ready for a date with his new, fancy girlfriend, and she hangs up, leaving me in total, all-consuming silence where I can hear the yacht creaking against the waves.

I set my phone down. I've been in the habit of not checking the news or gossip tabloids that love to report about my family. I prefer to live in blissful ignorance of what anyone has to say about me.

Still, I'm not sure what to do with my time on this boat. I haven't seen Logan yet this morning, but I didn't come up for breakfast. There's a small gym on board, but I much prefer a nice, long walk or shifting into my wolf form over pumping iron or sweating on a treadmill.

I start rifling through the closets and cupboards in the room, finding a stash of romance novels my mom likes to pretend she doesn't like, and choose one. When's the last time I had time to read a book? Normally, my days are spent following my mom and sister around, delegating tasks to the court, and ensuring Maeve is staying on track with her training and education to one day be queen.

In fact, my entire life revolves around Maeve.

I stare at the wall instead of the book, wondering when I last took a single day for myself.

It must have been… never. Because I have no hobbies, nothing I can say is my passion—and my passion alone.

I crack the book open just as a knock sounds on the door.

"Come in," I call out, expecting a stewardess with the coffee I ordered via the intercom twenty minutes ago.

But the shadow that passes over me can only belong to a man, and only one man in particular.

I stand, flustered, still wearing a lacy night dress and matching robe I didn't expect anyone but the stewardesses to see me in, and whirl toward Logan at the same moment he shuts the door behind him.

A tray with a carafe of coffee and a couple of mugs rest in his hands. He stares at me, and I stare back, both of us seemingly in shock for two wholly different reasons.

He braves a glance down my body to my bare thighs and back up again. I blush deeply and pull my robe around my stomach.

"I'm sorry—"

"You shaved," I blurt.

Logan holds my gaze. "I did."

He sets the tray down on a table by the door and absently rubs his now clean shaven jaw. It makes him look younger, more polished. He's wearing his glasses, too, which startled me almost as much as seeing him fresh-faced after a day spent directly in his company without them.

I notice the laptop bag hanging over his shoulder as he turns toward the coffee and pours two mugs, adding cream and sugar to mine. How he knows, I have no idea, but it's the exact ratio I would serve myself.

"Are you planning on staying inside today?" he asks, not looking over his shoulder.

"This morning, at least. I don't—I don't have plans," I manage to say without my voice shaking.

"I didn't see you at breakfast."

"I'm not a breakfast person," I admit.

"Well, neither am I," he replies as he turns to hand me my coffee, but he makes a point of not looking in my direction. "I'm just going to work for a while if you're going to hang out here."

He moves toward the far end of the room where a trio of armchairs faces the windows. I follow his progress, holding my mug like my life depends on it.

He's obviously uncomfortable. I can see it in the way his shoulders tense as he sits down and pulls out his laptop. His gaze lingers on my bare feet for a fraction of a second before he clears his throat and settles his laptop in his lap.

"I wasn't expecting company," I whisper.

"I wasn't expecting you to be wearing *that*," he whispers back, glancing at me—my face this time. His eyes are dark and... heavy with something I can't describe, but it makes me feel totally, completely exposed and all tingly….

"It's just a nightgown." Wait, why am I explaining myself to him? "And actually, you're in my space right now, uninvited, again."

"Would you like me to leave, Princess?"

I open my mouth with every intention of saying yes, but the word, *"No!"* rings through the room against my will.

I surprise myself by it, honestly, and feel that horrible blush creeping across my entire body once again. I quickly scurry to the bed and tug a new outfit out of the suitcase I failed to unpack right away and disappear into the bathroom to change, sipping my coffee while it's still hot.

When I emerge, dressed in casual but comfortable pants and a tank top to beat the heat seeping into the boat, he's still sitting in that armchair with his laptop propped on his thighs, his head bent and fingers occasionally clicking keys.

I peer at him, curious about what he's working on—research, it looks like.

"Are you buying a boat?" I ask, and he immediately shuts his laptop. I purse my lips and look elsewhere, feeling that crazy, impossibly thick tension start to fizzle between us again, just like last night at dinner.

I can feel him watching me as I move toward the windows, sipping my coffee and pretending like I didn't just totally pry into his business... but he is in *my* room, sitting in *my* chair...

When he doesn't respond, I sit on the bed, toying with the book I almost started earlier until he interrupted, and... can't help myself any longer. "I didn't know you needed glasses."

He sighs nearby–a sound etched with a flicker of annoyance.

"They're readers, not really glasses–"

"So you need them to read?"

"Yes," he deadpans. "Hence the name."

I look at him, finding him staring directly at me with an expression dripping with exacerbation. So, I shrug, crossing my legs and settling on the edge of the mattress. "I didn't mean anything by it. They look nice on you, just so you know." I take another dramatic sip of my coffee and meet his gaze again, kind of loving the way his jaw tenses at my compliment.

This isn't what I expected rejection to be like. It doesn't feel like anything anymore. We didn't know each other before the mate bond clicked into place–not in an intimate or even platonic, friendly way. Logan was just someone I knew of, someone who could, in a removed way, be considered a fringe member of my large circle of family. Rejecting him, and being rejected by him, hurt physically.

Not mentally. Not emotionally.

But now, I feel like we have an uncanny ability to get under each other's skin in ways others can't. Maybe that's just a remnant of the mate bond that used to be there.

Or maybe I'm just reading too much into this–far too much.

"I had to learn to not only speak but read and write your language," he explains, opening his laptop again. "As a teenager, I should add. It wasn't easy, and... I struggled. Ryan told me I have something called dyslexia. Cole confirmed it and glasses with a specific type of lens seem to help."

"They make the words stand out from the background?" I've heard a bit about this before.

"Yeah," he says with a shrug. "And they're not bad when it comes to picking up women at a coffee shop." He smirks right at me.

"You're a pig."

"Again, I've been called worse–"

"Give me an example." I shift my position so I'm facing him, gracefully crossing my legs and blinking at him in anticipation. "What's the worst thing you've been called?"

He lifts a brow, then smiles faintly, reaching up to remove his glasses. "I would have to say… well, I was interrogating a man once. It was the third day of it, and we were all exhausted, him included. He'd been calling me all sorts of names. *Fucker* being his favorite. I believe it might have been a term of endearment until I started breaking his–" He cuts himself off abruptly, running his tongue across his lower lip while throwing me an apologetic look. "Anyway, on the fourth day it became clear we had the wrong man. His cousin who bore an uncanny resemblance to him had thrown him under the bus, so to speak, and was picked up in Tarsian on other charges. I had to report all of this back to your father, who asked if I'd ever considered taking a day off from being an idiot, and I had no idea what to say, so I said no."

My brows shoot up to my forehead. "My dad calling you an idiot is the worst thing someone has ever said to you?"

"Yes, by far." A small smile touches his lips as he leans back, rubbing his temples like the memory pains him. "You see a very different version of your father than I do."

"I've called you a prick and a pig within a twenty-four hour time frame. Do I even make the list?"

"I think if you spoke your mind and said what you actually thought of me, you probably would."

He holds my gaze. I lose myself in his strange, hazel-green eyes for a moment, watching the way the sunlight reflects off the water and highlights flakes of gold and copper that weave throughout his irises.

"I've been called worthless," I whisper. I didn't mean to speak. It just came out, flowing like water. "And… useless."

"By whom?" his voice drops, going all gravelly and deeper than I thought possible. I notice the shift in not only his tone but his body language. He sits up a little straighter, which makes me sit up in turn, my spine turning to steel.

"No one you know. Not–not my family," I amend, laughing past the pain of the memory. "Just–just someone I was dating for a minute."

"A boyfriend said that to you?"

"Not–not a boyfriend, no. He was–we were considering marriage. His uncle is an Alpha in the Roguelands–powerful. Connected. Exactly the kind of man I–" I cut myself off as my cheeks begin to burn. Saying the words out loud makes me realize how ridiculous they are... but.... "He was his uncle's heir, and having him as a husband, having his pack behind not only me but my family... it would have thrown an impressive amount of support behind my sister when she ascended the throne. Allies, you know, when the crown is passed."

I look into my empty coffee mug to stop myself from looking at Logan, not wanting to know what kind of expression he's currently wearing. I wait for him to laugh at me, but he doesn't.

"He called you worthless?"

"He didn't mean it like that."

"What did he mean it like then? Exactly?" His tone is sharpened to a fine edge.

I risk meeting his eyes. They're nearly black, even in the sunlight. I shrug. "I don't have powers, Logan."

He holds my gaze with an intensity that makes me feel things I've never been able to put into words. It's like I'm under a microscope, and he's taking me apart piece by piece, studying places I've never allowed anyone to come near. My soul, for one. The pain and fear of rejection from those I love. The idea I won't live up to their unspoken expectations–expectations I'm not sure exist but can't move past.

"I don't have powers," I repeat, curling my hands around my mug. "I don't have anything to add to a bloodline other than my connections to my family. He had no idea I was adopted, and that mattered to him. I didn't blame him, you know. It's something to consider–"

"He rejected you because you didn't have powers to pass on to your future, *theoretical children?*"

"Yes," I whisper, turning my eyes back to the windows, to the ocean. "They all have."

I hear him rise, grunting softly under his breath. He doesn't move in my direction. His steps are soft on the carpet as he walks to one of the windows and braces his hands on either side of it.

"How many, Brie? How many have there been?"

7

BAD TIMING

LOGAN

BRIE KEEPS TOYING WITH HER COFFEE MUG. IT'S LIKE A NERVOUS TICK. Like she needs to do something with her hands at all times.

If I were in a different state of mind, I'd probably be thinking about what those hands would feel like braced against my chest. I would again be questioning why I rejected her, ignoring and damn near forgetting why I needed to in the first place.

But right now, I'm blinded by absolute, stunning rage.

"Brie–"

"Not many," she says under her breath. "Maybe… ten Alphas."

I close my eyes, trying to pull myself together. Of course, I've seen the headlines, which are normally dominated by Blake, who tends to put himself in precarious situations at night clubs and other seedy establishments in Crescent Falls… but whispers about Brie have been more common since she turned twenty-one.

She confirms where my thoughts are headed when she says, "The public has a special interest in us now that we're nearing maturity. I'm twenty-two. Blake will be twenty-one this winter, and Aris isn't far behind. Everyone wants to know who our mates will be. It's like a game to them." She unfolds her legs and brings them up to her chest, wrapping her arms around her knees. "But it's the Alphas I worry about. They're watching all of us closely, wondering how the dynamic in the kingdom will shift as we start mating, and marrying. Things will change. Allies will change. There's already an undercurrent of uncertainty now that my grandparents have announced Maeve is going to ascend the throne in three years. That sounds like so much time, but in the grand scheme of things, it's not. Three years from now, everything will be different in their eyes. There will be a full blooded Firestone witch on the throne again for the first time in… three thousand years. Some people aren't happy about it. It scares them."

She's not wrong about the undercurrent. Crime has risen across the board. New rebel groups seem to pop up every day. Alphas have been pushing buttons, warring with what were once peaceful neighbors.

Hell, Ryatt even tried to convince Cole, once the Alpha King of all of Tarsian after his father's death, to retake the territory after two of the three Alpha Kings there failed to maintain their thrones, falling to Alphas and rebels who split Tarsian into warring factions once again.

Cole and Misty had refused… for now, it seems. Their children are still in their teens and were born and raised in Crescent Falls. They're not throwing their own kids into the fire.

But it's not all bad. Many, if not most, of the people of Eastonia are rejoicing in Maeve's ascension.

A few bad apples with enough charisma to sway a larger crowd can have the biggest impact, however.

I've seen it happen. It happened to *me*.

"I have an advantage being a princess," she says, propping her chin on her knee while staring absently at the water. "Even without powers, I'm highly connected. Having a seat at my family's table is like winning the lottery. It means power and wealth. It means influence." She sighs heavily, looking down at her toes. "But it's just not enough. I'd settle for a Beta–"

"Do you hear yourself?"

She bristles. I regret the harsh tone, but I'm beyond thinking or seeing rationally. "I know how it sounds. I don't expect you to understand."

"You're essentially selling yourself for the benefit of your family."

"I'm doing this for my sister," she grinds out. "I still have three years. I have time to make an impact–"

"It's not your responsibility–"

"It is," she rasps. Her eyes suddenly well with tears that she quickly blinks away. "You don't–you don't have family so you can't understand."

The words hang in the air before crashing around us. I don't flinch, but she sure does.

"Logan, I didn't mean that." She wipes her hand over her face, tugging her legs closer to her chest. "I didn't mean–you just can't possibly understand what I'm trying to accomplish. It's why I rejected you, for Goddess' sake."

"Because I'm not an Alpha."

She sighs. "Precisely."

She's right. I'm not an Alpha.

I'm the rightful Alpha *fucking* King of Emberfyll.

But I can't get home, so it doesn't matter.

Silence settles between us, so heavy and thick I can taste it as I sink into the armchair again.

"Why did you need to reject me?" she asks on a breath, like an afterthought.

I close my eyes as her words work through my body, slicing into me like knives. Last night when she'd asked about Emberfyll, I hadn't told her the full story. Aviva and Ryan are the only ones who know. There are things I've told Aviva in particular that I doubt she ever repeated to Ryatt.

Brie doesn't know about the war in Emberfyll. I didn't tell her about losing everything, left to starve on the shore while the enemy crept closer, and closer, threatening my parents and the pack we had left.

But she knows I lost everyone. I washed up in her kingdom as an orphan and stayed one... by choice.

She'd also seen what I've been working on when I had my laptop out earlier.

"I am buying a boat," I tell her, nodding to myself. "Soon. I have something lined up."

"That's—that's great but an odd reason to need to reject someone—"

"You don't get to say that, considering your reasoning is you need to marry someone with a higher, more persuasive rank than I have," I cut back.

She frowns at me.

I roll my lower lip between my teeth, debating my next words. "I'm going back to Emberfyll. That's always been the plan. A mate would have just gotten in the way of that happening. I can't put down roots in a land where I don't mean to stay."

She stares at me, her face washed in a tangle of emotion that borders on pity, which I don't need. Not from her, especially. I rise, resting my hand on the top of the chair, and say, "I guess it was... a perfect twist of fate that we were mates. Neither of us wanted it. It made things easier in the end."

I meet her eyes. She looks just as secretly unconvinced as I feel.

"Yeah, I guess it was."

When the silence settles a second time, I start toward the door, pausing to pour myself another cup of coffee. "I'll be back later if you plan to spend the entire day here, in your room."

"You don't need to babysit me."

I close the door behind me, ignoring her comment, leaving my laptop behind, and walk into the hallway gripping the black coffee like a lifeline as my senses start funneling back to normal. Being in Brie's presence is unnerving, and we've already rejected each other. Maybe that takes time to fully dissipate, I'm not sure, but I'm in a totally foreign headspace around her.

And after this morning... I need to keep my head on straight.

I sip the coffee as I walk through the yacht like I'd done two hours ago when the crew started waking up for the day. I settled for the night in a stateroom a few doors down from Brie's, but honestly, it doesn't feel close enough anymore.

Not after walking into a conversation between two deckhands who'd immediately stopped whispering to each other the second I rounded a corner and dispersed, eyeing me over their shoulders as they disappeared into the recesses of the yacht.

But I'd noticed them. I'd taken in their details down to the way they walked, how their footfalls sounded on the polished floorboards.

I walk the length of the boat deck to deck before making my way upstairs to the cockpit where I find Charlie bent over the controls, monitoring a weather station. He looks up from the controls, swiping his dark blond hair out of his face. He's a few years older than me, likely in his early thirties. I notice the thick gold wedding band on his ring finger as he motions for me to enter.

"Where's the captain?" I ask, glancing around the snug space.

"Downstairs with the chief engineer, doing his rounds. I'm just… watching the weather." He glances at the control panel again with a sigh that immediately sets me on edge.

I look out the window at the perfect, unblemished blue sky. "What about it?"

"We've got some reports from boats two days ahead of us, currently skirting past KiloKilo, of a big storm system causing rough seas." He leans back in his chair, swiveling from side to side as he stretches his arms behind his head. "It's tricky, that stretch. The closer you get to KiloKilo, the worse the seas get, even on a perfect day. Try staying in shallow water, closer to the islands stretching out from Maatua, and you risk running aground. We're traveling through a straight, you know. To the north, you get sucked into KiloKilo's magical fields that can sink a ship in minutes. To the south, the water gets so shallow you end up trapped on a sandbar."

"So you're saying we're headed right into a storm without any options to go around it?"

He nods grimly. "A lot can happen in two days, though. The skies could clear if the storm dissipates, or it could head toward KiloKilo or

Maatua, and we'll miss it completely... but as of now, it's headed toward us."

I close my eyes, pinching the bridge of my nose. "What kind of swells are we talking about here?"

"Ten to fifteen feet, possibly more if we hit it head on. One of the cargo ships recently reported waves in the thirties, but they're in the storm as we speak."

"So, slow down," I tell him. "Give it some time to pass."

"Tell that to the captain," he laughs, shaking his head. "This is only my second year aboard this boat. Captain Louis has been ferrying this family since Queen Ella dropped the veil and made it possible for sea traveling between Veiled Valley and Maatua. He's seen a thing or two and doesn't believe this is anything to worry about."

I'm obviously not convinced.

I leave the cockpit in search of the captain but end up standing in front of Brie's door again. I knock before entering but find her curled up in bed, her body hugging a pillow.

She's fast asleep that easily, even after a cup of coffee.

I edge into the room, closing the door behind me and locking it tight. I watch the sunlight play over her face, remembering for a split second a memory of her as a little girl.

She'd been all puffed up about Maeve. I'd just returned to Silverhide with Ryan and Aviva after chasing that witch into the forest. My hands were raw and burned from Maeve's powers, but I'd saved her.

While the adults showered me with praise... Brie wasn't convinced.

I remember her looking right at me, her nose crinkled with distaste, but then she saw the bandages on my hands.

"You saved her?" she'd asked, and I nodded, somehow understanding every word she'd said despite not knowing a lick of her language yet.

I had no idea she was my mate back then. I wonder if I'm doing that little girl a disservice now. Would things have been different if we'd met a year ago? Would I have accepted our bond knowing what I know about her now, knowing how she'd sacrifice herself to what I firmly believe is a lost cause? Could I have talked her out of it somehow?

She can't prevent a theoretical civil war when Maeve rises to power. Even the Mystics can't foresee that.

If I hadn't been as close as I am now to finally returning to Emberfyll to see what's left of my kingdom, would I have considered staying?

For her?

I sit down on the edge of the bed, facing the waves, watching the perfect, clear blue sky, wondering if fate will get in our way, again, in two short days.

8

VIOLATED

Brie

I've decided I don't enjoy being on the yacht by myself. Normally, everyone is here. Maeve and I would spend mornings lounging in the sun while Mom and Dad sat nearby, talking about the books they were reading. Aris would be off doing something dangerous and naughty, of course, like threatening to jump from the roof of the cockpit into the hot tub.

We'd play board games, and my parents would tell us the family lore and secrets we weren't privy to as children. Taking the yacht to Maatua for Solstice has become a beloved family tradition that I look forward to every year... but being aboard is different this time.

I stretch my legs on the lounge chair, letting the sun fan over my skin. I tan easily. A few days of this kind of weather and my skin will be a perfect, golden bronze. I even squeezed lemon juice in my hair and brushed it out like Maeve does in the summer to give myself some natural highlights.

It's too quiet now. Even with music humming through a speaker nearby, I can hear all of my thoughts through the gentle rush of water against the sides of the boat. I lie down flat, closing my eyes and soaking in the sun, letting my mind wander back home to the castle, curious about what everyone's up to today.

It's been three days since we left the port. Yesterday, Logan spent most of the morning in my company, but I didn't see him otherwise until dinner, where we repeated his little ritual of deciding what I'd eat based on nutritional needs I didn't know I had.

But it had been the slice of chocolate cake waiting for me in my room later that night, after spending a solo hour in the hot tub reading the silly romance novel now resting at my side, that made me feel a sudden jolt of… regret.

Logan is actually a very caring, albeit sarcastic, man. I have no plans to give him credit for that, however. We rejected each other mutually, and that's something I need to live with, even if being in his presence makes me feel things I didn't think possible.

And seeing him walk out onto the upper deck in nothing but swim trunks that could be considered a bit too snug around his thick, muscular thighs makes those feelings tangle and thrum into something dangerous.

I remind myself *I am not* attracted to him. I remind myself a second, and a third time, while I watch under the camouflage of my massive sunglasses as he adjusts the other lounge chair, fumbling with the controls that lower the seat so he can lie down like I am.

His muscles flex and ripple with every move he makes. He's tan and tall and just… gorgeous. It's unfair, really, that someone could be so effortlessly perfect but also annoying and repeatedly in my way.

"I can feel you looking at me," he chuckles, and I blush so deep it could be mistaken for a horrendous sunburn.

"You're practically naked," I argue. "The sun is glaring off your back and blinding me, Logan."

"I'm not naked. Don't get too excited," he teases, and I find it best to bite my tongue instead of trying to come up with some kind of retort to that.

When he fails to flatten the lounge chair, he begins to lift it, shaking it repeatedly while grunting under his breath, being loud on purpose, I assume, just to annoy me.

I drag my sunglasses down the bridge of my nose, giving him a poignant frown. "Aren't you like, a super smart, strong, and capable warrior?"

Panting, he turns to me, squinting against the sun. "I don't get vacations, Brie. At all."

"You're being bested by a lounge chair."

"Would you like to offer your help or continue gawking at me?"

I push my glasses back up my nose and lie down with a dramatic sigh.

He groans, giving the chair one more kick of emphasis, and with a crack, it folds down. He chuckles to himself before settling with another dramatic groan, and then I'm just… getting a suntan… with Logan less than three feet away from me.

"Why are you out here?" I ask. "Don't you have better things to do than lie around?"

"I don't. This is my mission."

"What?"

"*You* are my mission," he amends, smiling wryly as he flips a pair of sunglasses open and slides them on. "I thought we'd accepted that by now."

"That doesn't mean you have to be where I am all of the time."

"There's not much else to do on this boat, and I'm technically not part of the crew, so I figured getting some sun and enjoying a moment where I don't have orders, and I don't need to give anyone else orders, would be a great use of my time."

I consider his words, suddenly curious about what his job entails outside of constantly hovering nearby. "What's it like being in the Ghost army?"

"I'm shocked you don't know everything about the Ghosts, given that your father commands us."

"You know my dad," I reply, running my fingers through my hair. The sun beats down on the two-piece bathing suit I picked out thinking I'd be alone today. It's far more revealing than I'd thought when I bought it online a few weeks ago on a whim, but if Logan's looking at me right now, I can't tell behind his sunglasses. "There's actually this unspoken rule my parents have. Dad doesn't talk about what he does for work in front of us kids."

"I don't blame them for enacting that," he says softly.

I turn my head to look at him. "So, what's it like?"

He shrugs, turning his head to look at me, too. I could reach out and touch him without issue from this impossibly narrow distance. I wouldn't even need to strain my arm to run my fingers over the scar on his right cheekbone, or the kink in his nose from what must have been a gnarly break at some point in time. It only adds to how interesting his face is, honestly.

He rests his hands behind his head, lifting a knee to stretch out completely, every fine muscle on display. I refuse to look down past his belly button, though. I won't. I can't.

"It's… policing, mostly. We step in when all other efforts to quell whatever strife is happening have been exhausted."

"But you're a spy, too, aren't you?"

"I've been in the field undercover, yeah," he admits, still looking at me. "I like that part of it, actually. I'd be happy doing just that, but King Ryatt and your father saw something in me, leadership skills or whatever and gave me a promotion a year ago. I left the Tarsian Navy for them. Now I send my own warriors undercover if needed. I sit behind a desk most days and strategize. Investigate. Boss people around."

"You must love the latter."

His bright white smile sinks into my bones, igniting heat that radiates like wildfire. Or maybe that's the unforgiving sunlight.

"I don't mind it."

"Are you going to miss it when you leave?" I ask in all seriousness.

That wry, cocky smile fades immediately.

I sit up a bit as a single cloud darts across the sky, casting a welcome shadow over the upper deck. I push my sunglasses to the top of my head and look at him. "You will miss it, I think, because you're really enjoying bossing me around, aren't you?"

He takes off his sunglasses as well, the corner of his mouth lifting into a half-grin. "I honestly am. It's almost too easy to rile you up, Brie. You need to work on that."

I try to frown but the way he's looking at me right now has my insides in a tangle. "You're annoying," I tell him.

"I'm going to take that as a compliment, Princess." He smirks, putting his sunglasses back on, and leans back with his face toward the sun.

I'm not surprised when an hour later, my skin prickling with the beginnings of a deep tan or sunburn, whichever comes first, Logan follows me through the yacht to my suite.

We've been making casual conversation just to pass the time, and I think after our conversation yesterday in my room, the so-called ice has been broken between us. I don't necessarily mind his company. I don't like to admit that the way he looks at me… especially when I'm wearing nothing more than a rather skimpy bikini and swim cover that rides low on my waist, hitting me mid-thigh… is tantalizing. Yeah. No one has ever looked at me like that before, and the idea that I can get under his skin in some way… it's… *fun*.

I like arguing with him, which sounds insane. I like his sharp comebacks and inability to see me as a princess, someone with higher rank than him. Nothing is formal when it comes to Logan.

It's like nothing I've ever experienced.

But so is finding a man I don't recognize in my room.

Logan's hand flies out, dragging me back into the hallway with his arm wrapped around my bare waist. He shoves me behind him just as the man turns to us, a toolbox in his hand.

He's… an odd looking man. He's older, maybe Logan's age plus a few *hard* years, but his hair is a gray-brown and thin, flying out in little wisps around his narrow face.

Dark eyes scan Logan as he goes totally, completely rigid in front of me. His arm is still twisted back, gripping my waist hard enough to leave imprints.

"What are you doing here?" Logan snarls at the man. It's a deck-hand, I realize. I've seen him around at least twice doing maintenance on the upper and lower deck during my daily walks around the boat.

The man licks his lips, craning his neck to get a look at me. I feel myself pressing closer to Logan to get out of his line of sight, my breasts brushing up against his mid back.

"Just checkin' the window seams," the man says in cracking, gravelly voice. "Big storm comin', I'm sure you heard."

"The windows are fine. Get out." Logan is so serious right now. Each syllable drips with malice. I've never heard him use this tone before.

"Logan, it's fine. He was just—"

The man starts to walk toward us, and Logan takes a step back, guiding me with him to give the man room to exit.

"How did you get a key to this room?" Logan asks sternly, his eyes nearly black with what I only describe as fury.

"We've all got a master key." The deckhand shrugs, but his beady little eyes move to my face, and the crooked, uneasy smile he gives me sends a lick of unease shooting up my spine. "Better tuck in soon. It's going to get rocky once the sun goes down."

The man hikes his toolkit up to his hip and saunters off, whistling. Logan doesn't move, he doesn't let go of me, either. He watches the man until he cuts around a corner and disappears.

"Logan, you didn't have to use that tone with him. He's just doing his job—" I yelp in surprise when Logan snatches me out of the hallway and practically picks me up, depositing me in my suite. He shuts the door behind him, locking it. The gentle click ripples through the ringing in my ears. "What's wrong with you?"

"Go over there," he says, pointing to the corner of the room farthest from the door.

"Why?"

"Now."

I bristle at his tone, throwing him a glare as I grumble and pad to the corner, turning to face him with my arms crossed as he starts to move around the room, checking the windows, the corners, tipping over the couches and chairs.

"What the hell are you doing?" I ask, scoffing as he throws open the closet door.

He moves on to the cabinets arranged around the bed, and that's when my heart begins to slow and sink.

I take a single step forward when I notice the clothes I'd finally unpacked and folded neatly in the cabinet are all in disarray. A jewelry box sits in an open position, my favorite stacking rings and dainty necklaces shining in the sunlight.

"I didn't–I didn't leave it like that," I stammer, meeting Logan's eyes as he looks over his shoulder at me.

"I figured," he grunts, taking the jewelry box out and setting it on the bed. "Make sure everything's accounted for."

"Do you think he was stealing?"

"I don't know. I know he doesn't have a master key, though." He closes the cabinet and moves to the others, finding them just as unorganized.

I look around in shock, unsure what to say, or feel.

It makes me feel even worse when I realize none of my jewelry has been taken. "What did he want, if not this?" I hold up the necklaces.

Logan stares at me for a long, long time, saying nothing. His expression is intense and dark as he scans my face. "Stay here."

"But–no," I rush out, shaking my head. "Stay with me, okay? I'm giving–I'm giving you an invitation this time–"

"Brie," he says slowly, darkly, "Do not leave this room. Do not open the door for anyone other than me, do you understand?"

"What are you going to do?" I ask, my voice trembling.

"Do you understand?" he repeats, looking and sounding every ounce the warrior he is.

"I do," I whisper, swallowing hard. "I'll stay."

9

———

TRUST ME

Logan

I stalk down the hallway at a near sprint, cutting around the corner that leads to a narrow stairwell to the bottom of the boat where the crew quarters are located. Down another narrow hallway, the engine room fades into view, but I'm not looking for the chief engineer.

I cut into a room, slamming my entire weight against the door, which pops open, revealing the man I'd just found in Brie's suite.

He jumps, startled, and presses his back against the wall of what looks to be a bunk room.

I slowly shut the door behind me, turning the lock. "Your name?"

"Now, why the fuck would I tell you that?" he growls.

I eye the toolkit on one of the bunks. The other three beds are unmade. The room is a mess, actually.

I slowly draw my gaze back to his. "Name." I crack my knuckles for emphasis.

"Trent."

"What pack do you belong to?"

"You think I'd be scrubbing the fuckin' floors on some rich bitch's yacht if I had an Alpha?" he sneers, snickering.

His tone betrays the way he's trembling, however, as I take a single step in his direction. "Give me the master key, you fucking rat."

Trent purses his lips, his eyes flicking from side to side like he's debating trying to move around me for the door, but there's no way in hell he's getting out of this room. I have him cornered between the bunk beds hugging each wall. I lift my arms, resting them on the top bunks, and smirk down at him.

"You know what I noticed?" I drawl, clicking my tongue. "It's small enough to be, I don't know, insignificant to the naked eye… but those scratch marks on the lock on her door weren't there last night, or this morning, were they?"

Trent pales, but his expression remains stony and cold.

"I'm willing to bet you don't have a key, do you?"

"I was just following orders from the captain."

"And what would he say if I asked if you'd been directed to check the window seams in the princess's room?"

"That I was doing my job–"

"Did your job include rifling through her things? Taking a little journey through her jewelry box? The drawer she keeps her… lacy little panties in?" I'm seeing red, and Trent knows it. "Do I need to go on?"

He bares his teeth. "Who the fuck are you, then? Parading around this boat half naked with the princess? Are you her little paramour, wolf?"

"I could be. It won't matter to you, in the end, if I ever catch you within twenty feet of her, or her room, again."

He smiles wickedly. I memorize his scent–like stale cigarette smoke and mildew, a rancid combination.

But something in those beady little eyes strikes a sense of familiarity. I tilt my head, smiling down at him with a bitter laugh. "Does the *Spider* know you're here?"

Trent's smile fades into a grimace. He stutters for a moment before saying, "I've no idea who you're talking about."

I lick my lips. They never do, do they? "Sure." I relax, briefly letting my arms fall to my side, but Trent risks a step toward the door, and I act.

I grab him by the back of the neck and slam his head into the left bunk. He gurgles a scream as I press the side of his face against the cold, hard metal and lean down so I'm speaking directly against the shell of his ear. "If anything happens to her," I growl, "I won't even bother killing you right away. I'll make it slow, Trent. I'll have you weeping for your mother while I flay the meat from your bones. Maybe I'll track her down and make her watch."

He grunts, trying to get out of my hold, but I press down even harder until the scent of blood fills the room.

"If you think you can escape me, I promise you, I'll spend the rest of my days hunting you down. You'll only be rid of me when I finally decide it's your time to go to the Goddess, if She'll even have you." I give him one more violent shove for good measure. "Stay away from the princess."

"You fucking bastard," he snarls, his teeth stained with blood from biting down on his tongue.

I let him go. He crumples to the ground in a heap, groaning and hissing curses as he cradles the busted side of his face, blood dripping from his swollen lower lip.

I back out of the room and scan the hallway, wondering where the other deckhands are, but I don't have time to track each of them down to interrogate them. I already know something's up, and with the storm approaching, I'm not taking any fucking chances.

I hike through the boat until I reach the cockpit. Both the captain and second officer are bent over the controls.

Louis and Charlie look up as I stalk into the room, but whatever I was about to say is stolen from my tongue as my gaze lands on the swirling black mass of clouds ten miles ahead of us, casting long shadows over the pristine water.

I spent the entire morning and afternoon on the upper deck with Brie. I'd seen a few clouds, but this…

My chest tightens as I grip the doorframe. Charlie gives me a knowing look before slowly looking back at his dashboard.

"It's nothing to fret over," Louis tells us both, noticing the tension in the room. "It's slowing down. The seas aren't as rough up ahead from what we've been told, not as bad as last night."

"How long until it reaches us?" I ask.

"We're headed that direction, but we've slowed down significantly. We won't hit any weather until midnight, at least. If the storm picks up again, it's going to miss us and move west, I believe."

Charlie stares at Louis before turning back to his controls. The guy looks nervous, and I don't blame him.

I came here for a different reason, though.

"The princess will remain in her room until we've safely passed the storm," I tell them. "I don't want any members of the crew near her suite."

Louis swivels in his chair at my tone.

I debate my next move. I have a hunch Trent might be here for nefarious reasons… or it could simply be the fact a man had gone through Brie's things, her intimate things, while I was nearby. My body should be aware that we're no longer mates, but for some reason, I can't shake the feeling of possessiveness. She's not mine, but she's in my care, and she was violated on my watch.

It will not happen again.

I eye the captain and his second officer for several seconds before saying, "One of your deckhands, Trent, is going to need stitches."

"Why?" the captain asks, his brows raised.

"Ask him, if you want. I doubt he'll tell you more than he told me." I turn out of the room, watching the waves crash against the boat before dropping back down to the main suite level of the yacht. I can feel the change in the waves. The boat rocks more than it has before, creaking painfully as it shifts from side to side. The air feels different, too—thick with electricity, like striking a match would set fire to the sky still painted in shades of deep blue as day slowly fades to night.

I stop in my room to grab my duffle bag, then I knock on Brie's door, leaning my forehead against it. I hear her moving within the suite, quick but nervous on her feet.

"It's me," I rasp, fighting a wave of exhaustion as the waves rattle the boat.

She opens the door immediately, just a crack, then opens it wide enough for me to step inside. I catch the door and shut it tight, switching the lock in place.

Brie looks up at me as I lean my back against the door. Her eyes are wide and full of concern as she takes me in. "What happened?"

I shake my head. "Nothing you need to worry about."

She crosses her arms under her breasts. She's changed out of that bikini I'd been admiring all day and into a cream-colored nightgown with thin straps. The hem brushes her ankles as she takes another step away from me, scanning my body. Her eyes lock on my hands, on the dark bruise forming over my knuckles on my right hand.

She sighs, looking up at me with those doe eyes. "Do I want to know?"

"No."

"What is the captain doing about it?"

"That's none of my business," I tell her, scanning the hidden emotions flaring behind her eyes. Fear. Concern. The sudden realization I was right about the chance she could be in danger, even here, on her parent's yacht. She hides those emotions well behind her mask of indifference, coming off as totally unaffected.

I almost wish the mate bond was still intact so I could physically feel what she's feeling right now.

"I can make that feel better," she says, blinking up at me.

"It's not bothering me."

"It looks terrible."

"The other guy looks worse."

Her mouth ticks into a smile she's desperately trying to tamp back down but jumps when a wave crashes against the windows.

I look over the top of her head, which is easy enough since she's at chest level, through the windows at sunset blocked by incoming swirling, angry clouds.

She follows my gaze, turning slowly toward the view of the storm.

The last strips of sunset filter through the windows, casting her a halo of light. The outline of her body is totally visible beneath as she walks toward the window until she presses her fingertips against the glass.

"We'll be in Maatua in four days," she says softly, cautiously. "What are you going to do next?"

"I'm on leave for a few months."

She turns her head to look over her shoulder. "Are you going to leave, then? To Emberfyll?"

I want to say yes. I want to tell her I have the boat lined up, that the bonus I'll receive for her safe arrival in Maatua secured it. I want to tell her I have bank accounts set up to automatically funnel money to the Silverhide pack despite the fact Ryan and Aviva don't need it... but I owe them something, at least.

"I'm not sure," I say, moving slightly in her direction.

She turns back to the window as the last rays of sun dip below the stormy horizon. The suite settles into darkness broken only by the soft light of the lamps on her nightstands.

We watch the storm funnel toward the boat, the black, angry sky erupting in strips of violet blue every time lightning flares in the distance.

I'm not sure how long we stand there in silence, but it's long enough for me to become acutely aware of the situation at hand. We're trapped on this boat with a man I'm not sure is actually here to scrub floors and perform basic maintenance. All of my training has my senses honed to the idea that he's here for Brie. I'd bet my life on it, in fact. I'm the only person standing in his way, and that should be enough.

But this storm is another animal entirely.

Over the rush of the waves I can barely hear the sounds of the crew preparing for the storm above us on the upper decks. Footfalls sound in the hallway sometime later as they return below deck to hunker down for the night.

Brie ends up in bed on her side facing the window, barely blinking as rain starts to pummel the boat. I sit in an armchair nearby, unsure what to say to her to make her feel better about the situation, but honestly, she doesn't seem scared at all.

"You like storms, don't you?"

In the faint light, I catch her fleeting smile. "I do. I find them calming."

I take a breath, relieved she's not the whimpering type, but then wonder what she is, in fact, afraid of.

But then I feel an overwhelming sense of unease rip through me, igniting my wolf powers like someone struck a match against my skin. The prickle of transformation makes me turn toward the door and rise.

"Brie?"

"Yeah?"

The ship abruptly powers down. Brie sits up, alarmed.

"Is that normal? It seemed like the storm was passing right by us–"

A screech echoes from below. I crouch, pulling a pair of black gloves from my duffle bag.

"Logan, what–"

"Do you trust me?" I ask, turning for her as she slides out of bed. She opens her mouth but her response is stolen by an alarm that tears through the air, blaring violently. "Do you trust me?" I repeat over the alarm, reaching for her.

"Uh huh," she murmurs, her eyes wide and finally showing me a glimpse of the fearful girl beneath that shell of impenetrable emotional armor.

Another scream rips through the air before cutting off abruptly.

I don't trust the silence that follows.

Something crashes against her door, splintering the wood. Brie's scream is the last thing I hear before shifting, the gloves transforming into my Ghost issued armor.

10

SABOTAGED SHIP

Brie

My vision blurs with fast moving bodies and... fur. Lots and lots of fur.

I stand on the bed, pressing myself against the wall as four wolves tangle with Logan, who's as black as midnight in his armor, his sleek, dark brown coat barely visible beneath.

But he's outnumbered. I watch in horror as one of the wolves sinks his teeth into the only soft spot in those impenetrable scales of metal, ripping into his lower back. Logan snarls, thrashing with the two other wolves, ignoring the pain that must be immense.

But the fourth wolf stalks toward the bed, beady black eyes locked on my vulnerable neck.

I should shift. That would be the smart thing to do. But instead of listening to that voice deep within my mind, my wolf, I leap off the bed with a jarring scream that echoes over the waves crashing against the boat and race out of the room, stumbling over the shattered remains of the door. The splintered wood bites into my feet, tearing my skin, but I ignore the sharp, throbbing ache as I careen down the narrow hallway, sliding from side to side with the ship.

Red light ebbs through the corridor as the alarm continues to sound. The air smells like smoke and is heavy with an electrical sizzle that heats my skin and blurs my vision as I trip, landing on my knees with a crunch.

Behind me, I hear another crash and several more snarls coming from my room. A wolf explodes through the doorway, yelping and then going perfectly silent as its back cracks against the windows, shattering the glass.

A shadowed, stumbling figure races out of the smoke coming from the lower level of the ship. I scurry to my feet, gripping the wall for support as the figure staggers down the hallway in my direction, shielding his mouth and nose with the sleeve of his soot stained shirt.

He trips over the dead wolf, shouting a curse as his knees bite the ground, but then I recognize him.

"Ron?" I shout, my voice cracking. "RON!"

Ron, the chief engineer of the yacht who I've known for years, looks up in shock. "Oh, my Goddess, Princess Brie. Get up–" He leaps to his feet, riding a wave of adrenaline when he sees me in one piece. "Goddess above, get up, Brie! Go to the upper deck, now!"

I can't catch my breath. The waves are tossing the silent ship violently as it drifts straight into the storm, leaning violently to one side. I hear furniture scraping across the ceiling above my head and more crashing, thunderous sounds coming from my room.

"LOGAN!" I shout, but it's no use. My dry, aching lungs are full of smoke, and my voice cracks painfully.

Ron grabs my arm and starts pulling me toward the stairs at the far end of the hallway that leads to the upper deck.

I cough into the crook of my arm, my eyes watering as smoke fills the stairwell. He shoves at the door at the top of the stairs, rattling the handle. We notice at the same time that the lock has been tampered with, jammed.

A shout rings out below, followed by a thunderous growl... then silence once again.

My heart beats out of rhythm as my lungs squeeze for air, but there's none to be found. Ron steadies himself on the wall beside me as the ship leans to the side. With one hand braced on the wall, Ron pulls a radio off his belt loop and desperately tries to contact Captain Louis, but it's silent.

He looks down at me, his eyes stained red from the acrid smoke. He looks entirely defeated, and my heart sinks to my bare toes.

I'm going to die here, in this stairwell.

"Move out of the fucking way!" Logan screams behind us.

I scream, startled by his voice but only have a single second to react before he races up the steps, and Ron snatches me away from the door at the speed of light. Logan throws his entire body against the door, spraying blood from multiple injuries, multiple tears in the armor that now hugs his human form.

The door groans, protesting.

Ron pushes me down until I'm halfway down the staircase, and together, he and Logan slam into the door until it pops off its hinges entirely.

Warm, stormy air spiced with ozone rushes in, sending the smoke cloud swirling in a frenzy. The smoke billows toward the fresh air, blinding me. I wheeze, unable to breathe at all, and feel my body start to go slack as my vision fails, dragging me into pure darkness.

But then someone grabs my arm just as I'm about to fall backward. Logan pulls me into the fresh, rainy air of the upper deck, catching me around the waist when my legs start to give out.

"They killed everyone downstairs," Ron pants, snarling and spitting as he tries to clear the smoke from his lungs. "The engine room is on fire–"

"Brie?" Logan groans, rolling me over on my side, his hand braced on my upper back. "Stop trying to breathe. Your throat is scorched. Give yourself a minute. Breathe through your nose–"

I tremble, blinking to clear my smoke-fogged vision. Logan kneels over me as the ship groans while it pitches dangerously to the side, sending one of the couches tearing across the floorboards in our direction. He takes the brunt of the impact without so much as making a sound.

I turn my head to blink up at him. He looks… wild. Bloody, torn to shreds, but otherwise whole. But his eyes are dark with mingled rage and worry as the ship tilts to the other side, sending even more furniture slamming against the railing, a few chairs disappearing into the angry, unforgiving sea.

I hear Ron run back in our direction. "There're two lifeboats."

"We need to find the captain," Logan rushes out, rising and lifting me up with him.

"I can walk," I whisper painfully, my throat burning like I've never experienced before. Logan sets me down but steadies me with an arm around my waist as we follow Ron across the deck to the metal staircase leading to the top of the ship. A cabinet fixed to the staircase is open, its metal doors snapping open and shut as the ship tilts. It snaps against his arm as he reaches inside for what should be a life vest… but there are none.

The look he gives me is telling. This attack was planned down to the most minute detail.

We aren't meant to survive.

But why?

Ron shouts from above us, and within a matter of seconds, we're standing in the narrow hallway lined with doors that stretches toward the cockpit.

The stewardess with bright red hair is lying face down in a pool of her own blood, bite marks and slashes from claws trailing down her back.

I close my eyes, stifling a sob.

Ron pauses at the entrance of the cockpit, hanging his head. That's when I know that Captain Louis is dead.

But a groan echoes from the second room to the left. Logan doesn't let me go as he picks his way down the hallway, carefully stepping over the dead stewardess before turning into the second officer's room. It's not big enough to house more than a bed and a few cabinets on the wall. Second officer Charlie is lying on his side, bleeding profusely from a wound to his neck.

"Oh, Goddess," I cry out, trying to kneel. Logan stops me, reaching for the officer instead with his free arm and manages to haul him upright.

Charlie's head bobs but his eyes open to slits.

"You're going to live, you hear me?" Logan shouts, shaking the man. Charlie nods as best he can, gripping his throat to try to stop the bleeding. His hands are swollen and bruised, his nails slightly elongated like he tried, and failed, to shift in time to prevent an attack.

Down the hallway, I hear Ron screaming, "Mayday! Mayday!" into a radio, followed by our coordinates.

The feeling in the air is heavy, however. The storm rages as heat begins to creep from the bottom of the boat where an epic fire is spreading.

We're going down. We're going into the water in minutes.

I look at Logan, unsure what to say, or do, except, "I'm sorry." He's never going to get his boat. He's never going to make it home to Emberfyll, his life's mission. It's over.

His eyes meet mine, holding there for what feels like an eternity. "Never say that to me again." He yanks me and Charlie out of the room in time to meet Ron in the hallway.

"We're going to the lifeboats now. We only need one with the four of us," Ron stammers, fear glazing his dark blue eyes. He's my father's age, at least, a man old enough to have seen and experienced the terrors of the sea during his long career. Seeing him scared is alarming and only adds to my own despair.

What is Maeve going to do without me? She's not ready. She's not ready to be queen.

"The life vests are gone," Ron continues, shaking his head, "and the boat is getting into the storm as we speak. We can't fight it. We have to go and hope for the best."

"I'm not leaving–leaving the boat," Charlie stammers, mostly out of it. His head bobs against Logan's shoulder.

"Take him," Logan tells Ron, passing him the half-dead second officer. "Let's go."

Logan turns for the stairs, taking me with him. He hasn't let me go at all, his arm still wrapped around my waist and lifting me to the point only the tips of my toes brush the ground.

The stairs are slick with rain. Wind rips across the deck, ripping against my thin nightgown that does nothing to protect me from the biting, glass-like droplets of water spraying sideways.

The boat tilts dramatically to the left and a wave crashes over the deck, soaking us to the knees.

Ron drags Charlie toward the opposite deck where a lifeboat slams repeatedly against the side of the ship. Smoke rises in a funnel of black from the lower staircase.

"My phone," I rasp, squeezing my eyes shut. "My family doesn't know–what if I never see them again?" I look up at Logan, desperate, my heart shattering with every second that passes. He holds my gaze and looks so… broken by my words.

"You will. You will see them again, I promise," he says, and he means every word. There's no teasing glint to his voice, no rough edges or attitude like usual. He's serious. Composed. Ready to battle whatever comes next.

And what comes next is in the form a battered wolf racing from below deck, its coat singed from the fire, teeth gleaming with blood as it sprints through the smoke in our direction.

Logan tosses me toward Ron, who slips as the boat tilts to the opposite side. He drops Charlie with a crunch, and the lifeboat gives way, one of the ropes holding it tethered to the boat snapping.

Ron grabs the lifeboat, not bigger than a small skiff, using all of his strength to hold its side while trying to slice through the other rope with a pocketknife. The lever apparatus that's meant to lower it has been purposefully jammed, of course.

But my eyes are on Logan. The wolf tackles him, hackles raised. They roll across the deck with Logan's arms around its neck, squeezing while the wolf tries to bite his head.

"LOGAN!" I scream as a wave rushes over the deck, sending them sliding back in our direction. "LET HIM GO! WE NEED TO GO!"

Flames start shooting from the lower stairwell. The boat groans, and a popping sound erupts all around me as the floorboards start to crack under the pressure of the building fire beneath and the force of the waves breaching the deck.

I hear the lifeboat drop into the waves, and Ron screams, "PRINCESS!" while extending his hand to me, motioning desperately for me to come to him.

"LOGAN!" I screech, hurrying to my knees, trying to find my footing on the slippery ground.

A strangled yelp sounds from the wolf. Logan's completely still beneath it with his arms still squeezed around its neck, holding tight.

"Logan?" I whisper, falling to my hands and knees as another wave crashes into the side of the boat, sending us spinning in a violent circle. "LOGAN?"

His arms drop to his sides before he shoves the wolf off of him, dead and still. He rises, panting, his eyes meeting mine in the stormy, lightning hued night sky whirling all around us. "Go to Ron, get on–get on the lifeboat–"

"You're hurt," I cry out, noticing the blood pooling out of his armor, across his chest.

He points weakly to the boat before bending to brace his hands on his knees.

I feel Ron grab my shoulders and yank me back. He's holding the rope to the lifeboat for dear life, and Charlie isn't on the deck anymore, so he must have been dropped inside.

I'm next.

I just can't go without Logan.

"Logan, hurry!" I shout, but Logan's swaying, unable to fight the pitch and roll as the waves batter the boat into submission. I feel my feet sliding as Ron drags me back toward the railing.

Logan looks up at me, nodding, "I'm coming–"

But my eyes are locked on the massive shadow thundering toward us on the horizon. My stomach flips, lifting against my heart as the yacht dips dramatically down. I feel like I'm floating as the shadow builds, and builds, while we sink into thin air. Lightning erupts overhead, highlighting the massive, otherworldly wave not yet reaching its peak.

It's three times the size of the yacht.

We're dead.

Ron gasps, loosening his grip on my shoulder in shock.

My body reacts before my mind has a chance to catch up, and I lunge forward, sprinting across the deck at the very moment Logan turns his head to look up at the wave.

The boat tilts to the side for the last time… rolling, falling into the water as the wave collapses over the top of us.

My arms wrap tight around Logan's waist. I feel him curl around me, dragging me to what's left of the ground… and then pressure.

Leagues, and leagues, of wet, endless weight.

11

SHE'S NOT DEAD

This isn't real.

None of this is happening.

I can't really be pacing the halls of the palace in Maatua, wringing my hands until they blister. I can't be craning to hear the voices drifting in from the foyer, where my parents talk in low tones, their voices so wrought with anguish they're unrecognizable.

This morning, before the sun rose, I woke abruptly to Mom screaming bloody murder and Aris shaking me awake, his eyes wide with shock. That was... hours ago. It's nearly nightfall now. The deep red sunset–the sky after a brutal storm that swept through the islands surrounding the capital of this sea-faring kingdom–paints the hallways crimson as my shadow stretches toward what's left of the sun.

I'm not sure my heart is beating anymore. How can it when it's lost at sea?

"Fuck." I sink into a crouch, bracing my back on the wall. I bow my head, pressing my face into my hands.

In the distance, I hear Mom's strangled voice as she talks to...

81

Maddy? Yeah. Maddy's still here. She was here when we arrived after we got the news that Brie's boat had lost contact with the mainland during the storm… right after a mayday had been sent from the ship's engineer.

"But we're going to find her, right?" Mom's voice cracks painfully. "Right, Evander? She's not gone. Brie isn't–she's our fighter, remember? She's going to be okay, right? She's going to come home? Please–please just tell me she's going to come back–"

I bite back a sob, trembling as her voice breaks over the words. I can't hear what Dad says in reply and I'm almost thankful for it.

None of this feels real.

Brie was just here, being all weird, all out of sorts. I'd teased her, hadn't I? She's normally so unfazed and serious.

Now she's just… gone.

I lift my head as hurried footfalls rush in my direction. Several warriors wearing the Maatua crest hurry by, stopping in the archway leading into the foyer.

"Your Highnesses," their leader says, a commander, I assume, of Alpha King Derek's naval guard… Derek being the dowager Queen Poppy's grandson, recently crowned Alpha King in the last ten years or so.

I rise, watching as Dad comes into view. Mom's behind him–pale and gray, like she's been standing lifeless all Goddess-damned day, her very heart ripped from her chest.

I can't hear what the commander just said, but several gasps echo from the foyer. Mom's face twists with anguish as she slumps, grabbing Dad's arm.

Dad just… stares at the commander, expressionless, but his eyes go wide and glassy. "Take me there," he rasps, his voice like gravel.

"The seas are too dangerous right now. The storm is passing, but our boats are having a hard time battling the waves. The debris has been pushed inland, washing up on the shore on the east side of the island–"

"Take me there, now," Dad demands, his voice dropping to a dangerous growl.

When the commander tries to argue again, Dad... hits him. Punches him directly in the face.

He's normally so composed. So serious.

Just like my sister.

"Oh, no," I whisper, bending at the waist as my stomach twists. "No, no, no..."

Footsteps hurry in my direction as all hell breaks loose in the foyer. I hear Isaac raising his voice over the crowd gathered in wait, shouting at the warriors to leave and for Evander to go outside, to take a breath.

Hands tug on my shoulders as I feel myself beginning to slide to the floor. Maddy's warm, rosy scents hit me, embracing me in a familiar hug.

I look up into her stormy blue eyes and see tears. Her dark red hair is dappled with streaks of creamy white–the only thing that gives away her age. She's edging on seventy, but beautiful as ever as she cups my cheek, a few of her own tears gliding free. She's as much of a grandmother to me as my own grandparents are, and I lean into her touch, my mouth tightening into a pained grimace as the despair and guilt echoes through my body and twists in my chest like I'm being stabbed in the heart.

"Come with me," she whispers.

"My mom–"

"She's okay. Sarah's here now. She's with her."

I close my eyes as Maddy guides me upright. I tower over her by nearly a foot. Other than my grandma, Ella, I'm the tallest woman in the family, but Lexa isn't far behind. She has a few years of growing left, I'm afraid, and will soon look down at me when we argue over nail polish the next time we see each other.

Lexa's memory forces my mind back to the tragedy, and I halt mid-step. Maddy turns and looks up at me, smoothing a lock of my tear-soaked hair away from my face.

"Do Ryan and Aviva know?" It's impossible to swallow past the vicious knot in my throat.

Maddy sighs, pursing her lips. "Y-yes," she croaks, her voice heavy with dread she's trying to contain. "Sydney is bringing them here. They should arrive within the next hour or so, and then we'll all gather at the beach house and wait."

"Wait for what, Maddy?" I sniffle, the numbness in my mind giving way to sudden fury. "Wait for someone to tell us they found Brie's and Logan's bodies?"

Maddy winces as she turns a corner in the massive, gilded castle. Maids rush around in a tizzy, carrying trays of tea and tissues to try to quell the tears. Maddy guides me up a wide, ornate stone staircase into the upper balconies of the palace, away from the drama below.

"Did you hear what the commander told your parents?"

I shake my head. She nods to herself, looking up from her feet as she guides me into a sitting room. We're not alone.

The dowager Luna, the best friend of my deceased great-grandmother Isla, sits in an armchair facing a massive set of ceiling height windows overlooking the turbulent water, watching the naval cruisers and speedboats rush away from the port to no doubt continue the search.

Poppy turns her head, giving me a soft smile despite the heaviness in her eyes. She's a very old woman. I honestly have no idea how old she is at this point, but she's outlived my own great-grandparents by nearly two decades. Her wrinkled face is still lovely. Her hair is a deep silver in the fading light of the sunset.

Maddy smiles sadly at her while escorting me to a chair and depositing me into it, pulling a blanket off a nearby chaise and draping it over my shaking knees.

"Two survivors were found," Maddy explains, smoothing the fabric over my lap.

"Who?"

"The yacht's chief engineer and the second officer. They are... in horrible condition," she manages to gut out, swallowing hard as she sinks onto the footrest of the armchair.

"But they're alive?" I ask, hope flaring behind my eyes, only to be extinguished like water to a flame when Maddy turns her sorrowful gaze back to mine.

She licks her lips. "For now, but it's not looking great for them. The boat is washing up in pieces twenty miles east, on a rural beach. It's hard to get to by land, but the navy is going to try."

"I can take us there, right now," I tell her, pleading.

She straightens her spine as heavy footsteps echo in our direction, and then my grandpa arrives, dashing any hopes I might have had.

Alpha King Ryatt looks both murderous and torn to shreds as he looks around the room before settling on me. "Maeve, you're going back to Veiled Valley."

"Why?" I ask, turning my eyes to him. His eyes are bloodshot with the darkest of circles lining them. "I want to stay here, with the family–"

"It's out of the question now. You're leaving in five minutes. I'm escorting you and Aris personally."

I rise, digging in my heels. "No–"

"The second officer is talking," Ryatt cuts in. "This wasn't a shipwreck. The storm wasn't the reason the yacht went down." His eyes flash with fury. "This was an attempt on your sister's life."

"What?" I rise, confused. "What the fuck are you talking about, Grandpa?"

Maddy stands, holding out her hands like she's going to try to get between us to diffuse the situation. Poor Poppy probably can't hear a Goddess-damned word we're now shouting at each other, old and deaf as she is.

"Brie wouldn't have just–have just let someone hurt her!" I scream. "She's not gone. I know she's not. And Logan was with her! Do you think he would have let anything happen to her? You've known him since he was a boy! He saved my life once, you know. You were fucking there!"

"Do not," Grandpa sneers, pointing his finger at my chest, "use that tone with me."

"I am not leaving this island until my sister is found!" I shout at the top of my lungs, my resolve shattering like glass at my feet. The moonstone necklace resting against my chest flares with crimson light, my powers crackling and clawing to the surface, desperate to be let loose.

Grandpa stares at it for a moment before taking a calculated step away from me. "You're going back to Veiled Valley. You'll be under lock and key until further notice–both of you."

"You can't keep neither me nor Aris contained."

"You will be queen soon, Maeve, but there's still so much you don't understand, and I don't fault you for it. You're young. This is your first taste of hardship, of heartbreak. If you think you're safe from the same threat that just killed–" His voice cracks. He closes his eyes, breathing deeply, but his entire body shudders.

Maddy, teary eyed and washed with despair, steps toward him and lays a hand on his shoulder, squeezing. "That's enough for now, Ryatt. We all need some time, I think, to just... be here, with each other, everyone together. We're safer that way, and you know it. Let her stay."

I eye the group, casting a wary glance at Poppy, who's back to watching the boats skid across the water, then I turn and race for the door, skipping steps as I jog down the stairs and hurry back to the foyer.

My parents are no longer there. I have no idea where they went, or where Aris is, but Sarah is huddled with a few of the castle guards, speaking in low tones.

Her violet eyes meet mine and she quickly dismisses the guards, turning in my direction.

"Oh, sweetheart–"

"Is Blake here?"

"No, he's in Crescent Falls. I don't know if he's going to be joining us–"

"I need him. I need him to use his powers to try to track her down."

Sarah hisses out a breath, closing her eyes for a moment before shrugging. "I know the thought also crossed my mind, but you... know him."

"I don't give a fuck if he doesn't want to use his powers, or whatever the hell his problem is lately. I need him here. I will go get him myself and drag him back, kicking and screaming, if I must."

Sarah blinks, then smiles sadly, giving me a weak shrug. "I wouldn't say anything to the contrary if you did just that, Maeve. He might need encouragement. However, meanwhile, I'm here now. If Brie's still out there, I should be able to find her. Your dad's making the arrangements now so I can scry."

The shine in her strange, violet eyes draws me back to memories of my cousin Blake when we were teenagers, and he came to live in Moonrise to train with the Mystics. Blake is like Isaac and Sydney-emotionless. Stern. Rational.

But he spent a year with the Mystics, and... something changed. It was like he left that training with missing pieces, like he'd been stripped down, broken apart, and badly put together again.

That emotional void only deepened as he matured.

I doubt he'd be any use to me... willingly. I'm not beyond forcing him to do what I need him to do, however, even if it involves a few threats to test my many, many powers on him. He's more powerful than his mother. If she can't find Brie, Blake can. *And will.*

My nostrils flare as I glance around. "Where did everyone go?"

"To cool off, I'm guessing. Your mother is...." She bites down on her lower lip. "Maeve, I don't know what to say. I am... so sorry-"

"Don't be sorry yet," I breathe. "She's not dead. I can't imagine a world where my sister is dead."

I won't accept her death.

Whoever is responsible for this... well, let's hope they're on their knees begging the Goddess to spare them...

From *me*.

1 2

SHIPWRECKED

Brie

Hot, bright, unforgiving sunlight burns through my eyelids. My body feels... shattered–and itchy. Incredibly itchy and dry and...

I open my eyes just enough to feel the grit of sand before I close them again, my stomach rolling and twisting. I cough once–a painful experience that has me moving quickly from lying flat on my belly to my knees where I choke and gag, spilling an exceedingly large amount of water from my lungs. My throat burns like fire. My teeth ache. My lips burn from several splits now packed with... sand.

I wipe my face which only spreads the sand further. I spit more water, gulping down air and choking on it like my lungs aren't used to breathing anymore.

My hair sticks to my face in wet, sandy clumps. My skin is raw and blistered from the sun.

It comes back to me in fragments. Fractured memories of a fire, of a fight, of death, hurtle to the forefront of my mind. I remember the wave last. I remember wrapping my arms around Logan's waist and...

"Logan?" I choke, sucking in another breath. His name leaves my

89

lips in a strangled whisper as I look around, the landscape before me coming into view.

It's impossibly bright. The sun reflects off snow-white sand to the point it blinds me temporarily, and I have to blink repeatedly to adjust my eyes to the sun's assault.

A tattered lump of black fabric comes into view. Logan's legs are completely free of the armor, which is falling off him in shreds of fabric, the sand around him dotted with those strange, metallic scales. The gentle surf brushes up his feet and calves as he lies face down in the sand, his back bare and vulnerable to the sun.

His skin is red—blistering just like mine, but his wounds are…

"Oh, my Goddess," I croak, crawling on my hands and knees roughly twenty yards to where he's lying. My sandy hands hover over his back, which is flayed in ribbons. Even the back of his legs are torn to shreds, like he went through a meat grinder.

A sob works its way up my throat, making it impossible to breathe. I gently take his shoulders, shaking him, but he doesn't so much as flinch.

"Logan? Oh, Goddess," I sob, trying to turn him over. A wave breaches the shoreline and rushes toward us, soaking me to the waist with warm, tropical water. The wave retreats, taking streams of Logan's blood with it, staining the sand beneath a dark, deep red.

"Logan? Please—" I grunt with the effort of rolling him over onto his back, ignoring the injuries that will now be caked in sand.

Water dribbles out of his mouth. I don't know what to do. I have no idea what I need to do.

"Help me," I whisper, my hands shaking as I take his face between my shaking hands. "S-somebody h-help me—" I can't scream. My throat is absolutely wrecked. Every word that leaves my mouth is raspy and dry, broken into pieces.

I turn his head to the side, giving him a rough slap across the cheek. Nothing happens.

I let his face go and lean down, pressing my ear to his chest, and close my eyes.

"*Please*," I whisper. "*Please—*"

I hear a gentle, slow thump, *thump*.

He's alive. He's alive, barely. But he's–he's still here, somehow. What do I do?

I kneel, raising my hands and curl them into fists, then slam them down on his chest. Nothing.

I do it again, as hard as I can, then again, and again, until my hands are bruised and starting to swell.

"Come on!" I beg. "Logan, don't leave me here by myself like this!" I slam my fists down one more time, then lean over him, taking his face between my hands.

I lower my face to his, my eyes wet with tears.

"Come on," I whisper, brushing sand from his cheeks with my thumbs. "Come on, you stupid bastard! Wake up!"

I do the only thing I can think of to save him. Without a moment's hesitation, I press my mouth to his, and blow.

His lips are… warm–and soft. He tastes like… salt, which is totally understandable given the fact we've just been tossed through the sea like clothes in a malfunctioning washing machine. I rear back and pump on his chest again, then press my lips to his, blowing hard, trying to fill his lungs with air.

I repeat this twice more, and the next time my lips meet his, I feel him twitch.

I don't stop. I blow more air into his mouth, squeezing his face between my hands. He groans against my mouth, choking just enough to tell me I succeeded. I did it. *I did it!*

His eyelids flutter while I whisper to him, telling him he's all right, to just… breathe. To breathe, for Goddess' sake, but he's still struggling.

I press my lips to his again, and his hand flies out, clasping the back of my neck and holding me there. I freeze.

He trembles slightly, his lips parting over mine. My heart skips as he takes a shallow breath, sharing the air I'm breathing. I slowly, ever so slowly, lean away, but his hand tightens, keeping me fixed only inches from his mouth.

"Logan," I say, my voice cracking. "Logan, it's me. *It's Brie.* You're okay."

His eyes open to slits, his pupils blown wide. "Brie?"

My mouth moves, but no sound comes out. His fingers drift into my hair, his thumb dragging up my neck like he's trying to feel me, trying to register that I'm really leaning over him, casting him in my shadow and guarding him from the sun.

My sandy hair falls around our faces, blocking the view of the unfamiliar tropical landscape, but my eyes are locked on his... even while he drags me back down to him and presses his lips to mine... *willingly*.

I'm frozen solid. My eyes are still open. My mind reels, wondering if he needs... more air, or something. Because, otherwise, why would he be kissing me right now?

His lips part, a soft, guttural groan leaving his throat that has my body unlocking places I never knew I could feel.

When his tongue sweeps across my lower lip I... melt.

I lean over him, bracing my elbows in the sand on either side of his head and lean into the kiss. It's my first. I doubt it's his because he can do things with his tongue that I haven't even read about in books.

I close my eyes, a moan leaving my throat against my will as his fingers weave through my hair to cup the back of my head, directing my face to the side to give him better access...

His other hand comes to rest on my back, traveling down my spine to my cup my–

I suck in a breath and lean away, my spine turning to steel. Reality crashes down around me, shattering like someone just hit me over the head with a vase.

I draw my hand back and slap the hell out of him. The sound of my hand meeting his cheek echoes across the beach.

But it doesn't erase the smug, cocky grin twitching to life on his lips.

"You pig!" I sneer, tears welling in my eyes. "I thought you were dead!"

He tries to take a deep breath, his lips parting with some snarky retort, but goes pale.

"Logan? Logan, are you okay?" Lo–"

He rolls to his side and coughs violently, water pouring from his mouth. His back is so terrible, so raw, blistered, and bloody. The sand has to hurt. It looks like it hurts. It has to–

"HEY!"

I look up, startled, as a male voice rips across the beach.

"HEY!!!" he repeats as two figures come into view roughly a quarter mile down the sand, running in our direction. The sun makes them look like an illusion, their bodies rippling with light.

I wonder, for a brief moment, if they're even real, but then one of them shouts to us again, and I know, for certain, we're not alone on this beach… and they're *not* from our boat.

While Logan continues to spew salt water, I rise on shaking legs, stumbling forward and snatching a long piece of sun-bleached drift-wood from the sand, wielding it like a sword. My nightgown is in tatters. It's holding on by a thread–one spaghetti strap, in fact, and the hem is frayed so badly I have slits up to my hip bones.

I'm sure my not-so-sexy cotton boy-shorts are on full display as I raise the driftwood and slice it through the air when the two men come into full view. "Get away from us!" I shout, but my voice cracks painfully. "G-go away! Don't come any closer!"

Logan sputters a rough, gravelly cough behind me, grunting as he tries to rise to his knees. My anxiety flares when I hear him hiss in pain. My gaze flickers to the bloody sand at my feet and back up again as the two men come to a stop, less than a car's length away.

I hold my piece of wood out in warning. "Get away."

The man in the lead, the one who'd been calling out to us, raises his hands in surrender, but his pale cornflower blue eyes scan my battered face then my body. He has bright, golden blond hair and a deep tan, but his cheeks are ruddy from the harsh sun. His compan-ion, a man in his mid-to-late twenties, has dark skin and long, softly curling, but insanely thick, black hair he has tied back in a loose bun that brushes his shoulders. His eyes are as dark brown as mine. Both men are similarly dressed in billowing, creamy white poet shirts and snug pants that taper at the ankles.

They look like… characters from a book I used to read as a kid. *Pirates.*

"Fuck," the guy with the bun grunts as his gaze flicks to Logan. His eyes meet mine again to ask, "What happened–"

"*Back. Up.*" I growl, jutting the stick toward them.

Both men take a step back.

The blond man lowers his hands, eyeing us with interest, maybe even morbid curiosity as he asks, "You washed up? Bad storm last night. We hunkered down around the corner–"

I open my mouth to cut him off, to tell them to continue walking backward until there's a safe distance between us, but Logan sways to his feet, his hand clasping my shoulder so hard I wince as I fight to hold myself up against his weight.

"Where are we?" he asks, his voice etched with pain. I glance at him, noticing how pale he is, how red his eyes are. He looks terrible–on the verge of passing out, actually.

"That depends on who's asking," the blond man says wearily. "Where were you coming from?"

I know better than to say anything. Logan, too, holds back, but what he says next shocks me to my core.

"My mate and I were traveling to Maatua to visit family," he says, trying to take a breath between the words. "We got caught in the storm. It was worse than–than anticipated."

"What are your names?"

Logan exhales, gritting his teeth as he sways.

Alarm bells ring through my head as he starts to lean into me, losing his balance.

I can't hold him upright. I try to grab him by what's left of his armor as he starts to fall face first into the sand, his eyes rolling back in his head.

The other men jump into action.

"What's your name, kid?" the blond one asks with a grunt as he lets Logan fall into his arms.

"Me?" I rasp, unsure what to do and if I should trust them. "B-Brie."

"And his?"

"Logan," I say, swallowing hard, still feeling sand on my tongue.

He nods, glancing at his companion. "I'm Alex, the Alpha of Tempest Valley," he says, then tilts his head to his friend. "This is Sawyer, my Beta."

I blink at them, trying not to burst into tears. None of this feels real.

"Where are we?" I ask, unsure if I really want to know.

Alex runs his tongue over his lower lip, squinting against the sun. "Welcome to Hell, kid. You somehow just washed up in KiloKilo."

13

RESCUED-MAYBE

BRIE

I'M NOT SURE WHAT I'M EXPECTING TO FIND WHILE FOLLOWING THESE two strangers dressed like pirates from the poorly illustrated fairy tale I used to make Dad read to me over and over again before bed.

Sawyer offered to carry me back to their… *camp*, but I refused, of course. In retrospect, I should have accepted. My legs are peppered with scrapes and bruises, and I'm sore in places I didn't know existed, but they have their hands full with Logan.

They're dragging him. They don't have any other option, I realize. Logan's a big guy–bigger than Sawyer, who has a few inches on his Alpha, and Alex isn't a small man by any means.

I feel childlike and useless in comparison as I drag my piece of driftwood, deciding if I'm going to put my trust in a pair of strangers, I should at least have a weapon.

Sawyer stops, panting, and says, "We should shift. One of us, at least. You could go back to camp for help. I've called through the mind-link, but they don't know exactly where we are."

"We're nearly there." Alex grunts under his breath, shaking his head. "He needs the healer, or he's going to die."

My face drains of all color. Both men turn and look at me apologetically. "Sorry, kid. Didn't mean that," Alex tries to say, but I turn my expression to steel, shaking my head.

"I'm not a kid." I clear my throat. "I'm twenty-two."

Alex and Sawyer ignore me and continue walking, dragging Logan between them.

The hot sand bites into my tattered feet, but I barely feel the heat. I'm locked on the trail of blood Logan's leaving in the sand, my heart sinking as the minutes tick by, and he doesn't wake up.

The beach stretches for what feels like miles. Beyond the beach, a thick, tropical forest hugs the single mountain that rises high above us but does nothing to block the sun. I've never been to KiloKilo, of course. Relations with the strange, secretive kingdom ceased to exist after my great-grandfather died. He'd been the buffer between the rulers in KiloKilo and Alpha King Antony of Maatua, and once Great-Grandpa Maddox was gone, KiloKilo abruptly stopped all trade and simply faded into the mist surrounding their island systems.

It's rumored they're a violent kingdom ruled by an even more aggressive king, but even I'm not well versed in their history and culture, regardless of my degree in history and second degree in politics and law.

I feel like I'm prepared for anything at this point, however. I've just been through hell. I went through an attack, a fire, and survived a sinking ship by the grace of the Goddess. Being stranded in KiloKilo feels like a cakewalk until we round a sharp corner and step into the trees, following a well-laid path through the forest.

When the forest opens up again, revealing the beach, my feet stop moving.

"Wh-what–" I stammer, unable to move.

Alex and Sawyer drag Logan, now groaning softly, through the trees and onto a beach that opens up to a lagoon, where three massive ships bob in the calm water.

They have to be… very old or exquisitely crafted replicas of the kind of ships Aviva mentioned used to sail the seas during the golden age of the Firestone witches. Several stories tall and made completely out of wood, they gleam like gold in the sunlight, their massive sails pulled in and anchors dragging on the seafloor.

Pirate ships. All three of them.

I might actually be dead. That would make more sense than what I'm seeing.

Skiffs zip across the water, weaving between the boats. The sound of tools and hammers echo across the lagoon, mingling with shouted commands. On the pristine shore, a city of tents and lean-tos greet us, smoke rising to the sky from a handful of small fires, the scent of roasting meat and coffee hanging low over the camp as I follow Alex and Sawyer out of the trees, my heart in my throat.

Wolves approach, yipping excitedly at their Alpha's return, but then they go silent with suspicion when they see the cargo he brought back with him.

An old, short, grouchy looking man comes tearing toward our group, his wild, shoulder length gray hair billowing in the warm breeze.

"Alpha Alex," he pants, his small brown eyes narrowed in both concern and annoyance. "What kind of emergency–" he cuts himself abruptly when he sees Logan, sucking in a breath.

I find myself stepping closer to Alex and Sawyer when the wolves start to circle around the group, eyeing me with interest.

"A woman, too? For Goddess' sake, man. We're already low on medicine–"

"She's fine," Alex cuts in, "but this man is not."

"He's dead," the old man says with a shrug. "Look at him–"

Logan groans, spitting blood. I bristle, wishing they'd hurry the hell up and help him. I should probably say something, right? Start begging and pleading?

My eyes begin to water, tears slipping free against my will.

"Bring him to my tent," the old man, possibly the healer, says with a sigh, waving a hand.

Several men rush toward us to help. I get shoved to the side at one point, stumbling through the powder-fine sand as a group gathers around Logan, and then he's just… gone.

My chest convulses, my eyes pouring with tears. I know I look pathetic. I feel pathetic, but seeing Logan–a fierce, highly trained warrior with a reputation of being a killing machine–like this? It's jarring.

What if he does actually die?

Why does the thought of that leave me in absolute shambles?

Probably because he warned me something like this could happen. I was ignorant. Arrogant–and sure I was safe.

No one has ever cared enough to put a price on my head until now.

"Is there something wrong with your lip?" Alex asks.

I nearly jump out of my skin. I hadn't realized he was still here. I drop my hand. I'd definitely been pressing my fingers against my lower lip, imagining Logan's mouth there, swiping his tongue and gently biting down…

"Do you want to go with him?" he asks, tilting his head toward the group taking Logan to the healer.

I nod, unable to form a single word. Alex purses his lips as he scans my face, then my hair, and my tattered nightgown. He sighs, motioning for me to follow as he starts moving toward the camp, toward the tents scattered across the sand.

He stops at one of the tents and flips the flap, talking rapidly to someone inside just out of sight. Shouting from the boats and the waves rolling across the nearby shoreline drown out his voice, but when I tear my eyes from the water to the Alpha, he turns, handing me a handful of neatly folded fabric. Clothing.

I run my hands over the white cotton dress and what I believe is probably a man's shirt.

"We'll get you a shower," he says under his breath. He reaches for me like he's about to take my hand to guide me through the camp but hesitates, looking down into my eyes. "How long've you been mated to your man?"

My chest goes impossible tight as I think through the lie and my options now. I understand why Logan said we were mates even though it's far more complicated than that. I would belong to him as a mate. He has a duty to protect me with his life and I his. No man would dare cross a mate unless he was prepared for a violent end.

The only problem is we rejected each other.

"Not long," I reply, my throat painfully dry and scratchy. "We were traveling to visit family to share the news."

"From where?"

I doubt it matters as long as I keep who I really am under wraps. "Veiled Valley."

"I'm not familiar with that," he replies.

"It's part of Eastonia–"

"Eastonia?" He grinds to a halt, turning to me. I have to dig in my heels to run right into his chest. "How?"

"What do you mean? There's a route from Veiled Valley, through the straight–"

"Eastonia's gone," he argues, arching his golden brows–bright and bleached against his suntanned face.

"Oh, no, that's not true." *Shut up, Brie.* "You're probably thinking about the veil, but that's been gone for… over fifty years now. Queen Ella took it down, and now Crescent Falls and Eastonia are united."

He doesn't believe me. His face is etched with skepticism. I wait for him to pepper me with questions I can hopefully talk myself out of, wondering if what I just said is going to come back to bite me, but he just shakes his head and walks off.

I follow close behind, letting him lead me through the camp to a canvas tent big enough to fit at least a dozen full grown men within its walls.

The second I step inside, my heart in my throat, I see the healer leaning over Logan's back with a knife.

"STOP!" I scream, lunging for him, but Alex snatches me around the waist and hauls me back. I claw at his arm, writhing against his iron grip.

Logan's limp on a crude stretcher only a foot off the sand. He's out cold, a strange, bluish stain around his mouth.

"What did you do to him?" I cry out, trying to rip out of Alex's arms.

"His mate, I assume?" the healer sneers. "Get'er out of here."

"Jackson," Alex says to the healer, his name, I guess, "can you explain what you're doing with that knife before she shifts and attacks all of us?"

I relax, but my heart is still thundering as Jackson lowers his blade. He's probably my grandpa Ryatt's age, somewhere around that, hardened by time and growing more impatient by the minute. He narrows his eyes at me. "Just cleaning his wounds. He's got some coral stuck in his back. I have to dig it out if you ever want him to be able to shift again."

I choke on a breath while trying to fill my lungs with air. "Wh-what? Coral?"

He nods, obviously annoyed with my question. "He got tossed through the reef. The water along the beach is shallow, you know. The reef can shred a man to ribbons if you get swept across it with the tide. I reckon he didn't try to save himself, swimming along the surface, while being tossed toward the shore because he had *something* in his arms that meant more than his own life."

My stomach sinks. Logan had been holding onto *me*. This is *my* fault.

Jackson rolls his eyes, shaking his head as he lifts what I realize is a paring knife and tilts it toward Logan's back. But he glances at me, then looks up at his Alpha. "She well? Any injuries?"

Alex looks down at me expectantly, but when I fail to answer, he says, "No major injuries that I've seen."

"Get her a shower, then. If she's not hurt now, the sand lice will change that."

"Sand lice?" My skin crawls, suddenly far more itchy than it was before.

Alex relaxes his grip and lets me go, motioning toward Logan. "When you're done, have him brought to the *Artemis* to recover." He turns us toward the entrance of the tent without another word.

I don't want to leave Logan. I don't want to be by myself, risking giving up our real identities and what actually happened to us by accident, but selfishly, the idea of being covered in little bugs has me on the verge of peeling off my skin and begging someone to shave my head.

Alex doesn't say anything, and neither do I. My mind is absolutely tangled by hunger, exhaustion, and stress.

The only consolation I have is that Logan will probably survive, and when he wakes up, he can get us out of here somehow.

We're nearly at the shore, walking toward a skiff tied off to a piece of driftwood, when a female voice rips across the beach in our direction.

"ALEX!"

"*Shit*," Alex says under his breath as a beautiful young woman charges in our direction. Her thick, strawberry-blonde hair falls in ringlets around her waist, bouncing with every quick step she takes.

"Care to explain," she shouts, still gaining on us, "what the *fuck* is going on? Sawyer said you found a couple on the beach and brought them back? Have you lost your mind?"

"Who is that?" I whisper, swallowing past the knot in my throat.

Alex smirks, shaking his head. "That'd be my mate. She's the real boss around here. You better get in the skiff before she gets here, though."

14

DESPERATION

I GASP AS COLD WATER RUSHES OVER MY HEAD AND SHOULDERS, FLOWING down my body in icy rivulets. The woman leaning against the doorframe nearby smirks at my expense as I shiver violently, trying desperately to cover my naked body with my arm braced over my breasts and my hand shielding the apex of my thighs.

Another bucket of water is dumped over my head, and I swallow some of it, choking.

"It's not that bad," Monica smirks, her arms crossed over her chest as she watches another woman, a young maid or something, start scrubbing sand from my hair for a fourth time.

"Wh-why is it-it so c-c-cold?" I stammer through chattering teeth.

"It's filtered water, that's why." She untangles her arms and knocks on the doorframe, her pretty, angular face shining with pride. "This ship might look like something out of the stone-age, but it's high-tech. We have running water aboard. Engines below if we need more power than the sails can provide."

"Do-do you have w-warm water, by chance?"

105

She smiles at me but her eyes flash with something I can only describe as distrust. "Yeah, we do."

The maid dumps a third bucket of cold water over my head to wash out the sharp, unscented soap that makes my skin feel incredibly tight and dry, but the sand is gone, swirling into a drain at my feet.

I'm in a wash room of some kind. Clothing hangs from a line stretching from wall to wall behind my back, where several large, circular windows are open to the warm, tropical sun.

This ship is just... massive. It's like a small city inside. Monica, Alex's mate, jumped into the skiff with us and gave her mate an earful that made me blush so deeply she asked if I was about to be sick, and honestly, I might have been.

I'm starving and tired to the point I can barely keep my eyes open despite having frigid water poured over my body repeatedly.

I'm also worried sick about Logan.

I'm worried about what kind of conversation we're going to have to have when he wakes up.

"Did Jackass send you up with some ointment for those wounds or anything?" Monica asks, stepping into the room and grabbing a fluffy towel from the line.

"J-Jackass?"

"Jackson, the healer," she amends, the corner of her mouth tilting into a wry kind of smile.

I shake my head, sniffling. "No, he didn't. He had his hands full with—with Logan."

"Your mate?" One of her blonde brows arches to her hairline.

I meet her eyes, the color of whiskey, and nod, but she doesn't look convinced.

Her gaze drops from my face to my naked body, paying extra attention to my neck. "I don't see a mark."

"It's—It's early," I grit out, wondering when she's going to pass me the towel. "We haven't gotten to that yet."

"Ah, I see." She gracefully drapes the towel over my shoulders. "No bother. He should live, I think. You'll have plenty of time to experience that."

I follow her back to the doorframe, which has been her perch for the last half hour while I had my body and hair viciously scrubbed until I was sparkling clean. The maid scurries out of the room, leaving behind the change of clothes Alex fetched for me, but when I move toward them, Monica shakes her head. "They're not going to fit. Come with me."

"In just this?" I wrap the towel around my body, still sopping wet.

She turns without answering my question, and I have no choice but to follow her through the winding, narrow hallways. Everything is made of wood. From the floorboards to the ceilings, the only color is a warm mahogany, polished and gleaming in the light spilling from vintage-looking sconces. Doors line the walls. We pass a few stairwells that must lead both up to the deck and down to the depths of the ship, but Monica just keeps walking, humming an unrecognizable tune. All the while, I follow her in nothing but a towel, dripping water all over the floor.

Finally, she reaches a room at the far end of the hallway. She turns the knob, and sunlight spills toward us as she steps inside, holding the door open for me.

I cautiously enter behind her, scanning the room.

"Alex insists you're good people in a rough situation," she says, walking toward a row of cabinets built into the wall. Just like the hallway, the entire room is made from warm toned wood. A large bed rests in the center, bolted to the floor, but that's it in terms of furniture. "We don't ever just… find people washed up on the beach, especially this one."

"I thought we were in KiloKilo," I whisper.

She pulls what looks like a robe from the cabinet. It's a thin material woven in shades of deep brown and pale cream. She hands it to me, meeting my eyes, then reaches back in for what looks like a nightgown.

"Oh, we are. KiloKilo has… hundreds of islands trapped within its veil. This one is… hard to reach, which means we're hard to find." A chill licks up my skin. She notices my skin pebbling before smirking and turning toward the windows, saying, "But you're safe here with us, however you got here. However you got through that veil."

I drop the towel and pull on the robe while she isn't looking but my senses are going haywire. Are we safe? She's obviously incredibly suspicious of me, and I share that same sentiment about her... but she's the Luna of this nomadic, sea-faring pack.

"You don't live on this island, do you?"

"No," she replies, turning, confirming my suspicions. "We'll be returning to our home soon, I believe. It depends on the weather and whether we're still being followed."

"Followed by who?" I ask.

"Don't worry about it now," she says with a shrug. "I've been told to let you get some sleep, it looks like you could use it." She glances down at my tattered legs. "I'll have Alex bring some medicine for that back from the camp. That's why you were washed with cold water, you know. Hot water would've burned something fierce."

She starts for the door, but I stop her by asking, "Logan–his mouth was tinged blue when Jackass–*Jackson* was cutting into his back." I swallow hard, closing my eyes against the image of Logan's injuries. "What was that?"

"Herbs to keep him asleep. They're harmless." Monica's eyes soften as she takes me in, smiling softly to herself. "You have a little sister, don't you?"

I freeze. "H-how did you know?"

"Just the way you carry yourself, how you're not showing how damned afraid you are." She shrugs again, but her expression flashes with a sadness I... find familiar. "I have one, too. Us older sisters, well, we carry the weight for everyone, don't we? We're naturally gifted in staying strong, acting like everything's okay."

"Is your sister here?"

"No, she's not." She smiles faintly at me, but her eyes say something else entirely. Hidden grief only someone like me would understand shines there, buried deep. "Rest. You're safe. Your mate will be brought up shortly, I assume." She glances at the bed and back to me, and I realize that she knows. Somehow, she knows we're lying, like she's one of those uncanny people who can sniff out the mate bond on others. "Do you want a cot brought up?"

"No," I reply with conviction, praying my cheeks don't go bright red. "That's unnecessary."

"Well, all right, then. If you need contraceptive tonics, just let me know." She winks at me before striding out of the room. Her pale blue, cotton dress hugs her trim waist, and she's tall. Nearly as tall as Maeve, I think. Her leather vest matches the leather belt she wears around her waist, several blades catching the light of the sun before she shuts the door behind her, and I'm suddenly, inexplicably, alone.

The only sounds that reach me are the soft creaking of the boat as it drifts in the gentle water.

I lie down flat on the bed.

I fall into a deep sleep before my head even touches the pillow.

I don't dream. It's the darkest, deepest kind of sleep imaginable. I feel like my eyes have been closed for mere seconds when I wake to darkness and a star filled sky twinkling through the windows over the bed.

I sit up as voices drift throughout the room, coming from the gap beneath the door. It takes me a moment to recognize the voices, and I stiffen as Logan's voice whispers toward me, low and hushed.

"It's unnecessary to drag her into this when I'm willing to tell you everything you want to know, right here, right now."

"She's part of this, too. You have to understand the position I'm in as Alpha. You are a stranger, an outlander, coming from a world I thought, until your mate revealed the veil around Eastonia has been destroyed, was gone. I have questions… for both of you."

I hear several steps in the hallway just outside the door, like both men are widening their stances, preparing for a fight.

Logan says under his breath, "She likely doesn't remember being in that water, but I do. I swam for hours through a storm from hell itself wondering if she was dead in my arms. *Let her rest.*"

"Who is she?"

"My *mate.*"

"Your insistence to get her back to her family… plus…" Alex chuckles, then sighs, "you're a warrior of some kind. No one with an easy life has as many scars as you do in all of the places they'd be found after repeated fights in both forms."

"Her parents will know by now that her–our–ship went down. They're looking for her."

"If they're beyond the sea barrier of KiloKilo, they won't be able to find her."

"That's why," Logan grinds out, losing his patience, "we're leaving. All I'm asking is that you're able to shelter us for a few days while I come up with a plan and she rests."

"And I'm asking how the fuck you got through that veil."

The tension rises. I imagine them on the verge of transformation in that snug hallway. My heart twists as I slowly switch my position, preparing to slide out of bed to fetch the nightgown Monica laid out for me, but then I hear Sawyer's voice.

"Alex, we should let them stay."

"I have no problem with that as long as I can talk to them both," he replies hotly.

"If she's awake," Logan presses, "We'll talk, but I want a moment with her."

"To plot? Scheme? I don't think so. I have my pack to worry about now. Everyone's questioning how you got here, where you're from–"

"And I have the impression you're hiding," Logan growls. "That's what's happening here, right? When I woke up, I heard the conversations happening around me. You're out of medicine, out of provisions. You've been stuck here in this lagoon for weeks. Why?"

The floorboards creak as someone, likely Alex, takes a cautious step. "My problems could easily be yours. That's why we need to be on the same page. I will help you both, if you help me."

"Help you, how?"

"You got through the veil. We need to, as well." My skin prickles with adrenaline as Alex continues. "You're a warrior with experience at sea, from what I understand, based on what you mumbled to

Jackson when you were coming down from the high of his herbs. I need you on my ship."

I slip out of the robe and slide the nightgown over my shoulders. It's short sleeve and baggy, but it covers my body to the knees, at least. I creep over the floorboards to the cabinet, wincing as I slowly open a drawer in search of underwear of any kind. I find something to wear, at least, tugging a pair of cotton shorts up my thighs and whirl back to the door in time to hear Logan ask, "And what do you need Brie for?"

"She's just extra cargo. Someone to keep you in line."

"You'd be holding her hostage to get me to do what you want? Do you really think I'm the kind of man who would willing put my fucking mate through something like that?"

"What are your other options, warrior? You have no boat, no maps of the islands, no idea where the veil rests, and no hope of crossing without getting wrecked, again, and sucked back into KiloKilo's hold. We are your only option. I am not holding you captive, Logan. I am pleading for your help." Alex's tone drops at the end, harboring an emotion I'm unable to place. Desperation lines his words, yes, but there's something deeper there.

Fear.

Logan takes several beats to digest Alex's words.

But then the knob turns, and he says, "If she's asleep, we'll wait until morning. There's nothing she can add to this–"

The door opens enough to spill light into the room, highlighting me standing there like an idiot, eavesdropping.

Logan's meets my eyes and hangs his head, murmuring, *"Fuck."*

He opens the door a little wider, light creeping toward my toes over the floorboards. Alex heaves a breath, nodding, and says, "Well then, let's all sit down and sort this out, shall we?"

15

TELL THEM EVERYTHING

BRIE

THIS GIANT BOAT IS SOMETHING OUT OF A FAIRY TALE... WELL, I'VE JUST found out that Alpha Alex not only has these three but two more tucked away in some island chain about as far from the capital of KiloKilo as he could get. It's hard to believe these boats even exist. It doesn't make sense. This room and its finery doesn't make sense.

I watch Logan resting only a few feet away, his large frame eating up the dainty armchair perched in front of a dormant hearth. He hasn't touched any of the food laid out for us, but I have. I'm on my second bowl of stew, swiping the nearly empty bowl with my fourth or fifth piece of rustic sourdough bread. With food in my body for the first time in what feels like days, I'm acutely aware of my senses and the room around me... and the people within it. The ship's ornate details come into startling view as I scan the room under the shadow of my eyelashes, carefully not to look directly into Alpha Alex's or Beta Sawyer's eyes.

We're in what I believe are the Alpha's personal rooms. It's exactly what I imagined it'd be—rich furnishings. Gold glinting in the light of a crystal chandelier. Treasures and books piled on shelves. There's even a hint of disheveledness to the space, like the Alpha can't be bothered to organize. He's probably too busy pillaging, of course, being a pirate, and all.

A flash of strawberry-blonde hair tears my attention from the space as Monica leaves an adjoining room, coming to a stop next to the couch I've been slouching in, eating as much as I can get my hands on.

Monica glances down at me, giving me a not-so-subtle once over before setting a stack of clothes beside me and waltzing away. Her red nightgown and matching robe makes her look like a beautiful... strawberry, especially with her almost pink hair spilling over shoulders. She gracefully perches on Alex's desk and crosses her long legs, looking slightly bored as she rolls her neck and fixes her mate with a scalding look.

I don't blame her. The grandfather clock taking up an entire corner of the room chimes 3:00 A.M., and the men are deep in conversation regarding the shipwreck and how Logan and I ended up on the beach. I'd love to be back in bed right now, too.

Logan hasn't said a word to me. He looks in my direction on occasion like he's confirming I'm still here, but otherwise, his attention is fixed on the Alpha and Beta.

Sawyer paces in front of the hearth, asking questions as Logan explains, in gory, vivid detail, the wolf fight and discovery of the dead captain then fighting with that last wolf on the deck.

"It was premeditated," Logan explains, "One of the lifeboats had been cut from the ship. The life vests were nowhere to be found, and the door leading to the upper deck had been purposefully jammed."

"Why would these men—these criminals, as you call them—want you dead?" Alex leans his thigh on the edge of his desk, reaching out to stroke his knuckles along Monica's arm. She doesn't look away from Logan, however.

Logan scratches his neck, casting me a glance under the guise of stretching out his sore body, and shrugs. "They likely wanted to rob the boat—"

"That's not true," I say, my voice wobbling.

Logan goes rigid, his eyes cutting to mine and holding with an intensity that takes my breath away, but I've had a long time to think about our situation while he was sewn back together again.

All eyes are on me, now. Even Monica, who I doubt trusts me at all, sits up a little straighter.

"What's the truth, then?" Alex asks.

"I'll tell you why we ended up in the water if you tell us why you're hiding out in this lagoon." I slide to the edge of the couch, setting my empty bowl down on the coffee table. With practiced grace, I cross my legs in a very lady-like fashion and knit my fingers around my knee. I straighten my spine and ignore the fact I'm wearing nothing but a shapeless nightgown and that my hair is totally out of control, channeling an energy that makes this situation seem like I'm sitting in front of some high-ranking members of a nearby pack to Veiled Valley, taking about the crime rates, or trade, or whether Maeve's temper tantrums will have an effect on their upcoming festivals.

Logan takes me in, watching the way I straighten my shoulders and shake my hair out of my face before settling the Alpha with a look of bored indifference right as I say, "I'm a princess of Eastonia. My mother is an Alpha, and my father is the commander of the Queen of Eastonia's–my grandmother, Queen Ella–of a very specialized faction of her royal forces, of which Logan happens to be a captain." I tilt my head in Logan's direction for emphasis. "We were traveling to Maatua through the strait when we were caught up in the storm. I believe the assailants were planning to rob me, or hold me for ransom at the Port of Maatua, but the storm gave them an opportunity for far more."

Sawyer stops pacing, now leaning on the far wall with his body turned toward one of the windows, but he looks at Alex, raising a brow.

Alex, however, has his eyes narrowed on mine.

Without skipping a beat, I continue, "Logan was right to hide my true identity when we were found. As you can imagine, I'd just been hunted down and trapped on a boat with men who wanted to hurt me in some way. He was protecting me."

"As a mate should," Monica smirks.

I ignore her, adding, "That's the truth. I am a royal. A princess. Logan is—is my mate." Well, that's a lie, but the truth is far more complicated than I'm willing to divulge. "We're now stranded here in KiloKilo." I lean forward, not allowing the group to jump in with their lines of questioning. "But I think you might also be stranded here in this lagoon."

Subdued fury flashes behind Alex's eyes. Sawyer bristles, and Monica… well, she's grinning at me like a cat.

It takes all my strength not to look Logan in the eyes. He's probably fuming right now, thinking I've put us in a precarious situation by telling these strangers who I am after barely surviving another group of strangers who wanted me for nefarious reasons. Who's to say Alex and his pack won't see this as an opportunity to do the same?

Alex leaves the desk and begins to pace, tapping his chin in thought. "And your family will be looking for you?"

"Of course. But… KiloKilo and Maatua are no longer allies." I watch him closely, noticing the way his blue eyes darken a shade as he glances at his mate. "Even if my family thought we'd somehow washed up here, your king—"

"Not my king," Alex cuts in sharply, and I've accomplished all of my hopes and dreams about this conversation. The Alpha shows me a single crack in his armor, and I lunge for it.

"So you are… on the run?" I tilt my head, giving him my most diplomatic smile.

"My pack, and a few others, cut ties with the royal family of Kilo-Kilo decades ago. We're as good as rogues. Anyone who doesn't fall under their… iron grip of dictatorship is deemed… criminal in nature. We've done what we've had to do to survive."

"So you live on these ships full time?"

"Not necessarily," he says, shaking his head. His eyes meet mine. "But recently, yes. We've been trying to make our way home for the past six months, but the royal navy has been making that... close to impossible."

"Why would they care?" I ask, curious. "If they deem you rogues, shouldn't that be that? You simply... don't get to enjoy the perks of having an Alpha King protecting your pack, ensuring peace?"

Alex swallows hard and closes his eyes. "It's complicated."

"We need to know what we're getting into," Logan says, his voice dry and raspy from lack of use, "especially if you're going to continue asking for my help—"

"What neither of you seem to understand," Alex cuts in, "is that there is no returning home for you, either of you. You cannot just... sail across the veil, the barrier, whatever you want to call it."

"Well, we got in," I counter, but Logan cuts me a look, and I purse my lips, biting back whatever future comment I'd been ready to make.

"And that's a mystery in itself I'd love the answer to because it would make leaving all that much easier." Alex takes several steps away from us, turning toward his Beta, saying, "Have them set up in a state-room, something bigger than they have now."

Sawyer nods and walks away. I watch him go then turn back to the Alpha as Monica says, "The rest can wait until morning, my love. Let our guests sleep."

I scan her face. While Alex showed me a glimpse of his emotions—showing me the stress behind his eyes—Monica is like stone.

Her eyes cut to mine, friendly but sharp, like she knows exactly what I'm thinking right now.

We have no choice but to trust them, and they want something from us, which means we're... safe, for now.

Safe, but with no way to contact my family. These people aren't going to turn us over to the authorities under the crown of KiloKilo, either, which might not even matter in the end. I don't know the ruling family or their politics. This place—this sweeping island system covering hundreds of miles all hidden behind rough seas and almost constant storms, is being kept a secret on purpose.

I have a feeling if whoever's in charge of KiloKilo finds out we're here... it'll be worse than this.

Alex runs his hands through his hair, mumbling something to Logan about speaking again tomorrow morning, and Logan rudely cuts back that speaking about this tomorrow was his idea in the first place, but I'm already halfway to the door carrying the stack of clothes Monica set beside me while she leads the charge.

I follow her down the hallway, which opens up to the main deck of the ship, and down a single flight of stairs where only a few doors line the wall this time.

I can hear Logan sauntering and stumbling behind me. We have so much to talk about, don't we?

A sudden jolt of apprehension flares in my chest when one of the doors opens, and a young woman, possibly a maid or something, hurries out of the room. Monica clicks her tongue at her before motioning to the dark space. "Well, this is you for the foreseeable future. Make yourself at home. Generally, breakfast and supper are served on the beach… but I imagine tomorrow is going to be busy, so go down to the galley if you're hungry. It's two floors down."

I nod along as Logan comes up behind me, slightly breathless with pain.

Monica looks him over before dropping her eyes to me with a smile that doesn't reach her eyes. "Goodnight. Or, good morning. I guess that depends on when you wake up." She whirls and sways back to the stairs, disappearing in a flutter of red, silken fabric.

I close my eyes, feeling Logan all around me, his hand on my lower back as he guides me into the dark room—our room.

I don't open them again until I hear him shut and lock the door, and light flares behind my eyelids.

I don't see the details in the room. That'll come later, I'm sure, when I've had a moment to process Logan and his bandages.

Blood seeps through some of them, painting him in streaks of deep crimson.

"Are you–"

He steps forward and takes my face between his hands, lowering his forehead to mine. He doesn't say a single thing to me, but his mouth… moves… and his eyes are closed, like he's praying.

I remember a conversation Aviva and my mom had a very long time ago, so long ago the details of where we'd been and why I'd been listening are hazy and fragmented. Aviva was telling her about Logan losing his parents, about a shipwreck and...

I gingerly wrap my arms around his waist, careful of his injuries, and let out a long, shaky breath. "We're okay, Logan. I think we're going to be okay."

He crushes me to his chest, and I finally, *finally*, allow the tears to fall in earnest.

16

UNEXPLAINABLE CHOICES

LOGAN

I DON'T REMEMBER FALLING ASLEEP. I DON'T REMEMBER MUCH OF THE past day, actually, not since washing up on the shore on some nameless island.

I slowly sit up, wincing as bright, fresh pain ripples through my back. I press my hand to my chest where the bandages cover most of my skin and find them damp with blood, but it's not fresh. No, I must have stopped bleeding like a stuck pig a few hours ago. That's one thing going my way, at least.

A soft murmur beside me steals my attention from my pain, and I turn to find Brie fast asleep, her hands tucked beneath her cheek. I don't think I've ever seen her wear her hair natural before. It's wild and... lovely. But looking at her–at the soft, relaxed expression on her face as she sleeps–has me careening back to going into the water with her and realizing that was it.

I'm not sure how we survived. Call it divine intervention of the highest degree because there's no other way we would have made it out without dying.

She's bruised, however. Dark spots of deep purple and blue are fading to a cruel greenish-yellow as I scan her body. She fell asleep on top of the sheets, and her legs are bare, giving me a glimpse of the scrapes and bruises that turn my stomach and have fury surging to life once more.

I hadn't been in my right mind yesterday, nor early this morning when Alex insisted he talk to both of us. Based on the sunlight filling the room, that was hours ago. It's likely late afternoon now.

I scan the room, taking in the details of warm wood and dark blues and greens. The room—a bedroom, with a few adjoining doors I'm sure lead to a bathroom, maybe closets or sitting areas—screams a kind of loud luxury I hadn't expected. Alpha Alex has money. He has power. Yet, there's something off about him, something I can't place.

I start to slide off the bed when Brie's eyes fly open, and she sits straight up, blinking blearily at me.

"Go back to sleep," I tell her, cursing internally at being careless enough to fall asleep beside her when there's a perfectly good couch taking up a nearby wall.

Brie rubs her eyes and covers her mouth as she yawns. "What time is it?"

"Don't worry about it." I stand with effort, grimacing as the bandages pull and pinch my skin. "I'll try to find some food—"

"You're not going anywhere without me," she argues, gracefully swinging her legs out of bed and storming toward me.

I allow her to rise on her tiptoes and place her hands on my shoulders. She presses down, forcing me back into a seated position on the edge of the bed.

"I'm going to fix you up, and then we need to talk," she says with a sigh. "Because a lot happened yesterday, and I highly doubt you remember most of it."

"Are you always so chipper when you wake up? It's rather annoying."

"I'm looking on the bright side, Logan."

"The bright side of what?" I ask, following her progress as she walks toward a dresser and fetches a stack of fabric, tucking it under her arm as she whirls back in my direction.

"We survived. Somehow, against all odds, we made it. Now, we might be trapped on a pirate ship–"

"Alpha Alex isn't a pirate–"

"I believe he might actually be," she counters, cutting me off. "And whether we trust him or not, we have no other options. It sounds like he's trying to leave KiloKilo, and we need to go home. So, we're stuck with him and his pack, which means we just need to–need to do our best. Starting with replacing the bandages." She taps the fabric. "I'm going to change and then I'll help you. Don't move."

She whirls again, her hair whipped into a frenzy at the movement, bouncing across her shoulders and back in a mess of tight ringlets and looser curls that follow no pattern. She tries a few of the doors until she finds a bathroom and shuts herself in, and the room falls into silence once again.

Sunlight plays over my thighs and hands as they rest in my lap. I'm in a pair of… boxers, perhaps. Shorts of some kind that don't belong to me at all, and I don't remember putting them on. I remember being in my Ghost armor while swimming with the current, trying to keep our heads above the violent waves. I remember how cold the water felt and how high the waves were as we drifted further and further from the lifeboat, and Ron's voice faded completely. I remember the sudden violence of reaching swallow water and rolling, hitting the reef over and over, practically drowning, before finally washing up on the beach.

It'd been pitch black when my body met solid ground again. I didn't even have the strength to make sure Brie was still alive before I succumbed to exhaustion and pain.

Then… I woke up again, briefly, to Brie's mouth on mine, and thought we were dead and I was… simply washed upon the shore of the Goddess's kingdom–with my mate.

I close my eyes at the fractured memories that come next. Being dragged back to a camp that smelled like smoke and the scents of dozens of other men, other wolves. Waking up flat on my stomach with a bitter taste in my mouth, listening to garbled conversation taking place around me. Waking up again on a cot to an old man peering down at me, fighting him, and being subdued by six others… and then Alex appeared, wanting to know who I was and how we got here.

My head pounds as I squint into the tropical sunlight streaming through the windows.

The only thing I remember clearly was Brie coming to life this morning in Alex's office. Her face had shifted from pure, unfiltered unease to a mask of… diplomatic grace as her spine straightened vertebrae by vertebrae. Even in a rag-like nightgown with her hair falling loose all around her face, she sat composed and unbothered, radiating a kind of unshakable energy that nearly brought me to my knees.

I don't know who Brie thinks she is, honestly, telling these strangers our secrets, but she spun her truth in a way that made her shine like a polished gem.

Maeve might be ascending the throne of Eastonia, but I wonder if fate chose the wrong sister, because Brie… she's a queen down to the marrow in her bones.

She rushes out of the bathroom in a dress of dark blue that brushes her calves and tapers tight around her waist. My throat bobs as I take her in, at the way her waistline and ample curves are on achingly full display in a dress that must belong to Alex's mate. It's just too tight in all the right places, and it takes all of my strength to tear my gaze from the cleavage the frock allows. The three-quarter sleeves leave her arms exposed enough that I can see the bruises again, which is enough to drag me back to the reality of our situation.

"These were left for us," she tells me, grabbing a length of cloth bandages and a jar of ointment from a table near the door. "Thoughtful, I guess. The healer must be sick of you after spending an entire day picking shells out of your back."

She starts to kneel between my legs, reaching for the bandages covering my chest, but I stop her with a hand on her stomach. "I can do it."

"Logan," she says slowly, drawing out my name like a curse. "You look like fucking shit."

Momentarily stunned, my lips part, sucking in a breath as I rasp, "I've never heard you cuss before."

"I'm hanging on by a thread," she admits, but smiles, even if it doesn't reach her eyes. "We're fine. We're totally, completely fine. I have to keep believing that, or I'm going to completely lose my mind."

She kneels, swatting my hand away, and begins unwrapping my bandages.

I stare at the wall over her head as she works in silence. I try not to wince when she slathers the sticky, slightly pungent ointment across my midsection with her bare hands, fighting the urge to lean into her touch.

But I notice the fine calluses on her fingertips and ask, "What did you do to earn those? I didn't take you as a fighter."

"I studied the wolf arts just like everyone else," she says, glancing up at me. "I'm sure my level of shifting expertise is equivalent to what you practiced as a teenager, but I'm not a warrior."

"What are you, then, Brie?"

She sighs, rising, her hands shiny with medicine as she looks back and forth for something to wipe them on. She settles on my pillow, ripping the case off and murmuring something under her breath to the tune of finding me a new one, and climbs onto the bed, settling behind me to start working on my back.

"I'm an older sister," she says lightly as her fingers begin to move over my sutures. "I braid Maeve's hair every day, sometimes multiple times if she's shifting between forms, that little witch."

"What do you mean by multiple forms?"

She shrugs. "Her favorite thing to shift into is a house cat. I'm not sure why, but she's silent on her feet when sneaking around the house that way. I've caught her lurking in the rafters of my dad's office a time or two in the form of a little gray bird–a pigeon. She's not very good at it, but she can shift to look like a different person, too, but the eyes always give her away."

I turn as best I can manage to look Brie in the eyes. "Are you serious?"

"Did you not know? That whole family knows by now. Our precious, shape shifting witch. She can do other things, of course. Her silver fire, her... banshee screams that deafen entire villages. What else? Oh, she's rather skilled as a warrior, but I think that has more to do with trying to keep up with Lexa."

I blink, remembering Maeve as a baby. I remember her fire, of course, but the rest must be new.

Brie continues, "Maeve hasn't even reached the peak of her powers yet. She will once she's pregnant with her first daughter-that's how it works. Firestone witches are their most powerful as mothers. Misty thinks it was a... biological defense mechanism to carry on their bloodlines. Men can't be Firestones, even if their mothers are, but they can pass gifts to their daughters. Firestone women can mate with shifters, etc., and still give birth to full blooded Firestone females." She sighs heavily. "Well, that's just a theory, of course. We'll know more once Maeve's line comes into existence."

"So you have calluses from braiding your sister's hair?"

"Oh, is that what we were talking about?" she laughs, shaking her head. I hear fabric tearing, and then she's nearly flush with my back as she reaches around me to start winding the bandages around my middle. "I suppose so. I do a lot of reading and especially writing. I guess it's from holding a pen all day."

"What do you write?"

"Nothing you'd find interesting. It's just studying-"

"Studying what?"

"Politics of past and present. Maps of territories from a time before now, and theorizing what things could be like during Maeve's reign and forward. Misty published an amazing history book a while ago. I've read it several times, so much so I'm sure I have it memorized by now, but there're others, especially in Veiled Valley. I keep our antiquities specialist, Arthur, busy."

I was right when I thought in another life that she could have been a commander. She has the brain for it, always thinking two steps ahead of everyone else.

I look down at my stomach as her hands weave the bandages in place with expert skill, like she's done this before.

I almost ask. I nearly pry, crossing a boundary I think we've inadvertently drawn in the sand.

We rejected each other. It was completely mutual. Nothing has changed for either one of us.

But I want to know her–even if it's against my will.

"I'm done," she says a bit breathlessly, sliding off the bed to examine her work. Her face is slightly flushed a rosy pink as her gaze lifts from the bandages to my face. "Does it feel better?"

I don't know what I'm thinking. I can't see past that moment when she ran to me across the deck of the yacht, forgoing the safety net cast by the lifeboat. She could have been home, with her family. Yet, she's here… with me. She chose me.

"Brie," I begin.

We both jump when a sharp knock sounds on the door.

17

———

A PIRATE'S LIFE FOR ME

Brie

Monica arches her brow as she plucks another petal off the flower she's been defacing for the last ten minutes in relative silence. She's precariously perched on the railing of the upper deck, with an insane drop to sudden death beneath her, yet she doesn't look the least bit fazed by it.

Me, however?

I adjust my position on a crate nearby, neatly crossing my legs and refusing to look over the railing and the lagoon below.

"Afraid of heights, Princess?"

"No," I rush out, but the word wobbles. I straighten my back, brushing invisible dust from my dress, and fix her with a cold look. "I'm not."

"Come sit with me then." She pats the railing, a cocky smile tugging on the corner of her mouth.

"I'm fine here," I counter, narrowing my eyes.

"Suit yourself. You're missing the show." She jabs a thumb at the water but goes back to plucking petals off her flower, humming a random tune.

All around us, people are readying the ship, the *Artemis*, to disembark from the lagoon. The two ships resting further back in the lagoon are also in preparation to leave. Skiffs zip across the water from the beach and back again, carrying supplies to the ships.

Monica notices me watching the two other boats and says, "The blue one is named the *Asteria*," she explains, tilting her head in its direction. "The one with the yellow sails is the *Atropos*."

"Names of the old gods," I murmur, and she nods, tilting her face to the sun.

"Goddesses, technically."

"I know," I cut back, but she laughs, her hair drifting in the tropical breeze.

It's nearly sunset. Logan and I slept most of the day. I'm shocked we were even left alone for so long after the Alpha's 3:00 A.M. meeting where I spilled the secret I'm sure Logan was wanting me to keep. After I'd changed his bandages this afternoon, Sawyer arrived with a stack of clothes for the both of us and told Logan he needed to meet with Alex again. For what, I don't know. I didn't ask. I was just… left behind.

I could tell Logan didn't want to leave me but we're not in charge here, and I think that's hard for him. Maybe it'll humble him a bit.

Eventually, Monica came to fetch me and fussed over my clothes and hair for an hour before dragging me up to the deck to watch the preparations, using me as her own personal form of entertainment.

She stretches out on the railing while people yell commands, scurrying across the deck carrying ropes and tools I've never seen nor could name. Men and women alike climb ratlines to start adjusting the sails. As it stands, Monica and I are resting in full sunlight, but once those sails expand, I'm sure the temperature will drop ten degrees, which would be a welcome relief from the sun.

My skin prickles from the heat. I was right about getting a tan. I'm starting to bronze wherever my skin's exposed, and I can practically feel the freckles starting to dot the bridge of my nose and cheeks.

"How long does it take to get to–wherever home is?" I ask Monica.

She tosses the flower stem over the railing. "Only four days with full sails and engines. We'll be moving at a full sprint as long as the weather holds. And if we're not followed."

I glance at her, but she's not looking in my direction. Her hair's piled on the top of her head in a bun spilling with ringlet curls that glow a pale pink in the sunlight, and she's wearing a dress similar to mine, but in a pale cream. A leather corset hugs her trim waist, and just like me, she's wearing leather boots. A pirate's outfit.

"Are you a pirate?" I ask, unable to help myself.

She snorts a laugh, squinting as she turns back in my direction. "What's that?"

"They sail the seas, pillaging and raiding."

"The only pillaging Alex has ever done is in our bed," she smirks without skipping a beat. My cheeks burn, but Monica's grinning from ear to ear at my expense. "We're not thieves or criminals, if that's what you're insinuating. Alex has a very large pack and has to travel on occasion for supplies seeing as we're not part of the KiloKilo pack-land network of trade. We're on our own."

"Is that who'd be following you? KiloKilo's... warriors?"

She nods, picking at her corset, her eyes holding on the water. "Why?"

Monica purses her lips. I can see the gears turning behind her eyes like she's mulling my question over, debating about telling me the truth, fragments of it, or everything. Finally, she meets my eyes. "Can you keep secrets, Brie?"

"I can," I reply honestly. "Just like you said, I'm an eldest sister. That's my job."

Her answering smile is faint and knowing. "I have to ask you something first."

"Go ahead," I say, sitting up a little straighter.

"Logan isn't your mate, is he?"

"It's complicated."

"The mate bond is not complicated at all," she argues, furrowing her brow. "It's very cut and dry–"

"We rejected each other about a week ago. He'd been an acquaintance of mine, of my family, since I was a child, and we hadn't seen each other in many, many years when we felt the bond. It was a mutual rejection." I wait for her to press me with questions as to why we did it, but she just nods, like she somehow understands. I add, "You asked if I can keep secrets. I can, and I hope you can as well, because Logan would prefer people think we're mates for my own protection."

"I understand. Your secret is safe with me. But does it not bother you sharing a space with him? Or even just being around him?"

"No, not at all. I actually enjoy his company a lot." I swallow, realizing I just admitted something out loud that I haven't allowed myself to accept internally, speaking the truth into existence. "I wouldn't want to be with anyone else in a situation like this."

She smiles, shrugging, "I always wondered if mate bonds were simply for breeding purposes or if it is more than that. Then I met Alex and I knew that the Goddess knows who pairs best with whom, regardless of how we feel about it."

I tilt my head, wondering what she means by that. "You and Alex call yourself mates. Are you saying… you're not happy about it?"

"No, not at all," she amends. "I only mean I was raised being told the mate bond was something that could be manipulated, chosen, so to speak. That whoever I was deemed to marry would be my mate based on being marked, and it didn't matter if I had a chosen mate out there, somewhere."

"We call that imprinting where I'm from. It's rare, but my grandparents on my father's side are mates because my grandpa marked my grandma."

Monica's expression is almost impossible to read as she toys with her fingers, the rings glinting in the sunlight, casting rainbows across her midsection. "Yes, precisely."

"You were… betrothed?"

She looks up at me, her eyes dark and wary. "I was born for a specific purpose, if that counts. And that purpose was to marry a prince within KiloKilo's royal family."

I notice a faint scar on her ring finger when she twists a thick, gold band inlaid with diamonds and sapphires around her finger. The scar is jagged, almost like a burn. I feel a sudden sense of dread as she continues, "Don't tell Alex I'm telling you, but I'm the reason his pack is on the run. They wanted to leave KiloKilo anyway, but... now they have to because every warrior in KiloKilo is looking for me and Alex. Me, and my fated mate."

"What happened?" I don't like this. My skin crawls as she looks over the water again, her expression edging on pained.

"My parents didn't marry because they were in love. They weren't mates like you and Logan were, or like Alex and I are. They were chosen for each other based on certain attributes valuable to the royal family. Attractive, lack of... intellect. Full, unwavering submission to the crown. Families like mine were rewarded for every girl their union produced. My two younger sisters were married into the royal network–to dukes and princes within the outer branches of their family. I was chosen to marry... the heir to the Grand Wizard. His son, a man three times my age. I was in the capital of KiloKilo for my wedding when... when I met Alex."

My stomach is in knots, but I don't press for information even though I'm dying to know more. So little is known about KiloKilo's royal family. My great-grandfather met the king's advisors but was never allowed to speak to the king, the Grand Wizard, face to face.

"But I was a bad egg, so to speak. Mouthy and opinionated, which isn't what the royals were looking for, of course. They tried to beat that out of me when my parents arrived with me, seeing my beauty tinged by what they called madness. My parents were... punished for raising such an intolerable daughter, and my sisters... already married, did nothing to stop them."

My throat tightens.

"One day, I was in the castle, being fitted for my wedding dress. It was the day after my parents were killed. I snuck away to the city, deciding it would be better if I... walked into the ocean and let the old gods decide what to do with me, but I bumped into Alex in the market and felt the mate bond click into place. Alex isn't the kind of man to accept defeat, and he wasn't going to let me go, whether or not it meant he'd be hunted for the rest of his life. He was looking for something, though. Alexandrite. The rare, purple hued crystals the wizard and his flock use to strengthen their magic. It's possible to travel through the veil with one of those precious gems on your ship, and my mate needed them to get his pack to safety. I knew where the royals kept them."

"So you stole them?"

"Of course. It was easy enough to do. Alex hated that he had to use me to secure the gems, but we had no other options. I had to wait until the day of my wedding, seeing him in secret. We'd… acknowledged our bond by then. He marked me on my breast." She closes her eyes as her fingers drift over her bodice. "High enough that the mark could be seen over my wedding dress to offend the wizards. But… things never go the way they're planned. I stole the gems–enough for every ship in Alex's armada and the two other packs and their Alpha's who wanted to leave KiloKilo as well. But I was caught. I had time to hide the gems in my room before a maid ratted me out after she saw the mate mark on my chest, and I was… held down, my finger cut to the bone and cursed to never heal, to always show who I really belong to. My–my betrothed told me our marriage would be a punishment worse than death for me. And Alex… burst into the ceremony, and saved me. We ran, taking the gems with us, knowing my sisters would likely be punished for what I'd done."

She closes her eyes.

"He has a death warrant on his head. Bounty hunters are looking for us in droves. Once we reach Tempest Valley, Alex's island, we'll be safe, but not for long. There's a system of reefs that surround Tempest and the nearby islands home to the rogue packs. We have our own witches and wizards who protect the reefs, keeping the royal guard out, but they're desperate to find us, knowing what we've taken and what we plan to do–"

"When we reach… anywhere, outside of KiloKilo," I cut in, "I can ensure your safety and that of your pack. You can settle anywhere you want. You'll have our royal family behind you. We don't tolerate things like that."

She gives me a wary smile. "Thank you."

I slip off the crate and go to her, taking her hand. "We'll make it out."

"You washed up just in time, Brie. Funny how fate works. Now, where are our mates?"

Shouting on the deck rings out, drawing out her voice. The sails expand, casting long shadows over the deck. They're magnificent.

"Time to go," she breathes, closing her eyes and saying a prayer for our safety.

18

SHAVE AND... NOT A HAIRCUT

Brie

Night falls on the trio of ships. During the course of the evening, the ships had been readied, and the camp on the beach had been totally dismantled, leaving no trace that Alex's pack had ever been there.

Now, against a blanket of silver moonlight, the *Artemis* bobs in the shallows just beyond the mouth of the lagoon, engines purring and sails drawn.

I lean against the railing and soak in the cool night breeze. It smells amazing here–like salt and tropical flowers. It's almost exactly like Maatua but far more rocky and mountainous. Beyond the mountain shielding the lagoon, nothing but calm, open water stretches as far as the eye can see… which means we'll be totally exposed to whatever enemies are lying in wait.

The deck teems with people waiting for the two other ships to silently leave the lagoon. It's a rough looking bunch–mostly hardened men with deep suntans and scars on their hands and faces, but a few women mill around, checking lines and making sure crates of supplies are secured. No one even looks in my direction. No one pays me any mind whatsoever.

I look up at the navigation deck where three shadowy figures huddle near the railing, talking in low tones. Logan looks down at me, his eyes catching the moonlight. He leans in to say something to Alex and Sawyer before making his way down the stairs, dressed in an outfit similar to everyone else's on the ship. The white, vintage looking shirt tapers at his waist, tucked into fine-fitting trousers tied off with a leather belt. Leather boots stalk in my direction, his dark curls rustling in the breeze.

He hasn't shaved since we ended up here. I'm reminded that he lost his glasses–everything he owns, I believe. His laptop and phone are gone. His clothes.

We're all we have left that came from our world.

That thought settles in my chest when he comes to my side, resting his arms on the railing.

"Things are going to move fast once the two other ships leave the lagoon," he says, dipping his head to brush the words against my temple, like he doesn't want to be overheard. "Will you stay below deck, please?"

I look up at him with a sly smile. "I've never heard you say *please* before."

"It's not normally in my vocabulary," he admits, smirking. "Will you stay below, in our room?"

"Only because you asked so nicely."

A glint of moonlight shines in his eyes as he gives me the softest of smiles. Something about the way he's looking at me right now makes my stomach feel all fluttery, but I could easily be imagining that look of what I can only describe as longing as something entirely unrelated.

His longing could simply just be for me to stay locked in our room tonight while we travel to open water, not... longing for *me*.

I shouldn't care how he feels about me, but after what we went through, it's impossible to continue to tell myself I don't care about him.

Just like it's impossible for me to see past Logan whenever I think about my plans when we finally reach home... my schemes to find a husband, an Alpha. When I think of that, I imagine him. I imagine us in the car the moment we'd rejected each other and wonder why the hell I did it.

I shouldn't be thinking like that. Maybe my feelings are changing, but his aren't. Logan doesn't want me. He can't. I'm not... pretty like the girls I'm sure he's been with. I'm stuck up and boring–too serious and stubborn. I doubt I have a playful bone in my body, and I know he's the kind of man who likes to laugh.

He'd never want me, of that I'm certain.

I just hate that now, all of the sudden, that knowledge hurts.

I follow him off the deck and down into the depths of the ship to our room. Anyone not working above is nestled below, tucked in for the night.

I expect him to leave right away, but he enters the room behind me, closing the door with a soft click.

"Do you want me to redo your bandages? It's been several hours."

"They're fine," he says, locking the door.

I wring my hands as I walk toward the bed and sit down. He slips out of his boots, setting them by the door.

"Are you not staying on the deck?"

He shakes his head. "Not tonight. Alex said the likelihood they're followed out of the lagoon is low. Open water is another story, from what I've been told."

I wonder if the Alpha told him about how Monica plays into this because I'm desperate to talk about it. I promised her I could keep a secret, though, and I plan to, even if it's eating me alive.

Logan continues, "I was told my services would be needed starting tomorrow morning, and that you and I will be moving to the *Asteria*. That ship needs a captain. Right now, a group of his warriors are making do, but none of them have the kind of experience on water that I have."

"Are we in danger?"

"I believe so, yes. I know you spent the day with Monica. Did she tell you anything about why they've been hiding out in that lagoon for months, and island hopping away from KiloKilo's capital for months before that?"

"They've been away from their territory for that long?" I ask in shock. I hadn't realized that.

He nods gravelly. "Monica is—was supposed to marry—"

"She told me," I tell him, grateful I have someone to talk to about this. "She told me about the royal family and the alexandrite."

"Good. I was hoping she did." He starts pulling his shirt free from his belt. "So you're aware the entire force of KiloKilo's navy is looking for them? Good. I told Alex that it's likely bits and pieces of the yacht washed up on this side of the veil, and if that's true, the navy will be busy investigating that versus trying to track Alex down. He's hopeful that time is on our side. We'll be traveling all night as fast as we can, and in the morning, we're switching boats and continuing what should be a four day long journey in less than two days." It's almost like he's talking to himself as he says it, going over the plan laid out using me as a sounding board. I nod along. I don't know anything about boats or maritime, but Logan does. Also, I just enjoy listening to him talk. He's not like my dad or brother, or any of the men in my family, really. He likes to tell stories. He can go on, and on, and I can just… listen forever….

He takes off his shirt and says, "I'm going to shower."

"Oh-okay."

"I'll sleep on the couch," he says, pointing to the sorry excuse for a couch on the far wall.

"You won't fit. Just sleep in the bed with me. We're grown adults. It doesn't matter." My heart flutters as he stares at me, his eyes darkening a shade.

I almost offer to sleep on the couch instead, but he nods and turns into the bathroom.

I use the time to change into a nightdress Monica supplied. It's beautiful and silken, like something I'd wear back at home. I slather the lotion she gave me on my skin and brush out my hair until it shines. I feel somewhat more like myself when I look in the mirror, like I finally have a routine again.

Logan exits the bathroom sometime later with a towel hanging around his waist–and nothing else. I dart into the steamy bathroom to brush my teeth, needing to put a bit of distance between us.

This has to be some echo of the mate bond, right? I told myself I'm not attracted to him, but that's obviously false. He saved my life. I can like him for that fact alone, feel grateful for him without that feeling bleeding into something more, something dangerous, but…

He re-enters the bathroom with a little black bag that he dumps on the counter. He looks down at the straight razor with a sigh, lifting it to the mist swirling around overhead. I set my toothbrush down, noticing the disappointment in his eyes as he lifts his gaze to the mirror to inspect the three day old beard growing in.

"Are you going to shave?"

"I was planning on it. I asked Sawyer for a razor, but I guess Kilo-Kilo isn't as evolved as Eastonia."

"KiloKilo doesn't have corner pharmacies selling razors and the like, I'm sure."

"I've never used a straight razor. It can't be that hard–" He lifts it to his face, but I snatch it before he can do any damage. "What, Brie?"

"You'll slit your throat! Or worse, slice a layer of skin off. Just keep the stubble."

"I don't like it," he says in a low growl.

"I like it," I retort with a shrug. Again, his eyes darken, his pupils blown wide in the hazy, foggy light. I amend, feeling suddenly short of breath, "But I can shave your face for you if you're that insistent on it."

"Why would you know how to use one of these?"

"Because Aris nearly killed himself with one on accident when he was thirteen. My dad uses one and tried teaching him, but Aris doesn't have the patience for it, so I learned."

"You shave your brother's face?"

"Don't be weird," I hiss. "And no, but I would if he could grow facial hair, poor thing."

Logan's mouth twitches into a smile. "Fine, but if you maim me beyond repair, I might have to reignite our mate bond because you'll be the only girl I'll ever get, scarred and disfigured as I'll be."

I do my best to ignore the fluttering sensation his words ignite as I command, "Go get a chair, Logan. You're too tall for me to do this standing up."

Logan scans my face before turning out of the room. I ready the blade and shaving cream while he drags a chair into the bathroom, sitting down with a soft groan.

"You have to relax," I tell him, standing directly behind him and tilting his head back until his head brushes my breasts. "And don't move."

He relaxes when I smooth the shaving cream over his neck and jaw but goes absolutely rigid when I swipe the blade in a practiced motion up his neck.

"Logan, relax."

He grits his teeth, peering up at me through narrowed eyes. "I'm not used to having a blade pressed to my neck."

I press a little harder, arching my brow. He exhales through his nose in warning, but I just smirk and carry on.

Within minutes, his neck is perfectly smooth, and he finally, *finally* begins to relax, allowing me to guide his head from side to side as I move with the blade like this is second nature.

I wonder if he's ever allowed anyone to take care of him before.

He leans into my touch while smoothing the razor over his jaw and cheek. His breath is warm on my hand, his lips dangerously close to my skin.

Unable to stand the silence and tension I feel creeping into the room, I ask, "What do you think the family's doing right now?"

"Panicking," he replies softly.

I've been trying not to think about it. Mom and Dad must be in pieces, and we have no way of contacting them until we pass through the veil. That could be… weeks from now.

"They think we're dead, don't they?"

Logan doesn't answer for a long time. "Maybe. It's only been a few days, though. They're still searching. They wouldn't give up on you that quickly."

"They wouldn't give up on you, either," I say, looking down at him. Those green-hazel eyes gaze up at me, and for a moment, the rest of the room blurs. I smooth my hand over his freshly shaven cheek, smiling sadly.

But then the memory of kissing him ambushes my brain, and I wince, rearing back and turning his head to the side. I clear my throat, swiping the blade on a hand towel before continuing the task at hand.

Logan chuckles, however, murmuring something under his breath.

"What did you say?"

"You were thinking about the beach, weren't you?"

My skin heats, but I manage to finish the last section of his cheek before my hands start to tremble. I step away from him, turning to the sink to rinse the blade. Through the mirror, I watch him rise and move the chair out of the way before turning to face the mirror, inspecting my work. But his eyes slowly meet mine, and that Goddess-damned bastard arches a brow, and I lose it.

"I was trying to save your life," I grind out through gritted teeth. "You drowned, remember? I wasn't going to let you die and leave me all alone on an island–"

"It felt an awful lot like a kiss," he chuckles.

"Well, I wouldn't know," I grit out, turning to face him. "I've never kissed anyone before."

"You kissed me," he shrugs, wetting another hand towel.

"*I did not kiss you.* If anything, you kissed me–"

He turns to me, leans down, and grips the back of my head. I gasp, but the inrush of breath is short lived, because one moment he's a comfortable distance away, and the next, his mouth is on mine–hot and firm.

His fingers tangle in my hair, tugging just enough I have to look upward into his face. He slowly pulls away from the kiss, which wasn't more than a peck but still made me feel like time was standing still. He looks down at me, his lips parted and eyes searching mine, waiting for me to react.

I should scoff. I should shove him away, calling him a pig again, or worse. I should smack him, actually, maybe even take the razor I'd just spend thirty minutes using to shave his face out of the graciousness of my heart and give him a new scar.

But I rise on my toes and press my lips to his.

19

MATE'S SCENT

Brie

AT FIRST, I FEEL NOTHING BUT HIS MOUTH ON MINE. HE INHALES, BUT otherwise, is still as stone. The tension between us is so thick I could drown in it, and I wouldn't bother saving myself by coming up for air.

I pull away just a touch–just enough to take a shuddering breath. Maybe this was a mistake. I'm not sure what I was thinking kissing him back, but... here I am, wondering when he's going to start laughing at me.

Logan's nose brushes mine as he closes his eyes. His hands drift to my waist, and my eyes flutter closed as his grip tightens. He takes a step toward me, then another, until I'm forced back, until my shoulders hit the wall. Time moves in slow motion as his lips brush the corner of my mouth, and he groans.

Logan presses me to the wall and kisses me hard enough to steal my breath away. I rise on my toes to meet him, my lips parting as I try to suck in another breath, but his tongue slides along my lower lip before gliding into my mouth. I have no idea what to do or think. Isn't there a specific way to do this? Something that makes someone a good kisser versus a bad one? *Because I desperately want him to think I'm good at this.*

His hands move from my waist to my back while he presses me closer, trying to deepen the kiss with our bodies flush against each other. He leans into me, pressing his body against mine in a way that makes me moan against my will. I'm losing focus with every slow, exploratory circle of his tongue. The room fades when he growls with satisfaction as he gently bites down on my lower lip.

I'm a goner, and the worst part is, I know… deep, deep down, that I want this more than anything.

My hand curls around the back of his neck, the other planted on his bare chest like I have any chance of pushing him away. He'll stop if I ask. I know he will. But I can't think of a reason why I'd want that.

"Come here," he whispers against my mouth, his voice low and gravelly with hunger.

He lifts me up like I weigh as much as a feather and deposits me on the counter, my thighs pressed against his hips. I have a single second to breathe, to reconsider what I've started, when he kisses me again so deeply my toes curl, and my body thrums to life with heat that radiates and settles in my core.

I gasp around his tongue. One of his hands slides up my back to cup my neck. He guides my head from side to side, curling his body into mine and kissing me like–like his life depends on it.

This can't be how everyone kisses, right? I know Maeve has kissed boys before because she gloats about it, and Aris is definitely the family slut as it stands, but this?

This is… *this is…*

His free hand travels up my thigh, taking the fabric of my nightgown with it. His warm, solid palm on my bare skin ignites a fire that burns through me, melting me into a puddle of want so deep I can't see past it. My heart beats out of rhythm, skipping and sprinting while our tongues dance, and he groans my name against my mouth like a prayer.

I squeeze my eyes shut and tilt my head back as his mouth moves from my lips to my cheek, brushing over my skin in a featherlight touch. His breath is warm over the ridge of my ear and into my hair, where he inhales deeply, his grip on my thigh tightening as he shudders. I feel my cheeks beginning to burn as his mouth finds my skin again, pressing a soft kiss just below my ear, and it's such a sensitive sensation. I shiver, gripping his arms for support as his mouth travels lower, down my neck, his tongue drawing a long, slow line to my sternum.

My nipples peek beneath my silky nightgown, and I arch toward him against my will, desperate to be touched.

But he pauses, panting against my skin, and slowly rises up to face me, so close our noses brush. I chase his mouth with mine, but he chuckles low, almost cruelly, and says, "That was a kiss, Brie. You should know the difference when you meet your Alpha husband."

Reality crashes down around me like a cold, wet blanket.

His eyes are as dark as polished obsidian as he pulls away, his mouth slightly red and swollen, and he looks…

Angry.

He turns and leaves the bathroom in a huff. I'm sitting on the counter with my legs splayed, his handprint a firm, red splotch on my exposed thigh. I teeter between heartbreak and righteous fury. His comment had been an insult, that's clear. A dig meant to make me feel… guilt, maybe even shame. Who the hell does he think he is?

I slide off the counter and rush into the bedroom.

He just finished pulling on a pair of pants and is reaching for a shirt when I yell, "What's wrong with you? Why would you say that to me?"

He looks over his shoulder, arching an eyebrow. "Say what? We're going home, and once we're there, you'll continue to try to make a match, won't you?"

My hands curl into fists at my side. I can't find an answer for him. Normally, *yes* would be resting on the tip of my tongue, but the look on his face is borderline shattered, a mess of emotion I'm shocked he feels.

He rolls his eyes back to the closet where he fishes out a shirt, shrugging it on, his voice muffled by the fabric, "It meant nothing,

Brie. Just a kiss." His voice drops as he moves toward the door, opening and closing it with a snap, leaving me alone and in silence with nothing but my thundering heartbeat as company.

I flop into bed and curl myself into a ball, unsure what to think. I hug my pillow, my eyes overflowing with hot, angry tears. I can still taste him—still smell the shaving cream and his rich, male scent beneath, and it hurts.

Worse, I think I just hurt him in some way, and I don't understand what I've done wrong because he wanted this separation—this dissolution of our bond—as much as I did.

As much as I used to.

I don't remember closing my eyes, but I fall into a fitful sleep and wake to pink-hued sunlight creeping through the windows above the bed. The door opening startles me upright. Logan steps inside looking worn and tired, like he didn't sleep a wink. The cool side of the bed he didn't occupy tells me he didn't return to our room last night at all. He scans my face, my body, determining that I'm in one piece, but that look is still in his eyes, that look I can't quite make sense of.

Something obviously shifted between us. I'm not sure when it happened. Maybe it's been like this from the beginning, and I've been too focused on ignoring my growing feelings to realize what was happening.

I liked him… I liked being his friend, but… my body is telling me with every passing moment I spend in his company that it craves more, and he just…

"Get dressed," he says sternly, turning from me to start gathering my things off the vanity.

"Why?"

"Brie, just do it."

I roll my eyes to the ceiling, cursing myself for kissing him back and ruining everything, and snatch another dress from the closet before rushing into the bathroom.

When I emerge a few minutes later, he's waiting by the door, his back pressed against it. His face is drawn, his eyes holding absently on the bed, like he's stuck in his mind.

"We're moving boats, right?"

"Yeah," he says, rolling his lower lip between his teeth. "We are. I'll be captaining the *Asteria* and you'll be... there."

"I can stay on this ship," I offer, a knot forming in my throat. "Logan–last night–I'm sorry. I don't know what–"

"That was all me," he says quietly, and his eyes rise to meet mine. "And so is what I need to do to you now."

I stiffen, confused. "What do you need to do to me now?" I nervously chuckle, but he reaches behind his back to lock the door.

My heart rate starts to skyrocket as he edges toward me, each step he takes like a predator stalking his prey.

"What are you doing?" I ask nervously.

He stops a foot away and reaches for me. I command my legs to move back, but they don't, and he manages to turn me around so my back is facing him. I shiver involuntarily as he brushes my hair away from the back of my neck and sighs deeply, saying, "I don't know the men who've been in charge of *Asteria*. They know I have a mate with me, but you... you don't carry my scent, Brie."

My cheeks flush. "Is that a problem?"

"I've been questioned about it already," he says quietly, his thumb tracing a line from the base of my neck down my spine until he reaches the zipper holding my dress in place. He gives it a tug and it pulls down.

I'm not naive enough to think this isn't a huge problem. He's right. I don't carry his scent like mates do when they've acknowledged their bond, slept together, marked each other... and I'm about to be in the company of strangers–strange men, from a pack that's not my own.

Logan has proven he'll do anything to protect me.

"Are you going to mark me?" I ask, the words wobbling off my tongue.

"No, but you need to hold still."

He walks us against the vanity. I can see his reflection in the mirror. His eyes are glassy, dark and conflicted while he winds an arm around my body to hold me in place as he bends me over the vanity just a touch.

I can't breathe. My body forgets how to function as he dips his head, and his mouth rests on the back of my neck. He takes a breath, inhaling deeply, his body shuddering just like it had last night when he pressed kisses into my hair.

Then he kisses my skin—light and tender. I close my eyes as he presses his tongue to my neck, drawing a line from the base of my head down my spine, leaving the occasional bruising kiss that has my body careening back to life again. When he's done, he slowly turns me around, his eyes briefly meeting mine before giving my neck and chest the same treatment. Slow kisses. Drawing his tongue over my skin. Sucking bruises just behind my ears. Nuzzling me like this is just—just what we do together. Every touch sends ripples of excitement across my skin and has that same heat from last night roaring to life.

I stand still as best I can and allow it to happen. He braces his hands on either side of me on the vanity, clutching it for dear life.

But I'm... melting again. I start to lean into his touch. When he licks across my collarbone, I gasp, a strangled moan leaving my lips, and he rocks into my body, breathless, like he's hanging on by a thread.

I've heard about this ritual before. It's ancient, of course, from a time when shifters were almost completely nomadic and constantly migrating, coming in contact with other packs. He's... scenting me. Marking his territory. And I've never felt more alive than right now.

When I start to slump, he presses a hand against my belly to keep me steady, my back biting into the edge of the vanity. He nibbles my collarbone and up to my neck again, gently biting my flesh—not hard enough to break the skin and leave a mark, but *close*.

Close enough I almost beg him to *just do it*.

"Am I hurting you?"

"No," I breathe, my hands leaving the vanity to clutch his sides. Another nibble of his teeth against my neck has me grinding my hips against his in an almost involuntary movement. Desperation clouds my senses. My wolf is in agony, which is something I've never experienced before, even when we rejected each other.

When he turns me around again to face the vanity, and leans down to continue his ministrations, I begin to whimper.

"I know," he breathes, clutching my hips to steady himself as he kisses up my skin, causing gooseflesh to erupt all over my body as a heated chill licks down my spine. "I'm almost done–"

"Don't stop," I rasp, unable to stop myself.

His lips part against my skin, a straggled sign escaping. "Brie, I–"

A thunderous rap on the door jolts us both. Logan lifts his head as Sawyer's voice rings out, alerting him that the skiff is here to take us to the *Asteria*, and we need to hurry.

"We'll be there in a minute," Logan says as firmly as he can, but his voice still shakes. He holds perfectly still with me bent over the vanity, totally prone and at his mercy, until Sawyer's footsteps recede.

I catch his gaze in the mirror. He's disheveled, breathless, his cheeks stained a ruddy pink as he looks down at me. He closes his eyes, whispering a curse under his breath, biting down on his lower lip like it's taking all of his strength to pull my zipper back up and step away.

He manages it, gently helping me upright.

I can't look at him right now. I can't let him see how much that just affected me. My inner thighs slide together–wet and aching for him, and I'm… suddenly desperate to get away from him. Far away.

"Do not wash my scent off until I tell you to," he says under his breath then takes my hand and moves toward the door.

2 O

IN THE SHADOWS

MAEVE

THE HALLOWED HALLS OF THE PALACE IN MOONRISE ARE QUIET AND somber. Normally, light would spill through the ancient stained glass windows lining the foyer, casting sunlight that made the golden walls gleam, but today everything is dark. Gray. Lifeless.

Rain thunders across the glass ceiling, echoing down hallways usually alive with conversation and bodies bustling from room to room. Now, my only company is my shadow, and even that's trying to curl away, just as worn and empty as I feel.

It's been nearly a week since we lost Brie. I couldn't stay in Maatua for another second waiting for news.

I walk up the grand staircase, wearing a hoodie, jeans, and sneakers, a far cry from the sweeping, luxurious gowns of silk I normally dress in when visiting my future home.

Yes, one day all of this will be mine. I've known it—felt it in my bones since I was just a little girl. I will be queen. Soon. Three years from now, I'll stand on the balcony and wave down at the people of

Moonrise—of all of Eastonia—but in the visions I had for myself, the dreams I manipulated?

Brie was always beside me.

I close my eyes, raising my face toward what little light there is to be had, and curse her name for leaving me behind to do this by myself.

That bitch. Honestly, I mean, really, Brie? You had to die in a *shipwreck*?! You couldn't have just—just been normal? Been cool? Stopped your madness about finding a husband for a single fucking second and—

"Maeve?"

I whirl, blinking back tears as my grandmother's voice drifts toward me just as lightning pierces the sky, blanketing the corridor in violent blue light. Queen Ella—Grandma—walks toward me, cutting a corner from another shadowed hallway tucked just out of sight. Her cloak of crimson trails behind her in the shadows, but her eyes are wide and glittering like polished sea-glass as she reaches my side, laying a hand on my shoulder. My hoodie's slightly damp from the rain, but she doesn't seem to notice the cool chill. Instead, she squeezes, her dark brows furrowing slightly. "What are you doing here? I wasn't expecting you. Or anyone."

"I got sick of Grandpa pestering me constantly in Maatua." I sniffle, reaching up to wipe the tip of my nose with my sleeve. "Aris left for Veiled Valley and convinced Mom to go with him, and I..."

"Your grandpa told me what happened," she says under her breath, one of her brows arching toward her hairline. "I didn't know you knew that kind of language."

"I'm sure Grandpa has been called worse than an overbearing, annoying *motherfucker.*"

Grandma's lips part like she's about to reprimand me for calling her mate of over forty years, the Alpha King of the Roguelands, and the scariest, most powerful man to walk our realm a horrible name, but her mouth curves into a knowing smile.

"Ryatt is having an especially hard time with this," she admits sadly, her eyes glistening in the gray light.

"Brie was his favorite," I murmur, my heart wrenching at even the thought of her.

Grandma bites her lip and curls her hand around mine, wordlessly leading me away. The palace is a maze to most people, but I know the winding hallways and shadowed alcoves like the back of my hand. My feet know where we're going without needing my eyes to confirm it. Within a few minutes, I'm tucked in her office on the third floor, surrounded by the familiar crimson wallpaper and dark wood finishes.

Her paintings cover the walls in thick, golden frames. Grandpa kept everything she painted down to sketches on napkins.

Once, I tried to explain the concept of love to Brie. I used our grandparents as an example. They have the type of boundless love that spans realms, lifetimes. Something so deep it could never be broken, even by death.

Maybe one day Brie will understand that feeling for herself. I never will because I'm technically not a shifter. I'll never feel the mate bond. I'll never know what it's like… but Brie could have. I imagined living vicariously through her great love story one day.

Now, I'll have to settle for Aris and whoever is unfortunate enough to end up as his mate, bless her soul.

Grandma sits on a leather couch, reaching for a tea set, but before she can utter a word, I blurt, "I need you to force Blake to come here as soon as possible. Have your mystics reach out to him in their divine way, I don't care how it's done."

She stiffens, blinking once, then turns to me with a puzzled look flashing behind her eyes. "Why?"

I perch on the armrest of the couch, my legs splayed in a very unladylike fashion, my pants also damp from the rain. "Because Sarah failed to find Brie and Logan by scrying, but Blake can do it. He's just a lazy, rotten imbecile and needs an extra push. That's why I'm here. I need him, and he's ignoring me and everyone else."

She sighs heavily, abandoning the teapot she just reheated with her powers. Powers we share. "Blake isn't lazy nor rotten, Maeve. He's grieving like the rest of us."

"You know that's not true. Everyone in the family seems to be keen on giving that asshole a pass, but I'm not. I need him here. I need his help."

"Blake is a grown man, and if he's choosing not to use his gifts, that's his business—"

"Brie is missing," I grind out.

"Brie is likely dead," Grandma says with heartbreaking effort.

And just like every day for the past week when the crushing truth is mentioned, I ignore it, rising and turning away from the possibility that my sister is gone, and there's nothing I can do about it. "I'm staying the night. Possibly for the next few days. I'll bring him here myself."

"Maeve," Grandma says, shaking her head at me when I turn to look at her over my shoulder.

"Is everyone just okay with this?" I ask through tears. "Everyone just… we're just accepting that she's gone?"

I've always known Grandma to be a woman of many words. I love that about her and have craved just sitting with her and listening to her stories, her opinions, her plans but… for the first time in my life, she has nothing to say.

I see the grief written all over her face. Grief for me and especially for my mother, her only child. Grief at the loss of the glue that held our family together. I doubt Brie knew how much we all relied on her. I doubt *we knew* until she was gone.

I leave Grandma in her office. I have no destination in mind as I walk out of the castle into the dreary night air. I just need a minute. I need a moment to think outside of the walls of my family's many castles and fortresses.

I pull my hood over my head, shielding my face with its shadow. I don't bother masking my identity with my magic, not when the normally lively city is in the deepest kind of mourning, every flag lowered and door veiled with black fabric in honor of the princess who's not coming home. No one is out on the street tonight in the inner city. It's silent, save for the pounding rain.

My feet carry me to the village of Old Moonrise on their own accord. It's nothing in comparison to Moonrise. The buildings are lopsided and ancient compared to the polished marble and crystal of the city my grandma pulled from the lake forty some-odd years ago. Old stone greets me in a warm embrace. The smell of food from the vendors lining the narrow, cobblestone streets remind me I haven't eaten much in the past few days. Old Moonrise is busier than the city with its night market and bar scene flourishing despite the somber undercurrent scenting the air with grief. It's a welcome relief.

Rain drips from awnings where patrons of taverns and shops stop to smoke cigarettes and catch up with friends and neighbors. I walk through puddles reflecting neon light, keeping my head low against the downpour. I reach a small tea shop, its doors open to the storm. I stand in line, watching the TV in the corner of the shop as the news plays in a pixelated loop. A news anchor from Crescent Falls, dressed in a khaki suit, speaks against the backdrop of the official royal portrait of Brie, taken only a year ago when she graduated from college.

"The search for Princess Brie of Veiled Valley has concluded its seventh day with no new information to report," the report says solemnly. *"The Kingdom of Maatua's naval forces have extended their search to the ocean borders of their closest neighbor, the Kingdom of KiloKilo, but sources state that the leaders of KiloKilo aren't cooperating with search efforts."*

The person waiting in line behind me taps on my arm. I blink, moving up in line, but my eyes stay glued to the TV.

"While the royal family of Eastonia has remained quiet on the details of the search and continue to ask for privacy at this time, Alpha King Sydney of Crescent Falls has spoken out,"

I close my eyes.

"The full force of the royal army of Crescent Falls is now joining with the Order of the Ghosts to aid King Ryatt and Alpha Kenna's search for Princess Brie and Captain Logan Atrayis of the Silverhide Pack. According to the two survivors of the wreck, there's reason to believe that this was a targeted attack on the princess, and the mastermind behind the plot was Hannibal Arachnis. Sources out of Eastonia recently confirmed that warriors have been deployed in all major territories–"

Another tap on my elbow has me moving up to the counter where I murmur my order and step aside to wait.

The image of the anchor from Crescent Falls fades to an anchor reporting from Eastonia, and images of my family in Maatua fly across the screen. Paparazzi pictures of my parents leaving the castle in Maatua. Me speaking to Aris on one of the balconies. I should be used to feeling like I'm under a microscope every waking minute, but this...

I shift to the side to turn from the TV, grabbing the tall paper cup tea off the counter–and miss. I swipe the cup instead, sending its contents spraying over the stomach of a man standing less than a foot away.

He doesn't flinch away from the hot, chamomile scented water.

"I'm sorry," I rush out, fisting a handful of napkins and thrusting them in his direction, but he grabs my wrist before I touch him. Tattoos stretch from his wrists to his fingers. Stars, I realize. A map of the heavens. Constellations and planets in faded black ink.

I look up into his face, but he's... wearing a mask. It's a black mask that covers all but his mouth and the outline of his sharp jaw. His eyes shine behind the fabric, but it's otherwise... simple, yet jarring.

He looks at the woman behind the counter and says, "Another chamomile tea, with honey. A *ridiculous* amount of honey, apparently." He snatches the napkins from my hand and dabs at his shirt with an annoyed sigh. I move away just a touch, bending to pick up the cup I knocked on the floor. When I rise, he's turning toward me with a new cup of tea, his mask cast in the shadow of his hood.

He's taller than me by a foot, which is no easy feat, even for a man. He's broad in the shoulders but lean in the waist, a build that makes me think he's a long distance runner, or something of the like. I take him in, tilting my head as I scan his worn, tight wash jeans, thick black leather boots that match his black leather jacket.

He's wearing a hoodie similar to mine beneath–brand-less and a dark gray now soaked with tea and honey.

I hold out a hand to accept the tea but let my powers simmer, sending a spray of heat toward the stain, which dries in a matter of seconds.

He just stands there, looking down at me through his mask. I can feel him scanning my face, taking me in, just like I'd so unapologetically done to him less than a minute ago.

"I can… buy you a new hoodie," I offer, reaching to take the tea from him.

"You shouldn't do that in public," he whispers.

I go still, unsure what to make of his tone. It's casual but laced with warning. I never use my powers in public, but I'm so rarely in public these days, especially this close to my coronation. Well, I do go out, but in disguise, using my powers to give myself… blonde hair, a shorter build, or something like that.

I hadn't done that tonight.

"Habit, sorry," I murmur, clutching my tea for dear life as I slowly turn away from him. We're the only two people in the snug tea shop now. A few others linger under the awning, but the three vinyl tables are empty, and the TV's still blaring the news on an endless loop. "Thanks for this." I hold up the tea. I reach into my pocket, rolling a few coins in my palm before extending them to him.

"It's fine," he says, his voice low. He glances at the TV. I wonder how well he can see it through the mask. I wonder why he's wearing a mask. It's not unheard of in these parts, but it's still a little… odd.

The anchor has moved on from my family to another story coming out of Tarsian.

"Alpha John Yarris was found dead three days ago after a lengthy search. His body was located ten miles from his pack territory. Local officials have deemed his death a murder, but the motives are unclear–"

The stranger slowly lifts his cup to his mouth but doesn't take a drink. I'm watching him, however, watching the way his jaw flexes as the anchor continues, *"An official statement from the Royal council of Tarsian has been released regarding the investigation, confirming this was a targeted attack by the assassin Blade, supposedly the right-hand of the criminal under lord Hannibal Arachnis, a wanted fugitive in both Eastonia and Crescent Falls."*

The stranger cracks a small, tight smile.

"*Blade*," I whisper, rolling the moniker over my tongue. "What a stupid fucking name for an assassin. So uncreative." I sip my tea.

The stranger chuckles, then turns, walking into the downpour.

I follow his progress, noticing a silver glint around his wrist when he lifts his cup to his mouth again. It's a bracelet of some kind, which is odd, because that's actually silver, I'd bet my life on it, and if he's a shifter, that would hurt like a son of a bitch–

He looks right at me, giving me a slow nod, and disappears into the night.

My powers surge then settle, and I'm left with an overwhelming feeling that I know him.

I sink into one of the plastic chairs and watch the man with the mask until he's no more than a shadow disappearing through an alley on the opposite side of the street.

2 1

LET'S JUST BE FRIENDS

Logan

Sunlight pours over the deck of the *Asteria*, glinting off the sails. I watch the *Artemis* drift past, Alex waving from the upper deck before fading into the bright glare of the sun. I grip the railing, closing my eyes for a moment and taking a much needed breath that catches in my throat the second footsteps sound on the stairs nearby.

Sawyer grunts softly as he reaches the top of the steps and turns in my direction, squinting against the sun but smiling as he says, "You settled in?"

I nod, biting back that breath I desperately needed and all the other feelings threatening to make themselves known the next time I see Brie, which is hopefully several hours from now after I've had a chance to cool off.

"The *Asteria's* the oldest and slowest," Sawyer says under his breath, joining me at the railing. "But she's a solid ship. A good girl. My favorite of the fleet, actually."

"Why aren't you captaining her, then?"

He grins and shrugs. "The same reason I'm not on the *Artemis* with

Alex. I'm his Beta. If anything happens to him, I'm taking over the pack. He has no heirs yet as it stands, and… I can't captain a ship in the event we start sinking because I can't go down with it. That's your job now."

I smile to myself. "So you're not just here to keep tabs on me, then?"

"Not exactly. Although I think Alex might be acting too cautious when it comes to you and Brie. You're stuck here, and I don't think either of you are dumb enough to try to breach the veil on your own."

I glance over my shoulder at the men scurrying around the lower deck, climbing rat lines to adjust the sails. Just below where I'm standing, there's an indoor cockpit. Unlike the yacht, it's basic, with almost archaic engine control systems and no weather station at all. It's easy enough to make this ship move, however.

I would know because my parents died on a ship exactly like this one.

"I gotta ask," Sawyer says quietly, his hair pulled back away from his face. His dark skin shimmers in the sunlight as he turns to me, leaning his hip against the railing and crossing his arms. "How do you know how to sail? You're not from here. What I know about Crescent Falls makes it sound like it's mostly landlocked."

"That's true, but you know I'm not from Crescent Falls. I'm from—from Eastonia, technically. I was in the navy for a while."

Sawyer nods but still looks unconvinced. I spent most of last night, after the kiss that might have ruined both of our lives, talking with Alex and Sawyer, as well as some of their higher ranking warriors, about Eastonia. I answered whatever questions they had about the history, about the downfall of the kings and the rise of Ella and her Firestone line that will soon rule.

I told them about the Deadlands and Tarsian, where I'd served under the crowns of what used to be the Three Alpha Kings… now whittled down to only one, seeing as Tarsian has fallen back to rebels. But their navy is the definition of elite, and joining their ranks gave me three years of experience in the same sea I washed up in seventeen years ago.

But with all of their technology and maps at my fingertips, I couldn't even get close to Emberfyll. I have no idea where it is. Just like passing through the strait heading to Maatua, the sea beyond the shores of Tarsian and the southern Deadlands grows rough, damn near violent, before becoming unsailable altogether. Storms rage constantly. Winds from hell and rain so intense it could sink a ship make journeying more than fifty miles off the coast impossible.

A week ago, I didn't care. I was buying a boat, for Goddess' sake, planning on making the journey despite it being a death wish, knowing I'd never return and likely never land on the shores of Emberfyll.

But now I... I've started to question sailing into an inevitable death. I could have a life here–in Eastonia. I could lean into the love Aviva and Ryan offered me that I rejected at every turn because I didn't want to hurt them when I eventually said goodbye. I could have a house instead of continuing to live in the barracks. I could have a warm bed, and long, lazy mornings spent tangled in the sheets with the same woman who's likely raging in a stateroom below me *right now*.

It was easy enough to reject her. It was just a few words. *I accept your rejection.*

It was the worst thing I've ever said.

I hate that it took nearly dying to realize it. She deserves more.

"Logan?"

"Yeah," I rasp, running a hand over my face. "Did you say something?"

Sawyer chuckles, "I asked about your experience on a ship like this, but you were somewhere else."

"I didn't sleep last night. Likely won't tonight." I lean on the railing.

Sawyer purses his lips and nods, apparently agreeing that for the next forty-eight hours, we're tethered to the helm, sailing as fast as possible through endless, but so far calm, open water.

"KiloKilo has some high-tech boats in their armada. Cruisers and speedboats, mostly. Nothing like this, not anymore. Everything they use on the water is powered by the magic of the wizards on the main island, which is roughly three hundred miles from here. But still, their armada is everywhere—an infestation. We're gonna see 'em, soon, I think."

"And what do we do when they make themselves known?" I ask, turning my head to look at him.

Sawyer shrugs, shaking his head with a sigh. "There's nowhere to hide now, not until we reach the reef that protects Tempest Valley. So, we run, and we pray."

I run my hand through my hair, narrowing my eyes at the endless waves. I got the full run-down on the *Asteria* this morning right after boarding the wooden ship. Brie had been there, standing stoically beside me in the cockpit while I inspected every dial and lever, and followed me through the ship's hull, her hands neatly tucked behind her back and her shoulders squared.

Ever regal, ever calm, ever collected, she didn't make a sound. Her expression never cracked from the mask of cool indifference. Only when my inspection ended, and the trio of ships started off again, heading deeper into open water, did she close herself in our state-room—the captain's quarters.

That was hours ago. I know she hasn't eaten a damn thing today.

The worst part of this day had been her scent mingled with mine. I can't think past what that felt like… what doing that to her made me feel like, and I… nearly just marked her and took back what's mine. It's been weighing on me all day.

I leave Sawyer on the deck with instructions to keep our course and speed. My legs feel heavy with a strange mingled sense of both extreme fatigue and a desperate, nearly overwhelming desire to shift.

It's been over two weeks since I last ran free in my wolf form. It's not good for anyone to go that long, especially after a rejection and several near death experiences.

I pause with my hand curled around the doorknob of the captain's quarters. There's not much to be had in terms of food at this point, it seems. Some stale bread, fruit, and fried fish sit at the bottom of a basket I fetched before deciding to check on Brie after all this time. I did manage to snag a bottle of red wine from Alex before departing the *Artemis*, however. I know she prefers red over white.

I shouldn't care. I shouldn't feel this way, but I do. Every minute that has passed since the rejection has been torture, like deep in my soul I knew it was a mistake of my own making. Yet, I did it anyway.

Because I… care about her. I want to–to see her smile more than anything. A real smile–not the practiced regal smile of a diplomat. No, something genuine and sincere with me as the cause.

I already know I've changed my mind about Emberfyll but can't admit to it yet. I feel it in my bones the second I open the door and find Brie perched by the windows overlooking the water, the sun casting her in a halo of light.

I would stay.

But even then, even if I gave up on what I believed to be my life's purpose, Brie wouldn't. That was painfully clear last night when I kissed her. She held back, even after returning the kiss. She held back yet leaned in, like it was practice, like she was looking for a taste of what romantic affection is supposed to feel like in anticipation of someone else.

That had been… my undoing, to say the least. The idea of her with anyone else makes me want to do unspeakable, violent things.

Brie looks up at me, sliding off the window seat with her hands woven together over her stomach. I set the food down on a table near the door and tuck my hands in my pockets.

"We're moving again," she says, "I can feel it."

"We're going to be sailing as fast as possible for the next… day or so. It might be bumpy. If you start feeling sick–"

"I don't get seasick," she cuts in, her voice low. "You don't have to worry about me. I'll stay here the whole time. I have no reason to be out and about."

"While I appreciate your sudden submissiveness," I reply with a hint of skepticism, "I would like for you to be on the deck." I meet her eyes. In the sunlight, they glimmer like her irises are inlaid with flakes of gold. "As much as possible, actually."

"Why?" she asks lightly, smirking, which... makes me stiffen defensively.

I'm not in the right mind. I need to shift to clear my head. I can feel my wolf clawing at the barrier that separates me from that form. This back and forth between us since the day we met has to stop, or I'm going to lose control, I know that much. I'm teetering on the edge of saying fuck it, fucking her, marking her, and dragging her to Emberfyll with me knowing we might not survive the journey... and if we did, that she'd never see her family again.

"You need fresh air. Sunlight." I wave a hand toward the window. "Sitting behind that glass doesn't count."

"You're always so concerned about me when you don't need to be," she remarks with a huff, turning and pacing toward the far side of the room where a door opens to the bedroom... with a four-poster bed nailed down to the floor. Just one bed, of course.

And there are no couches on the *Asteria*. I checked.

"Eat something, and come up to the deck when you're done." I turn for the door before I do something I'll regret.

"How did you learn how to–" She cuts herself off abruptly, turning a bright pink.

I glance at her over my shoulder before turning to face her, leaning my back against the door. "Scenting?"

"Yeah, that." She leans on the bedroom door. The distance between us–the space of the entire room–doesn't feel like enough.

I could light a match, and the tension in the room would erupt into flame.

"I can read, Brie."

She rolls her eyes, but her mouth twitches into a smile. "You never know with warriors."

Now, I'm fighting a smile. "Aviva's people–the tribes–it's a custom of theirs. They don't mark their mates until after they're married at the harvest festival, but sometimes that's months away. They would do that ritual if mates were separated between tribes until the festival... so their scents mingled, warding off other suitors." I clear my throat, my gaze honed on the way her blush creeps down her neck.

We had it out about the kiss. I was an asshole, I know. That's the only part of it I regret.

Brie's lips part like she's about to say something but thinks better of it. I have to dig in my heels to stop from asking her if she still plans to hunt for and marry an Alpha after everything that happened to us, if the shipwreck didn't flip a switch in her brain that finally made her start to think rationally, maybe even selfishly, telling her it's okay to have wants and desires that only benefit her and not her sister.

"I can't be down here for much longer," I tell her. "I can't mind-link with Alex and Sawyer. I need to stay in the cockpit or at least on the deck."

"What about sleep?"

"I don't need it. We'll be in Tempest Valley in two days. I'll be fine until then."

"You didn't sleep last night." She holds my gaze with an accusatory glint in her eyes. She's right. I left after the kiss.

"I didn't trust myself to stay in here with you." My words hang in the air between us. I watch her take a breath—watch the way her chest rises, pauses, then falls.

The column of her throat bobs as she swallows—hard. And that blush... deepens.

Her reaction is enough to make me curl my hands into fists to stop from stalking across the room and kissing her again.

"You—you didn't have to kiss me to prove whatever point you were trying to make," she hisses.

"You acted like you enjoyed it."

"What I enjoy," she says, breathless, "is being your friend."

It's like a knife to my heart. It's the confirmation I needed to know that this... feeling... it's more than just want. It's more than what the mate bond could have ever offered us.

I am fucked.

"I can't be your friend, Brie."

22

REGRETS

BRIE

I can't be your friend.

I lean my forehead against the railing, closing my eyes as I dangle my legs through the rails. What feels like fathoms below me, the ocean stretches toward the milky light of the last minutes of what had been the most spectacular sunset I'd ever seen in my life. Stars flicker into view overhead, nestled against a blanket of deep orange and crimson, and behind me, I listen to Sawyer and Logan pouring over a map spread out on a table bolted to the floor just beside the helm–the massive wheel used to steer a ship only a pirate would have.

Logan doesn't want to believe we have, in fact, been thrust through time and now sail the open seas in the company of pirates. In his rational defense, I haven't seen a single person with a peg leg, a parrot, or an eye-patch, so he's probably right.

It's a fun thought, though. I kick my legs, my bare toes chilled by the wind whipping into the sails as we practically fly over the water.

I like this better than the yacht.

"Why aren't we cutting between these islands?" Logan asks nearby, his back bent and elbows resting on the table. "If the current moves between them, we can stay at this speed even without the sails aiding the engines."

"It's a narrow passage and shallow," Sawyer replies. "We'd have to raise the propellers and coast at half-mast—any faster and we risk running aground."

"If my math is correct, *which it is*," Logan says in a snarky tone that makes me smile despite myself, "it would cut the journey by *ten hours*. That's significant. We'd be in Tempest Valley by tomorrow afternoon instead of the next morning."

"Alpha Alex wants to stay the course. It's up to him."

"Look," Logan sighs, "all last night, Alex talked about the royal armada and how they're waiting for us in open water, how they've been searching for weeks knowing you've been hiding out on one of the islands. You got fucking lucky you haven't been found yet."

Sawyer shifts his weight, crossing his arms over his chest. I risk peeking at them, pretending I'm simply resting my cheek against my shoulder, but seeing Logan all puffed up and… bossy… it does something to me. Something I'd rather not admit.

He presses a finger to the map, arching a brow at Sawyer in a silent challenge to argue his point.

"If they're waiting for us where Alex says they'll be, we'll be trying to outrun them in the dead of night. It'll be a new moon then, too, which means if it's even the least bit overcast, we'll have no light. If we take this other route, it'll put us directly in the path of the reef you've all been boasting about. And if we get past the reef, we're safe. Is that correct?"

Sawyer sighs again, scrubbing a hand over his face. "Well, you're not wrong."

"Tell him, then." Logan motions at Sawyer. "Tell him right now, through the mind-link."

"You shouldn't challenge an Alpha you've just met," I say, rolling my head back to look at him upside down.

Logan frowns at me. "Would like to add to this conversation, Princess? Or are you happy eavesdropping?"

"I have nothing to add. I know nothing about boats and navigation."

"Then butt out," he says, each word clipped and firm.

I roll my head back, leaning my forehead against the railing again like a child who was just told to go stand in the corner after being naughty.

The boredom is starting to sink in. Without having Maeve's day-to-day life and countless plots and schemes to worry about, I've found that I am more boring than I realized. I don't paint. I don't knit or embroider. I don't know how to wield a knife to spar. I've been sitting around all day, kicking my legs, following Logan around like a lost puppy, and he's been distant.

He's lost that sarcastic, teasing edge to his tone. He looks at me like I'm the last thing he wants to see, always curling his hands into fists and acting like being around me is torture.

I understand why he's upset. I didn't believe him when he said something like this could happen. I'd been sure of my safety to the point I chastised him for being so up-tight and always in my space.

Now look at us.

"Alex said we'll stop in the morning, at six sharp, and discuss the change of route then," Sawyer says after several minutes.

"Fine," Logan replies, annoyed, his voice dripping with exhaustion.

"I'll take over the ship for a few hours," Sawyer adds, but Logan shakes his head. "Just a few hours. You sleep, I'll keep us on course. That's what a second—what did you call it? Second captain? Is for." He claps Logan on the shoulder hard enough the sound echoes over the flapping sails.

Logan almost flinches in pain from the injuries to his back but holds himself together, wincing only slightly as he shrugs Sawyer's hand away.

"Second officer, technically," he murmurs, eyeing Sawyer wearily before glancing at me. The bastard clicks his tongue at me like I'm an actual dog and tilts his head toward the stairs leading to the lower deck.

I frown at him but rise, smoothing my dress over my thighs. I keep my mouth firmly shut until we reach our room, and he shuts and locks the door behind us.

"I'm going to shower–" he begins.

"What's your problem?"

Logan looks down at his boots, midway through running his fingers through his hair. He sighs heavily, looking down at me with an exhausted expression casting shadows across his face. "Where do I even begin?" he asks sarcastically.

"With me, specifically."

He flexes his jaw. I watch as he starts to unbutton his shirt, his eyes holding on mine. "I don't have a problem with you."

"You're acting like you do. You wanted me to be on the deck, so I spent the entire day near you, and you barely said a word to me."

"I was busy captaining a ship we're not supposed to be on because you should be in Maatua by now, and I–"

"Should be on your way to Emberfyll," I cut in hotly, the emotions I've been holding in all day simmering to the surface. "Right. I get it." I brush past him, grabbing a nightgown I left on the bed and balling it between my hands.

"Brie–"

I pause in the doorframe of the bathroom but keep my back to him.

"Brie," he repeats firmly, but his tone is thick.

"What?" Everything I want to say–that I want to ask–nearly brings me to my knees. "I just–we kissed. Things feel weird now."

"I know."

"You kissed me and acted like–like I offended you in some way."

His eyes are like green gems in the fading light of the sunset. "You didn't offend me."

"Then what is this?" I ask, waving to my chest like he could possibly understand the feelings currently raging through me like a firestorm. Doubt. Confusion. The startling, unspeakable realization that I've made a terrible mistake and likely ruined my life by rejecting him. "I don't understand. I–" I bite back my words before I say too much.

He can't feel the same way I do. He can't regret rejecting each other like I do. He can't. A man like him wouldn't go for someone like me–someone boring. Someone plain. Someone who got us in a terrible situation because I can't fathom a situation where I'm not right. Someone without powers who can't offer him more than–

"Don't you dare look at me like that," he says heavily, his clipped words bringing me out of my mind and back into the present in an instant.

"What?"

He points an accusatory finger at me. "That. *That* expression. I never want to see it again."

I run a hand over my pinched brow, trying to relax my muscles. "I–I don't know what you're talking about–"

"What were you just thinking about?"

"Logan–"

"What," he breathes, losing his patience, "were you just debating in your head, Brie?" He takes several steps in my direction before stopping short, his shirt half-unbuttoned and hanging off one shoulder. He looks… incredibly disheveled. Like he's on the verge of shifting or losing his mind entirely. In fact, I've never seen a man so undone, so raw. His eyes are wild with emotions I can't define, and his jaw is set, his hands curling into tight fists at his sides.

I swallow hard, teetering on the precipice of making a fool of myself. I wanted this. I wanted to break my bond with him. I had a reason to do so, but now… after everything….

He sucks back a breath before saying, "When we return to Eastonia, are you still planning on marrying an Alpha?"

"What are you asking?"

Logan edges toward me, holding out his hands in surrender. "Are you still planning on marrying an Alpha?"

"What does that matter?" I ask, sniffling. "Of–of course I am. I have to!"

He shakes his head. Goddess, he looks angry. "What are you trying to tell me, then? Are you asking why I kissed you? Covered you with my scent? Are you asking why I balked when you told me *we were friends*? Because I doubt you'll accept the answer." His voice is a growl that laces through my body, making my skin pebble.

"Why would you do that? To–to tease me? To make some point–"

"Isn't it obvious? Or are you so lost in your own head that you can't see what's right in front of you?"

I stiffen, taken aback by his tone. "I don't understand–"

"Have you ever looked in a mirror?" he asks, taking another step in my direction. "Do you not see what I see when I look at you?"

"Don't do this to me," I whisper, my chest going so tight I can't breathe. I wait for the inevitable–for him to say I'm plain, that I'm boring, that I have nothing to offer because that's all these men have ever said to me. It's all the tabloids ever say, although they're far more colorful in their choice of words when comparing me to my family members.

"You are *stunning*," he says slowly, almost painfully, gritting out the words through clenched teeth. "Just–*beautiful*."

"You don't have to say that to me–"

"Someone needs to," he cuts in sharply. "I've listened to you berate yourself, tear yourself down to make yourself smaller, and I can't fucking take it anymore, Brie. I can't do it."

We stare at each other. I'm not sure what this feeling is, this overwhelming sensation that's been plaguing me all day. His scent is everywhere, driving me absolutely out of my mind. I want to hate him. I want to push him over the railing of the ship. I want to never see him again, but the thought of a life without him in it, annoying me, constantly in my space, arguing with me… it hurts. It has hurt since we rejected each other.

"Do you want to know the truth?" he asks hotly, his eyes wild and full of emotion I can't put into words. "I kissed you because I wanted to. Because I've been thinking about it since the moment I saw you in your parents' breakfast room. I've been wondering what it is about you that has infected my mind and turned everything I knew about who I am, and what I want, inside out. I thought rejecting you would end this suffering. I thought it was the mate bond, Brie. Remnants of it that were left behind when I pushed for the rejection–"

"You didn't push me. We both wanted it–"

"We made a mistake," he says firmly, clearly, each word clipped and exaggerated. "I regret it."

23

TAKING BACK WHAT'S MINE

BRIE

I TAKE A STEP AWAY FROM LOGAN, THEN ANOTHER, UNTIL MY BACK HITS the wall just outside of the bathroom. The room blurs, the soft cream fabrics and dark wood turning dreamlike and hazy. We could be anywhere–any kingdom–any room or darkened forest, and I wouldn't know it because right now it's just me and him, and I'm utterly, wholly exposed.

I'm sure my family and those others who know me well would say I'm a complicated person. They'd be right. Below the surface, beyond my mask of resilience, I'm like ice, and within that icy fortress is something akin to fear.

No one has been able to penetrate those walls. Not even Maeve.

But Logan is looking right through me, shoving those walls down, clawing at them until they topple and shatter.

"If you don't feel the same," he says, his tone softening, "I... I understand. I know our situation is complicated, Brie, I get it. I have an... obligation to return to Emberfyll, and you–"

"I regret it." My voice shakes, but my gaze stays locked on his. "Logan, I regret it–"

He closes the distance between us in three easy steps, his hands caressing my face as he leans down, his nose brushing mine. I close my eyes against a torrent of emotion that washes through my body like the current flowing beneath our ship, carrying us toward an increasingly uncertain future. There's so much we need to talk about, so much that needs to be said, but this–his touch–it settles in my bones and erases any words that may have been trying to materialize on the tip of my tongue.

His lips brush mine in a featherlight touch. I chase his mouth, my hand curling around the back of his neck as I inhale, taking in his cedar scent. That smell… Goddess, it reminds me of the shores of the river beneath Veiled Valley. I used to sit down there as a child and throw rocks into the river, collecting the prettiest, smoothest stones to bring back to my dad. He keeps them all, still, in a drawer in his desk. Logan is a constant reminder of that–of home.

Logan cages me in against the wall and kisses me, dragging my lower lip between his teeth. He trembles as my hand slides up his chest beneath the fabric of his half-unbuttoned shirt, tugging it free of his belt. He lets out a rough sigh, releasing me from the kiss to nuzzle my neck, inhaling and exhaling sharply. His hand curls into a fist at my side, his other arm bent and resting against the wall over the top of my head.

He's hot to the touch. Almost fevered. His chest is still peppered with scrapes from the shipwreck, but he doesn't flinch as my hand glides over the hard, smooth muscle of his abdomen and back down to his belt. My fingers dust over the leather toward the buckle. I look up into his eyes. They're closed, and his expression is…

"I've never…." I taper off, my cheeks suddenly blazing with heat as a blush soars through my skin. "I've never been with a man before."

A soft, wry smile touches the corner of his mouth, but his pupils are blown wide when he opens his eyes to slits. "I can't take you right now. I–" He sucks in a breath, chuckling darkly as he licks his lips and leans in to brush the next words over my mouth, "I wouldn't be able to stop. I'd hurt you. I need to shift first–I need to run, and get off this fucking boat."

I swallow hard, my hand leaving his belt to travel up his chest again. He likes this. He closes his eyes, his chest rising and falling slowly, like he's trying to calm himself down. He opens his eyes again, scanning my face, then pulls away, clasping my hand and whirling me around to face the wall. He cages me in again, pressing a heated kiss to the crook where my neck meets my shoulder. I close my eyes as his hands drag down the gentle curve of my waist to my hips before he reaches for the zipper of my dress.

It's dark in the room now. It's the main room of our suite–the captain's quarters. As he pulls the dress from my shoulders, sliding the fabric off my arms and down to my waist, I'm suddenly acutely aware of the soft light coming from a nearby lamp–the only light to be had.

He explores my bare stomach as he presses his body against mine. He nuzzles my head to the side to press kisses to my temple, down to my jaw, like he's trying to distract me from where his hands are moving now.

I'm not wearing a bra. I wasn't given one, and the dresses Monica supplied had built in boning to keep my ample breasts in place, but now there's nothing between us but skin, and when he cups my breasts, they overflow around his large hands, and he... groans, pressing his mouth into my hair and whispering what I can only assume is a prayer of thanks to the Goddess Herself.

My dress slides off my hips without his help, the fabric falling in a heap around my ankles.

"Tell me to stop," he whispers, his thumbs brushing over my nipples in a way that makes me jolt awake, alive and burning with desire. "Brie, push me away."

"No," I moan, sucking in a breath as I fist my hands against the wall. "Please, don't stop."

"Goddess," he curses, trying to regain control of himself. I wonder if he turned me to face the wall because looking at me might send him over the point of no return. He said he'd hurt me, that he wouldn't be able to stop, but I… want that. I know what he's capable of. I've seen him fight without mercy. I've watched his mouth move when he speaks with that sharp, unfiltered tongue. His roughness and wit is what drove me toward him even without the bond in place to speed things up.

I want him just the way he is.

But he's right about shifting. It's been a while for me, too. Normally, it's not a problem, but now I'm hypersensitive and desperate for any kind of stimulation I can find… which includes the filthiest thoughts I've ever had about what this man–this warrior–could do to my body… and I'd love it.

I lean against him as his hands press into my breasts, kneading while rolling my nipples between his fingers. The sensation is almost too much to bear. I lean my head in the crook of his shoulder, my face tilted toward the ceiling, my lips parting as I moan again, unable to stop myself.

Before I can even think of catching my breath, Logan moves, roping an arm around my waist and hoists me off my feet. I yelp, taken by surprise by his swift movements as he carries me a few steps toward the bedroom door, which he kicks open, the door slamming violently into the inner wall and nearly smacking us as he carries me inside the room and promptly tosses me on the bed.

I gasp as the door slams shut on its own accord, and we're coated in darkness, his body nothing but a dark shadow as he stalks toward the bed.

Faint moonlight drifts through the window on the far side of the room, but it's not enough for Logan. He looks down at me then glides around the bed and flips on a lamp on one of the bedside tables.

I wince as soft golden light ghosts through the room, highlighting my naked skin. My simple, cotton panties are all that covers me, and he's here, seeing me, seeing nearly all of me…

I bring my arms up to try to cover my breasts, but he grabs my wrists.

"No. Let me look at you."

I look into his eyes expecting to find… at best, morbid curiosity, but it's more than that. Lust shines bright, turning his already rugged, handsome features into something dark and dangerous.

A part of him I think only I have ever seen.

I know Logan's been with other women before. A man like him wouldn't have trouble in that department. He's older than me at nearly thirty. He knows what to do, whereas I'm… totally unprepared when he unbuttons his shirts all the way, his gaze locked on mine.

He rounds the bed slowly, his gaze leaving my face to travel hungrily down my body. When his eyes meet mine again, I feel my body relaxing, my arms going slack at my sides, my lips parting as mingled excitement and a feral kind of heat sweeps over me.

He notices the change. His nostrils flare, a cocky smirk twitching at the corners of his mouth as he says, "Come here."

My heart races as I sit up. He's barely even breathing as I crawl to the end of the bed and rise on my knees.

For the first time in my life… I feel… beautiful.

He pulls the pins holding my hair away from my face loose. Curls and waves roll down my back and shoulders. He cups my cheek, his thumb drawing a line along the underside of my jaw as he tilts my face upward to look at him. He kisses me fully, his tongue dancing with mine in a slow, laborious circle that makes my toes curl and my body hum to life.

But Logan's rigid. His muscles stay flexed as he guides me onto my back, his hands roaming freely over my skin. I tangle my fingers in his thick hair, losing myself to his touch, his scent, until my brain shuts down completely, and I'm nothing but a puddle of desire that makes rational thought impossible… until he pulls away to start kissing down my body.

When his mouth grazes past my belly button, and he begins to drag my panties down over my thighs, I freeze, my breath catching in my throat.

"Wh–what are you doing?" I try to sit up, but he presses a hand to my stomach, forcing me back down.

I try to squeeze my thighs together, but he kneels on the floor at the edge of the bed, wrenching them apart.

"Logan–"

He presses a kiss to my hip bone, shushing me, pulling my panties down my calves, and I'm… lost to him. Completely, utterly, at his mercy. He looks up at me, his eyes shining as his mouth curves into a smile. He presses a kiss to my thigh, then lower, toward my center.

Grunting, he adjusts his position, my thighs resting on his shoulders, and tugs me further toward the edge of the bed.

I arch a brow, mimicking the cocky look he's giving me. It's like he's challenging me to say no instead of offering me an out, and I'm….

Logan presses his tongue to my thigh and licks upward. I shiver, my head rolling back and hips arching into the sensation. Another lick has me locking my ankles behind his neck, my hands traveling up to cup my own breasts like I've been taken over by some demon—some siren desperate for touch.

He chuckles darkly against my skin, rasping my name like a prayer before his tongue parts me.

I gasp, my hands leaving my breasts to clutch the sheets.

"You're mine," he says against my aching folds, licking another line and circling his tongue over my clit. "From this moment forward, you are *mine*."

2 4

NEARLY UNDONE

MY KNEES BITE INTO THE FLOORBOARDS, BUT I DON'T FEEL A GODDESS damned thing except my tongue sliding through Brie's wetness. The taste of her is... my undoing. I might regret this in the morning. There will be consequences for this, of that I'm sure. We both know this can't happen. I am stronger than this–I was stronger than this–able to shut any feeling down the moment it tried to flicker to life, but Brie has this otherworldly effect on me that I can't shake.

I've given up trying.

She whimpers and trembles as my tongue draws lazy circles over her clit. Her thighs flex while she grips the sheets, her eyes squeezed shut as she chases a feeling I know she's experiencing for the first time. A sense of pride swells in my chest knowing it's me between her legs. It's my face she's squeezing between her soft, supple thighs. It's me kneeling for her, a queen in her own right.

There's so much I want to do to her. So much I could show her, make her feel, but she's... new at this. And I'm on the verge of losing

183

my mind against her taste, her scent, the way her inner walls grip my fingers when I carefully slide two of them inside her.

Brie arches her hips at the intrusion, her breath coming in a short, surprised exhale. I swipe my thumb over her clit, kissing her inner thigh and watch the way she relaxes into my touch again.

"You're beautiful," I whisper against her skin, closing my eyes as she rocks her hips toward me, moaning low in her throat. She's close. Her body jerks, her moans become soft whimpers, and her hands drift into my hair, tugging ever so slightly while I press kisses up her thigh.

My mouth continues its dance, sucking and lapping at her clit while my fingers pump in, and out. She's soaking wet. The thought of being buried inside of her makes it almost impossible to focus on the task at hand–making her come.

I have to see her at her most vulnerable to truly understand her mind. I know who she is, what she's capable of. She's not the type of woman to sit quietly while the world turns. No, she's a leader. A commander. A queen.

She's mine.

"Logan," she whispers, my name a soft, airy whimper against the creaking of the ship as it sails through a world where we're just… Brie and Logan. Not the sister of the Firestone Queen. Not the displaced Alpha. Just us. "Logan!"

I open my eyes to slits to watch her unravel, sucking deeply, groaning as her walls clench my fingers and pulse erratically. She arches her back and bites back a scream, her fingers pulling my hair like I'm the only thing keeping her here, in this world.

She comes down slowly, struggling to catch her breath. Her breasts tremble, her rosy nipples peaked in the cool night air, her skin washed in starlight. Her hair is loose and spread around her on the mattress, and her face… Goddess, she's stunning. Raw and suddenly, finally, at ease.

I release my fingers, pressing another kiss to her clit before my mouth begins a slow exploration of her hips, her belly. I climb back onto the bed, straddling her, looking down at her while I lick my fingers clean, and I... I have to leave the room as soon as possible before I do something we'll both regret.

"How did you–" she whispers, sucking in a breath, "That was–"

I lean down and kiss her, stealing her praise. I don't need it. Seeing her flushed like this is enough, but her hand rests on my chest and begins to slide down to my belt. "We can't," I breathe, meeting her eyes in the darkness. The lamplight does little to light the room, but her eyes glow like polished mahogany and are heavy with desire.

"Because you think you'll hurt me?" Her fingers graze my belt buckle.

"Because I'll mark you."

Brie exhales slowly, her lips curving into a seductive smile that rewires my brain and makes me forget why we can't do this.

"We shouldn't," I whisper, lowering my body to hers.

"Because we have... a lot to discuss."

"Yes," I say against her lips. Her scent wraps around me. All warm things, spice and honey. It's intoxicating. She's intoxicating, and I think she knows it. I think I haven't given her enough credit for being a closeted vixen because she kisses me deeply, passionately, her tongue gliding over mine while her hands travel up and down my sides, mapping my body like I've just mapped hers.

I have her pinned to the bed. I have her caged in. I should just roll us over, keep her pressed against my chest until she falls asleep and releases me of this torment, but... something shifts in my chest. A flicker. A song I know by heart without ever once hearing the melody. It's like a shadow of what was once there–our bond. The bond we broke against our better judgment.

I look down at Brie and see stars in her eyes. I see a woman I could love deeply, madly. I see a woman who would run my life down to the second, and I'd let her do it. I'd crawl for her.

I see my mate as I should have seen her before.

BRIE

. . .

MY BRAIN IS A TANGLED MESS OF FATIGUE AND CONFLICTING FEELINGS when Logan falls asleep on top of me, lulled into a stupor by my touch. I just... held him there, comforted by his body on mine, listening to his heart as it slowed.

Eventually, he slid to the side and pulled me to his chest where I fell asleep with my cheek pressed to his shoulder, his heartbeat a lullaby that rocked me to sleep with the waves.

But I dream. I rarely ever dream. When I do, it's never good. I dream about being pressed into the depths of the ocean with Logan's arms around me. I dream of walking the hallways of the castle in Veiled Valley, alone, while my father and brother are off fighting in the civil war I failed to prevent.

I dream in startling detail of being... freezing cold. My back is bare and pressed to an altar, and fire is everywhere, the crackling flames breached by the screamed pleas of a young man who looks a whole lot like Sydney, but... far younger. Twenty or so years younger.

I dream of hazy conversation where I feel like I'm underwater. I feel... fear. Guilt. Shame... and above all, hatred. Hatred directed at me, this stain. This reminder of the man who held her down, forced her. She knew I'd meet the same fate. She tried to stop it. She had one chance to escape, to save me, and she did it.

But I killed her.

Sobs choke me away. Someone's calling out my name. A hand caresses my cheek, but I flinch away from the touch.

"Stop! Don't–don't touch me–"

"Brie, it's me. It's Logan."

I blink rapidly, my eyes wet with tears. The darkness doesn't fade. It's the dead of night, maybe the earliest hours of the morning, and the entire room is blanketed in black.

But Logan's face comes into view. He's pale, his brow furrowed and body rigid, his arm muscles flexed as he holds me to the bed. I've been thrashing in my sleep, haven't I?

How many times have I woken up to Mom or Dad holding me down just like this, begging me to wake up?

I'd always walked it off, laughed about it while blinking away my tears, saying I couldn't remember what the dream was, often blaming it on some stupid, scary movie Aris insisted we watch together.

I didn't want them to know. I didn't want them to carry the guilt. So, I buried it.

But the way Logan's looking at me right now... he sees it. He sees everything.

"I'm sorry," I whisper through tears.

He shakes his head and shushes me.

"I'm–I'm sorry–I–"

His mouth meets mine in the darkness, firm and *real*. This isn't a nightmare. This isn't a stupid dream about my future, of the peace in the world I'm trying to attain. This is just... him. My mate. The mate I told myself I couldn't have because there was too much at stake.

The bubble of delusion bursts.

I gasp, wrapping my arms around his neck and dragging him down to me. He's still shirtless and I'm wearing... nothing. Absolutely nothing. There's something different about this kiss–something untamed and wild, something born out finally, saying to hell with it and letting myself have something I want, damning the consequences.

Logan groans against my mouth, hissing as he bites my lower lip. He whispers my name as his hands rove down my sides, his body shifting to position himself over mine. Whatever resolve he had to hold back vanishes in the space of a ragged breath as he clutches my thighs, spreading them apart.

I'm willing to beg. I have no idea what I'm in for, but I need it. I have to have him.

I close my eyes as his mouth travels over my breasts, peppering me with rough, bruising kisses. His teeth leave marks as his tongue dances over my nipples, sucking and biting his way down to my belly, but I hear his belt catch against his belt loop before it lands on the ground somewhere near the bed, falling to the ground with a thud.

The button on his pants is cool against my inner thigh, but his fingers are warm when he frees it, and then he's…

I choke on the air trying to leave my lungs. He rises up on his knees and leans down to kiss my lips again, but I'm acutely aware of his nakedness, even in the pure dark.

I reach down, my fingertips grazing the head of his cock. He shudders when I touch him–featherlight–before curling my hand around his shaft. I can't wrap my hand around his width completely, and a jolt of sudden apprehension clouds my senses.

But not for long. That siren song taking over my mind wins, burying any doubts. My core throbs, my hips arching toward him on instinct. A needy whimper escapes my lips as I pump my hand up his shaft.

He sighs–a deep, guttural sound that stirs my wolf.

He reaches over the bed to turn on the lamp, and the room floods with muted golden light.

Seeing him like this, with my hand wrapped around his dick stimulates me in a way I didn't think was possible. The way he's looking at me right now is almost enough to send me over the edge even without him touching me. I swipe my thumb over the head of his cock, trembling with heat. I feel like I'm fevered. The rest of the room is hazy, and my heart pounds out of rhythm as I writhe, desperate for him.

Logan gives me that cocky smirk, one of his brows twitching as he rolls his lower lip between his teeth. His pupils are wide, his eyes nearly black in the lamplight. Just like me, he's on the verge of transformation. He told me he wouldn't be able to stop, to hold back. He'd mark me if we did this before he had a chance to get off this boat and shift to clear his head.

"Needy little wolf," he rasps, reaching between my legs. He drags his fingers through my aching, throbbing folds, chuckling darkly with satisfaction as he looks at his glistening fingers. He nudges my legs further apart, bracing a hand on the bed near my shoulder, and looks down at me once more before lowering his body to mine.

His cock teases my entrance, sliding in a fraction of an inch. The stretch is already too much to bear.

His lips part as I whine, biting down on my lip to stop from whimpering. I meet his gaze, and his eyes have softened just a touch.

"Can you handle it?" he rasps, pulling out and fisting his cock before sliding it again just enough to tease me.

"Yes," I breathe, "*Please!*"

He grips my hip with his free hand, his mouth crashing into mine. We're on the precipice of no return when Logan goes very, very still, and lifts his head.

"What?" I whisper, reaching for him.

He slowly turns his head to look behind him at the bedroom door. I can hear his heart slowing as the room falls silent all around us, but then he moves with a predator's stealth, sliding off the bed and grabbing his pants, roughly pulling them up to his waist.

"Stay here," he whispers, his eyes meeting mine in the lamplight.

"What is it?" I ask, unease curling through my body.

He doesn't have a chance to reply. The boat careens sharply to the side, shifting direction so swiftly it sends whatever's not nailed down to the floor sliding across the room.

Through the window, against the early morning sky still full of stars, purple lights blink on the horizon... speeding toward us.

GOOSE CHASE

BRIE

"LOGAN!" I FLY OUT OF BED AS THE BOAT TILTS DRAMATICALLY, SEVERAL books, a pair of boots, and a hairbrush sliding across the floorboards as I dart toward the closet and snatch a pair of pants from a hanger. Logan hastily buttons his shirt, turning his head from side to side trying to locate the boots that just flew to the opposite side of the room.

I pull on the pants and grab the first shirt my fingers graze–a men's shirt, but it doesn't matter. Logan rushes to the far side of the room for his boots, pulling one of them on, cursing under his breath while the purple lights continue speeding in our direction.

"Logan," I hiss, tossing his other boot at him.

"Why are you getting dressed?" he asks, pointing to the bed. "Stay here–"

"No, I'm not going to stay here." I growl, shrugging the shirt over my shoulders and doing my best to button it with trembling fingers. Echoes of pleasure still thrum through my body, mingling with the adrenaline now pumping through my veins. "I'm going with you."

Shouts from above split the air. He mumbles something under his breath before whirling toward the door and rushing out. I catch the door before it slams shut.

"Stay here, Brie. I'm not fucking around."

"Neither am I!" I rasp breathlessly, struggling to keep up with his long stride. "Look me in the eyes and tell me I'm safer in our room than I am with you, on deck, while we have what looks like over a dozen royal armada ships heading in our direction!" I stumble on the stairs leading to the upper deck, yelping in pain as the wood bites into my knees.

Logan jerks me upright but doesn't let me go. His eyes darken, shifting from his usual golden hued green to that wolfish, inky black as his pupils expand. Moments ago, we'd been on the verge of... something we couldn't take back. He would have marked me. I would have marked him back, reinstating the mate bond we threw away.

My breath catches in my throat as his gaze scans my face. He's rigid, his grip tightening on my arm as emotion floods his eyes, sending shadows over the planes of his face. "We're not going into the water a second time. I promise you."

"I trust you," I whisper, rising on my toes and pressing a kiss to the corner of his mouth.

He shudders. His scent shifts, that cedar smell changing to something deep and heady, reminding me again just how close we'd come to the point of no return and how badly I wish we were still tangled in bed together.

Logan pulls away, grabbing my hand and yanking me through the door to the upper deck. The change is immediate. Electricity crackles in the air as people dart across the deck. The sails flap in the wind, and the boat groans against the choppy, white capped water despite the sky being clear and starry, not a single storm cloud in sight.

A man I don't know rushes toward us, grabbing Logan's shoulder. "I was just sent to fetch you. We have royal armada ships coming in quickly from the east. They see us."

"Where's Sawyer?"

"The helm—"

"Cut all power to the ship," Logan says hastily, tugging me along as he glides across the deck, the other man struggling to keep up with us. "Power the engines down completely. Cut the lights."

"Why?" I ask, but the other man disappears, running at full sprint into the depths of the ship.

Logan doesn't let me go, nor does he answer my question. He races up the stairs to the helm, where Sawyer turns, casting a wild look at the two of us.

Logan pants as he rasps, "I pledge my loyalty to the pack Tempest Valley and its Alpha and Beta." I rear back, my heart skipping several beats as he says the unthinkable, "I renounce my affiliation to the pack Silverhide, of the Deadlands, and it's Alpha."

"Oh, my Goddess," I whisper. Logan's hand unravels from mine, my arm falling slack at my side.

Sawyer clasps his arm, nodding grimly.

And then Logan… changes. Sure, I've seen his warrior face. That look of cold, icy death. I've seen him fight. I've seen him kill.

But I haven't seen this man captain a ship and lead over a dozen wolves.

I have no choice but to press myself to the railing as the man I've started to fall head over heels in love with begins to shout orders. Everyone in the vicinity obeys him—a stranger—someone they don't know well enough to trust, but his voice echoes over the panic like a death knell, commanding obedience.

He's an *Alpha*. It's in his blood, in the marrow of his bones. This is what he was born to be.

My eyes water as Logan turns to Sawyer, toward the map nailed to the table fixed beside the helm. I watch his back straighten, his spine turning to steel, as he braces his hands on either side of the map and hangs his head, scanning the illustrations before reaching for the helm again.

Silence settles between the three of us. I understand why he just denounced his loyalty to Silverhide. He needs to be able to mind-link with Alex, but still…

I turn to the railing and look out at the water, at the two shadows and their sparkling lights ahead of us, heading straight toward the armada.

But my gaze catches on something I can't make sense of right away. In the distance, against the starry sky, what looks like a mountain stretches against the horizon, but it's moving, crashing back against the water.

My stomach sinks as I look back at the stars, at the hazy rope of violet light as the sun begins to rise, and it's all wrong. The constellations are upside down, tilting at odd angles.

I wasn't alive during the time of the veil that used to hide Eastonia behind its massive, unexplainable magic shield. The stories from the time describe it as this… forcefield. An impenetrable barrier made of mist.

But my grandma and grandpa used to tell us stories about passing through it—the only two people in the world with that ability. Grandma Ella described it like being pulled through space and time itself in a place where everything was upside down and skewed, a place where time knew no end or beginning.

Grandpa always described it as the birthplace of violence.

Here, it's just… waves. Waves taller than buildings. Waves that would drown and consume these ships in seconds.

How had Logan and I survived that? And if there's a similar ocean barrier between Eastonia and Emberfyll, how did he survive that *twice?*

I watch the *Asteria* and *Atropos* go dark against the sea, their lights shutting off completely, turning their wooden bodies to starlit shadows. The armada is still a mile or so away, but closing in with every passing second.

Logan turns the boat violently west, tipping dangerously to the side. The *Asteria* and *Atropos* fade into the background.

I turn to look at Logan, wishing we had the ability to mind-link and cursing myself for rejecting him once again, but he says to Sawyer, "That group of islands six leagues away, which direction does the current run during low tide?"

"You're joking, right?" Sawyer asks, leaning toward the map with his arms crossed tightly over his chest. "We'll run aground. There's a reef there and sandbars that stretch more than a mile at low tide!"

"We have no weapons on these ships," Logan asserts, "No way to defend ourselves. Your only defense so far has been hiding, but we're in open water, and there's nowhere to hide now. If we cut through this island system and continue west, we'll reach that strait I noticed yesterday before noon tomorrow."

"We can't risk the engines-"

"We won't be using any powers but the sails and the current," Logan cuts in sharply. "The armada has speed on its side in open water. Their ships are smaller. They can't see the sandbars. They'll get caught in them, but we won't."

"You won't be able to see them either!"

"I can, and we have enough weight to burst through them, over them. They don't," Logan says, and I might be imagining it, but I swear his eyes glow. "We're doing it." He yanks on the helm, sending the ship into a spin so abrupt I have to clutch the railing for dear life.

My hair whips against my cheeks like little knives. I peek through the railing, watching as seven purple lights break from the group, speeding in our direction instead of chasing the *Artemis* and *Atropos*.

The five other armada ships whiz in all directions like they're trying to decide which boats to hunt, but eventually the entire group settles on *us*.

My heart slips into my stomach, which pitches and rolls with the boat as we bank heavily west, the sails snapping taunt against the wind. "Logan!" I shout, pointing at the purple lights. Logan looks over his shoulder at me, his eyes wild and full of starlight as he spots the boats tearing in our direction.

But then he meets my eyes again and exhales slowly, reaching for me. I hold his gaze while stumbling to my bare feet. I didn't have a chance to put shoes on, but if we end up in the water again, it won't matter much, anyway.

Logan pulls me against the table, steadying me with my back pressed to his chest. Everyone on board realizes that the entire might of what is either the royal armada or bounty hunters are now heading in our direction. They must have seen us turn, cut our lights out abruptly. We're flying across the water at the speed of light away from the two other boats. They must think we're carrying something–or someone–important.

The Alpha himself.

I glance over Logan's arm at the shadows drifting in the distance. Alex and Monica are on the *Artemis*, which is leading the charge in the opposite direction from where we're heading, but those purple lights dart past the two other ships, chasing us instead.

Logan's tricking them, leading them back into the swallows on what will be a wild goose chase through reefs and sandbars while Alex and his pack stay safe in open water, continuing their journey while we bear the brunt of the violence.

I wonder what Logan and Alex have been talking about through the mind-link, but the sunrise begins to bleed over the sky, casting the sails in shades of purple, gold, and pink as the water sparkles with morning light, camouflaging the incoming shallow patches and sand-bars beginning to sprint past the boat.

Even without the engines, the sails carry us with the wind at an incredible rate of speed. The sunrise illuminates several small islands, some of them are only raised blobs of sand, others with a handful of trees, some with rocky hills and multiple beaches. Logan speeds past all of them, steering the ship toward a larger island chain whose mountains cast shadows over the sparkling water.

My heart is in my throat when I look over my shoulder again at the sleek, silver boats finally coming into full view.

They're like speed boats–small yachts, perhaps. Narrow and long, they sprint over the water, their engines roaring over the waves and wind, but their length makes it hard for them to maneuver around the sandbars jutting from the ocean floor. The salty smell of low tide hangs heavy in the air, a warning sign that not everything in the water is what it seems.

Floors below us, I can hear the scraping, crunching echo of the *Asteria* sliding past the sandbars.

Logan was right to cut the engines. The current is carrying us, pulling us through the islands as the tide retreats.

"Stand over there, Brie. Hold onto—onto something," he grits out.

I step away from him, swaying toward the railing as he turns the helm from side to side. Sawyer grabs my arm and yanks me toward him at the same moment the *Asteria* slides across another underwater sandbar that nearly catches us, causing the ship to lurch painfully, the sails clapping and groaning in protest.

A sharp crash and explosion behind us makes me scream in surprise. Sawyer whirls with me in his arms as one of the armada cruisers hits a sandbar and launches into the air, soaring and diving into one of the other armada ships. A shockwave of heat bursts toward us as the two ships explode into a fireball that consumes four other cruisers, knocking out half the fleet in one go.

I gasp, choking on my breath as I turn to Logan, who's smirking at the fire blazing behind us. The *Asteria* continues forward toward the island chain, and the single gap between the islands that opens back up to clear, open water.

But then, with a violent jerk, we slam into a reef.

2 6

INTO THE GREAT WIDE OPEN

Brie

One second, I'm standing, my feet firmly planted on the floorboards of the uppermost deck, and the next, I'm flying through the air with Sawyer, our bodies colliding with the railing and then bursting through it, the wood splintering painfully across my back and spine.

Logan shouts my name, but his voice drowns out, nothing more than a flicker of breath against the sound of the incoming ships trying to burst through the wall of fire so close to us I can feel the heat on my skin.

I'm... dangling. My legs are slack, my arms burn and stretch, and my head... aches, hurting so fiercely I can barely open my eyes. A sharp, heady, metallic taste fills my mouth. I try to breathe in, but the scent of blood is so heavy it makes my stomach roll with nausea. I can't breathe. *I can't breathe.*

"Someone grab her! Help them!" Logan shouts, his voice lined with desperation and utter rage. My arms go numb, but my belly slides against the side of the ship as I'm dragged upward, and only

199

when I'm roughly pulled back onto the upper deck do I realize I've been hanging precariously over the side, Sawyer holding my bruised, swollen wrists the only thing keeping me from dropping into the ocean, into the fire starting to creep toward us carried by the oil leaking from the wreckage.

The *Asteria* groans as the engines sputter to life, sending a hum across the floorboards. I'm suddenly on my back, my eyes lifted to the stars, and the hurried, desperate shouts of the crew on the deck below fade as Logan appears overhead, his hands resting on either side of my face.

Sawyer groans weakly, his shadow passing over me as he sits up, but my eyes are on Logan and the ring of light cast by the sunrise painting his face in shadows.

The ship lurches painfully, followed by more frantic shouts. The engines whirr, and the scent of oil and smoke fills the air, cutting through the blood staining my tongue.

"She all right?" Sawyer asks, his voice choked with his own pain.

"Broken nose, maybe. Brie? Can you hear me?"

"I'm okay," I reply to the best of my ability, but the words fall from my tongue in a garbled whisper.

The ship lurches again and bursts free of the reef's hold so abruptly Logan has to brace his hands on either side of my head to stop from flying forward over the top of me. The helm spins out of control just a few feet away, but Logan's looking down at me, his eyes wide and heavy with concern.

"I'm okay," I say again, unsure if it's the truth, but I figure we have bigger things to worry about, especially the roaring engine noise sprinting in our direction as the few surviving enemy boats race through the wall of fire behind us.

"Get her downstairs," Logan commands as he rises, looking at two men unfamiliar to me standing nearby.

I don't fight it when I'm lifted and tossed over the shoulder of a man I don't know like a sack of potatoes. My vision goes in and out while blood races to my head, and the sunrise fades to warm wood and the smell of wax and oil burning sconces. The inner sanctum of the *Asteria* is incredibly loud with the engines running full blast through the shallows. I'm carried down to our stateroom and deposited on the bed… the bed that still smells like me–and Logan.

"Let's have a look at that," the man who carried me down here says, sitting me upright against the pillows while the boat lurches and jerks across the waves, its hull scraping over the reef.

I blink blearily up at him, his face coming into view. He's young– likely my age, maybe even a little younger. He presses a wadded up piece of cloth to my nose and holds it there, forcing me to breathe through my mouth. My head pounds as I take in his details–the scar on his cheek that looks deep enough that he likely needed stitches, healed to a faint silver line against a patchwork of dark freckles. His skin is fair and tinted pink from the sun, and his hair is a mousy dark blond but unruly, touching his shoulders in rough waves.

"Who are you?" I mouth, unsure if the words make any sense. I think I might have bit down hard on my tongue because it's swollen and throbbing with echoes of dull pain.

"Jake," he says simply, casually, shrugging one shoulder. He has a teenager's build–tall and lanky, like he hasn't quite caught up with his height yet. "And you're Brie, the captain's mate."

"Yeah," I reply, my voice like gravel.

He pulls the cloth away and grimaces, shaking his head ever so slightly. "Your nose isn't broken but you bit your lip."

"What exactly happened?" I reach up to rub my forehead where a bruise is forming right between my eyebrows.

"You went through the railing. Beta Sawyer had a hold of you, though, caught you by the wrist when you went airborne, and you slammed face first into the side of the ship. All of us on the ratlines saw it."

"Oh," I breathe, embarrassment prickling across my cheeks as a blush burns to life.

"It's not serious. You're fine. You can obviously take a beating." He presses the cloth to my nose again. I take it from him, dabbing my swollen face. "Well, you're supposed to stay down here–"

A crash echoes from above. He winces, clutching one of the

posters on the corner of the bed to steady himself as the boat scrapes over what feels like another sandbar. I slowly turn my head to the windows. The sun is up, the last moments of a stellar sunrise fading into the purest of blues.

Jake's dark-brown eyes follow my gaze.

I gingerly slide off the bed to my feet, sniffling against the cloth. "I'm going back up."

"Captain Logan–"

"I don't care what he told you to do. I'm not going to sit down here by myself." My body aches as I hobble toward the door. Jake makes no moves to follow me until I've reached the door to the belly of the ship. However, I hear him grunt with resignation before turning on his heel, his boots echoing across the hallway and stairwell to the deck.

He's behind me on the stairs when another crash reverberates through the boat, then another, and shouts from above cascaded down to us when I hurry up the last steps, Jake following close behind. I burst through the doors, blinded by bright sunlight. It takes several blinks to adjust my eyes to the brightness, but finally, I see why everyone's shouting, and it's not because we're being boarded.

I lower the bloody cloth in awe as the boat sprints between two mountains through an incredibly narrow straight. The boat vibrates as it surges across what must be sand, only a dozen or so feet of water acting as a buffer. The sails are pulled in tight, and the engines shut off abruptly as the bright green mountains speed by.

We're being carried out to open water again by the tide, just like Logan said we would be.

Tears well in my eyes, but not from the pain of slamming into the side of the ship..

Logan looks out over the water, panting, his arms braced on the railing as he watches the islands slip by, shaking his head in awe as his mouth pulls into a smile.

He looks wildly happy. Like this was where he was meant to be, what he was meant to do.

Beyond the islands, behind us, fires dance across the water like a flaming scar. It's all that's left of the armada–oil and smoke.

Everyone is cheering–from the lower deck to the top of the sails. Their voices ring out as they pump their fists. Logan whirls to the crew, his wide, brilliant white smile glimmering in the sunlight as his eyes crease with pure, unfiltered joy.

I've never seen him smile like that.

He laughs at something Sawyer says but then goes rigid as he slowly turns to look down at me, and that smile fades completely.

I try not to think about what that means.

He says something else to Sawyer, pointing at the helm, before starting in my direction. He skips stairs on his way down to the lower deck and stalks toward me. Jake gets lost, disappears into the crowd gathering along the rails to watch the fire as it fades from view, replaced by leagues and leagues of open ocean again.

Logan grabs my upper arm, and I wince at his touch. Something feels different now, but I'm not sure how to explain it. It bubbles up inside of me as he turns me back toward the stairwell, silently leading me to our room. He says nothing, and I'm thankful for it, because all I can see as he shuts the door behind us is that fading smile, like the sight of me robbed him of the happiness he felt in that moment.

"Let me see you," he says gently, turning me around and gingerly prodding my jaw, my cheeks.

I wince away from his touch. "I'm fine–"

"I'm shocked you're upright," he says with a hint of confusion in his voice, which is low and heavy with emotion I know he won't name. "You slammed–"

"Jake told me."

"Are you okay?"

"I'm fine–"

"Brie–"

"You–you severed your ties with Silverhide," I burst out, knowing full well it doesn't matter to him, but for some reason, it matters a whole hell of a lot to me.

He takes a breath, his eyes scanning mine before he runs a hand through his dark hair. "I needed to be able to mind-link with the crew of this ship–"

"I get it."

"But you're angry?"

"You're not coming home, are you? After this, after we get out of KiloKilo somehow… you're not going back to Eastonia."

His cheeks go a pale pink as he swipes his tongue along his lower lip, "Brie–"

"I asked you if you were going to do it–to go back to Emberfyll. You never answered the question. You asked me if I still planned on finding an Alpha to marry."

"And you said of course, you will." He steps toward me, raising his palms in surrender. "And then I told you I regret it–"

"That doesn't matter if you're–if you're leaving."

"Brie–"

"What were you going to do, Logan? Fuck me and then drop me off in Veiled Valley like–"

"That's not what's happening here–"

"Then what?" I snarl, the force of my words sending fresh pain across my split lip and swollen nose. I'm sure I look insane right now, with my nose smeared with blood and my face bruised, but to hell with it. "What is this, Logan?"

"You wouldn't have me if I did go back to Eastonia with you, Brie. Don't act like that's not still the case. I have nothing to offer you but the life of a captain's wife in your own father's army. I don't bring support behind me. I can't pledge a pack to you, to *Maeve*. And I know for a Goddess damned fact you wouldn't choose me over her."

He could have slapped me, and it would have had the same effect.

"And I would never ask that of you," he says quietly, sternly, his eyes holding mine. "But I spoke to Alex. I'm sure the same kind of magic guarding KiloKilo wraps around Emberfyll. It felt the same when we went through it." His voice is barely above a whisper and rough, like it's taking all of his strength to get the words out. "Alex has enough stones to get us out of KiloKilo. He has just enough to get us to Emberfyll after that."

My heart quakes. "You told him."

"I offered his pack a lifeline. A home–"

"If he offers you an army in return!"

"My father was Alpha King!" he shouts. "I am, by blood, the Alpha King of Emberfyll. I have a duty to whoever's left there to return, to take back what's mine."

It's the most selfish thing I've ever said, but I can't stop myself when I say, "What about me? What about Aviva and Ryan? Lexa? Nora? Your family? What about *us*?"

WHY WOULD SHE DO THIS?

BRIE

"What about us?" My voice hangs in the air between us. The room goes so quiet and still I can feel the Asteria gliding back into open water, the rocky, uneven bounce of sailing through the shallows finally settling.

I wait for him to tell me to come with him. I wait, and wait, my heart squeezing with each second that passes, but I already know he won't.

His eyes already paint his answer clearly.

He's sacrificing the family he was given—the family he loves that loves him in return. He's not going to ask me to make the same mistake.

My body slumps against the weight of it, like I'm being dragged underwater, unable to fight the current. I'm exhausted. I'm in pain—physical and emotional pain, like my heart is being plucked from my chest and tossed into the ocean to drown.

I promised myself, long ago, that I'd never beg and plead on my knees to be loved. I would simply accept my fate. I knew my worth to the world the moment I was old enough for the tabloids to start questioning my future mate and the future alliances that union would make. That's when I knew all eyes were on me, the eldest sister of the future Queen Maeve.

My duty is, and always has been, to her.

Logan's duty has always been to the kingdom his parents died for, nothing else.

He reaches out and smooths his thumb over my cheek, brushing away a tear. I shiver, leaning into his touch as he caresses my face.

"We'll talk about this later," he says softly, his voice breaking over the words. "When we've both had some rest and the opportunity to shift."

I pull away, turning my body to face the bedroom door instead of him. "This has nothing to do with shifting–"

"You'll be thinking with a clearer head."

I close my eyes, biting my tongue to stop from lashing out at him, from telling him all the emotions battling for dominance and threatening to explode into a fireball bigger than the one his expert maneuvering during the royal armada's assault produced.

"Brie?"

"What?" I turn to look at him over my shoulder. His eyes are glassy, and his mouth is slack with unspoken words.

He tilts his head slightly to the side, mulling over whatever he's about to say before exhaling deeply, his eyes meeting mine. But he shakes his head, mumbling, "Just don't lie down for a while. You probably have a concussion. I'll be back with food and medicine."

"I don't have a fucking concussion," I grumble under my breath, but he's already leaving, the door snapping shut behind him.

I sink into the window seat, watching the waves rush past the boat, the water sparkling and crystal clear all the way to the horizon.

I wonder what Maeve's doing right now. I press my fingers to the glass, wondering what she'd do in this situation. Probably nothing. I don't think Maeve is capable of romantic love. She doesn't understand it, even when it comes to our parents. She curls her lip and snarls at any man who looks in her direction with a curious glance lately.

She wouldn't understand why I'm so torn to shreds. My mate found me, and we ended it. Yet, fate kept us together, proving at every turn that we made the wrong decision.

But fate hasn't stopped either of us from continuing to think logically about our situation, no matter how badly it stings.

Emberfyll was his home. He's spent his entire life preparing to go back, and now he has a real shot at making it happen.

But when I think of home… I think of him.

My eyes pinch shut as a sob tightens my chest, my hand curling into a fist against the window.

LOGAN

SHE'S CRYING. WHIMPERING, ACTUALLY, TRYING TO STAY QUIET. I WISH she'd let it out. I wish she'd scream and curse the world for the hand she was dealt, but Brie is still the composed aristocrat she'll forever force herself to be.

I lean against our door, repeatedly running my hand over my face, unable to tear myself away, yet unable to go back inside. I'll snap. I'll actually lose my fucking shit if I have to look at her, mangled with tears in her eyes, knowing I'm the cause.

Jake, the teenage deckhand whose father is one of Alex's high ranking wolves on the *Artemis*, clears his throat from the middle of the staircase where he's been perched for Goddess knows how long.

"What are you doing?" I ask—and not kindly.

The kid pales for a split second before puffing out his chest and gripping whatever he'd been holding in his lap, which turns out to be a pile of bandages and some of the herbal remedies Jackson, the grouchy old healer, packed aboard the *Asteria.*

"For the princess." He stretches his arm through the railing.

"Take it to her. I need to speak to the Beta." I do not want another man in her room, even one who likely hasn't grown his first chest hair, but that's just my wolf talking–howling and screaming not to walk away from her door. Jake's shocked look when I pass him on the stairs burns into my back as I throw open the door to the deck and storm out, scanning the crew for Sawyer.

He remains at the helm where I left him, looking worn but thankful just to be alive. His look of careful cheerfulness fades when I walk up the stairs to the helm, motioning for him to move so I can look at the map.

He says nothing, but I can feel him watching me, inspecting the tightness in my muscles and the furrow of my brows. I keep my eyes on the map, my finger gliding in a nearly straight line toward Tempest Valley, through a second, narrower straight... but a straight shot nonetheless.

"We'll be there in six hours at the latest," Sawyer says, sighing around the words. "You were right. I bet Alex is pissed right now. He takes great pride in his navigational skills." His chuckle is stolen by the stiff, steady wind helping the *Asteria* glide effortlessly toward home.

I spend the rest of the morning on the deck, staring at the water, wondering what the hell I'm doing and why. When I spoke to Alex about Emberfyll, wanting to know more about the veil around KiloKilo, things had just clicked into place for the first time in my life. It's the same magic. The same impenetrable field. Alex had been excited, damn-near buzzing with energy when we hurriedly hatched a plan in the dead of night while under duress from the knowledge the royal armada would be catching up to us eventually.

It'd be perfect. A sign from the gods, honestly.

But then I ended up in bed with Brie, and everything I thought I wanted, everything I thought I knew, failed to matter.

I can't take her away from her family. I can't ask her to come with me and sacrifice everyone she loves and her home in the process. We can get into Emberfyll, of that I'm certain, but once there... we wouldn't be able to get out.

She'd be stuck. She'd be with me, my queen, my mate and Luna of her own kingdom but at the cost of everyone she knows and loves.

"You fucking bitch," I whisper to myself, cursing the Goddess for doing this to us. She had to know, didn't She? When She interlaced our souls knowing that Her divine plan would either tear us apart or force us to make choices that would break us beyond repair?

I find Brie right where I left her, but asleep.

"Shit. Brie? Brie, I told you not to fall asleep–"

She snarls and swats my hand away, but I haul her upright, her body cast in the midday sunlight pouring through the windows over-looking her perch–the window seat.

"I'm fine, really." She sniffles as she bunches her hair into a bun on the top of her head, tying it off with a ribbon. She won't meet my eyes. The bridge of her nose is horribly bruised, and her under eyes are yellow with the beginnings of what I know will be two black eyes.

I crouch, balancing on my heels while knitting my hands in the fabric cushion she's resting on, but she moves away, crossing her arms under her chest. "Are we there yet?"

"We're about to go through the strait. It'll be rough for a few minutes, but then we'll be in Tempest Valley."

"What then?"

"We stay a night or two, ready the ships with supplies for a much longer journey, and cross the veil. Alex is within mind-link range and said he believes the royal armada won't have time to regroup and send out new boats by the time we're on the water again, so we're safe."

She looks out over the water, the sun turning her brown eyes the color of polished mahogany with flakes of honey within. "And then you'll go to Emberfyll?"

"I don't want to talk about this now."

"I do." She faces me, giving me an expectant look. "I want to talk about it right now. I think it's a terrible idea."

"You know why I have to. And you have to go home."

"Will I ever see you again?" she asks, suddenly tearful, that carefully crafted dam finally cracking. "Or is this just it? We were mates, Logan. Why would She choose us if this was always the outcome?"

Come with me. Come with me. Come with me.

"I don't know."

She turns back to the window, swallowing hard. "I just need to shift. You're right. Everything will be clearer when I shift."

I hope she's right because I'm ready to crawl out of my skin. I've been on the cusp of throwing caution to the wind and marking her for days now.

I rise and sit on the opposite side of the window seat, stretching out my legs, boxing her in against the window with my size alone. She hugs her knees, her lower lip quivering as she starts to come undone at the seams. I feel it in my chest—the same pain she's feeling. The confusion, grief, and utter heartbreak neither of us have been able to put into words so far.

"I miss them," she whispers, her voice cracking painfully over the words. "I miss my parents."

I reach for her, taking her hand, silently inviting her to come closer, to come to me, and she does.

I gather her in my arms, resting my chin on the top of her head as she cries silent tears into my shirt. I close my eyes against the pristine, turquoise water. My hand drifts down her back and back up again in gentle, lazy strokes as she clutches my shirt. She smells like everything I love, everything that ever made me feel calm and at home.

Going back to Emberfyll feels pointless if she's the sacrifice I have to make to get there, but I'm so close, and she... she wants to marry an Alpha.

I'm not an Alpha again until I set foot on those shores. I won't be who she truly wants until then, and I can't stand the idea of her living with that regret for her entire life if I do stay.

She slumps against me after a few minutes, her grip on my shirt going slack. She's asleep—fast asleep on top of me, lying between my legs. She fits perfectly, like she was built for me, and I... wonder if the Goddess was trying to tell me something by matching us.

"I'll come back for you," I tell her, opening my eyes to lush greenery as the boat passes through the strait. "One day, I'll come back for you. I swear."

28

BRIE FOR ONE NIGHT

BRIE

TEMPEST VALLEY IS EVERYTHING I'D BEEN TOLD IT WOULD BE. IT'S rocky, mountainous, but with flat, sprawling beaches with pristine, white sand that shimmers against the shallow, turquoise water. Palm trees bend at odd angles along the beach as the sunset sets the small village in shades of gold and crimson. Small houses made of wood stick out of the trees and along the rocky rise of the mountain. The village spirals upward against the mountain, small trails connecting each house and shop.

On the beach, several huge bonfires erupt as the sun finally drops below the horizon, the sound of lively, thrumming music and conversation mingling beneath the twinkling stars.

I'm looking down at it all beside Monica, both of us in our wolf forms. We've been out in the mountains for hours–sprinting. Jumping off of rocks, skirting around trees and chasing small tropical creatures and birds–anything to burn off some serious nervous energy.

Another group of wolves rushes up behind us, but she pays them no mind. She's a strange looking wolf–a color I've never seen before. Her strawberry-blonde hair makes her nearly pink as her wolf counterpart, and she glows in the starlight while she licks her pale yellow paws.

Comparatively, I'm dark brown. My fur is thick, just like my hair, and even though I trained in the heat and humidity of Veiled Valley, I'm having a hard time keeping my temperature regulated here in KiloKilo. It's hot as hell, and I'm damp with sweat when the group of male wolves comes up to bug us, yipping and chittering at Monica, who snarls at them, pawing their leader with her claws until they finally give up their game and leave us alone.

She shakes her head, her amber eyes meeting mine. I don't need the mind-link to know what she's trying to say to me. I think it goes something like, *"Men, huh?"*

I bark a wolfish laugh, rising from my belly to stretch out my aching legs, feeling like myself again after what feels like weeks on the water.

In fact, I think it has been weeks. I have no idea how long it's been since the yacht went down. Time is a construct on the water. Some days felt like they sped by, while others dragged. Monica tilts her head back to the beach, beckoning me to follow with a little friendly nip to my shoulder, and I do, letting her lead the charge down the rocky wolf trail that flows toward the village.

She comes to a stop near a large wooden house with giant windows overlooking the water below. It's higher than the rest–the Alpha's house, obviously, positioned on an overlook that takes in the entire view of the village, the docks, and the sprawling ocean beyond.

We arrived several hours ago. I'd woken up tangled on the window seat with Logan, his fingers drawing lazy circles over my scalp as he gently woke me up.

After that, it's a blur. We arrived to excited chaos, the first ship out of the trio, and in the worst wear. The *Asteria* needs work–repairs that could take days, if not weeks. The *Artemis* showed up an hour later followed by the *Atropos*, and the entire village broke out in song and dance in celebration for their Alphas' long awaited return.

I lost Logan in the fray. That was hours ago. I haven't seen him since.

Maybe that's a good thing because I'm... so incredibly conflicted as to what to do, to say, and to feel right now.

My chest feels heavy and tight as I shift back to my human form, accepting the robe Monica holds out for me, helping me into the sleeves.

"You have a beautiful home," I tell her, and she smiles softly, shrugging as she laughs.

"I do, don't I? I've never been here before."

I watch her face as she guides us through the open concept house, passing the windows overlooking the beach and bonfires below, and into a room set up like a walk-in closet, where her exquisite clothing already lines the racks and shelves, sent up and put away while we were shifting.

She grabs a few things off a shelf, handing me a bikini and swim cover, saying, "I had some stuff sent down to your cabin. Shirts, pants, toiletries... the works, but let's go down to the beach, to the party."

I give her a short smile, but she turns before that smile shatters, that tightness in my chest growing worse and worse as the minutes tick by. We walk side by side through the village, stopping every few feet when unfamiliar people approach us, approach her, their new Luna. She had six months to get to know the crew of Alex's three ships. The women and children don't know their new Luna yet, but Monica's met with excitement and gratitude I think makes her feel more at ease with the situation.

It must be hard for her. I know how she feels, actually. She left the only place she knew as home–lost her family, her home, possibly even whatever friends she could trust, and chose her mate.

While our situations are different, I get it because I'm on the precipice of choosing Logan knowing my life will change forever, and that there's a chance I'll never see my family again.

The worst part is... that I will choose Logan, if he lets me.

The air is hot despite the darkness. Fires burn toward the stars as music drifts through the air–chaotic and beautiful in a sensual way that sets heat coursing through my veins. It's the kind of music that would play in a club deep in Moonrise, when the lights would dim and the air would shift to dark and dangerous, lust fueled by alcohol thick in the air.

I wouldn't know, seeing as I've never been to a club, even during my trips to visit family in Crescent Falls, but I've had to go fetch Maeve enough times to know that I'm drawn to it. I've just never let myself give in.

Freshly shifted, showered, with my hair piled on top of my head and a belly full of delicious food, I rest on the sand beside Monica, who watches the group dancing along the beach, Alex being a part of it.

"He's so happy to be home," she smiles, stars in her eyes. "He's been talking about this for so long."

"Does he have family here?"

"No. Not really. Friends he considers family, yes, but he was an only child, and his mother passed when he was young, and his father never mated again. But Sawyer's parents are here and his sisters and their families." She sighs heavily, glancing at the village. "Everyone loves it here, but…we have to leave—soon, I fear."

"You said you have your witches and wizards that live here?"

"We do, but they're not as powerful as the royals. Their magic can only stretch so far, and if the royal armada can break through their shields and find this place, we're dead. It's that simple. So, we'll leave—because of me."

"It's not totally because of you. Alex and the other Alphas on this chain of islands wanted to go."

She nods, looking down at her lap and taking a deep breath. "It doesn't matter now. We're home, we're on land, and we can rest. But first, we dance."

She grabs my hand and yanks me upright before I have a chance to prepare myself. I dig in my heels, and she laughs, tugging me along the sand.

"Don't be such a sour puss, Princess. Dance with me! Have a little fun." She laughs, spinning me in a rough circle. "I know you can dance. I've seen you move. Just loosen up, Brie. You've been through hell, what's the worst that can happen? You enjoy yourself? Goddess forbid!"

We spin past a group of men resting on the sand. I catch Logan's gaze out of the corner of my eye where he's sitting next to Sawyer, shirtless, his skin bronzed from several days spent in the sun.

I tighten up immediately as Monica spins us through the sand, the gentle waves lapping at our feet. She notices my sudden stillness and stops, grabbing my arms. "What is with you and him?"

"I–I don't know what you mean?"

"Are you joking? You're the sharpest female I've ever met, the smartest. I mean that. You act like you're totally oblivious to the fact that he loves you–"

I pull away, shaking my head as the light of a nearby bonfire illuminates her face in shades of amber and crimson, the rest cast in shadowy starlight.

"He doesn't love me."

"He's looking at you right now," she hisses, keeping her voice low. "*Longingly.*"

I close my eyes for the space of a breath. I've never had close female friends. I was too busy–always going to meetings with my mom, my grandma, always tending to Maeve and her schedule. My social life outside of what I made my royal duties was non-existent.

I'm not used to this–being prodded, shaken, by someone who... wants to be my friend. Who wants to help me come to my senses and break out of my delusions.

"Look at him," she says, gripping my upper arms. "He's looking at you like you are the center of his world–"

"Did your mate tell you where you're going after this? Where your new home will be?" I interrupt.

"Yes, of course. Logan's taking us to Emberfyll, where he's Alpha King–"

"A war torn kingdom trapped behind another veil."

Her grip on my arms tighten, her face washed with sympathy, which isn't what I expected.

"It's better than here. And you'd be his Luna–"

"My family," I whisper, shaking my head. "My sister–she needs me. She'll be queen in three years, and she's not ready–"

"Are you her keeper?"

"What?"

"Is her success your responsibility? Are you not allowed to have your own life?"

"Logan and I rejected each other. It has nothing to do with her–"

"Why did you reject him?" Her hands fall to her sides. She arches her brow, shooting me an expectant look. "Why would you reject him? I take you as a religious person, am I wrong? Do you not believe the Goddess knows what She's doing when She pairs mates?"

"I do–I–you don't understand."

"Make me."

I suck in a breath, losing my patience. "I'm a princess. He's a warrior. We can't–we're not–I just–" I hate myself for this–for feeling this way, being torn in two different directions. Being pulled apart by my love and worry over my sister and my... love for Logan.

Love. The words barrels through my brain like a heated blade, cutting me to ribbons.

"He won't take me with him," I tell her through gritted teeth. "He won't take me away from my family, I already know. It doesn't matter what I want, Monica. It's not up to me. He knows that once we reach Emberfyll, the chance of me ever going back to Eastonia is slim, and that's if we survive the journey. You have to understand... I made a mistake when I rejected him, but it wouldn't have ended in a different way. We'd still be separated. He made his choice to return to his homeland."

She looks... conflicted. Her brows raise as the gears turn behind her eyes, thinking my predicament over. "You want him to stay. Stay in Eastonia with you?"

"I do but... he'd always long to see his home again. Years from now, when we're settled with a family of our own, he'd still wonder if he made the right choice. He'd resent me for it eventually, and I can't live with myself knowing that. That I made him choose between me and what he actually wanted."

"Then go with him."

"My family," I whisper, shaking my head. "They think I'm dead. I can't do that to them after everything they've done for me." She has no idea I'm adopted and how that came to be, but it doesn't matter. "And... even if I told him that I wanted to go with him, he wouldn't allow it. I already know."

She takes my arms again, her touch sailing over my skin as she knits our hands together. "Then... love him now. Are you going to let this opportunity pass you by? You have him now, Brie. This moment, this night, this... journey ahead us. Are you going to take that opportunity, or live with the regret of not experiencing being with your mate–forever?"

I look into her eyes, unable to answer her question, but something shifts inside of me.

She's right. We've wasted so much time already.

"Just dance with me," she whispers. "The rest can wait until tomorrow. We'll be sad and worried tomorrow, okay?"

I feel Logan's gaze on my back as she tugs me toward the fire and lets me go, holding her hands high above her head as she spins with the music. I let the beat seep into my bones, let my mind wander to a quiet, empty place, and give in, letting myself be... *Brie*, for the first time in my life.

And it feels good.

Like I'm forever changed.

29

MELODY REMEMBERED

Logan

Brie moves like the water, like a tree swaying in the wind, the most natural I've ever seen her. Her full, luscious curves are on achingly full display in the bikini she's wearing, which does little to hide what… what I want to claim as mine. Her body, her mind, her soul…

Even after spending the majority of the afternoon and evening in my wolf form, thinking finally having the opportunity to shift would clear my head, it only made those feelings worse.

Feelings that tell me I'm making a mistake. Leaving her behind, choosing Emberfyll over her…. It's the worst thing I've ever done.

Sawyer sighs beside me, lifting his drink to his mouth. It's rum, which I'm not a fan of but have been drinking since the boats pulled up to the dock, mostly against my will.

"She's beautiful," he says, nudging his shoulder against my arm.

"I know." I wish she knew. I wish I could show her that, make her believe it somehow. Show her how much she's worth, but… I'd be crossing the line we nearly crossed already knowing the consequences of our actions.

"You're really gonna just… give her back to her family? Let her go?"

I've told Sawyer practically everything. I didn't have a choice when I explained the Emberfyll situation to him and Alex, and they agreed to go. Brie won't be coming with me. I can't separate her from her family and just… take her away.

Doing that would hurt everyone I love back in Eastonia, not just her.

I watch Brie raise her hands in the air, moving her body with the music. She looks… incredible. Just… everything I've ever wanted, and I realize, in that moment, how little Emberfyll actually means to me if she's not there.

I wrap my arms around my knees and watch her dance, watch the light of the bonfires paint her bare skin in gold, wanting my touch to be painting her skin instead.

Alex and Sawyer already know they can settle anywhere. The Deadlands would have room for them, and the two other packs in tow, to spread out and settle with enough land to expand their numbers. They could stay along the coast like they're used to now. They could be happy there—secure and protected by Ryan as their Alpha King.

And I could… take Brie back to Silverhide. We could set up our life in the village with our family and be only a few days' travel away from Maeve in Moonrise, from her parents in Veiled Valley.

But I wouldn't be an Alpha. Would I still be enough to marry a princess?

Because I could just… go home. Home to Eastonia, where I spent… the majority of my life, honestly.

If she'd be happy enough as a captain's wife.

Brie turns so I can her face as she winds her hips to the music, and I… fold.

I rise, and Sawyer snorts a knowing laugh behind me as I stalk forward through the crowd of dancers. Brie looks up at me with those round, wide eyes full of flames. I don't think. My brain goes blank, save for the undying need to just... be with her.

"Logan," she breathes, blinking up at me.

"We're going home to *Eastonia*," I tell her without thinking through what I'm saying, what I'm offering... deciding in the moment. "You and I–are going home. As mates."

Her mouth forms a perfect O. She takes a shallow breath, her hands pressing against my chest as she starts to shake her head. But I scoop her into my arms, throwing her over my shoulder and turning from the bonfires.

A few men hoot and holler at us as I march through the party, carrying my mate off the beach and into the trees where a small cabin rests nearby, overlooking the water, tucked into the shadows.

"Logan, we need to talk about this–"

"No," I rasp, adjusting her weight while she tries to squirm out of my grasp.

I walk up the steps onto the porch, throwing the door open. It's a single room with large windows overlooking the water, but the curtains are drawn, thank the Goddess. There's a single door leading to a bathroom, but that's it.

"Logan?" Brie whimpers, struggling to push herself upright, bracing her hands on my shoulders, but I deposit her on the dresser. She gasps, her chest rising and falling with a rough, shuddering breath, but we're eye to eye now as I lean in, bracing my hands on either side of her thighs.

"We're going home," I assert sternly. "To Eastonia."

"But–but you'll never be happy, Logan. You'll always be wondering about Emberfyll–"

"No," I tell her, leaning in to brush the word over her lips. "Brie, I was wrong. I thought my parents left to give me a chance to go back one day, to rule again but... they just left. They ran away praying I'd never return. They died so I could have something better."

"Something better?" she asks breathlessly, gasping as my teeth graze the tender skin of her neck.

"My mate," I whisper, pulling back enough to look her in the eyes.

"You."

She scans my face before reaching up to caress my cheek. "Logan…"

"Will you have me, even though I'm not an Alpha? Even if I can't give you a pack that can throw its support behind Maeve when she becomes queen?"

"Will you resent me for being the reason you'll never be able to go back to Emberfyll?" she asks painfully, her eyes watering.

"Never," I breathe, pressing my lips to her. "I'd never resent you, Brie. Goddess, you have to know—you have to know by now that this is just… we shouldn't have rejected each other."

"I know, Logan, I know—"

I kiss her again, deeply, my tongue swiping over hers. She moans, wrapping her arms around my neck and dragging me closer, leaning into the kiss when neither of us can breathe.

My hands travel to her thighs, wrenching them apart. My wolf takes over, and I let him, let everything go until it's just me, her, and the choice we're about to make that we can't take back.

BRIE

LOGAN'S HAND MOVES BETWEEN MY THIGHS, HIS FINGERS PULLING MY bikini bottoms to the side. I arch my back, my head lolling against the wall while he strokes my clit with his thumb, two of his fingers gliding through the wetness pooling at my entrance before he presses them inside—roughly. I gasp out a breath, my heart skipping a beat before surging. Heat floods my body, turning every thought and feeling into a desperate kind of want.

Desire has a chokehold on my mind. Nothing else matters. Nothing we just talked about matters, not now, not with his fingers inside of me and my body reacting to his touch like waves being pulled out by a vicious tide.

I'm lost to him, and I know it. I'll let him do whatever he wants, whenever he wants.

"Goddess," he breathes against my temple, gritting his teeth and nuzzling me as he works me with his fingers until my inner walls tighten around him in warning that I'm already close. I'm perched precariously on the edge of the dresser, and he's standing between my knees, pressing his body to mine, each stroke of his fingers forcing whimpering moans from my lips.

"I want to finish what we started," he rasps against my cheek before kissing me deeply.

"Please," I whimper, losing control entirely as my body tightens, begging for release.

He nips my jawline, pressing kisses down my neck to my collarbone, where his teeth graze my skin. I can still hear the music outside. It sends a gentle hum of vibration through the cabin as the beach party rages on without us, everyone lost to music, dance, and copious amounts of rum.

I haven't had a single drink, but I feel like I'm moving in a haze when he lifts me off the dresser and deposits me on the bed, pulling my bikini bottoms off and tossing them across the room.

He steps back to look at me, drinking me in. This time, I don't shy away from his gaze. I let my legs fall apart while I reach behind me, untying my top, letting the thin fabric fall away from my breasts, and he... exhales sharply, his pupils blown wide, his face etched with so much longing it could bring tears to my eyes.

Tears of happiness. Thank the Goddess for giving me a man like him. A man that looks at me like I'm a meal, and he's been starving for his entire life. No one has ever looked at me like Logan does–has, from the beginning.

He shoves his shorts down and steps toward the bed, his cock hard and proud as he fists it, his gaze dropping to my sex.

I've never done this before. My sex education came from Misty, Aviva, and Sarah–seeing as my mother's soft disposition made it nearly impossible to describe what this was supposed to be like, to feel like for me.

I know it's going to hurt, but I want it to. I don't want him to be gentle. I want him to show me what I'm capable of feeling. I want him in full control. I want him to force me to let go of the reins for once.

He must see that behind my eyes because he crawls on the bed, pressing my hips to the mattress, and kisses me so hard it steals my breath away.

He nudges my legs further apart, settling his hips against mine, his cock teasing my clit, swiping through the wetness, before he presses inside of me, and I feel the stretch of him….

"Ohhhh," I whimper, closing my eyes as his mouth finds my neck. He rolls my nipples between his fingers as he pulls out slowly, like he's savoring the feel of me, even if he's barely inside.

"You feel *so good*," he whispers breathlessly, pressing in again and not stopping until I whimper, raising my hips to meet his. He chuckles low and dark when I arch again, writhing beneath him. He's teasing me, isn't he?

"Are you enjoying this?" I ask hotly, my voice cracking with desperation as he slowly pulls out. "Teasing me?"

"Yes, I am," he answers, his lips parting as he exhales. He slides his cock inside me, filling me and stretching me to the point of pain but hits the barrier and stops.

"Please," I whimper as the pain fades to a kind of pleasure I've never felt but need to chase. "Please, Goddess, Logan, just–" I gasp, fighting back a scream as he pulls out roughly and thrusts hard, the headboard clapping against the wall behind us.

"*Fuck*," he growls, lowering his forehead to mine and rolling his hips, grunting and groaning, refusing to hold back the sounds of his own ecstasy.

He holds me down as he thrusts inside of me again, and again, taking his time as I adjust to his size. He presses hard kisses to my neck, my breasts, sucking my nipples into his mouth and nibbling until I find it hard to catch my breath. My body is on fire. Every touch is both too much and too little. My skin is suddenly so sensitive, like a single swipe of his finger across my belly will make me come unglued, fraying at the seams.

I grip his neck, my other hand braced against his chest as he rolls into me in short, quick thrusts. My inner walls clench around him, and he slams a hand down beside me, curling his fingers into a fist. "Fuck, Brie. If you do that again, I'm going to knot in you."

"I can't help it," I breathe, my voice coming out in a rasp as I moan the words, crying out when he presses into me so fully he fills me up to the brim and can't go any further. I arch my hips toward him, giving him deeper access, and he groans my name, panting as he grabs my hips to hold me there before splaying my legs apart to absolutely devour me with his cock.

His fingers find my clit again, drawing quick, perfect circles. I start to tremble as tension builds in my thighs and lower belly. I lock my ankles behind his back, crying out his name incoherently as the word bleeds into moan and gasps.

It's like a wave that ripples through my entire being. The tension breaks in a snap, and I'm flooded with tingling warmth. I spasm around his cock, my legs shaking as I grip his shoulders, my vision filling with stars.

He grunts, slowing his movements. I can feel him looking at me, watching me come. I open my eyes to slits as one of his hands slides up my belly, past my breasts, and clutches my throat. He's breathing heavily as he starts to move again, sending new, fresh ripples of pleasure through my body. But he's moving slowly, savoring the feel of me—of us where we're joined, and the look on his face just...

"Mark me," I whisper, unsure of whether he can hear, but the words settle between us, igniting a new fire behind his eyes, and I know, in the moment, he's about to hurt me... in the best way.

"Oh, Brie. He closes his eyes and rolls his hips against mine. Logan lowers himself on top of me, balancing with one elbow on the mattress while his free hand gropes my breasts. He starts to tremble, his movements more erratic. He hits a spot so deep within me it sends me into spasms again as my pleasure skyrockets.

"I'm going to come again," I whine, turning to face him, our noses brushing, but then I feel... pressure. Pressure that turns to an intense feeling of fullness that takes me off guard. I gasp in pain, my legs shaking as I try to pull away, but he presses his hand to my belly, forcing me back down.

I've heard about this. Knotting. It's happening right now, and it hurts. I can't–I can't move.

"I know," he whispers against my cheek. "Brie, it's all right." His hand moves down, his fingers reaching my clit and stroking gently, turning the pain to pleasure that feels totally new and just... overwhelming.

"Come for me," he commands, his eyes on mine. "Come for me while I mark you."

I suck in a breath as he thrusts as deep as he can go, trapping us there as the knot forms and binds us together, and then he spills himself into me, filling me with his warmth.

An orgasm builds and erupts. "Logan!" I scream, his name shattering on my tongue at the same moment he kisses down the slope of my left breast and bites down hard, hard enough to make me wince and whine.

But the effect is... immediate. The pain ceases, turning to ecstasy that washes through me, making me go slack. My hand curls around the back of his neck as I pant against the rim of his ear, closing my eyes as a strange sensation ripples through my chest–like little strings plucking into place, creating a song only we know.

A song we tried to forget. It's been there this whole time, waiting for us to remember.

"Oh, my Goddess," I whisper, nuzzling him as he holds me, his tongue sliding over the mark he left on my breast–his mark.

He rises, the tips of noses touching as he looks in the eyes. I gasp for breath, tracing his cheekbones with my fingertips before kissing him tenderly, a single tear falling down my cheek. I kiss his jaw, then his neck, my wolf taking over the moment my mouth reaches that tender patch of skin where his neck meets his shoulder.

"Right there," he breathes, his hand cupping the back of my head. "I want it right there, where everyone can see it. Mark me, Brie. For the love of the Goddess, *please*."

I bite down, claiming Logan as mine, whatever comes.

3 0

YOU'RE GOING TO HELP ME

MOM STANDS WITH HER ARMS CROSSED ON THE BALCONY OVERLOOKING the ballroom in our castle. In the city below, the once beautiful, tropical landscape is cast in shadow. The crystal bridges lined with greenery are now painted in banners of black. A field of flowers stretches beyond the gates of the castle, left by mourners. Left for my sister.

Veiled Valley has never been this quiet and dark. The sun has barely shown itself since Brie left us. The castle itself has barely stirred in that time. It's magic just… can't handle Brie's loss. It mourns with the rest of us, sometimes sending a low, choked groan through the corridors that make the lights flicker, like the magic is crying.

"I'm not ready," Mom says quietly as she watches the women below mingle in small circles, most, if not all of them, dressed in dark fabric–mourning gowns.

"I'll tell them we're waiting. It's not a problem," I reply, gliding to her side, reaching to lay my hand over hers as she grips the balcony, but she turns and walks away, disappearing behind a curtain.

My chest quakes while I watch the curtain fall back into place. I've never seen Mom like this. Yes, she's an anxious person by nature but... seeing her shattered is...

I blink away tears and turn back to the group of high-ranking ladies, all of whom have gathered to offer their help with a memorial service for their princess. It's been over a month, after all.

I take my time walking down the steps to the ballroom. I only have to say three or four words before the women bow and take their leave. No one steps up to me to speak privately or offer me condolences. In fact, everyone gives me a wide berth, some glancing wearily over their shoulders in what I can only describe as fear.

The doors shut, closing me in with my own grief once again.

I've never felt alone in my life until now.

The corridors are quiet. Gray daylight slips between the folds of the curtains. Everything is dark, gray, and damp as rain pours and thunder booms overhead, like the Goddess Herself is rejecting Her decision to take Brie from us. I find myself in Brie's room, pacing in a circle along the walls, running my fingertips over her things. Her books, her skincare products, and little knick-knacks. The magazines she likes to hide between the mattress and the bed frame—magazines that said such awful things about her. She still read them, though. She drank that criticism in, turning her hard and icy until she believed herself unlovable unless she did something worthy.

Like marrying a fucking Alpha.

I sit on the edge of the bed, grabbing a notebook off the bedside table, flipping through it and finding it totally empty. I smirk. That's such a Brie thing to do. She seems like the kind of person who would write in a journal, but she doesn't—not about herself. Nope. I glance at her desk, at the piles of textbooks pertaining to history and law, and the scattered notebooks with so much wear she had to tape the spines multiple times to keep the pages together.

I lift a finger, and a pen goes whizzing off her desk, landing in my open palm. I cross my legs, sucking in a breath as I wrack my mind for all the names of the men—the Alphas and their heirs—who ever rejected her.

I don't think I'll kill them. That sounds a little... extreme, doesn't it? I mean, I want to. I want to hurt each and every one of them... slowly. Painfully. I want them to live with that pain so that someone in the world might know how it really feels to lose her because they had no idea what they were giving up, did they?

I scribble the names then rip the paper, folding it neatly and stuffing it in the front pocket of my jeans. A slow rush of air flutters through the room before settling as quickly as it came. At first, I think the scent I'm smelling is just... Brie's things. Her warm, soft, clean scent is everywhere here but... this is different.

My skin prickles as I rise, glancing around like she's going to jump out from behind the curtains or out of her closet to say, "Surprise! I fooled you. I've never been missing, you idiot!" But...

I feel her. I swear on the Goddess Herself... I *feel* Brie.

I don't think. My mind goes blank as my powers erupt around me in a whirl of red light and stars. Paper catches in the storm, swirling around the room as I'm sucked into oblivion, into darkness, where I float in a vat of nothingness, where time stands still.

When my powers fade, and the light creeps in again, I'm standing in an apartment in a towering high rise overlooking Crescent City, the kingdom of Crescent Falls stretching out all around me in a shimmer of blinking lights against the starlight overhead, through the glass box where Blake hoards himself away.

A blue fabric sectional stretches along pale gray tile floors. A large television blocks an entire corner of the room where a rather violent video game is sending shockwaves through the apartment, the floor beneath me vibrating.

The dark-haired man sitting on the couch has his back to me, resting his elbows on his knees. He doesn't stop the game or look in my direction.

I look around at the spotless apartment. It's clean. So clean I could eat off the floor.

"What do you want, Maeve?" Blake grumbles, his voice deep and dry—monotone—not a flicker of emotion behind the words.

"Where have you been? You never came to Maatua. Nor Moonrise. I know you haven't said a Goddess damned word to your own aunt and uncle about the loss of Logan."

"Why would I?" His fingers fly over the controls, his glittering violet eyes reflecting the game as I round the sectional, tracing my fingers over the top. His eyes weren't always that color. They used to be a dark, stormy blue, like his father's. Unlike some of his siblings who were born with eyes the color of a pale purple lilac, Blake's... changed, and now radiates power he can't turn off. It's unsettling looking at him, honestly.

He's handsome, sure. The most, if I'm being honest. He's like me—tall with dark hair and chiseled, sharp facial features. We take after our great-grandfather, Maddox. In fact, I've seen pictures of Maddox in his youth... Blake is his spitting image—except for those eyes.

There's a reason Mystics wear masks. They're frightening creatures. Looking into their eyes is like seeing the future against your will, or seeing the deepest, darkest parts of yourself reflected in full color.

Sarah is a Mystic too, but Blake?

He's... a fucking *god*, and he knows it.

"Turn that shit off before I break your TV," I growl.

He finally looks up at me, running his tongue along his lower lip before he smirks, rolling his eyes back to his game. "What do you want? Is this just a friendly visit, cousin?"

"We're not friends."

"Then why are you here?" He shuts off the game, tossing the controller to the end of the couch and slouches, stretching his arms behind his head. "To chastise me for not blubbering with grief with the rest of the family?"

"I called for you. I called for you to come help. Your mother couldn't find Brie and Logan—"

"Because they're dead."

I arch a brow. "You'd know. Are they dead, Blake? What have you seen?"

He searches my eyes, the corner of his mouth lifting into a cruel smile. I wish I knew what fucked him up all those years ago. He'd wanted to train in Moonrise with the Mystics so badly. I remember it being a point of contention between him and his parents when they refused, telling him he needed to wait until he was older, but then he started targeting his siblings, stretching those developing powers on his own, and Sarah and Sydney had no choice.

Blake is… incredibly powerful.

He's the only person in the entire world who would be able to match *me*, power for power. One day, he'll be king of Crescent Falls while I rule Eastonia.

If those kingdoms ever go to war against each other… it will be because of us. We've never gotten along. Ever.

"I haven't seen anything because I haven't looked."

"Why not?"

"Because I don't want to glimpse my cousin dead on the ocean floor, being eaten by crabs–"

"She's not dead," I assert, pointing a finger at him. My voice trembles as emotion I'm desperately trying to keep tamped down echoes to the surface. "I felt her, Blake. I need you to look. I need you to read between the realms for me."

"No."

"I didn't ask if you would," I snarl. "I'm demanding it. Find her!"

He rises, towering over me by more than a foot. I'm not afraid of him. I'll topple this entire skyscraper if he so much as moves in my direction aggressively, and he knows it.

"You need to accept what happened so that your parents can move on." His voice doesn't vibrate, but his eyes change, going a shade darker, some of the power fizzling out. He looks more like a person all of the sudden and not a demon from my nightmares, but I'm not backing down.

"She's not dead. I don't care what you think. I don't care what anyone else thinks, especially you, you fucking bastard! Help. Me. *Right now!*"

"No."

"You care this little for Brie? You loved her. I know you did. She was the only person you truly ever cared about."

Blake's mouth tightens as he blinks, his expression softening to grief for a split second before he turns his features to ice-cold steel. "Shut the fuck up, and get out of my apartment."

"Fuck you! You're a monster—you always have been. This is my *sister*! And I feel her, Blake, I swear to the Goddess and the old gods. I swear on Isla and Maddox's graves—"

"I do not take looking between realms to read the stars lightly," he grinds out, his tone edged with fury. "You cannot ask me to do so. You can't, Maeve. I'm not afraid of you. I'm not going to let you bully me in my own home. Swear all you want. Spirit away, to the depths of the sea, if you feel that she's alive so strongly!"

My nostrils flare, desperation clouding my senses. "Help me. Please, Blake." Tears well in my eyes for the first time since the day we found out Brie's ship sank. I haven't let myself cry since then. "Please. *Please*. Just try. Just try to locate her. That's all I'm asking."

He takes a step toward me, his shoulders rigid and jaw flexed. "I won't risk seeing something else while going on a wild goose-chase for you, Maeve."

"Is that what you're afraid of? Seeing something you won't like? Using your fucking powers like you're meant to? For fuck's sake, Blake. You have to try. If not for me, then for my mom. *Please*."

"I can't." He turns away from me.

"She—I think she found her mate shortly before she left for Maatua."

He stops, slowly looking at me over his shoulder.

I exhale, wringing my hands as I continue, "She was acting so strange the day before she left. She smelled different, too. You know how people smell different when they find their mates? I don't know how else to explain it, but she wasn't herself. Then she just… left. And for the past month, I've been thinking that… if she were alive, and she had a mate, that would be… she could finally be happy and feel like she belongs somewhere, you know? I think me closing in on my maturity and ascension has been hard on her. She's—she puts so much of herself into our family and has never, ever, had anything for herself."

"She's been your little assistant, and you miss that," he sneers.

"That's not what it was," I retort, but his bitter laugh bounces off the sterile, dark gray plaster walls.

"You are blind to what Brie was doing for you, aren't you? Her little marriage scheme? I can't be the only one who knew the real reason she was practically begging every Alpha she met to marry her."

"What are you talking about?"

"She saw something no one else did. Powerless as she may be, she noticed something even the Mystics in Moonrise couldn't have deciphered... and that's the rift your upcoming crowning is going to cause in Eastonia."

I feel my cheeks burning with righteous fury and disbelief. "You have no idea what you're talking about."

He laughs again, bitterly, his eyes glowing that intense violet once more. "She wanted to marry someone powerful who could throw their support behind you so her kingdom didn't topple the second you sat on your pretty, golden throne. You didn't realize it because your head is so far up your own ass that you're blinded by your own ego and prowess! You are not as untouchable as you think you are." He steps toward me again, closing in on me. "And you know what, Maeve? I *am* going to help you. I'll show you what you think you want to see. Because you deserve it, whatever it is. But I swear to the Goddess, if you force me to look upon her dead, decaying body, *I'll kill you.*"

He grabs my hands, squeezing tight as his eyes shine with the brightest light—starlight, raw and unfiltered.

It only takes a few seconds. I'm not sure if that's a good thing. Dread washes through me as his scornful expression shifts to sudden confusion.

"Blake? Blake, what do you see?"

His grip on my hand tightens as he says, "Take us to Veiled Valley, *now.*"

3 1

NOTHING CAN CHANGE IT

BRIE

"There's four main ports on the continent," Logan says, bending over the crude, illustrated map of Crescent Falls and Eastonia for Alex. "Here, in Maatua. Just south of that is Avalone, in Veiled Valley. I believe that's where we'll be closest. However, if we come out of the veil far south, there's a port here, in Tarsian, which is part of Eastonia. And if we're somehow north." He breaths, tapping the map with his knuckles. "We'll be here, in Crescent Falls."

"And Emberfyll is… where?" Alex asks.

"Somewhere… over here, I believe." He drags a finger south from Tarsian and sharply east. I follow it, my chest tightening as I look up at him.

We're on the *Artemis* right now, tucked away in Alex and Monica's private quarters. Behind us, the *Asteria*, the *Atropos*, and two other grand ships bob in the water. Beyond them, an entire fleet of ships of varying sizes follows our progress away from Tempest Valley and into the open, toward the veil.

We've been on the water for two weeks. Before that, we spent an

239

entire week in Tempest Valley preparing for the journey. It's been a whirlwind of activity. I helped where I could. I went into homes to help families pack their things, determining what was important to take with them to a new life, what was irreplaceable. I followed Monica around while taking stock of supplies. We'd sit together, trying to comfort nervous mothers with infants and young children, all of them wary about the journey.

Logan and I wouldn't see each other from dawn to dusk. He was out with the men—fixing the ships. Loading supplies. Alex didn't bat an eyelash when Logan told him they were going to Eastonia instead. I think it was easy enough to convince the Alpha of the change after witnessing several tense pack meetings where his people were nearing a split, some wanting to stay and fight, other's desperate to go—to go anywhere to escape the royal guard.

Now nearly five hundred people have boarded these ships, following Logan's lead. He's nervous about crossing the veil. I can tell. We'd lay in bed together at night talking about anything but that.

I walk around him slowly, resting my hand on his lower back. He relaxes a touch, but not much, as he says to Alex, "Once we reach any of these ports, we're going to be met by warriors. You need to let me lead and explain the situation."

"Will my people be detained?"

"No, but it's likely that you, Sawyer, Monica, and the Alphas of the other two packs will be. I'm hoping we're closer to Avalone because Veiled Valley is Brie's territory. She'll be able to see everyone to safety without much… fanfare."

"Logan, it's going to be chaos," I tell him. "We've been missing for… a month, at this point."

"That's actually on our side," he replies, meeting my eyes. "You're right." He turns to Alex. "It'll be chaotic, but once Brie and I explain everything, you'll be safe."

"And then what?" Alex rounds the armchair Monica's sitting in, resting his hand on her shoulder. She looks at us expectantly, but she's a lot calmer than Alex is right now.

"My plan is for you and your allies to settle in the Deadlands. It's summer. There's still time to build villages, even if the buildings aren't permanent, but there's space and my–my Alpha King is kind to those wanting to settle in his lands."

I think of Ryan with a smile.

"But," Logan says with caution, "the reality is… these boats will likely act as pack houses until we're cleared to travel the river out of Veiled Valley and into Eastonia freely."

"They're stocked for it," Alex grumbles, running a hand over his face. "We've never moved this slowly before. We're all weighed down with supplies."

Logan straightens his back, eyeing the couple. "And you're positive the Alexandrite will see every single ship in this fleet through the veil? You have no doubts?"

"Yes," Monica says simply, nodding her head. "It will work."

Rain patters against the windows. Thunder booms nearby. We all turn to look, to try to glimpse a peak of the veil through the rain, but that's its little trick, isn't it?

The boat groans all around us as it's sucked into the storm.

"We're fine," Alex says as if to calm the tension starting to soar toward the ceiling. "I've sailed along the edge of the veil before."

"But you've never sailed through it," Logan says under his breath. His eyes shine, turning a dark, deep green against his white shirt and bronzed skin. He's no longer the clean-cut captain of my father's army. He's suntanned and war-torn, roughened from weeks spent in physical, and honestly, emotional turmoil. I know he hasn't slept much. Even when he's had the chance… we've been doing other things in bed that have little to do with getting any rest.

I feel my cheeks burning at the fresh memories of being with my mate. My mate. Our bond, reignited, burns through me. Logan glances at me, his pupils expanding like he can see right through me, see into my mind and the images flashing there like I'm turning pages in a book.

He clears his throat. "Wake me up if anything happens."

Alex nods, running a hand over his face. "We have a few hours before we pass through the veil. You should be on the deck to witness it. I'll have someone… wake you up?"

"Fine," Logan replies shortly, grabbing my hand and pulling me out of the room, into the maze of narrow hallways.

He wasn't given the *Asteria* again. It wasn't any fault of his own, but Alex wants us close, on the same ship as him, when we leave Kilo-Kilo and come into waters protected by our people, our kingdom, so we can do the talking when the time comes. It's cramped in the ship now, however. Every stateroom is taken, down the smallest box with only a cot to sleep on. A lower deck has hammocks, but thankfully we still have a room of our own.

It's the second room we were given when we first stayed on the *Artemis*. It's spacious and comfortable, and the bed is… going to do what it needs tonight because the second Logan shuts us into the room, he turns to me, pinning me to the wall.

"Did you think I wouldn't notice what you were just thinking about in there?" he whispers, smiling wryly as he brushes my hair out of my face and plants a kiss on my kiss. "It was very… graphic of you, Brie."

"You're enjoying the perks of having a mate I see," I giggle, smiling then gasping as his hand travels up my belly to cup my breast, his thumb flicking over my nipples.

"We were in the company of others," he growls against my neck, nibbling gently.

"I couldn't help it."

He smiles wickedly against my skin. "You're in heat."

I pull away, pressing my hands to his chest. "Heat? You can't possibly–how do you know?"

"Another perk of being your mate." He presses his lips to mine, but I lean out of his way.

"Logan, we haven't been using any type of protection and… oh, Goddess. What if? What if I'm–"

His hand lowers to my stomach again. "The thought of you pregnant with my child–"

"We're getting ahead of ourselves." I chuckle nervously, but to be honest, my life isn't necessarily flashing before my eyes at the thought. The past week with him has been... *amazing*. A dream. It's just been us. No distractions. Nothing burdening us except for helping Alex's pack prepare for their journey. It was easy to forget about everything else and just be in the moment with him.

I rise on my toes and kiss him, my lips brushing his in a featherlight touch, but I feel the shift between us at the same moment the thought of my family–the family we inadvertently share in a weird, removed, *adopted* way pops the bubble of delusion for good.

"What are we going to tell them?" I ask, my hands brushing down his sides.

He leans his forehead against mine, his eyes closing as he sighs. "I've been thinking about it, trying to decide the best course of action."

"I'll do the talking."

He opens one eye, his brows raised. "Absolutely not."

"Why not?" I slide free of his hold, walking across the room while picking the laces securing my dress in place loose.

"Because you'll make this far more complicated than it needs to be."

"But *it is* complicated." I sit on the edge of the bed to remove my boots and socks while he moves toward me. "We're mates, Logan. We accepted that, acted on it, and now have to–have to tell our family the news after being missing for a month!"

"They're going to know the moment they see us."

"You don't know that." I laugh, shaking my head as I rise and pad across the floor, trying to pass him to get to the bathroom.

He turns to follow, chuckling under his breath while I continue to fumble with the laces of my dress.

"I do know it." He catches me around the middle as I breach the bathroom. His fingers deftly untie the laces, and the dress slides free from my shoulders. "And it won't matter to them, not then, at that moment. We've been gone for a while. They'll just be happy you're home." He presses a kiss to my shoulder. I close my eyes as tingles of warmth flood my body. His hand rests against my stomach, pressing me to him. It's almost enough to make me forget what we were talking about, especially when he kisses the crook of my neck, then upward, before turning me to face him.

He gently pulls the dress down to rest around my waist, his hands cool against my heated skin. He exhales deeply as his hands move up my body, his lips brushing over mine. "Whatever happens," he whispers against my skin, "It won't be worse than what we've already been through. We're going home, together, and that's all that matters."

I close my eyes when his mouth meets mine in a hungry kiss. He backs me into the bathroom until my hips hit the counter, slowly sliding the dress down over my hips until it pools in a heap of fabric at my feet.

I unbutton his shirt, my fingertips brushing over his skin. There's nothing hurried about this, not like the times before, when we were just desperate to be together and exhausted from days spent preparing Alex's pack to leave their islands. Now, it's the calm before the storm, literally. Thunder cracks through Logan's soft groan as he lifts me on top of the counter and spreads my legs. Rain pelts the windows, pinging off the glass, while his hands travel to my breasts. He knows where and how to touch me to set me on fire. Every stroke of his fingers has tension curling through my body, my skin tingling and electric, like the lightning casting the sky beyond the ship in ribbons of blue.

"I was going to take a shower, you know." I breathe, fanning his neck, closing my eyes against the sensation of his cock slipping effortlessly through my folds. My toes curl, and I inhale sharply when he buries himself deep, his body trembling in satisfaction.

"Later," he says breathlessly, his hands steadying my hips as he rocks into me in deep, but slow, thrusts.

It goes on like this for some time, and when I'm tucked in bed an hour later, my hair damp from the shower I ended up sharing with Logan, I reach over to smooth my hand over his chest while we watch the storm.

"I never found them calming until you mentioned it," he admits, his voice barely above a whisper. He exhales, toying with my fingers while his gazes hones in on the distant glare of lightning. "On the yacht, during the storm. You just... watched it. It was the first time I ever saw you relaxed."

"There's just... nothing anyone can do to change it," I whisper, pressing my lips to his chest before nuzzling closer. "Not us. Not my all powerful family. Not *me*."

He gathers me in. "Everything's going to be all right. When we return, I mean. I'll handle it."

"I know," I whisper, trying not to close my eyes and inadvertently fall asleep, but he's so warm and I'm so tired...

And moments later, a knock sounds on the door to our room. Logan leaves the bed, pulling on a pair of pants as he walks to the door, giving me a bit of a show as the stormy darkness casts shadows over his toned back and legs. Sawyer's voice is soft but serious, muffled by distance, but there's only one reason he'd be here.

We're about to go through the veil.

3 2

WHEREVER HOME IS

Logan

Brie folds her arms under her chest against the sudden, humid chill in the air. Thunder booms around us as the *Artemis* creeps toward the towering waves that should be crashing down on the deck but seem to hang in midair, casting long shadows over the ship. I rest my hands on the railing, caging Brie in against the wooden slats while we look up at the waves, neither of us breathing.

In fact, everyone aboard the *Artemis* is standing on the deck, watching the unnerving sight in absolute bone-chilling silence.

The waves simply vanish ahead of us, rolling back into the depths, allowing the fleet of over a dozen boats to pass.

It's unreal. It doesn't make any sense whatsoever.

"Are you all right?" I ask my mate, resting my hand on her upper arm. She nods but is beyond words at this point. I don't blame her. I feel like I've been holding my breath for the last half hour as the *Artemis* leads the charge.

Several men scale the ratlines to hang from the masts, keeping an eye on the ships just starting to make their way through the storm guarding the veil. A few shouts ring out from above but are quickly muffled by the groaning of the sails and lull of the engine.

Alex turns from the veil and looks up, then across the deck where the view of the other ships spreads out at least two miles behind us. A great distance away, purple lights breach the darkness, flickering in and out as they hang back beyond the storm's reach.

"We've got company," Alex murmurs as he passes us, clapping my arm.

Sawyer steps up beside me, crossing his arms as he watches his Alpha race down the steps to alert the rest of the crew and passengers on board.

"They won't catch up to us," Sawyer says under his breath. "They're in the thick of that storm now, and we're...we're–"

"We're already in the veil," I finish for him, my chest tight with unease. Even the water is silent here. It's like we're moving over glass. The ship casts no wake. No waves brush against its hull. I'm not sure we're even in the water anymore. My mind can't grasp this, and I've been wondering for several minutes if we're flying, but a strange suction-like sensation peppers my skin with gooseflesh. Even Brie shivers, backing her body closer to mine as she trembles.

Her hair lifts from her shoulders as the air suddenly, inexplicably thins. Several people gasp, and murmurs of concern ripple across the lower deck, but then we're... rocking again, moving against increasingly rough water.

"What's that sound?" Brie asks with a wince as wind whips over the deck. Thunder booms overhead like a violent drum beat.

"Rain," I breathe, shrugging out of my jacket to drape it over her head as a sheet of heavy rain barrels toward the ship, violently crashing down over the deck.

Sawyer races to the helm to steady the boat as we rock against the surging waves.

I clutch Brie close, trying to edge away from the railing, but her iron grip prevents me from moving as she looks over her shoulder, her lips parted in a gasp.

I follow her gaze, watching in awe as the *Asteria,* then the *Atropos,* come into view, appearing out of a haze of dark mist nearly invisible to the naked eye.

I look down at her, pressing a kiss to her forehead as other boats start to appear. I have to squeeze my eyes shut against the rain, but I pray, and I honestly can't remember the last time I called upon the Goddess, but I pray in thanks.

Alex's voice follows his heavy tread on the stairs as he pants, "Hold steady in this position. We're just going to ride out this storm while the rest of the boats catch up to us."

Sawyer nods from the helm, shielding his face from the rain. Brie turns to follow Alex's progress across the uppermost deck, clutching my arm. She's shivering and already soaking wet, but I can feel in my bones that the moment I ask her to come back to our room with me, she's going to say no.

Alex says, "If the KiloKilo armada follows us out of the veil, we're going to have to run. Full engines, full sails. Logan, I'm going to drop you in a skiff to join the crew of the *Asteria* if–"

"That won't happen," Brie cuts in, viciously shaking her head. Lightning crackles overhead, illuminating her eyes in shades of brilliant, vivid blue. "Eastonia and Crescent Falls have no current contracts or treaties of peace with KiloKilo. There isn't anything pertaining to whether they're allowed in our waters. They'd risk the might of the Allied Kingdoms naval fleet, and they know that." She looks up at me, a delirious smile stretching from cheek to cheek. "We're not in KiloKilo anymore. We're home. Oh, my Goddess, Logan, we're home–"

I steal the words with a kiss, clutching her face between my hands as rain falls all around us. Shouts and hollers from the masts bleed into the storm as more boats breach the veil. Within an hour, every single boat has passed through unscathed.

It's like... It's like a weight I hadn't realized was there has been lifted from my shoulders. *Brie is safe.* Yeah, Alex and his people made it out, but I brought my mate home, and she's safe. Thank the fucking Goddess, she's safe. That's all I ever cared about.

The boats sail through the eternal storm that guards the veil, racing toward the sunrise. The clouds part, the rain turning from a torrential downpour to sheets of warm mist, and finally, *finally*, the sea calms.

Tropical water stretches as far as the eye can see as the first light of morning paints the horizon in throws of pale pink and yellow. A ribbon of crimson sparkles on the edge of the water as the sun rises like it's being pulled from the sea itself.

I watch it in silence, gripping the railing on either side of Brie. She leans forward, the soft, warm breeze making her hair flutter around her head. She stretches her arms wide and laughs. I love that sound. It's like *music*.

I wrap my arms around her waist and bend down to rest my chin on the top of her head. "I love you."

The words… well, I didn't necessarily mean to say them. It's not that I don't mean it, because I do, with every fiber of my being, *I do*, and it also has nothing to do with the mate bond. I love her. I have since the first time she mouthed off at me on that grimy, rusty ferry.

Brie whirls in shock and blinks up at me, her eyes turning a bright, polished amber as the sparkling sunrise descends over the deck. "Why?"

My lips part in a groan. "*That's* why."

She arches a brow, smoothing her hands down my sides before wrapping her arms around my waist.

"Because you question *everything*. Always. You always get the last word, too," I amend.

"Those don't sound like good things." She laughs.

"They are for us. We'll never have a boring conversation in our lives."

"You do like to talk. *And* argue," she says pointedly, smiling wickedly as she presses her chin into my abdomen.

But I'm… in awe. Overcome, if I'm being honest. I was so wrong. Wrong about damn near everything for most of my life. I used to think my purpose was finding home again, taking back what's mine.

I should have known the moment I saw her and our bond snapped into place that home was *her*.

"Do you want to go back to our room? I'd like to get into some dry clothes." She slowly unravels her arms, taking a step away from me.

I open my mouth to reply, but Alex appears at the top of the stairs, glancing at the helm I've been guarding while he and Sawyer took reports coming in from the other boats.

"Everyone's accounted for. Every ship made it through," he says absently, moving toward the crude, hand drawn map Sawyer splayed out on the table after the rain stopped. He's trying to remain cool and collected, but he runs his fingers through his sandy blond hair, his brows pinched with unease. "So, where do you think we are?"

I hold out my hand, motioning for the compass he keeps in his pocket. He casually drops it in my hand, glancing at the stairs as Sawyer jogs up to meet us.

I smooth my thumb over the bronze circle, over the etched symbols I can't make sense of, then flip it open. "We're positioned south as it stands." I scan the water for any sign of islands or other boats, but we're alone in open water. "We need to move east. We'll meet land that way eventually."

"Where do you think we'll land?" Brie asks, leaning against the railing, the sunrise casting her in a halo of light.

"I don't know. Not yet, at least, but it's warm here on the water, which means we're south of Crescent Falls, for sure. I'm willing to bet we're close to Veiled Valley, however." I squint as I look up at the sky, at the fading stars. It's too light out now to catch any glimpses of the constellations I know so well, constellations that could tell me our exact positioning. "We'll know in a few hours–"

A crackle of energy splits the sunrise into pieces. The boat lurches, the masts groaning as a gust of violent wind crashes through the sails. I stumble before catching myself on the railing, snatching Brie to my chest with a grunt.

"What the hell was that?" Alex snarls, rushing to the far edge of the upper deck to look at the water. "Did we just hit something?"

Another shockwave bursts over us, knocking Sawyer and Alex to the ground. The sails strain against their lines, against the sudden pressure building in the air. My ears ring painfully. It's a... familiar feeling. When that dark mist begins to trickle in, shielding us from the sun, I realize we're either saved—or royally fucked.

The tension snaps, and another shockwave bursts over the boat, causing it to rock side to side. People on the deck below shout in confusion as they grip whatever they find to hold themselves steady. A whirl of air sends anything not nailed to the ground flying from the ship. Paper, the lids of crates, and a few hats sail into the water.

Inky dark mist curls over the floorboards of the lower deck. People are screaming, trying to jump out of its way. Several people shift—likely by surprise, their clothing shredding to ribbons and hanging around their necks as they jump to safety anywhere they can find, but I'm... I'm not even breathing as the young, dark haired woman who just appeared in the center of the mist slowly turns her head, scanning the strangers clambering to get away from her. Her cloak of deep, dark crimson looks like a waterfall of blood as her sea-green eyes catch the light of the sunrise.

She whips her head in my direction before settling her gaze on Brie.

Brie gasps, tears in her eyes, her mouth stretching into a smile as her body slumps in my arms.

But Maeve scowls, her eyes narrowed and... gods, I can feel the fury radiating from her even though I'm standing above her, looking down at her, watching in horror as her expression shifts to dark, dangerous, rage.

Maeve swishes her cloak and stalks toward us. Alex draws a short-sword from his belt, but she lifts a hand, her magic ripping it from his grasp and sending it flying into the water. He doesn't have a single second to react before her power has him and Sawyer pinned painfully against the railing, both of them gasping for breath and writhing to get out its invisible hold.

"Maeve," Brie breathes, looking wildly around before settling her gaze on her sister, who's just reached the top of the stairs.

Maeve stops short of her, her chest rising and falling in a rapid breath. I catch a single, fleeting glimpse of tears in Maeve's eyes before she blinks, her eyes slowly dropping from Brie's face to her... chest.

Brie's wearing a men's shirt and loose trousers—another borrowed outfit that doesn't fit her. But her shirt is unbuttoned just enough, and the breeze formed by her sister's magic has pushed the shirt further apart—apart enough to see the beginnings of the mark I left on the upper slope of Brie's breast.

Maeve stares at it, her expression unreadable, before she slowly, *slowly*, turns her gaze back on me.

On my neck.

The Firestone witch doesn't say a word to us. She tears Brie out of my arms with inhuman strength, and I... lose it.

"Get off her," I snarl, grabbing Maeve's thin forearm and twisting hard. She tries to yank her arm away, but I'm stronger, even against her powers. I've dealt with her before. I also know the searing pain in my hand well. I have scars that tell our story, from when she was a baby, and I saved her life. She can burn me all she wants.

Her eyes dance with... light. Crimson light, the same light now dancing in the moonstone necklace around her neck. I keep my grip on her arm, squeezing tight enough to break bones.

"Don't you fucking dare," I growl. "She can't handle the jump. You know that."

"Maeve," Brie says hotly, trying to get her sister's attention. "Let go. Please, we need to explain."

"Dad's naval forces are their way," Maeve says, then blinks, and I have a single second to catch, and notice, the apprehension flaring to life behind her eyes when she says, "Hold on."

And the world around us goes pitch black.

33

MY MATE

Logan

I HIT SOLID GROUND WITH A CRUNCH THAT REVERBERATES THROUGH MY body, shocking me back to life. Dark stone and stained glass come into view, and it's all familiar. We're in Veiled Valley, in the castle.

I blink, sucking in a breath, then curl to a seated position before swaying to my feet, my vision blurred, but I can just make out the outline of Maeve clutching Brie to her chest as Brie slumps over her arms.

I run, slipping over the stone floor, and pull Brie out of Maeve's grasp just as she begins to fall to the ground.

"What is wrong with you?!" I shout at Maeve, kneeling and cradling Brie as my knees hit the ground. "What were you thinking?!"

I smooth Brie's hair out of her face. Her eyes are closed, and she's pale, barely breathing.

"Hey, Brie? Brie, come on–" I run my hand over her face, smoothing pale silver tears from her eyes, but she remains frozen.

I look up at Maeve, who's panting, a horrified look on her face. She shakes her head over, and over, mouthing something I can't decipher, but then rapid footfalls echo from one of the corridors leading off the foyer.

I blink rapidly to clear my vision, squinting into the shadows. Aris appears, his face etched with confusion as he spots Maeve standing shellshocked against a backdrop of stained glass. "What the hell was that?" He turns his head to me and Brie, his eyes going wide. "Oh, my fucking Goddess–Maeve, what the hell? Brie? *Brie?*!"

"Get Mom!" Maeve screams. "Get a fucking healer, Aris!"

Aris shakes his head, at a loss for words, his dark blond hair falling around his forehead in soft curls as his eyes start to water. "She's–she's alive? You're alive?" His silver eyes meet mine. Aris is only a year younger than Brie, but he's always seemed so young, like he's unable to shake his teenage years. He stumbles backward into the shadow of the corridor and whirls, shouting at the top of his lungs for help as he disappears from sight, but his voice carries.

A tingle of air rushes over the floor. The stained glass windows stretching to the domed ceiling rattle and a groan whispers from the shadows, like the castle is waking up, coming alive again after a long slumber.

Maeve wrings her hands, her cruel, murderous expression from the *Artemis* shifting to worry so extreme I think she might be on the verge of exploding into sobs.

"You're an idiot," I sneer, gathering Brie close. She's cold to the touch, her head lolling back over the crook of my arm.

"Where the hell have you been?" Maeve snarls, her tears sliding over her lashes. They glow a pale crimson in the light drifting through the glass. "Who were all those people?"

Rushing footsteps cut through my words as I answer, "If you'd given us a moment to explain–"

"BRIE!" Alpha Kenna's shriek of disbelief echoes through the corridor. Kenna sprints in our direction, her beautiful, tear stained face twisted in both agony and joy as she falls to her knees and slides toward us. More shrieks follow as people rush into the foyer. Some, I recognize. Aris hurtles toward us dragging a very old woman with startling white hair–his great-grandmother, Cressendra, a witch–

who is honestly very spritely for closing in on ninety years of age. Her mate follows at a slower pace, a man I'm very familiar with being a captain of the Ghost army.

Adrian Westfall, Ryatt's elderly father, whispers either a prayer, or a curse, as he says in a voice like gravel, "Has anyone called for Ryatt?"

The voices in the room blur as Kenna looks at me, her eyes heavy and grief-stricken as I lift Brie and place her over her lap. She smooths her trembling hands over Brie's face, her fingers dipping into her hair. Her eyes meet mine again, wet with tears, and says, "Thank you, Logan. You kept–kept another of my daughters safe."

Cressendra kneels with effort at Kenna's side, resting a withered hand on her shoulder. "She needs to be moved upstairs. You know how little she tolerates the herbs. She'll be sick when she wakes up."

Kenna nods, blinking rapidly as tears stream down her cheeks.

I feel a sense of being watched and look over the heads of the women gathered in front me.

Blake stands in the shadows, his violet eyes glowing as he takes in the scene. I bristle under his watchful gaze. I might not be afraid of much, but that young man… yeah, he can fuck right off.

Blake glances at Maeve before fading into the shadows, his footsteps receding before going shockingly silent.

More footsteps echo toward the foyer, and soon, a sea of people are tending to Brie. I rise on unsteady legs as Ryatt appears with a haggard looking Evander, who sprints toward his mate and their child, not even looking in my direction as he cups Brie's face and whispers rapidly to his mate.

It's the woman standing in one of the archways that steals my attention. Wild, unruly red hair sticks out of a bun on the top of her head as she moves cautiously into the light with a teenage girl at her side, both of them looking at me in shock.

"Logan!" Lexa screeches, blubbering my name as she tears in my direction with her arms spread wide. I catch her, but barely, as she throws herself in my arms, sobbing while squeezing her remarkably built, muscled arms around my neck.

But I'm looking at Aviva. She takes a shuddering breath, shaking her head, obviously at a loss for words. I extend my hand in her direction–a silent invitation–and her expression crumbles. I catch her as she crashes into us, lifting both women off the ground, which isn't an easy feat with Lexa's height.

Ryan appears next, woozy as he stumbles into the foyer with Sydney at his side. It didn't take long for word to get out. Family members start appearing out of thin air before other's with the capability of jumping through time and space disappear again to fetch others.

Ryan sees me and takes an audible breath before stalking in my direction. He throws his arms around us, smashing Lexa and Aviva between us to the point they grumble and gasp for breath. Out of the corner of my eye I notice a tearful Nora holding back. She's sixteen–turning seventeen this summer. Her dark amber eyes glow as she slowly steps to my side and rests her forehead against my upper arm, silently sobbing.

Ryan pulls away, clutching the back of my head and leaning his forehead against mine. "You scared the hell out of us."

He releases me, turning when Sydney calls out his name to help move Brie upstairs.

I lower Aviva and Lexa to the ground but watch the group gathered around Brie instead of listening to Aviva and Lexa rail on me for disappearing. Ryan lifts Brie into his arms without much effort, cradling her, but then, as if in slow motion, Kenna's arm darts out and clutches Brie's shirt.

My heart stops beating as Kenna folds the shirt down, the mark on Brie's chest a pale pink crescent shaped scar on her sun-tanned skin.

The room goes completely, utterly silent.

"It's a mark," Kenna says breathlessly. "How–who–"

Aviva's fingers grip the collar of my shirt and pulls, hard, until I'm forced to bend down, gritting my teeth as the fabric bites into the back of my neck. She looks at the identical mark on my neck for several seconds before her eyes meet mine, one of her red brows slowly rising to her forehead.

I glance at Maeve, forgotten in the corner of the foyer. Her eyes are dark, unseeing, as she stares at her sister.

No one says a word. No one moves. The air becomes so thick I feel like I'm going to choke when Evander looks right at me.

Ryatt is the first to do anything. The moment he takes a step in my direction, the foyer bursts into activity again, voices raised to the rafters. It's obvious no one knows how to feel right now. Ryan takes a deep breath, rolling his eyes as he turns with Brie in his arms and starts walking away, Kenna hot on his heels. I try to take a step in his direction, my senses going haywire as Brie falls out of my line of sight. Aviva presses her hand against my chest, dropping her voice to say, "She's fine. Brie is going to be fine."

"I want to go with her," I tell her, but she presses harder, shaking her head.

Ryatt cuts through our group, his hand clasping around my upper arm in an iron grip and yanks me away. I'm pulled roughly into a darkened corridor, Evander and Sydney's footsteps sounding out in the background as they follow.

I try to shrug out of Ryatt's grip, but he holds firm, pushing me roughly through an archway into a sprawling room painted in sage green with dark wood accents. It's a beautiful day. The sunlight warms the space, but I'm chilled to bone as I whirl on the three men, my hands curled into fists.

Ryatt approaches me, his silver eyes searching mine. "What happened? From the beginning."

"We were attacked. There was a group of men on the yacht with ties to Hannibal Arachnis, I believe. I'm almost certain." I growl, planting my feet and crossing my arms over my chest in a show of defiance. "We were skirting a storm in the strait, a day or so out of the waters of Maatua. They sabotaged the ship. I don't know their motives–whether they wanted Brie dead, or if we were being followed by another ship, and they meant to kidnap her, but the storm would have made the latter impossible."

Ryatt glances over his shoulder at Sydney. His dark, reddish-brown hair trembles as he gives Ryatt a short nod in confirmation of… something.

"We ended up in the water," I tell them, narrowing my eyes as I glance between Ryatt and Sydney. "Brie and I. Ron, the Chief Engineer, and Charlie, the second captain, were able to get on a lifeboat before the wave–" I close my eyes against the memory of Brie sprinting in my direction, her eyes wide and wild with grim determination as she risked her life for mine. I roll my lower lip between my teeth, exhaling deeply before finishing, "Brie and I went under. We washed up in KiloKilo."

Silence descends on the room for several seconds.

"We were found and rescued by Alpha Alex of Tempest Valley…" I explain everything to them in regard to Alex and his pack, and the other two Alphas in his charge. Ryatt and Sydney barely blink during my recounting, but Evander starts pacing, repeatedly running his hands through his hair and glancing toward the archway, torn between this conversation and his daughter.

I understand how he feels. I want to crawl out my skin with worry as I yank on the threads of our bond. I can barely feel her now, like she's lost in the ether between realms and I… I can't take it anymore.

"I need to see her," I say, cutting off whatever question Ryatt was asking that I'd totally ignored. "Now."

Evander looks right at me, his dark green eyes sparkling with an unreadable emotion as I take a single step in Ryatt's direction, raising my hands in surrender.

"Listen," I rasp, losing my patience, "you've got hundreds of innocent people bobbing in the water looking for a place to land. Brie told them they'd be safe here, in Eastonia. They got us out of KiloKilo. You need to honor her promise. That's the priority right now, not questioning me. There's time for that later."

Ryatt narrows his eyes in warning, but I don't really give a fuck how he feels about being bossed around by a nobody.

"I'm going to go see my mate now," I say through gritted teeth, forcing the words out on a sharp exhale. "*My* mate. Brie is *my mate*. Is that clear to everyone in the room?" I look at Evander, her father. "We knew. The bond snapped into place during the luncheon before she left for Maatua. I kept my word to you that I'd keep her safe, and I did. I'm going to go see her now." I try to step around Ryatt, but he stops me with a hand to my chest. I glare, teeth bared. "Let me pass."

"Brie is being tended by a healer. We have matters to discuss," the Shadow King, the Alpha King of the Rogues, snarls.

"I'm not afraid of you," I quip, and my eyes meet Evander's, who crosses his arms and exhales slowly. "The only man in this room that I need to discuss anything with is *him. Back off.*"

"Would you guys just fuck off and drop the act for a few minutes?" Ryan's voice rings out from the archway. "Let him go. These kids have been through hell and back. Give them a fucking minute to catch their breath."

Sydney turns to his twin brother, narrowing his eyes in annoyance, but Ryatt doesn't budge. His eyes hold mine, glowing with that strange, dark power of shadow and mist.

Evander, however, moves aside, his shoulders relaxing as he says, "Come with me, Logan. The rest can wait."

34

IN MY OWN BED

Brie

At first I think I'm dreaming that I'm in my room in Veiled Valley. Familiar smells and textures unravel my senses, shielding me in a sense of calm serenity I haven't felt in a very long time. Sunlight trickles through the curtains as they lift in a soft, warm summer breeze. Birdsong flutters through the air, breaking through murmured conversation nearby, but it sounds like a gorgeous day outside. The kind of summer day I'd spend in the garden before shifting and running into the mountains to that overlook, where a waterfall funnels back toward the city of deep, emerald green and crystal.

The vision fades for the space of a breath, my eyes growing heavy once again. I wonder what I'll dream of next? I hope it's a good dream.

But my stomach rolls and pitches, and I choke on a cough. Bright pain tingles through my body, settling at the base of my neck where a headache of epic proportions explodes, and suddenly wherever I am is too bright and far too loud.

I groan, twisting into the pillows behind my head, trying to shield my eyes from damning sunlight that makes me feel sick to my stomach. "Ohhhh," I moan, whimpering against the sharp ache radiating through my skull. I wait for the ship to lull me back to sleep, praying it happens soon to put me out of my misery, but hands grasp my shoulders, hurried voices coming in all directions.

"Brie, honey?" Mom says, her hand cool against my fevered skin as she slides her fingers into my hair. "Sweetheart?"

I open my eyes to slits, turning my head ever so slightly to look up. She's hazy, but she's here…. My mom. What–what happened? Where am I?

My lips part to ask, but the pain bursts again, shimmering across my brain like tiny, hot needles.

"It's a migraine," Misty says nearby, but I can't see her through the haze. Lights dance in my eyes, distorting the room. "She's going to be okay–"

"From the jump?" Mom whispers to her. "That's new–"

"She's so stressed, Kenna. It doesn't surprise me at all–"

"But what if it's not just a headache? What if something happened, and she's–"

Fingers curl around my forearm. My skin pebbles as tendrils of what I can only describe as ice fan over my skin, sinking into the pain and gnawing at it. It only takes a second for the pain to ebb away, replaced by that cold sensation that feels incredibly refreshing, but still I shiver, my teeth chattering as my vision abruptly clears, and the room finally rushes into view.

The mural on my ceiling, the stars and the moon cycle, distract me from the women bickering nearby and the shuffling of feet. I slowly turn my head, watching as Misty ties her long, golden hair away from her face and plants her hands on her hips, speaking to my mom in low tones.

"She's fine, really. She's just exhausted. Maeve's powers are…" Misty licks her lips, shaking her head. "I'm going to stick around for a few days, all right? Just in case."

"You should go back to the kids, Misty."

"Cole's got it handled. He's worried sick, but just—we're all just so happy she's home. Everything's fine." Misty squeezes Mom's arm before glancing at me, her eyes wet with unshed tears as her lips pull into a watery smile. "Hey, honey. I'm glad you're home. We missed you so much." Her voice splinters, a single silver-blue-hued tear catching on her eyelashes before rolling down her cheek, her healing powers riling inside of it.

"Hi," I manage to murmur but my voice is a shattered mess. My throat is dryer than the desert of Tarsian when I try to swallow. Misty's powers continue their slow journey through my body, easing aches and pains I hadn't realized I suffered from.

Misty leaves the room and Mom comes to my side, sniffling as she brushes my hair away from my face, her silver eyes shining with shreds of grief but mostly a desperate, undeniable happiness. "We thought we lost you."

"I'm sorry," I manage, swallowing past the lump in my throat. Memories flood back. Maeve brought us here. I remember the moment her powers enveloped me in their madness, their darkness, and I fell to pieces under the weight of it. "How long have I been out?"

"Just a few hours," she says breathlessly. "It's just past lunch. Are you hungry?"

I shake my head.

"Tea, then? Anything?"

"Tea would be fine—"

A crash bounces through the room as a tea-tray drops from thin air, rattling as it settles on my bedside table. I close my eyes, smiling as a rush of air lifts strands of my hair off the pillows in a strange, paranormal embrace. "Thank you," I whisper to the castle as it groans and creaks in answer, followed by a rogue sugar bowl that drops onto the tray so hard it nearly knocks the steaming tea-pot over. Mom steadies the tray at the last second, exhaling sharply as she eyes the trembling curtains.

"The house is a bit worked up. We all are. It's a been a—been an interesting, slightly overwhelming day."

She helps me into a seated position, her hands shaking as she smooths the duvet over my lap. I notice quite abruptly that I'm wearing my favorite pajama set–sage green silk with little tortoise shell buttons on the shirt. I pick at it, meeting her eyes.

Her cheeks flare with a soft blush as she shrugs, reaching for the teapot. "Your clothing got a little scorched when Maeve spirited you here." Her eyes brush over the spot on my chest where... Oh, gods. Oh, Goddess of above–

"Mom," I breathe, but she shakes her head, clasping my hand.

"We'll talk about that later–"

"Is he here?" My heart squeezes painfully. Misty's lingering healing powers rush into my chest to try to fix whatever they think is wrong with it, but panic feels my body with dread so deep I might drown.

"Logan?" Mom asks, and nods. "Yeah, he's here. He's downstairs with Aviva and Ryan. He spent–he spent most of the day here, but Aviva was adamant he eat something so–so, well, she had to drag him out by his ear in the end, but he's here, honey, in the castle. He's okay."

I slump against the pillows. She sinks to the side of the mattress and pours me a cup of tea. I watch her add four spoonfuls of sugar, then think better of it, and add two more before stirring in an enormous helping of cream.

"Drink this. You'll feel better instantly. It's those nasty herbs I make your father take, but they help."

I obey, closing my eyes against the bitter, acrid taste she tried to camouflage with sugar, which barely takes the edge off. She rises and flutters around me like a mother bird, picking at my hair, adjusting my blankets, fluffing my pillows, always keeping at least on hand on me like there's a risk I'll up and disappear.

"Are you okay?" I ask after several aching minutes spent watching my mother start to come apart at the seams.

"I am," she says tearfully, giving me a smile that I know is forced. "I–I am so sorry that happened to you again. I–I couldn't stop thinking about the first time, you know, while you were gone. Your father–Goddess, he was just...." She can't finish. Her grief is painted over her face in harsh, deep lines that make her look decades older than she is. I realize she hasn't slept at all in the month we were gone.

My heart sinks to my stomach, splintering into pieces. "I'm not going anywhere ever again. I promise."

Her mouth quivers into a smile. She takes a few breaths to calm herself, her lips parting to speak, but footsteps echo toward us in the spiraling stairwell leading out of the tower.

We both turn as a looming shadow darkens the doorway. Logan steps into the light, dressed casually in clothes similar to the outfit he wore that morning on the ferry. It's almost like we've gone back in time to the morning that changed everything for us. I half expect to look down at the floor and see my suitcase there, or to hear the soft hum of the engine of the car parked in the driveway–the same car we were sitting in when we rejected each other.

That feels like a lifetime ago.

Logan braces his hands on the doorframe. Aviva peaks around his side. I always forget how small she is until she's standing near one of the incredibly tall men in the family.

"Are you okay?" Logan asks, his voice trembling a bit.

I nod, giving him a watery smile, my breath catching in my throat as I watch his shoulders relax and his expression soften.

He looks at my mom like he's waiting for her permission to enter my room. Mom rises from the bed, dabbing her eyes with the back of her hands, "Aviva, is Evander still in the dining room?"

Aviva brushes under Logan's arm, shaking her head. "He went with Sydney and Ryatt to Moonrise for the rest of the afternoon. I'm not sure why. Ryan's downstairs, though. Do you need help with anything?"

Logan's still looking at me, his eyes locked on mine as Aviva and my mom talk about... well, I'm not even sure anymore. Their voices fade as Logan breaks away from the doorframe and edges in my direction, throwing the women a quick glance before picking up his pace as he closes in on my bed.

"Hey," he rasps, eyes wide and dark as he takes me in. He breathes heavily–like he's been holding that breath for ages–and sinks onto the edge of the mattress.

"Hey," I reply weakly, reaching for him. The moment my fingertips brush his arm, he launches at me, curling his arms around me in the tightest squeeze.

I bury my face in his shoulder as he hauls me into his lap, kneeling on the bed–my bed–in my room, in Veiled Valley.

We made it back against all odds, and it's overwhelming.

Mom and Aviva go totally silent. I hear the softest chuckle and a whispered murmur before their footsteps retreat, and my bedroom door softly, slowly, closes with a faint click.

I burst into tears, babbling words and rushed apologies that don't make sense. He kisses the words away, his cheeks damp with my tears, or his, I can't tell.

But we're home. Home–and together.

He pulls away only slightly, resting his forehead against mine as he gasps for breath before saying, "Misty came downstairs and told us you'd woken up. I wanted–I tried to stay here. I wanted to be here when you did, but Aviva insisted I eat something and I just–" He closes his eyes, whispering a soft curse under his breath. "Are you feeling okay?"

"I'm okay, really. You don't have to worry about me."

"I think I always will."

My arms brush over his shoulders, curling round his neck. He nuzzles me close, pressing a kiss to the top of my shoulder, then my temple, whispering that he loves me, that he's sorry.

"We won't be alone for long," he whispers, laying me down against the pillows. His expression shifts, his eyes going dark and wolfish even in the sunlight. I catch the shadows dancing behind his gaze, the concern.

"What happened?" I ask, knitting my fingers in his to prevent him from getting off the bed.

"Nothing you need to be concerned about–"

"They know we're mates, though."

"Yes," he says simply, his gaze holding on mine. "They do." I watch the column of his throat bob as he swallows.

I arch a brow. "How… you look nervous."

"I really pissed off your grandfather," he admits, shrugging one shoulder.

"Grandpa's always pissed off about something."

"He is… not happy about this," he continues.

My heart sinks.

"But everyone else is. Your father offered me a promotion," he says on an exhale.

"To what?"

"Commander," he says, pursing his lips. His gaze is far away, like he's lost in thought. "I–it hasn't been that long since we arrived, so I don't know what else is happening, not really. I know Veiled Valley's naval fleet went to meet Alex to guide them into the port of Avalone. I know your parents want to speak to us, and that your grandmother will be here tonight."

He absently strokes his thumb over my knuckles, looking a bit lost in his thoughts.

"I love you," I tell him firmly, passionately, letting the words ring out loud and clear.

"I know," he says. "I love you, too."

"Have you changed your mind about staying?"

"No," he says with conviction, breathing the word like a promise. "No, Brie. I'm not leaving you."

He winces, reaching up to rub his temple.

"What's wrong?"

"Ryan wants to talk. He's been trying to handle all the women in the house today while your dad, Sydney, and Ryatt do whatever the hell they're doing."

"I'm fine here if you need to go."

"I'll be back. I'll bring you something to eat." He rises, pressing a lingering kiss to my forehead before pulling away and stalking toward the door. He slips through it, leaving it open a crack as his footsteps descend the stairs.

I decide to test my legs, finding them weak and wobbly as Misty's powers fight against the lingering sensation of Maeve's magic in my blood, but eventually, I hobble toward the bathroom to catch a glimpse of my myself in the mirror, where I wince, turning back to my bedroom deciding it was a horrible idea.

But a man stands by the window in smart, expensive dark gray slacks and a white button-down shirt, his dark brown hair flaked with hints of a deep, almost cherry red in the sunlight.

My mouth pulls into a shocked smile as Blake turns to me, his violet eyes sparkling from within.

"Blake? What are you doing here?" I run to him, throwing my arms around his neck, but he only gives me a slight, half-assed squeeze in return, quickly stepping away to put some distance between us.

"We need to talk," he says under his breath, his voice deep and unnerving. "When you're rested and ready."

I notice the sparkle in his eyes—that hint of the powers raging within him—and feel dread wash through my system.

"About… what?"

35

HE'S NOT LIKE THE REST OF US

Brie

I pull the stool out from under my vanity, sinking down and facing Blake. I'm older than him by a few months. We've always been close, even when we were younger, and he tended to want to play rowdy boy games with Aris. He always sat quietly and played tea-party with me, though, without fail.

He's also the pariah of the family and knows it. His powers rival Ryatt's, which is a terrifying thought. In fact, I often question who's more powerful–him or Maeve?

But that's not a fair question at the moment, given that Maeve's powers aren't even fully developed yet. Blake, however... he exudes energy that makes my skin tingle as he sits in my desk chair, resting his elbows on his knees.

"You found us, didn't you?"

He nods, a flash of guilt darkening his irises. "I admit I didn't even look until Maeve cornered me. She felt you, she said. Sensed your arrival back in our waters."

I wonder how much Logan told the family. Probably everything,

I'm sure. That man can talk, and I love that about him, which means I don't have to fill in any gaps.

It's a relief, to say the least.

"You know we were in KiloKilo, then?"

He knits his fingers together and rests his chin on his knuckles with another nod. Blake barely blinks. I can see why people are so unnerved by him. He just… gazes into peoples' souls, against their will and his, I think. It's just who–and what–he is.

"The media has no idea you're home and safe, and the family is going to keep it that way for now. My dad is in Moonrise today preparing a joint statement with Ella and Ryatt about your return, but the details of what happened are going to remain private." He takes a breath before continuing, "So is the news about the first of our generation finding their mates."

"Well, I would hope so. That's not the public's business–"

"It is, and will be, especially when a wedding is announced."

"You sound like your father right now."

"I'm telling you what I know, what's been discussed in your absence."

"What else did I miss?"

He untangles his fingers and smooths his hands over his thighs. "The men who attacked you on the yacht were Hannibal Arachnis's men. Do you remember any of their details?"

"You should ask Logan. He was the one who fought them off." I clear my throat as the memory spins through my mind. "I remember one, but the others… I never met them."

"What did he look like?"

"Like a rat," I murmur, swallowing hard. "Short, spindly. He barely had any hair." I notice an odd emotion sweep across Blake's face, something akin to relief. That's probably not what I'm exactly seeing, though, knowing Blake as well as I do. He's always been impossible to read.

"When you were dead," he says, "or, at least, presumed to be floating at the bottom of the ocean–" I frown, but Blake continues without skipping a beat, "the Allied Kings moved their forces into

Eastonia to try to locate anyone even remotely suspected to be aligned with the Spider in an effort to locate him, to make him pay for this."

"Are you saying he's been caught."

"No, he hasn't. Nothing the Ghosts, or the spies and warriors my line of the family has in their arsenal, have come up with any leads. We hit dead ends at every turn."

"Can you just… find him?"

Blake's expression goes completely blank, void of emotion whatsoever. "It doesn't work like that."

"You found me."

"You're family. We're connected," he says. "I couldn't locate you in KiloKilo because of the magic veiling that kingdom and its waters, but otherwise, I could slip into the stars and find you pretty much immediately."

"But not Hannibal? Doesn't the family have piles of evidence against him and his cronies by now? He's been terrorizing the packlands for the past decade!"

"He's… different. Some kind of magical being. It's rumored he has witch blood somehow–whether a direct descendant of a witch, or something else, but he has the ability to shield himself, or his lair is somewhere my powers–the family's powers–can't reach."

I tuck my hair behind my ears, taking a deep, restorative breath. "I don't care about the Spider–"

"You should, because everything he's doing right now is to undermine the royal family of Eastonia–your line, Brie–in an attempt to split the kingdom as Maeve comes into power."

"And you know that for a fact?"

"Yes. The assassination attempt on you was the nail in his coffin."

"Why are we talking about this right now?" I ask, rising and smoothing the wrinkles in my pajamas. "We just got back–"

"It's highly likely Logan will be deployed with the Ghosts into Tarsian."

"No, he's on leave for the rest of the summer," I reply, but unease prickles over my skin, causing it to pebble. "He isn't active again until after the harvest festival in the Deadlands–it's always been that way for him–"

"Things have changed–"

"How?"

"We'll find out when our dads return from Moonrise," he says under his breath. His tone is ragged with guilt that sends warning bells skirting from one side of my skull to the other.

He rises, his arms crossed over his chest as he paces to the window overlooking my bed and stops, his eyes on the city below.

"Where's Maeve?" I ask, watching the fabric of his shirt flex as his broad shoulders tense.

"Downstairs, I assume, with the rest of the family. They're waiting for you to feel well enough to handle being bombarded with attention–"

"Thank you for finding us. For helping her do it. I know how–I know the two of you have a hard time getting along."

He chuckles low and dark, shaking his head, his dark hair rippling as he turns his head to look at me over his shoulder. His lips part like he's about to say something cutting, but I stop him, raising my hand to silence him.

"She's a teenager, Blake. She's young. She'll grow up eventually."

"She'll be younger than us when she takes over Eastonia. She's not ready. She won't be ready."

"I know, but she has to be. It's not our fight, you know that."

"You made it your fight. Your whole life's purpose. What changed?" There's an edge to his tone that I don't like–it's sharp, meant to ruffle my feathers.

I don't fall for the bait. "You know what changed. He's downstairs, right now, fetching his *mate* something to eat."

Blake stares at me, scanning my face. I wonder what he sees when he looks at me–at any of us. I wonder if he can, truly, see our futures. That's what he's rumored to be able to do. Sarah explained it to me once, that is like seeing an option in the future. A single deviation from the timeline could change everything–from taking a different street to the coffee shop to deciding to wear jeans instead of a skirt.

It's why the Mystics can only prophesize, I suppose, and everything they say is taken with a grain of salt.

But Blake is different. He sees more, feels more, and gets lost more in his powers, in the stars that constantly call him home.

I edge toward him, resting on the edge of my bed. "Have you talked to Marianna recently?"

He abruptly looks away from me, turning his eyes to the window. "No. I haven't spoken to her in years."

"What? Why not? She's your best friend–"

"I'm not sure what gave you that impression," he murmurs as he moves in the direction of my bedroom door.

I shake my head, imagining the dark-haired, musically gifted beauty in my mind. I only met her once when I'd gone to Crescent Falls for a visit with my parents. She spent maybe ten minutes at the castle talking to Blake in the driveway. I'd been curious about her, seeing as Blake didn't stop talking about her the entire trip, but whenever I asked him about her, he clammed up, unable to tell me exactly what the two of them did, what they were up to when they hung out, which seemed to be pretty often.

That was… years ago. It was after he'd gone through his training in Moonrise, and unless he was talking about Marianna, he was just… broken.

He opens the door, trying to make his way out like he's running from this line of conversation, but I say, "I heard she's a violinist now."

His shoulders tighten as he grips the doorknob.

"She's brilliant," I press. "I've never heard her play in person but–"

"She is," he cuts in, glancing at me over his shoulder. "She is brilliant."

"You should reach out to her. I don't understand why you haven't spoken to her in years. Blake, that's so weird to me. She was your only friend." I bite my lip, internally cursing myself for saying that last part to him, but now I can't stop myself as I add, "I kinda thought the two of you might have been mates–"

He steps through the doorway, shutting the door behind him.

I roll my eyes to the ceiling, cursing myself for being so insensitive, but honestly, this is just Blake. He has a habit of just disappearing when he tires of a conversation or activity he doesn't like.

Wrapped in silence, I change my clothes, choosing a comfortable sundress to try to escape the growing heat of the day. I pull my hair into a messy bun on the top of my head and take in my surroundings, remembering that at one point, I didn't think I'd ever see this room again.

The castle's magic rushes around my bare feet, urging me in the direction of the door. Logan hasn't returned yet, which doesn't surprise me. If the entire family is here, gathered below, he's likely trapped in conversation with someone–likely Sarah or Misty, who can talk just as much as he can.

I slip my feet into a pair of sneakers and head downstairs, careful on the steps. My legs still feel a little wobbly as Maeve and Misty's powers continue to roll through my body, fighting for dominance, but that feeling is fading with every passing second.

Voices drift from the informal dining room on the third floor, which is where my family normally takes meals. Logan laughs, backing out of an archway with a plate of food balanced on one hand while he tries to free himself from a conversation with Sarah, just like I thought.

He turns, sensing my presence, and smiles faintly, his shoulders slumping in relief.

But Logan doesn't have a chance to say anything to me. Sarah beams, poking her head around the archway, and then a thundering of footsteps across the stone floors blares in warning that I'm about to be trampled.

My view of my mate is blocked by bodies as Sarah, Misty, and Lexa rush out of the dining room. My mom follows at a slower pace, rounding the corner and tripping over her own feet. Conversation erupts around me, everyone peppering me with questions I can't possibly answer all at once, but through the fray I catch a glimpse of Maeve moving into view, standing beside Logan, who says something to her before picking up the sandwich on the plate meant for me and biting into it, walking back into the dining room.

I watch Maeve, watch her face pale and shift as tangled emotions drift behind her eyes. She finally meets my eyes, and I smile at her, my heart squeezing.

But she looks... so sad, so lost. A jolt of panic rises in my chest when she quickly looks away and turns, walking down the hallway and turning out of sight.

"Can I eat something now, please?" I ask over the barrage of questions being hurled at me from every direction. "Please? I'm starving."

36

NOW LIE IN IT

Logan

Brie looks exhausted, but otherwise... *happy*, thank the Goddess, as she sits between her mother and Misty, listening to their conversation and picking at a sandwich.

I lean my elbows on the table across the room where I'm sitting in silence, alone, still waiting for my mind to catch up with my body after Maeve jumped with us from the middle of the ocean to Veiled Valley.

A shadow moves into view, crossing through the doorway before a shadow breaches the informal living area. Ryan looks around before turning the corner, beelining for me, waving away several rushed questions coming from the group of women on the couches nearby.

He braces his hands on the table beside me, leaning down to whisper into my ear, "I need to speak to you in private before Ryatt returns. Can you come with me?"

I glance at Brie, who's watching us with her brows furrowed in worry. I suck my teeth before nodding, and Ryan moves back a step so I can stand.

Brie and I have been using the mind-link as much as we need to, which hasn't been often, seeing as up until a day ago, we were together almost constantly, but I send her a quick message through the bond, telling her I'll be back shortly.

My footsteps echo on the dark stone floors as I follow Ryan through the woven, interlocking hallways of the ancient castle. I haven't spent much time here at all. I've only ever been in the more formal rooms downstairs and Evander's office. Ryan takes me all the way downstairs and out into the front garden, which is in full bloom now. It's mid-summer. Brie and I were gone for the first truly hot, sunny month, having spent it on the sea instead.

Ryan sighs with relief as the sun beats down on his face. He's finally starting to look his age–a man in his mid-forties with two teenagers daughters constantly giving him hell. His dark brown hair has gone a soft, pepper gray around his ears and forehead, and his neatly trimmed beard is almost completely gray, but I've never known him to keep a beard this long.

Smile lines are deep set around his eyes and mouth, a map that highlights the good years more than the bad ones. I know he went through hell when he was my age. Younger than me, actually. He nearly lost Aviva twice–the second time dying beside her and their unborn child on a desert battlefield.

The thought of them makes my chest squeeze with regret, but Ryan's motioning me to follow him to an outdoor seating area surrounded by the overgrown, wild front garden. Vines wrap around the wrought-iron benches as the sun filters through the trees over-head, but it's shaded and cool here.

"That's better," he grunts, sitting in one of the chairs. It groans under his weight but he ignores it, spreading his legs while running a hand over his face.

I lean against the trunk of the tree shading the garden, breathing in the smell of flowers and fresh, summer grass. "What'd you want to talk to me about?"

"Nothing that hasn't already been said. I figured you'd probably want to get out of a house full of women as much as I did, though."

I chew my lower lip to stop from smiling. "Where's Mom?" The word falls from my tongue without thought, without any care of the connotations behind it. It's not the first time I've slipped up and called Aviva my mother but it's definitely the first time I've said it in front of him.

Ryan, to his credit, doesn't do more than smile faintly. "She's around. Nora's having a rough go of it. It's a lot, I think, going from one extreme to the other–thinking you were dead and then... being yanked out of bed and jumping here to see you alive."

"I'll talk to her," I whisper, guilt ripping through my chest.

He nods, his stormy blue eyes going a shade darker than normal. "Did you have a chance to talk to Evander?"

"Briefly. But not about–about the fact that Brie and I are mates. It was... glossed over. I don't think it's hit anyone yet, honestly. He needed to know about Alex of Tempest Valley and his pack, first and foremost."

"That's been dealt with. Alex and his mate are here in Veiled Valley. Their pack is docked in Avalone."

"Are they safe?"

"Yes," he says with a nod. "Kenna already set them up, and she's making long-term arrangements for them. It sounds like they'll be staying here in Veiled Valley for a year, at least, unless–" Ryan cuts himself off, his eyes raising to meet mine. "Logan, what's your plan now?"

My back slides down the trunk of the tree until I'm in a seated position, stretching out my legs in an entirely casual fashion that betrays all of my training as a warrior.

"Brie and I have discussed a few options," I admit. "It's mostly just... dreams, I guess." I lick my lips, trying to find the words, the solutions, but everything feels different now that we're home. I peer through the trees at the tall gray fortress just within view on the other side of the valley, its windows shining in the sun's glare. "I'm a warrior, Ryan. I'm a Ghost. A captain," I begin, meeting his eyes again. "I have some money set aside. If she wants to stay here, in Veiled Valley, I'll buy a house for us. Something comfortable for her. I'll be close to the barracks and my offices, close to Commander—"

"Evander, your soon-to-be father in law?" he cuts in with a smirk.

"Still my commander as it stands, but I was promised leave… a long enough leave that we could stay in Silverhide for the remainder of the summer to help with the harvest before truly settling down."

He nods but says, "You know we have everything settled in Silverhide—"

"But we could always… come to live there," I cut in, and his eyes meet mine in the hazy glow of summer sunlight. "I could come home, Ryan. I—I had to sever my ties with you, with Silverhide, when we were in KiloKilo. I had to pledge my allegiance to Alpha Alex, but it meant nothing more than a formality needed to be able to communicate with the crew I was leading at the time. But I could come back. I could live in Silverhide, start a farm or something—"

"Is that what you want, Logan?"

"Yeah," I breathe, smiling around the word. "I do."

I've rarely seen Ryan show any type of emotion beside… happiness. He's always been a content, easy-going man. I know he can be scary and vicious when it's deserved and is a tough, commanding Alpha, but he spared us from that side of him growing up. Right now, his eyes are dark, however. "What about Emberfyll?" His words ghost through the air between us, creating a void I can't climb out of.

There's so much I could say on the subject. I could spill my heart out, telling this man who raised me like his own son while I balked at his leadership and affection every step of the way, that I can't see myself leaving, that my life has been spent here, and wasted, and I don't want to waste another second on a what if, on a fairy tale.

"The second I saw Brie," I tell him, my voice low, "I knew that whatever future I had planned for myself didn't matter anymore. I fought it. I fought it for weeks, but she's my mate." I meet his eyes. "I want to be here—with her. She is the only thing that has ever felt like home."

Even in my fractured memories of Emberfyll, I can't conjure the same feelings of warmth and togetherness. I don't remember sunlight.

I don't remember soft skin and a warm bed. I don't remember love until the memory of my father crying out for my mother as she washed away sprints back to the forefront of my mind.

He'd held me until he couldn't, and the waves separated us. That was the only kind of love I knew in Emberfyll, and it's a reminder of why they left in the first place.

"I was meant to be here, in Eastonia. Brie was always what I was meant for. I spent years training," I continue breathlessly, holding his gaze, "to be able to protect her. The Goddess put me in your path, Ryan, you, and Aviva, so I could learn how to *love her*. That's what I was always meant to do, and I was fucking stupid when I let her reject me, when I accepted her rejection. I'll live with that for the rest of my life, and I'll spend the rest of my days making it up to her."

Ryan hides his smile, and maybe even a few relieved tears, while bowing his head and chuckling, "Then come home, Logan. To Silverhide. Bring her with you, even if it's just for the summer."

"I will."

Aviva's voice rips through the air, "Ryan? Are you and Logan out here?"

He chuckles, leaning back in his chair. "We are."

She huffs under her breath as she fights through the overgrowth, popping into the clearing while shielding her face from the sun. "Are you hiding? Is that what's going on?"

"We're talking." Ryan corrects her but rises with a soft groan. "We'll head back in now. Logan and Brie have something to discuss before we all leave for Silverhide in a few days."

"Silverhide?" Aviva's dark brown eyes catch the sunlight and turn a bright, shimmering amber as she narrows her gaze.

"I think it's time I went home," I tell them, gripping her shoulder. "I'll be bringing my mate home, too."

Her eyes glisten before she turns her expression to steel. Her tongue darts over her lower lip as she glances from me to Ryan. "Ryatt returned from Moonrise. He's back, and so are Evander and Sydney. They arrived a few minutes ago. I came out to find you, to tell you because–because they need to speak to you and Alpha Alex of

Tempest Valley. Warriors have been dispatched to fetch him and his mate from where they're staying in the barracks across town"

I bristle at her worried tone. She shakes her head, her eyes downcast on her sandals.

"What's going on, Aviva?" Ryan asks, stepping to her side with his hands braced on her upper arms.

Something like the deepest, sharpest sense of unease prickles through my body. I rush away, cutting through the garden, leaping over stones and what remains of a toppled fence. I stalk across the driveway where, once, what feels like a lifetime ago, I drove Brie away from this very castle and the paths we laid for our futures fractured, blurred, and wove together.

I've barely crossed the foyer when I hear raised voices coming from Evander's office and catch a glimpse of Brie as she slips out of the doorway, her face pale and eyes dark.

"Brie," I rasp, reaching for her.

She looks up at me with wide eyes, shaking her head.

"What's wrong?" I pull her against me, smoothing a hand down her spine as she coils her arms around my waist, burying her face in my shirt.

Just out of view, I hear Sydney say, "These stones change everything. You have to understand that."

Kenna scoffs, followed by Misty raising her voice to a near yell. "You can't be serious, Sydney! They just got home!"

My stomach twists as Brie clutches me close, her tears soaking into my shirt, and I realize our bed has been made.

"He's an Alpha King. He has to return to Emberfyll. This has been laid out and planned for since he was a boy, and now we have a way to support him in taking over his rightful throne," Ryatt says. "With Hannibal Arachnis trying to undermine our family's monopoly on the Allied Kingdoms at every turn, we can't risk such a strategic territory going unclaimed, especially with KiloKilo now breathing down our necks. Logan will return and claim his lands as Alpha King of Emberfyll. That's final."

37

THE PROPOSAL

BRIE

LOGAN STEPS INTO MY DAD'S OFFICE. ALL EYES TURN TO HIM AS HE scans the men–Sydney, Grandpa Ryatt, my father, a few others that serve both my father and grandfather as generals, captains, and commanders. Logan's eyes are like polished, imperfect emeralds as he eyes my grandpa wearily, like he's not entirely sure he understands what Ryatt just said to everyone in the room.

"Brie, you don't need to be here for this," Aviva whispers behind me, knitting her fingers in mine.

But Logan growls, "She stays."

A silent, heavy, creeping hint of tension scatters around the room. The entire castle would explode if someone lit a match right now, I'm sure. My spine tingles as Logan turns to Ryatt and says, calmly despite the bite in his voice, "There's nothing in Emberfyll."

"Quite the contrary," my grandfather replies immediately, rounding my father's desk, his shadow powers simmering and coiling around his fingers, "Debris has been washing up on the southern shore of Tarsian for decades now. You might not remember much

285

from the war there, given how young you were, but if there are survivors–"

"There was an illness," Logan cuts in, shaking his head, "I'm the last of my pack. I swear."

"But you don't know that for sure," my father says with calm quiet. His eyes meet mine through the crowd of family gathered, family starting to trickle in from the hallway, curious about the raised voices. "And if there are people left in Emberfyll, Logan, you are the king, by blood, by birthright."

Maeve brushes past me into the room, settling silently near the far window, her body cast in shadow, but her eyes glowing.

"The Allied Kingdoms," Grandpa Ryatt continues, "will expand to include Emberfyll, with you as Alpha King."

Logan is rigid beside me. I feel Aviva tugging me back toward the door. I feel my Mom's hand grip my shoulder, but my eyes are on Logan as Grandpa Ryatt explains, "Alpha Alex of Tempest Valley was able to cross through the sea veil of KiloKilo using alexandrite, and you will do the same to cross into Emberfyll, but with a legion of Ghost warriors with you. Four armored ships from the royal Tarsian fleet have already been ordered and will be ready in three days' time. You'll take two-hundred men with you."

Logan's lips part, but he doesn't say a thing. His eyes… Goddess, I know that look. It's the same look I saw aboard the *Asteria* when he'd been looking out over the valley, his eyes shimmering with… purpose, but he's… conflicted, like he can't decide whether he's happy about this or not.

"Alex of Tempest Valley and some of his pack mates will accompany you with the promise of setting up a new pack territory within Emberfyll, with you as his king. He's already agreed," Grandpa continues, but the rest of his words begin to blur together as my head spins.

Logan blinks, shaking his head. "And what about Brie?" he says to the group, and the whispered murmurs floating through the room cease abruptly. "What about my mate?"

"She stays here," Dad says, sighing, his eyes flicking to mine and full of empathy, pain, and possibly regret. "Brie, I am sorry–"

"You can't do this to us," I rush out, my voice cracking. "We–we just got home. We just found each other, and now you're separating us?" Anger courses through my body, making my skin tingle. "You can't force him to leave!"

"He'll return, Brie," Grandpa Ryatt says sharply, but his eyes betray his tone. They're soft, full of the same regrets I see in my dad's eyes, but neither man is willing to tell me the truth.

"How long?" I ask, looking from them to my mate, who's now bracing himself on the back of the couch across from my father's desk. "How long is he going to be gone?"

Logan exhales deeply, closing his eyes as he shakes his head. "It'll take three months to get there once we cross the veil."

My chest quakes, my breath catching my throat. "Three months?"

"Then another…three months to get back, but that's if we turn right back around."

"*Six* months?" I say under my breath, a silent sob choking the words. I feel myself beginning to lean into my mother, who is just as still and solemn as everyone else in the room watching two mates get torn apart… again.

"We think it would be wise to set up a small colony–a base–on the shore. Even if Emberfyll is empty, we'll need a place to return–" Dad's voice fades as my heartbeat hammers in my ears. I've been looking at the floor, but when I lift my head to Logan, he's staring right at me.

His expression is so… broken. Conflicted. Worn-thin.

I turn from the room and run like my life depends on it, racing up one of the back staircases, ignoring the people shouting my name. But just as I reach the top of the stairs, footsteps echo behind me as someone rapidly climbs to my side.

Long, pale fingers gently wrap around my wrist and tug me into the light of a window overlooking a sweeping view of the city below.

Grandma Ella tucks my hair behind my ears before tilting my chin so I have to look into her eyes. I've never seen her cry. I think this is the closest I'll ever come to it, honestly.

"You're stronger than this," she says in a low whisper, nodding, like she's agreeing to her own statement. "This is temporary."

"It's unfair."

"It is, but deep down, you know this is right. Your mate is an Alpha King, Brie. You were meant to be his queen–it was destined by the Goddess, and he was always destined to return to his homeland."

"He'll be gone for months while I, what? Sit here. Wait for him? What am I supposed to do?"

"He'll return."

"You weren't in the room," I argue. "My own father and *your* mate are forcing him to go back. We decided we'd settle in Eastonia. He told me he'd be happy–"

"Do you believe that? That an Alpha King could be happy giving up his title, his territory, for the rest of his life?"

"Cole did it for Misty," I grind out.

"Cole never wanted it," she whispers. "Cole wasn't meant for it. Logan is, and he'll be king. And you'll rule beside him, rebuilding his pack."

I step away from her. "You act like this is right–like separating us is what's good for us, but this is only because Grandpa and my dad feel threatened, don't they?"

"Not by Logan."

"Obviously not," I sputter, tears filling my eyes. "But Hannibal? Is it really bad enough that they need an Alpha King stationed that far away on an island lost to time?"

"KiloKilo is threatening war on Maatua and their alliances if the Luna of Tempest Valley isn't returned. I spoke to her directly–Monica–and our family is standing behind her fully. She will not be returning, and I've already tried to reach out to KiloKilo for a convention, to try to find a way to move past this, but they're digging in their heels, which makes me, and your grandfather, believe they're hiding something behind that veil that threatens us. If Logan's assumptions about where Emberfyll is located are correct, KiloKilo isn't that far away from there, and if they attack and gain access to that territory with their stones , they'll have access to both Eastonia to the south and Crescent Falls to the north. We are doing what we need to do to protect our people, Brie. I know you understand that. You're smarter than this–smart enough to see the pieces in play in this game. You always have been."

"I'm going with him."

"No."

"Why not? I'm his mate!"

"You," she says, stepping toward me, "are needed here. You will be his Luna when you marry. You'll be building his pack from the ground up. You need to stay to prepare for that moment because once Logan returns to Emberfyll, he's king. Whether he has to… fight for that title, or not."

Dread coils in a knot in the pit of my stomach.

"We don't know anything about Emberfyll. Aviva's new memories of the Firestone era make no mention of it. It was lost millennia before that, we believe, somehow. Logan needs to go home to find out the truth, and in time, you'll join him." She squeezes my upper arm before leaning in to say, "Unless… something else works out in your favor."

"What? What do you mean by that?"

Grandma turns and walks back down the stairs, her footsteps mingling with the hushed voices coming from the hallway below. My heart thunders as I watch her shadow descend, then disappear. My head starts to pound and I'm reminded that twenty-four hours ago, I was on a ship, watching pristine water rush by as Logan and I sailed into an uncertain future… but one thing was clear.

We made a choice to reignite the bond we originally wasted. We choose each other, no matter what.

I guess this is *what*, huh?

I walk up to my room in the tower and calmly shut the door. I take a shower, using my familiar shampoo, conditioner, and body wash for the first time in over a month. I change into my own clothes, not the homespun dresses of a pirate, and sit at my vanity, where my lotions and potions smell familiar, scenting the air with vanilla, lavender, and honey.

But my face in the mirror has changed. Weeks at sea bronzed my skin and bleached my hair to a soft honey-gold. My loose waves are tighter as I run a comb through them, holding my gaze without so much as blinking.

I don't feel the same as the last time I sat here. I don't feel the same at all. Maeve's reign is the furthest thing from my mind. Hannibal Arachnis and his continued terror of the Allied Kingdoms ceases to matter.

I couldn't care less about the heightened strife with KiloKilo and what it could do to our sea trade relations with Maatua and Crescent Falls.

I've changed. I can see it, notice it in the way my eyes shine with rest and love. I can see it in the smooth skin no longer marred by heavy, dark circles beneath my eyes.

I can see it in the way my expression shifts as my bedroom door opens, and Logan appears, his eyes on the floor as he leans against the door to close it tight, turning the lock.

The magic of the house whispers through the room—pulling the blinds, fluffing the pillows. The magic drifts away on a phantom wind, and then we're truly alone… for the first time since we arrived home.

"Brie," he says, swallowing hard as he lifts his face to meet my eyes.

I take a deep but painful breath, swiveling on my stool to face him. It's obvious neither of us have the words to convey our feelings about our situation, but he steps toward me, his eyes never once leaving mine. I rise as he closes the distance between us, taking my face between his hands. I close my fingers around his wrists as he leans his forehead against mine, and silence settles around us.

We stay like that for a long time—holding each other. Finally home but not knowing how long we actually have before we're separated again.

Eventually, I whisper, "I understand why they're doing it. Why you have to go."

"I promised you I'd stay."

"You never promised. You didn't have to."

"Brie, I don't want this. I wanted–I wanted to bring you home to Silverhide for the summer and then… use my meager captain's salary to buy us a house here, somewhere we could settle."

"We'll have all of that when you come home," I breathe, squeezing my eyes shut against the influx of tears trying to breach my eyelashes.

"It could be a very long time before we're together again," he admits. "Months. A year."

I press my face into his shirt, struggling to breathe as a sob tightens my throat.

"But I'd be an Alpha King. Someone worthy of you–"

"You've always been worthy of me. It's me that hasn't ever been worthy of you." I tighten my arms around his waist.

"Marry me," he whispers into my hair.

Tears slide down my cheeks, soaking into his shirt. "Yes. I will. Of course, I will–"

"Tonight," he adds, tilting my chin to look up at him. "Marry me *tonight.*"

3 8

ALWAYS

BRIE

"TONIGHT?"

"Yes, tonight."

"How?" I laugh, taking a step away from him. "We-we can't."

"We can," he says breathlessly, shaking his head. "The temple stays open all night. We'd just need to find a priestess."

"We'd need a witness," I whisper as the cogs in my mind start turning. "I'd need a dress–"

"I'd marry you like this," he says, taking my hands. "But please, for the love of the Goddess, marry me before I go."

I blink up at Logan, my heart swelling and squeezing simultaneously. There's still a whisper in my mind that warns me that he could change his mind, that he can't really want me, but I… banish it, giving myself to him fully.

"Are you sure?" I ask, scanning his eyes.

"I've never been more sure of anything. I want you to be my wife, Brie."

"I'm already your mate."

"It's not enough." He brushes my hair out of my face and kisses me, but a rush of air alerts us to a visitor making their way up the stairs to the tower. I pull away as a soft knock sounds on the door.

Neither of us move as the lock begins to turn on its own accord.

Maeve steps into the room, her fingers curled around the door. Her eyes meet mine, a soft blue-green in the sunlight, but her expression dances with shadows as she asks, "Can I come in?"

I nod, but Logan moves away, taking a few steps toward the door. "We'll meet up later–"

"You're going to the temple tonight," Maeve cuts in, and he stops in his tracks. Before either of us can talk our way out of it, she continues, "I overheard."

"You couldn't have," I laugh. "We weren't–"

"The castle told me," she whispers, shrugging. "Like it wanted me to help you."

I stare at my sister, trying to gauge whether she's serious, or scheming to tell but... Maeve looks forlorn as she closes the door behind her with a soft sigh.

Logan stiffens as Maeve guards the door. "Why would you help us?" he asks, his tone low.

"Because I don't like what's happening here–that you're being sent away, and Brie has to stay. I think it's unfair. And, she's my sister. If you're going to elope, I can't stop you, but I still want to be involved in some way."

"You won't tell?" I ask.

"If that's what you want, no. I'll... I'll be the witness." Her eyes briefly slide down my body, lingering on my stomach. I turn from her, shaking my head.

"It's too risky. We haven't thought it through," I whisper, breaking my own heart. "Our parents will want to be there. Everyone will."

"It could be months until the two of you are together again," she says.

"I know that."

"If you're serious," Maeve continues, looking at Logan, "I'll help, but you have to keep this a secret until you leave."

"What's the catch?" Logan asks, his voice sharpened to a knife's edge. He steps toward her, ignoring the power flaring in her moonstone necklace. "I haven't forgotten how you looked at me when you spirited us here, nearly killing her. Is this a trap? A way to separate us for real, by turning me in to your father and grandfather for marrying your sister in secret?"

Maeve scoffs, power flaring behind her eyes, "No, it's not!"

"Logan," I hiss. "Maeve!"

He steps toward her, but she doesn't back away. He stares her down, and she looks up at him, her eyes narrowed in a cat-like glare.

"You can think what you want of me, but I'm doing this for my sister, who loves you, even if I think—even if I think you don't deserve her. No one will ever deserve her, but I suppose you come close."

"Maeve," I growl, looking around in hopes I'll find some kind of weapon—a broom, a candelabra, anything to use to separate them by force if I have to.

"Do you promise you'll take care of her?" Maeve asks, her voice cracking. "When you take her back to Emberfyll?"

"I will," Logan rasps.

"I want you to swear it," she replies darkly, and holds out her hand.

"What are you doing?" I ask, my voice rushed as I watch Logan curl his hand in hers.

Inky, dark magic fills the air, scenting the room like blood as she squeezes his hand, her eyes glowing crimson as she says, "Do you vow to protect her with your life if it comes to it?"

"I do."

"Do you vow," Maeve asks, "to lay down your own life for her sake and the sake of her future children if you must?"

"You know I would."

"Say it," she hisses, and the magic scenting the air becomes too much to handle. I feel it creeping over my skin, ringing through the mate bond. I feel Logan's silent pain as Maeve's powers curl through his body like tiny snakes, burrowing into the very marrow of his bones. Black mist rushes over his skin, up his arms, under his shirt…

"I swear on my life. I swear on the Goddess, I will keep her safe. I will lay down my life for her, and our children. Always."

She lets go of his hand, and the pressure in the room snaps, the mist fading. The magic of the castle, which had shied away from Maeve's powers, returns, making the curtains flutter violently in protest, but what's done is done.

I've never seen anyone do this before–a magical oath. I notice the crimson stain on Logan's hand as he wipes his palm against his shirt, looking momentarily disgusted, but then I catch a glimpse of the wound on Maeve's hand. Blood.

Blood magic.

My lips part, my mouth dropping open. Blood magic is very dark magic. Only a few witches in Moonrise get to learn it, and Maeve was one of them.

"Why did you do that to him?" I shout.

"Because he'll drop dead if he ever lets any harm come to you," she rushes out, opening the door. "Go, Logan. Go to the temple and secure a priestess for tonight."

He looks at me, but Maeve clicks her tongue at him.

His jaw tenses before he exhales deeply and tears himself out of the room, his footsteps thundering on the stairs.

"A blood oath? Really? Do you hate him that much?"

"I don't hate him, but I trust him as much as I trust any other man–"

"He's *my mate.*"

"And you're *my sister.* You'd do the same for me if you could," she remarks. "Enough of this. The rest of the family have decided they've put you through enough and are giving you and Logan some space, which works in our favor. No one is supposed to disturb you. But, I still have to sneak you out of here somehow so we can find you a dress."

"I probably have one–"

"No, we're going to get a new one, or I'll raid mom's closet, and Blake is going to get Logan what he needs–"

"Blake knows? How is that possible?"

"Blake told me where to look to find you, and… he might have foreseen something like this happening."

I exhale, closing my eyes. "Is anything private in this family? For Goddess' sake."

"Do you want my help getting ready for your wedding or not?"

"Can you ensure no one knows? Not even Mom? Not yet."

"Yes." She waves a hand around the room. A soft groan echoes from the ancient stone while the curtains flutter. "The castle will keep everyone busy."

"Am I making a mistake? Eloping?" My voice cracks, but Maeve closes in on me, shaking her head.

"If this is what you want to do, do it. You've always taken care of all of us, Brie. It's your turn to just… do what's best for you and be selfish. Let them throw a grand second wedding or something. But this is for you and Logan."

I nod, swallowing past my nerves, and say, "Okay. Okay, we're doing it."

"Let's get ready then. It's nearly sunset already."

It's raining again. I've heard it's bad luck to get married on a rainy day, but this feels… overwhelmingly right.

"This way. Hurry," Maeve whispers, clutching my hand as we sneak through the garden, our bodies and faces shielded from the rain by our thick cloaks.

I slide to a stop when a trio of guards appear near the front gate, guarding the castle, but Maeve tugs me forward, her necklace glowing as she waves her hand in a wide motion toward the guards and they slump. "Come on," she whispers, giggling as she rushes us toward the gate.

We slip through it, but I look back at the castle at the flickering lights and towers cast in rainy shadows.

Maeve and I had to act like everything was normal for the rest of the evening. We looted my mother's closet, finding an old creamy-white gown that Maeve quickly turned into something I could wear. It's beautiful—with long, flowing sleeves of cream satin and a drop waist. Pearl beads and lace dust the hem. I think she wore this for some ceremony when I was kid, but I can't remember seeing it on her since.

I also didn't know that Maeve had the ability to sew, but I figure I can ask her about that, and other hidden, secret talents, later.

We had dinner with the family. Logan didn't return to the castle, and I made up an excuse for his absence that everyone seemed to understand, saying he was dining in the barracks and meeting with the warriors under his command as captain, readying them for being dispatched to Tarsian, where they'll soon board ships heading into certain death if the alexandrite doesn't work.

I felt guilty for keeping this a secret, but my heart is racing as we rush through the rainy streets under a cloak of near absolute darkness.

"What if he doesn't show up?" I breathe heavily, my muscles straining as I climb the steps to the temple.

"He will. He's already here," she says, throwing open the heavy, ancient wooden doors to the temple and leading me into darkness once again.

It's a small temple, a very old one. Dark stone is illuminated by nothing but candles as we walk inside, our footsteps echoing. Maeve turns me to face her in the little alcove of the entrance.

"I'm happy for you," she murmurs, but her mouth tilts into a girlish smile. "I wanted this for you, Brie."

I nod, unable to find the words I need to tell her that I… I love her, and to thank her for making this possible.

Instead, I turn and walk out of the darkness. It only takes me a few steps to reach the archway where the inner sanctum of the temple opens up, revealing pews, and an altar… where Logan's already waiting.

He looks nervous, but he smiles at me, his eyes creased with a wild kind of excitement, which is exactly how I feel. I have to dig in my heels and slow my pace to stop myself from running into his arms, but this is our wedding. Probably our *first* wedding, given that I'm a princess. Maybe even the first of three weddings, if he wants to do this again in the Deadlands during the harvest festival, but tonight, this is just about us.

Everything else fades as I walk to him. Blake is nothing but a dark shadow with glowing violet eyes as I pass the pew he's sitting in, wrapped in silence.

I feel like… nothing is real until I'm standing in front of Logan, my fingers sliding into his hand.

"Are you ready?" he asks.

"Are you still sure?"

"Always," he whispers, and two unwilling, headstrong, stubborn, communicatively challenged mates turn to the priestess patiently waiting to marry them.

39

INTO THE RAIN

Maeve

Brie is... radiant. She glows in her simple white dress of lace and satin, her hair falling loose over her back and shoulders as Logan slowly, tenderly, lowers the hood of her dark blue cloak. The temple is quiet and dim, moonlight flooding the altar. Logan knits his fingers in Brie's and brings her knuckles to his lips, pressing a kiss against them. They're bathed in silver, the windows behind them dancing in starlight. It's beautiful, really. It's what I envisioned for her, one day, what I thought would be… years from now.

I watch my sister–the person I love the most in all of the world–intertwine her soul with someone else, forcing myself to unravel the ribbons binding my heart to hers.

She doesn't belong to me anymore.

Logan looks at her as they kneel before the priestess in her silver robes. They lean into each other like being inches away is too far apart. And the look on his face as he brushes his lips over her temple… he loves her. He's devoted–body, and soul.

My heart is in my throat as I sink into the pew beside Blake at the very back of the temple. We watch in silence as the priestess begins the late-night marriage ritual, taking her sweet time.

But there's no rush. I could sit here forever just to witness the smile tugging on Brie's mouth–a smile of complete and utter happiness.

"This isn't fair to them," I whisper without realizing I've said the words out loud. "This is just… grossly unfair."

Blake sighs heavily, his voice low and monotone, "You understand why they're sending him to Emberfyll. You must."

"Because they have the means to cross its veil? That doesn't matter to me. I'll be watching my sister's heart get torn from her chest when he leaves, Blake. And he–he doesn't want to go. He changed his mind."

"It doesn't matter. He's an Alpha King by blood. The family needs him to claim his seat–"

"His seat at our table, you mean?" I hiss, meeting his eyes as the ceremony continues without our undivided attention.

"If there's a threat of any kind in Emberfyll, it needs to be dealt with. I don't blame our fathers and grandfathers for making that decision."

"By sacrificing her mate to the cause."

"With an army behind him," he whispers sternly, but his eyes remain on Brie and Logan, a soft purple against a sea of stars.

My quiet scoff is nearly silent. "You weren't in the room when it happened–when they told him he was going back. It wasn't a question of if or when. He wasn't given the choice. His face, Blake, I can't describe it. He looked at her and just… crumpled. I could see it in his eyes."

"I didn't take you as a romantic."

"I'm not. I know my place in the world, I know my purpose. But Brie… Brie was meant to love and be loved, and that's been taken from her the moment it began, and I'll never support it."

"You love her."

"Have you ever once questioned that?"

"I think she's the only person in the world you're capable of loving."

"Then you understand where I'm coming from," I say, swallowing hard past the knot in my throat. "Seeing her hurt makes me want to… burn the world down and spread the ashes at her feet."

"You have the ability to do so if you wish."

"Don't mock me. I'm not in the mood."

"I'm not mocking." He stretches out his legs under the pew in front of us. His head tilts to the side as he watches the priestess say her blessings, her voice a gentle, rhythmic hum. "I just find it odd you haven't… stuck your nose where it doesn't belong."

I scowl. "What do you mean by that?"

He shrugs one shoulder, picking an invisible piece of lint from his finely tailored suit jacket. He sticks out like a sore thumb anytime he visits Moonrise or Veiled Valley–Eastonia in general, honestly. Wearing only drab grays, blacks, and dark blues. Never white. Blake wouldn't be caught in a white shirt even if his life depended on it. It's like his very soul was sucked from his body once, erasing whatever creativity and joy he had, leaving behind a shell of a person.

He reminds me of rain, the kind that pours without ceasing, the kind that thunders, knocking the leaves from the trees. The kind that leaks through nail holes in ceilings, leaving scars in its wake.

Blake washes reminders of life away. He's an incubus–a sucking, consuming, soulless being.

Yet, he says, with a glimmer of his own heartbreak, "She's pregnant."

"I know."

"She doesn't know yet. It's too early."

I nod, biting my tongue for a moment. "She'll be so happy when she finds out. I can't bring myself to tell her. Logan will be… at sea. She won't be able to tell him for months, if she's able to at all before the baby comes. It's a boy, too."

"I know."

I look at my cousin–the only person in the world who truly understands my burden–my powers. We're alike in a lot of ways, especially when it comes to guarding the people we love, even if that means pushing them away, hiding things from them. Even if that means our own people fear us instead of adore us.

"Can I ask you something?" I ask.

He gives me a short, knowing nod, like he's already aware of what I'm about to ask. At the altar, the priestess directs Brie and Logan to rise. She binds their hands with a length of fabric, murmuring prayers to the Goddess. The couple bows their heads. Brie's eyes are closed as she repeats the prayers, but Logan… he's watching her in awe, like he can't believe this is his mate, his wife.

I blink back tears as I ask, "What do you see when you look into their futures?"

Blake takes a shallow breath. "They'll have a handful of sons, no daughters. I can see their children's timelines well."

I continue watching the ceremony, smiling sadly to myself as Blake continues, "Logan will outlive her. It will destroy him, but he'll be an old man by then—with grandchildren, great-grandchildren. He'll follow her into death within days."

My heart quakes. "Will they be happy?"

"Yes. But the time they'll have together won't feel like enough. I doubt it ever feels like enough for anyone."

Tears spill down my cheeks, glinting in the moonlight as the priestess places a silver coin on the fabric joining their hands, an old tradition meant to test their bond. Blake shifts his position beside me, settling against the pew. We watch the rest of the ceremony in silence, neither of us blinking as the priestess blesses them again, and Logan kisses Brie— the kind of kiss that makes her smile and giggle against his mouth.

I've told myself I'll live vicariously through her great love story. I'll never have one of my own. I can't feel the mate bond. I'm not a shifter. I'm the only one of my kind, and my purpose has been, and will always be, to be queen, and to give Eastonia as many Firestone daughters as I can. It doesn't matter who their father, or *fathers*, will be.

The man in the mask from the tea shop invades my mind. I blink, banishing him before his memory can fester. I'll admit I haven't thought about him since that night. Why would his image spring up now? A man whose face I haven't even seen?

I think of the tattoos on his hands and fingers. I remember them vividly, like they're tattooed in my own mind, forever cemented in my memory.

I shove the stranger's image away, tucking it deep in my memory and locking it away for… later, maybe.

Brie and Logan rush past us in a flurry of white fabric. The priestess disappears into the recesses of the temple, which falls quiet and dark again, but neither Blake nor I make any moves to leave the pew.

We sit in companionable silence for several minutes, listening to rain, letting our powers simmer beneath our skin, like our energies are calling out to each other, speaking in a hidden language only they know. Eventually, we leave the temple, walking side by side into the rainy night air.

"Where do you think they're going after this?" I ask him when the silence becomes too much.

"I'd rather not think about what a newly married couple does on their wedding night," he replies pointedly.

I roll my eyes. "Oh, please. You spend most of your free time in underground clubs."

"I like the music."

"You like the topless women."

Blake chews his lower lip. I like to think he's doing it to stop from smiling, from showing a single ounce of emotion, but then he replies, "The music, it–it helps."

"With what?"

He taps on his temple, his powers shuttering behind his eyes. "It turns things off, makes me feel normal, stops me from… seeing things I don't want to."

He steps away from me until he's nothing more than a hazy outline of himself in the shadow of night, rain falling in droves all around us.

"You should find that thing that shuts you off from time to time, Maeve." With that, he disappears into a swirl of dark mist.

Alone on the empty, rain-soaked street, I stare at the cobblestones where Blake was just standing only seconds ago, mulling over his words.

I turn in the other direction, toward the castle, which casts a long, shimmering shadow over the street. Glowing amber light pours from a few of the windows, and as I look up to the towers, I watch as Brie's bedroom lights flickers on then off.

I gather my cloak against my body, blinking rapidly to try to dry my eyes as I stand alone in the downpour.

Eventually I find my nerve and start to move, but when I close in on the gates of the castle, I abruptly turn on my heel and walk back into the city, bundled against the rain. Thankfully, it's warm, but my clothes are damp, and my cloak is sopping wet when I reach the inner city, a trio of streets stacked on top of each other on the rise of the mountain overlooking the valley below.

I close my eyes, feeling the warmth of my necklace radiating over my skin. My clothes dry instantly. My skin tingles as power rushes through my veins, curling and stretching until I feel myself changing.

I open my eyes, splashing through puddles while passing a restaurant, a diner, one that stays open all hours of the day and night. I catch my reflection in the glass door before yanking it open. On close inspection, it's still me. The porcelain, flawless skin. The pointed chin. The blue-green eyes that shine like polished sea-glass. But now my hair is a deep red and pin straight. My face is rounded, less hollow in the cheeks. It's enough to get by without being recognized.

But I can't keep this disguise for long. My powers are already simmering, stretching to their limits when I slide into a booth, ordering a cup of coffee and nothing else.

Rain streams down the windows. I can't see much beyond the flickering fluorescent lights of the diner casting a glare against the glass.

The thought of going home right now is just... impossible. Maybe in the morning. I'll face a future where I rule without Brie by my side tomorrow.

I curl my hands around the stale, but hot, coffee, keeping my hood on despite the dry warmth radiating from the kitchen across from the diner bar. Smoke spices the air as a group of men walks in—warriors, it looks like. I recognize a few of them. They pass me without so much as looking in my direction, but I turn my face to the window just in case.

Another group of men—younger men, men dressed in jeans and worn-in T-shirts, murmurs in a booth in my direct line of sight across the diner. They eye the warriors wearily before rising, shrugging into coats.

I glance at one of them in particular as he slides his muscled arms into an old, brown leather jacket, his head bowed, his face just out of sight. Black gloves catch my attention. Ghost issued gloves. I'd recognize them anywhere.

It's not uncommon, I guess. The Ghosts are everywhere, but they don't just… wear their gloves in public. He has dark, chestnut brown hair. It curls softly, the ends shining a golden blond like it's highlighted from the sun… or the unforgiving fluorescent lighting.

"Probably a good call," one of his friends says as the group moves toward the exit, having to pass directly in front of my booth to do so. "What about grabbing a drink at Raleigh's? They're open until, like, 3:00 A.M."

The other guys nod, mumbling in agreement as they raise their hoods or slip on ball caps to shield themselves from the rain, but Gloves shakes his head.

"Not tonight. You guys go ahead. I have to meet up with someone in like twenty minutes."

The other guys tease him, oohing and awing as the group brushes past my table.

I turn my face to the window again, a sudden jolt of panic rushes through me when I catch my reflection. My usual features are already bleeding back into view. I pull my hood down over my forehead, fishing in my pocket for a few coins for the coffee as the men reach the door.

Out of the corner of my eye, I notice Gloves hesitating at the entrance, he looks over his shoulder, his face cast in the shadow of his ball cap. Only his mouth and jaw are visible as he glances at my table. He's halfway out the door, but he goes still. He reaches up to the collar of his shirt and pulls what almost looks like a scarf from the base of his neck and pulls it over his face until the length of thin black fabric covers his eyes and nose.

My heart stops. I turn to look at him, shock reverberates through my system as the man from the tea shop steps out of the diner and into the rain.

Did he see me? Even if he had, he wouldn't have recognized me, right?

I wish I'd gotten a better look at his face, taken in some kind of detail other than his hair color.

He's a Ghost. Why else would he have the gloves?

I wait a single minute before darting from the diner into the rain, my powers flickering out as they weaken, my disguise fading into my normal features. Rain pounds the top of my head as I look around wildly, but I'm alone in the street.

40

THE MARRIAGE BED

BRIE

THE MOMENT MY BEDROOM DOOR CLOSES BEHIND US, LOGAN'S MOUTH is on mine. The lock slides into place with a soft click, and an even softer groan leaves his mouth when I reach up to run my fingers through his damp curls.

He smells like rain and leather. Like the promise of warmth and comfort through another stormy night.

And now this man–this loud, obnoxious, opinionated man... he's mine.

He presses a kiss to the ring he bought today on a whim. It's a simple band of gold–that's it.

"I'll give you a better one when I return," he promises, kissing the palm of my hand before his lips find mine again. "A ring with a diamond the old gods can see from the heavens."

"I don't care about that." I giggle as his hands glide down my sides, pulling me close. Outside, thunder booms, the room lighting in ribbons of blue as lightning splits the clouds, but in here, it's warm. It's private. It's just us.

He removes my cloak. It falls to the ground in a heap at my feet. He's careful with the dress, unfastening each button like they're made of glass, his eyes never leaving mine.

"You're beautiful," he whispers into the darkness.

"You're my husband." I smile as the dress falls away, leaving me in only a lacy shift.

"Any regrets?"

I laugh as he scoops me up and deposits me on the bed. "Not yet."

"Well, we have the rest of our lives together…. That may change."

"You're teasing me on our wedding night?" I sit up as he starts unbuttoning his shirt. He eyes me, his gaze slipping to my breasts–full and aching beneath the silken fabric of my shift.

One look at my hardened, peaked nipples has that feral look sweeping over his eyes. His pupils expand as he roughly pulls his shirt off then slides his pants over his hips until he's in nothing but his boxers.

He pushes me flat on the bed and covers me with his body, lowering himself to kiss him. Logan presses kisses to my lips, my neck, and then my chest, growling with satisfaction as his hand cups my breasts, kneading until I needily moan his name.

His cock is hard against my thigh with nothing but his boxers separating us. He grinds against me, pulling the straps of my shift over my shoulders and down until his mark on my skin is exposed. It tingles when he kisses me there, and I sigh with soft, featherlight pleasure that ripples through my body, numbing my senses.

"You smell different," he murmurs against my skin, kissing down my belly as he slowly drags the shift down with him. The silky fabric makes my skin pebble as the chill in the room brushes over me, and then he's kneeling, pulling the fabric down my legs. He hooks his thumbs in my panties and takes them next, hungrily scanning my body until our eyes meet.

"I had a chance to use my own shampoo and conditioner today–"

"It's not that," he says softly, lowering himself to me again and caging me in against the mattress. "You…" he presses a soft kiss to my lips. "I don't know what it is, Brie, but the way you smell makes me… want to be gentle with you."

I laugh, but he's being totally serious right now. There's a soft glow in his eyes–something tender and deep.

"You smell the same to me," I say, shrugging.

He smiles, kissing the corner of my mouth, but then wraps his arms around my waist and flips us over so I'm on top of him.

I spread my hands out flat on his chest, admiring his hard muscles. He lifts his hips, hissing in a breath as I grind against him. He still has his boxers on, but he's growing impatient, especially with me on top of him, his view nothing but my skin, my body.

I rise, giving him room to slide his boxers off, and in a smooth motion, glide my folds up his shaft.

He lets out a low, satisfied groan, closing his eyes for a moment. "Fuck, Brie, you're so wet."

I'm enjoying this–being in control, watching his face as I reach between us and position him where I need him before sliding down onto his cock. The noise he makes is… everything. It ignites that fire in my blood that makes me heated all over. I writhe, grinding my hips as I ride him, my hands planted on his chest.

"That's good," he says breathlessly, grunting as he closes his eyes again and relaxes into my movements, his hands resting on my hips to set my pace, but every movement has me climbing toward the peak already. My body thrums, my skin suddenly too sensitive to every touch, every kiss, every whispered word of praise. He pulls me down to him, kissing me fully, tenderly, clutching my body to his.

"I'm going to come," I warn him, but he shakes his head.

He slowly rolls us over without pulling out then thrusts hard, burying himself so deep my toes curl, and I moan.

He clamps a hand over my mouth, shushing me, shaking his head. But he speeds up, trying to match my progress toward his release, lowering his lips to my ear to whisper filthy things that have my body tightening.

"You're such a good girl," he growls, thrusting into me again.

I moan, whimpering his name as tension coils and snaps, and that pleasure builds rapidly until I fall over the edge, taking him with me. My headboard claps against the walls as he thrust inside of me in time for me to ride out my orgasm on his cock, my muscles locking and spasming around him while he pumps, spilling himself inside me without restraint.

Breathless, we both slump on the bed, tangled in each other's arms beneath the sheet. I'm warmed to the bone and already falling asleep under his weight, but he gathers me close, nuzzling my neck.

"Why did you shush me?" I ask out of sheer curiosity.

He rests his head on my shoulder, his curls tickling my cheek as he traces lazy circles over my bare stomach. "I didn't want to be overheard. I feel like a teenage boy trying to sneak in to see you here at the castle."

"Did you ever sneak around behind Aviva and Ryan's backs? I find it hard to believe you didn't, honestly."

"I didn't. In my defense, it wasn't because the opportunity never arose... Lexa and Nora normally ended up in my room at night. They were scared of the dark. In fact, I didn't sleep in my own bed past the age of sixteen."

"Where did you sleep, then?"

"On the floor, while Lexa and Nora curled up on my bed, with my pillows, my blankets." He smiles at the memory. "I tried to carry them back a few times, but they'd wander back in, and I'd wake up between them normally, with Lexa snoring in my ear and Nora draped over my legs. When I was fourteen, I did my first warrior training course over the spring in Moonrise. I was gone for three months, home in time for the harvest, and found out that they had miraculously started sleeping in their beds while I was gone. But that first night back, I woke up to Lexa's elbow in my neck and Nora trying to burrow under the covers. I just... laid there, and felt... happy to be home."

I run my fingers through his hair, absently separating the curls as he tells me it was the first time he realized that he hadn't been thinking about Emberfyll and plotting to leave. He'd felt guilty about it and spent the rest of that summer trying to be cold to his adoptive sisters, but they saw right through him.

"They cried after I left for good, when I was a bit older. Coming back to visit was one thing, but they were so young. Lexa was only four or so, and Nora was even younger, so me going away for nine months at a time was forever for them. Years passed, and they started forgetting me, acting shy when I'd come home to visit, and… I hated it. I let that hate fuel me, convincing myself that it was a sign that I was on the right path–training to leave. To go back and claim what was meant to be mine when I could have had a much fuller life here."

The words unsaid hang in the air between us. I can taste them. They're bitter and terribly hard to swallow.

"And now I'm going away again."

That's what he's thinking.

"I won't forget you," I tell him sleepily, but minutes pass between words, and he begins to feel rather heavy, his arm draped over my waist and face resting against my breasts. I wrap around him, sighing deeply as rainy air spiced with ozone drifts through the windows I leave open out of habit because there's always someone–or something–here to close them for me.

"You can come back now," I whisper to the house. I'm answered by a timid, creeping rush of air, like the magic spirit is trying to gauge whether it's about to see something that it doesn't want to see, like me in a precarious position with the first man that's ever been invited into my bed.

But the air is warm as it tickles my skin in what I'd consider congratulations, and the windows close, and the thick curtains draw back against the rainy, early morning sky.

Hours later we wake up slowly, naked and draped in my warm quilts. Logan pulls me to him and makes love to me slow and tender, every touch honed to my needs, my pleasure. I want to stay like this forever with him–joking and smiling as we shower, dress, and get ready for the day. I watch him button the shirt the house left out for him, laughing as he mentions getting married again at the Harvest Festival this year, in a few short weeks, knowing that's impossible but pretending like he's not leaving, and I'm not being left behind.

Logan leaves the room, telling me he'll be at the barracks with my grandfather and dad most of the day, but tonight we'll shift, maybe grab some dinner before at whatever restaurant I'd like to go to.

Like a normal couple would.

But we take off our rings, forced to keep this secret until he returns.

I'm biting back tears all morning. Sitting at the breakfast table in the fancy breakfast room with a view of the valley, I dab at my tears with a napkin, telling Misty and my mom I have allergies, which they apparently believe, but I glance at Maeve and notice her staring blankly at the sweeping view beyond the balcony.

Her eyes are a soft sea-green in the sunlight as she watches the clouds, watches the slight glimmer of magic in the sky just over the mountains. Veiled Valley has a veil around it, but the magic guarding it is ancient, something my mother, brother, and grandfather guard, using their powers to ward the sacred valley from enemies.

But I notice a change in Maeve's eyes.

I slowly put my fork down. I've seen that look before. She's scheming, the gears in her mind whirling as her eyes brighten.

"Maeve–"

The screech of her chair across the tiles cuts through my voice as she darts from the table.

Mom and Misty look after her before dropping back into their conversation.

But I watch her disappear at a full sprint, her long, dark hair billowing out behind her. I've never seen her run like that. Not unless she's in some silly competition against Lexa.

I turn back to the valley, squinting at the magic shield. What had she seen?

41

ONE LITTLE HITCH

Logan

Ryatt and Evander walk out of sight across the bridge connecting the barracks to the main streets of the city. I look out of my old bedroom window at the sunny glare casting shadows over the valley. The shadows move as the clouds dart across the sky toward the castle, toward my wife, who I'd much rather be with right now than here.

I... I don't have anything to pack. Anything that meant anything to me—my laptop, my *fucking* glasses—were lost in the shipwreck. I have the clothes on my back, and even those were borrowed from who-knows-where, left on the dresser in Brie's bedroom by the ghost that haunts her house.

She's all I have, and it's not like I can pack her in my duffle bag and take her with me.

I crank open the window to let in some fresh air to cut through the overwhelmingly male smell of the barracks. I turn to my empty duffle bag with a sigh, bracing my hands on either side of it on the bed, and hang my head, but a whoosh of air rushes out behind me,

315

and I turn in time to see a tiny gray bird sweep across the ceiling before falling to the floor.

I wait for the impact, but instead of a confused bird diving to its death, Maeve appears in a burst of crimson light. Her moonstone necklace glows against the fabric of her dark green sweatshirt. She's wearing clunky sandals and athletic clothes, a far cry from the silken gowns I equate her memory with.

Her hair is piled on top of her head as she pants, wiping sweat from her brow. Her eyes fix on mine as she bends to brace her hands on her knees.

"What are you–"

"Give me a minute," she pants, breathlessly, sucking in several lungfuls of air before straightening and waving a hand toward the window in dismissal. "I flew–flew around the building like eight times looking for an open window."

I eye her wearily. Brie mentioned Maeve's powers of transformation, how she could turn into a little bird, but I hadn't really thought about it that deeply. "Why don't you turn yourself into a bigger bird? An eagle, or something? It would probably make flying easier."

She scowls, still trying to catch her breath. "What do you know about flying?"

"Nothing."

"Yeah," she hisses, rolling her eyes. Steely silence settles between us as she glances around the room, pursing her lips as she takes in my meager belongings, the old calendars tacked to the walls. "So, this is where you lived?"

"Whenever I wasn't on a mission, yeah." I zip up the empty duffle bag. "Can I help you with something? If you're looking for your dad, you just missed him."

"I'm here to see you. To talk to you."

I freeze then turn to her. "Why?"

She licks her lips. I always forget how young she is. She just turned nineteen. She's still a kid, honestly. A kid with little real life experience about to be thrust onto a throne she's not ready for. I know Brie still struggles with separating her life from her sister's, and I get it. Seeing Maeve, standing face to face with her… she's still the same little girl I followed into a forest. The same girl who killed a witch and burned the fuck out of me when I came to her aid. I glance at that necklace, rolling my lower lip between my teeth as I wait for her answer.

"What if… what if you didn't have to travel to Emberfyll by boat? Would you do it?"

"What do you mean? Swim?"

"No, idiot," she says under her breath, her eyes shining like sea glass in the sun. "You say it's a veil. A veil like the one around KiloKilo, like the one that used to be around Eastonia."

"It is."

She wets her lips again, her eyes locked on mine. "I can break a veil."

"No," I breathe, shaking my head.

"But I can. You can't deny it. I'm a Firestone. I'm a full blooded Firestone witch, Logan."

"You're nineteen, Maeve. I don't know much about Firestones, but I know you don't come into your power until you've had a baby, right? Motherhood trips something in your mind." I point to my temple before shaking my head, dismissing her. "No–"

"Just hear me out, okay? Look–" She waves at me, trying to get my attention as I turn for the door, which is wide open. "Logan–"

I shut the door and lock it, turning back to her with my arms crossed. "You can't. Breaking a veil is… incredibly difficult magic. You should ask your grandmother about it."

"I'm not like her, okay? She had a few drops of Firestone blood in her veins in comparison to what I have. Same with my mother. I'm different. The stars aligned at my birth. I am the compilation of generations of Firestone blood converging. I can do it."

"Even if you could," I cut in sharply, "we'd still have to take boats. The journey could take months–"

"Maybe," she hisses, losing her patience. "Even you don't know how far away it is, and what if the alexandrite fails, hmm? What if it's not the same kind of veil as the one around KiloKilo? You'd die. All of your warriors would die–"

"You know this isn't my idea."

"And I'm here to offer you another solution." She holds her hands out in surrender. "I can get you there. Both you and Brie. I can do it. I could take us there tonight. It's a full moon. My powers are at their height. Will you at least hear me out?"

I stare at the teenager. My sister-in-law. The same young woman who made it possible for me and her sister to elope last night. The same young woman who spirited dozens of miles away to pluck us from the ocean.

"Fine. What's your plan?"

BRIE FIDGETS BESIDE ME IN A DARK, HOLLOW SPACE ON THE BACKSIDE OF the castle. It's well after midnight. Moonlight drifts through windows that spiral above us toward the ceiling of what must be another tower, like Brie's room. But it's cold here. It shouldn't be. It was a hot day and an even hotter evening. The family gathered here had dinner inside in the AC instead of out on the deck, where I had to sit next to my mate like her sister hadn't just offered the lifeline of a lifetime.

Brie said yes to Maeve's asinine plot immediately, and I've learned over the last month or so to keep my fucking mouth shut when it comes to these sisters and their schemes.

But watching Maeve dart around the room, moving dusty chairs and discarded end tables against the only door into this creepy, shadowed space makes me wonder if she can, in fact, get us to Emberfyll with only her magic.

She left out a very important piece of information, though.

"You are crazy," Brie hisses as Maeve thrusts a thermos into her hands.

"Just drink it, Brie. Every drop. You have to."

"You're going to open a portal?!" Brie clutches the thermos full of that strange, bitter tea her family uses on the members who don't have the power to jump from one place to the other.

"Like it's hard?!" Maeve hisses, whisper fighting in an effort to not get caught.

I glance around, wondering if the spirit of the house is going to jump in and end this, but the air remains still. My eyes land on the sheet of dark velvet covering something tall and ominous in the center of the room, something flooding the area with a dark, twisting kind of energy that makes my skin crawl.

Something I figure Maeve is planning on using in her plan, which is now a lot more complicated than it was before.

"It's simple. It really is," she tries to explain. Brie scowls but pops the lid of the thermos and drinks deeply, gags, and continues chugging the lukewarm liquid. "I'm going to use the mirror. I'm going to syphon its powers to strengthen my own. I know what the shore of Tarsian looks like. I know what the sea looks like. I can get us there–"

"You can get us into the water–" Brie tries to argue, but Maeve cuts her off with a wave of her hand.

"Logan made a blood oath to me. We're bound by that. I'll be using that bond, that oath, to get us to Emberfyll. He has memories of not only Emberfyll but the seas coming out of it, of passing through the veil. I have everything I need. Well, almost." Her voice drops at the end as she grimaces.

Brie sucks down the rest of the tea, fighting for her life as she sucks in a breath, then asks, "What else? What else do you need?" But the look on Maeve's face must tell Brie exactly what Maeve needs to complete her insane plan because Brie yelps, shaking her head. "You can't be serious."

"It'll work, and you know it."

"Maeve, you can't. That's–that's the darkest kind of magic–"

"What are you talking about?" I ask the sisters. I'm losing my patience and will power with each passing second. I could be upstairs in bed with Brie right now, enjoying the precious few nights we have together, but instead I'm standing here, listening to them whisper fight.

"She's talking about *The Book of Whispers*." Brie snarls, her voice flashing with fury.

Maeve's nostrils flare. "It will work. You know it will."

"It'll take pieces of your soul–"

"It won't. Richard of the Arcane Umbra wasn't a witch. He didn't have any power to counteract the book's power, but I do. The book was made for someone like me, someone with the ability to read and cast spells without having to give anything back to it in return."

"Even so, how are you going to get it? It's not here–"

"Misty has it."

"She has the copy. *The Book of Whispers* was destroyed!"

"I can still say the spell. I can open a portal just like Richard did. I'm going to do it, and I'm going to use the mirror as a base for the spell. It'll be like jumping, Brie. We can travel thousands of miles that way just by stepping through the glass!"

I run my hand over my face as they fight over the logistics of it, but Brie's voice is starting to slur as the herbs take hold, and she stumbles. I catch her as her body starts to relax.

She pants, "You're going to kill yourself, Maeve. You're not powerful enough for this."

Maeve stares at her sister, her chest heaving as she inhales sharply. "I am powerful enough. I'm going to prove it to you. Do you want to sit around for months while he's gone? And you–" She turns to me, pointing an accusatory finger at my chest. "Do you want to be separated from her? Risking death if the stones don't work?"

I don't. I really don't.

Brie shakes her head but continues to slump in my arms like she's losing the ability to stand upright.

"How much of the herbs did you give her?" I ask, concern washing through my system.

"Enough to keep her comfortable," Maeve answers matter-of-factly, tilting her chin up to me. "And a little extra."

I sneer, but Brie can barely keep her head up, and Maeve takes that as a win.

"I need you both to trust me. I can get us there. We'll reach

Emberfyll in a matter of minutes. Once we're there, Logan can do whatever he needs to do while I work on bringing down the veil. The family will realize we're gone and likely figure out exactly what I did in a matter of hours, and the whole strength of our families armies will be heading to Emberfyll to fetch us within the day. By the time they arrive, I'll have destroyed the veil around Emberfyll, and the two of you can live happily ever after, or whatever. Or, we play the long game and spend months waiting to hear if Logan died or not."

Maeve taps her foot, checking the dainty wrist watch on her arm.

Before either of us can argue, she continues, "It's eight o'clock in Crescent Falls now. Misty's here in Veiled Valley, which is one less thing to worry about."

Brie exhales, nodding, her head pressing into my chest.

"I can do this," Maeve concludes, nodding, like she's still trying to convince herself she can, in fact, do this.

"Your powers will be completely spent when, and if, we reach Emberfyll," I tell her, my voice steady despite the nerves making it almost impossible to focus. "I'm not sure what we'll find there. There wasn't much left when my parents abandoned the place and took their pack with them. If I'm remembering correctly, a few people chose to stay. My uncle was still raining havoc. If he's alive, we could be walking into a war zone with only me to protect the two of you."

Brie nods against my chest like she agrees, but I feel her starting to slip away as the herbs take control, rendering her mind and body useless.

"We'll deal with it. You made a vow to me to keep her safe."

"I mean to keep it."

She looks at Brie, saying, "She'll perk back up in a few minutes. The drowsiness is a side effect of the herbs, but it doesn't last long. I'll be back in ten minutes at the most. Stay here. Do not leave this room."

With that, Maeve disappears in a soft shimmer of crimson light.

4 2

I CAN DO THIS

MAEVE

COLE AND MISTY HAVE A BEAUTIFUL SUBURBAN HOME IN SHADOWCREST. It's always the same—always smells like freshly baked cookies and the flowers she keeps in vases all over the house. Tonight, as my toes brush the ground, and my powers funnel back into my body, it smells like... popcorn.

"You pig! You're not going to eat all of that." Josie's voice, so similar to her mother's, drifts down the hallway. I landed in the foyer, which is dark, soft moonlight drifting in through the windows and casting the stairs and framed photos of the family in silver shadows.

"If you wanted more, you should have added it to the order," Adrian argues then yelps after a smacking sound reverberates toward me in the gloom.

"Give me one of your tacos—"

"Or what?"

"I'll tell Mom."

"She's in Eastonia, dumbass. Hey!" A scuffle ensures. I have two seconds to jump into the shadow of Misty's study just off the foyer when Cole walks down the stairs, still wearing his hospital scrubs. The sound of a shower running upstairs follows him as he lumbers into sight, looking exhausted.

He doesn't see me lurking in the shadows as he passes within feet of my body, walking down the hallway where Adrian and Josie are apparently fighting over dinner in the kitchen.

"What's up with you guys? You've been at each other's throats all afternoon. Knock it off, okay? I miss mom just like you guys."

"Adrian ordered me the wrong thing," Josie snaps.

"Josie," Cole says breathlessly, "Just order another delivery. I really don't care. Just don't start the movie without me, okay?"

I hold my breath as he stalks back down the hallway. I wait until he's upstairs and his bedroom door closes before I creep into the foyer again, listening to Josie and Adrian whisper-fighting down the hall.

"I can't wait for you to go back to Wellington," she hisses, but then her voice changes to something bright and amicable as she places another food order.

The microwave beeps, and Adrian howls, hissing under his breath as what I assume is steaming hot popcorn is dumped into a bowl, but I'm not here to eat and watch a movie.

I look back into the study, my heart hammering. Where would she keep the book? Not out in the open, for sure. It's the only copy left of the grimoire, *The Book of Whispers*, the recipes within capable of undoing the fabric of time.

My necklace glows and warms against my skin, it's light faint as it bleeds through the fabric of my sweatshirt. "Show me where it is," I command my powers.

I close my eyes as I move into the study, stretching out my hand. Faint whispers drift toward me in a language long lost to time. Ageless, genderless voices that mingle, hissing and chanting as my fingers brush over the spines of books, over Misty's stationary computer, her notebooks.

I open my eyes and look up at the ceiling where the voices seem to gather, calling out to me in hushed tones.

"Fuck," I hiss through gritted teeth and look toward the stairs.

I back into the shadows and wait what feels like an eternity for Cole to return, dressed in sweatpants and a faded T-shirt, his hair damp and swept away from his face while he presses his phone to his ear.

"They miss you, is all. They wanted to go with you to see Brie," he says, to Misty, I presume. He turns the corner and falls out of sight.

"Please have it out in plain sight," I whisper to myself before darting across the foyer and racing up the stairs as quietly as I can. The house has a simple layout, which works in my favor as I run into Cole and Misty's room. Steam billows out of the ensuite bathroom, and their walk-in closet is open, offering the only light to be had in the room.

Panting, I send my powers drifting through the room, and the voices return.

I turn to the closet. "Bingo," I smirk, tip-toeing into the snug space full of Misty's fine, designer clothes and Cole's less flashy shirts, white coats, and scrubs.

I dig through the drawers in their built-in dresser, clawing through rolled up socks. I leave the drawers open as I move on, snatching folded sweaters off shelves and tossing them on the floor in my haste as the voices grow louder and louder.

"Where are you?" I hiss, crouching to sift through the bottom shelves and drawers. I pull the lowest drawer of the dresser out of sheer frustration, reaching against the wall and feel... something hard.

A lockbox is fixed to the wall–built within it.

The room blurs. I forget where I am as I send my powers into the lockbox. Metal sizzles until the frame comes loose from the wall, and the little metal door falls into my hand. I toss it behind me and reach inside, praying, my fingertips grazing cash and jewelry before finding... the book.

"Yes," I hiss, smiling deliriously as I pull the book from its hiding place, clutching the small, black leather cover and rocking back on my heels. I flip through the pages, confirming it's the copy, the only book of its kind in existence.

This book has none of the power of its predecessor... but that's fine. Because *I do.*

"What are you doing here?"

I whirl toward Cole's voice. He's standing a few feet away from the entrance of the closet, which is now in total disarray. He picks up his wallet off the bed, narrowing his eyes as he scans my face, then his gaze drops down to what I'm clutching in my hand. "Maeve!"

"Don't be mad!" I shout, then disappear in a burst of crimson mist, my powers ripping all of their clothes off their hangers and sending socks and sweaters into the air. The world twists painfully, falling apart and pixelating, then rushes into view again within seconds.

My feet slam to the floor in the mirror room, where Brie and Logan are waiting right where I left them.

"I got it," I breathe, showing them the little black book. "But Cole caught me. We have to go now."

Brie nods but looks at Logan with a wary expression. He looks nervous, too, but not for the journey. Brie doesn't spirit easily–it's terribly hard on her body, her senses. Even with the herbs, this is risky, and they both know it.

"How is this going to work?" Logan asks.

I glance at the door to the room, which is closed, still locked tight and blocked from within like I left it. I lick my lips, sighing deeply to try to calm my nerves before I open the book. "I just–I just need to say the spell. That's all I have to do." My voice cracks as I glance at Brie and Logan, trying to swallow past the knot in my throat. I can do this. It's just a few words–a few words that nearly brought our world to its knees twenty years ago. Words that... words that a madman said to try to flood our lands with evil.

The original book was full of magic–ancient magic. Dark and endless. It stole parts of his soul every time he said words he didn't understand.

But I understand these words as I crack the pages–printed in neat ink on simple printer paper, not weathered, yellowing papyrus.

Misty's scribbles leave indents in pen under the printed symbols—a translation done to the best of her abilities. I have to trust her. She's the brightest mind of the family, but if she got one single translation wrong… and I say it?

I look at the couple in front of me again, taking in the way Logan places his hand on Brie's back. I look at her face, taking in her features like I'm memorizing them. What if I fail and we die? What if I fail, and we get separated between the realms?

We don't have to do this. Logan could leave as planned. He'd return, months, maybe a year from now, and meet the child they still don't know about.

But I'd watch my sister get her heart torn from her chest. I'd witness the agony of her finding out she's pregnant with no way to tell him. I'd hold her hand while she brought her son, my nephew, into the world without her mate by her side.

I offered them this lifeline.

I cannot mess up.

I close my eyes as the warmth of my powers begins to bleed out from the moonstone around my neck. It's a simple necklace, something I've worn since I was a little girl to keep most of my powers locked away. But now, I'm calling on them—calling on the ancient bloodlines, my ancestors, witches and wolves alike.

Hear me. Obey me.

The pages of the book flutter as I begin to speak in tongues—the tongue of the people who lived in an age of magic even the modern people of Eastonia can't comprehend. An age of gods and goddesses that walked among us. An age of monsters and untapped power.

My powers surge, and my skin is suddenly chilled as I push, and push, my Firestone gifts to the limit.

My grandmother was able to pull a city from the lake.

I can do more, and my powers aren't even mature yet. I can feel it.

"Maeve?" Brie asks, her voice trembling. "What's happening?"

A splintering, crackling echo bounces from wall to wall. I open my eyes as wind begins to whip my hair into a frenzy. The mirror—the ancient, Shadowsynger mirror, shatters, creating a void of... nothing. Nothing and everything. The beginning and the end.

"Maeve!" Logan shouts over the chaos as my power booms and thrums. Debris skitters from the ceiling, crashing to the ground as bricks of stone begin to crack, bouncing and rolling down at our feet.

I keep saying the spell. I imagine the route in my mind. The shore of Tarsian. Further, into the sea. Into the waves and storms, but past it. *Take us past it. Take this king home.*

Pressure on my forearm almost snaps me out of the powerful haze. I'm so cold. I taste ice on my tongue as my powers drain, but I keep repeating the spell. I keep saying the words as my vision blurs with tears, my body choked with pain as Logan tightens his grip on my forearm, tugging Brie close, his arm locked around her waist.

My eyes are open to slits when he nods at me. "You got this. You're doing it."

Brie can't catch her breath. She starts to slump over his arm, already overwhelmed by my power, and we haven't even jumped yet. The herbs... they'll work. I did the calculations on the dosage myself. She'll survive.

If we survive the jump.

I strain and cry out in pain, my screech cutting the spell. I'm so close. I can feel the void forming in the mirror–the portal, but it's taking everything I am–everything inside of me–to open it.

"MAEVE!" Logan screams over the thunderous, throbbing whirl that bursts my eardrums. "DO IT NOW!"

Blood trickles from my ears as I restart the section of the spell my scream of pain interrupted.

Hear me. Obey me.

The book flies out of my hand as the room shatters. We're sucked into a vacuum of sound. It's like being trapped in a boom of thunder–so loud I can't hear my own scream when the room fades into darkness. The sound stops. The movement stops. I feel nothing–like I'm suspended in a void. I open my eyes and see... stars. Yes, stars gliding past me in streaks of gold, purple, and blue. The pressure on my body is insane. I can't move. I can't breathe.

It's too much. This pain... this doesn't feel right.
Logan and Brie... they're not here, wherever we are.
I'm alone.
I'm alone–and I'm trapped.
The stars fade into darkness again.
The quiet kind.

43

WASHED ASHORE... AGAIN

BRIE

I OPEN MY EYES AS I'M FALLING THROUGH THIN AIR. I DON'T EVEN HAVE time to scream before my body drops into water. Deep, rough water that drags me under the second I suck in a salty breath. I flail against the waves, trying to find the surface, but the undercurrent drags me down again, pulling me by my dress and tossing me upside down.

My head hits something hard, and I screech, but the sound is empty. I suck in water, choking, and realize quite suddenly that I'm drowning.

I go as still as possible, using the last of my energy to start moving with the current instead of against it, which turns out to be the best idea I've ever had, especially under duress. I open my eyes underwater, staring down at the shallows. It's sunny. Daytime. And below, seaweed waves between large, gray rocks. Pockets of sunshine dance through the water, illuminating seashells in shades I've never seen before.

Another wave crashes over the top of me, sending me rolling into even shallower water, and finally, I'm able to breach the surface.

I suck in a desperate breath as waves continue crashing into my back, over the top of my head, but I fight against the current and stand. I'm pushed down, my knees biting into the rocks and coarse sand, but I keep moving. Each step takes an enormous amount of my energy. I blink into the sunlight, into the sky blotted with dark, gray clouds moving against a stiff breeze, and force myself to keep going.

After several minutes fighting through the shallows, I reach the beach.

I fall to my knees in pure exhaustion, ignoring the waves pressing into me and trying to pull me back out again. I crawl on my hands and knees, sputtering water, sniffling as blood drips down my forehead and neck from a cut to my hairline.

I can't hear much of anything. The sound of waves crashing along the shore is blurred and warped, but a single touch to my ear informs me that they are both bleeding. I stare at the crimson streaks on my fingertips, and my chest convulses.

I wobble to my feet, soaking wet and covered in sand. Swaying, I blink at the unfamiliar shoreline. It's rocky, barren, and nothing more than a blackened cliff like whatever was atop it was scorched long ago, and nature never took it back.

I brace my hands on my knees and pant, trying to catch my breath. I glance down the beach, sniffling and reaching up to wipe blood from my cheeks and lips.

I'm alone.

I look along the shoreline, whirling as the sudden realization strikes me like a dagger to the chest. "Logan?" I croak, whirling back around. "Maeve? LOGAN?!"

My voice echoes against the cliff, bouncing down the barren beach.

"MAEVE!" I scream, turning to the water. "LOGAN!!!"

A large, funneling storm rages in the distance. Water spouts dance along waves. I can hear the thunder, see the lightning from where I stand but… there's no one else in the water.

"LOGAN!" I scream again, but his name cracks into pieces as I fall to my knees in the sand and weep.

"No," I mumble, shaking my head. "No, no, no–"

A sharp shout breaks across the shoreline, followed by several others. I look in their direction, trembling uncontrollably as dark shadows move across the beach in my direction. Five wolves, their leader at the front of the charge. They're all a dark brownish black.

I should… I'm not sure. Prepare to fight? Defend myself? Plead for help?

My body and brain are still hazy from the herbs. My jaw goes slack, whatever words I had for the wolves now padding in my direction, their ears flat along their heads, don't materialize.

I just stare at them, my heart slowing, and my ears pounding with my heartbeat.

Their leader is an elder, that's clear. His body is terribly scarred. His face, especially. Jagged, wide silver scars stretch across his snout. One of his nostrils is completely split open. He reaches my side and sniffs the top of my head.

I just allow it to happen because what can I really do at this point other than accept my fate?

"Where did she come from?"

"She doesn't smell familiar. She's obviously not from the villages."

"She's soaking wet. And look, that's blood. Did she–was she trying to swim, or something?"

I jerk away from their leader as unfamiliar voices skitter through my head, tickling the inside of my busted ears.

"She's cold. We'll take her back with us, warm her up. Have someone treat those injuries," a deep, rumbling male voice says. I peer up at the leader, watching his hazel eyes as he scans the wolves. *"She's probably just lost. That storm was something else. She was likely out in it, got swept off the cliff by the wind–"*

"Who are you?" I ask through the mind-link.

The leader nearly jumps out of his skin. He leaps back, turning to face me and lowers his head in confusion, and maybe fear.

"Why can I hear you through the mind-link?" I ask.

The group stares at me in shock. I stare back, unsure what to do or say.

"Where are you from, girl? What village? You're not part of our pack."

"What pack are you?"

The leader eyes me wearily, his hazel eyes… are shockingly familiar. He doesn't answer my question. So, I ask another, but my heart contracts as the words whisper through my mind, and into his. *"Am I in Emberfyll?"*

He looks back at his companions before meeting my gaze again. *"Can you shift?"*

It's confirmation, I guess, that I made it.

But where the hell are Maeve and Logan?

"I can."

"Shift then. We have several miles to cover."

"I'm—my mate and my sister. They were supposed to be with me, but I'm here alone, and I—" Tears roll down my cheeks as the elder wolf looks down at me. *"My mate—his name is Logan. He's from here. We came here because—"*

"Logan?" The elder's eyes narrow.

"Yes, Logan. My mate. He had to leave Emberfyll as a boy. He was—his parents died during the journey—"

The wolves behind him look wildly around then begin to sprint up and down the beach, howling and yipping like they're calling out for someone.

"What is his last name?"

"Atrayis," I whisper into his mind. *"Logan Atrayis. He's—he has eyes like yours. Hazel-green."*

"And you are his mate?"

I reach along my collarbone, absently feeling for his mark on my chest. *"I am."*

The elder takes several steps away from me as his companions return, the mind-link filling with their voices as they say they didn't see anyone else on the beach, or in the water, but they stop when they see their elder kneeling with effort, his front legs tucked under his scarred body as he… bows.

To *me*.

The other wolves follow suit. The breeze coming off the water rustles through their fur as I wait, breathless, for someone to say something.

The elder rises, and the word he says next is a whisper through my brain that feels... odd. Misplaced. A dream, honestly. Maybe I am dreaming. Maybe I'm dead because the elder wolf looks me in the eyes and says, *"Luna. We've waited an incredibly long time for your arrival."*

I WANTED TO STAY ON THE BEACH, BUT EVEN AS–AS *LUNA*–I DIDN'T have much of a choice in the matter. Cold, bruised from being thrown through the surf like a rag doll, and hazy from the herbs in my system, I shifted, following the group of wolves ten miles across the rocky shoreline and up above the cliff where a barren, scorched landscape greeted us.

I find it hard to wrap my mind around what happened here as I pick at a plate of fire-roasted venison, root vegetables, and a foraged salad. I'm served hot, spiced tea that has an odd, bitter aftertaste I'm not familiar with... but it's all these people have to offer.

The elder wolf is named Seamus. He's tall and built almost exactly like Logan. They're cousins in some way. Distantly related by great-grandfathers or something. And this fortress? This castle of toppling stone and overgrown vines? This was where... where my mate was born, where he grew up.

It was beautiful once. A beacon of white and silver against the sea. I look out the window–nothing more than a ring of old stone, the glass long shattered, and watch the water–watch for any sign of Logan and Maeve.

A fire burns nearby in a hearth of the same light gray stone now stained so thickly with soot I can't make out the detailing carved into each brick.

Furs line the floor like rugs. I'm wearing a borrowed dress–something homespun but soft and comfortable, even if it's a bit big on me.

Seamus walks back into the cozy room I've been given for the night and turns to the kettle hanging over the crackling embers.

"I have men out on the beach looking for him and your sister," he says under his breath as he wraps a length of fabric around his hand and plucks the kettle from its hanger. "If he's found, you'll be the first to know."

"They're in the sea," I whisper to myself, closing my eyes. "Or they're not here at all."

Seamus pours hot water into my tea cup but says nothing until he puts the kettle back and crouches near the dwindling flames. It's hot enough in the room now to be mildly uncomfortable, but the sun is setting, and I was told it grows cold at night, even in the dead of summer.

To his credit, he didn't pepper me with questions. He didn't ask if Logan was actually my mate, but he didn't have to. The fact I can mind-link with him, and everyone else that lives in little hovels around the remains of what was once a great palace, is enough.

I am their queen. The mate of their Alpha. An Alpha they didn't think would ever return.

Seamus simply showed me around, introduced me to the thirty or so people who live in the castle, and brought me out onto a balcony where three villages were visibly spread out along the top of the cliff, separated by sparse, spindly trees–a new growth forest.

That's it. That's all that's left of Emberfyll. Three villages. One castle. One pack without a name. Without an Alpha.

I don't ask Seamus what happened for it to have come to this. I'm barely functioning as I pull a fur over my shoulders and slouch in my chair, suddenly chilled to the bone as the herbs start to wear off.

Seamus works in silence after glancing at me and sees that I'm trembling. He stokes the fire until it shines bright, casting amber light throughout the room as the last of the sunset fades over the water.

"My father," I say in a near whisper, "and my grandfather are–are sending ships here with warriors and supplies to build a colony. Logan was supposed to be with them. They had the ability to cross the veil and… we were impatient. My sister offered to help."

"And your sister has powers?"

I nod. I told him about Maeve in the event she was found and accidentally hurt someone with her gifts, but he doesn't seem affected whatsoever.

"Did you know you're locked in here? That there's a veil around Emberfyll cutting you off from the rest of the world?"

"It's always been like that," he says, rising and then sitting on a stool by the fire. He's in his fifties, I imagine. His hair is just starting to gray, and he keeps it cut short, nearly shaven down to the scalp.

"Why?"

He shakes his head. "The truth has been lost to time. We have our stories, our myths, as your people probably do. We follow the Moon Goddess but not everyone in Emberfyll did. That only changed after the last war, the war that… killed everyone." He shifts his weight, resting his elbows on his knees as he looks at me. "You look tired, Luna. You should rest."

"He's not dead," I tell him absently. I'm not sure if I've even spoken the words out loud, but my throat tightens regardless. "The bond is still there. I can feel him."

"He'll return for you. And, like you said, your father is sending boats."

"It will be months before they get here."

"Maybe," he says with a shrug. "I've never been out on the water before. We fish along the shore, but that's it. Any boat that left never came back."

"Why didn't you go with his parents and their pack?"

His eyes meet mine and hold. "Some of us stayed behind as bait so the prince could escape. I've spent the last two decades wondering if we were successful. And, we were, weren't we?" His smile is soft as he rises. "Sleep now, Luna. If we find them, I'll wake you."

His footsteps echo as he turns out of the room, leaving the door open just a crack.

I stare into the fire as the herb's hold on my senses finally wane, and I… feel everything again, like I'm still battling waves, being tossed in all directions and unable to come up for air.

I crumble into myself, sniffling, too tired to even lift my arms to wipe my tears.

44

EMBERFYLL

LOGAN

"BRIE!" I SHOUT TOWARD THE TREES. MY VOICE CARRIES THROUGH THE night but doesn't bounce back to me. It just keeps going, and going, and I'm at a complete loss as to where we are or where my mate could be.

Maeve murmurs at my feet where she's lying flat on her back. I woke up five, maybe ten minutes ago in so much pain I could barely breathe, let alone stand. Now, I'm stumbling from spindly tree to spindly tree, using them to steady myself as I scream my mate's name into the night, but she doesn't answer.

Through the trees, I can just see the ocean, the storm raging in the distance. Lightning in shades of crimson and deep violet split the clouds as wind rushes toward the mainland. I can feel the electricity in the air, even from miles away. I can taste the thick, metallic stain of magic on my tongue. That storm… Maeve created it. It's her powers drifting away from us, stirring up the sea.

But Maeve is currently unable to even speak as it stands, and she's cold to the touch when I kneel and take her by the shoulders, shaking her.

"What did you do? Where is she?"

"Give me a minute," she rushes out, the words slurred and jumbled. Her lips are blue, and her skin is an odd, pale gray. That golden luster to her skin is totally gone, like her powers light her from within, but now she's drained.

Totally, completely drained.

I've heard of this phenomenon. I know what I need to do for her, but I'm torn between my duty to Maeve and finding my mate. I look out over the distant water again, my chest convulsing. Is Brie in the sea?

I press my hand to my chest, finding it hard to breathe. The bond is still there–still strong–but I'm weak. Weaker than I've ever felt. I couldn't shift right now if I tried, if my life depended on it. I can't summon the mind-link or even see through the darkness.

"Did we make it? Are we in Emberfyll?" Maeve asks, her teeth chattering violently.

I can't bring myself to answer her. I have no idea where we are as I shrug out of my shirt, laying the thin fabric over her trembling body. We're dry, which is good, but she's cold, and the warm night air isn't doing a damn thing to fix that.

"Stay here," I command and rise, stumbling several yards before my legs start working properly again. I gather sticks, stopping to scream Brie's name every couple of seconds, until my arms are full, then carry the bundle back to Maeve, who hasn't moved at all.

I start a fire and drag Maeve closer to the flames, which are too new to give off heat yet. I repeat this process, stacking more sticks onto the fire until the flames begin to warm us. I keep Maeve close to the flames, watching her for signs that she's warming up. When she turns her face from the flames, wincing at the heated bite, I drag her a foot away, and make the fire bigger.

I'm not sure how long this goes on. The watch on her wrist is busted, the glass shattered and the face within burnt to a crisp. The clouds hanging low above us promise rain, but the wind moves them across the sky before they dump water over the fire, and the sky opens to stars that... that I know. That I remember.

Maeve continues lying flat on her back. Her coloring is better, so I leave her side again, and walk through the woods, keeping the sea in my sight. The moonlight breaks through the clouds and begins to trickle through the new-growth trees. Some of them are shorter than me, actually. Just a few years old, so skinny I could snap them in half, and I realize why.

The ground beneath is scorched. Moss and pockets of grass have begun to poke through the thick layer of soot left behind by a fire that absolutely ruined the forest that used to be here, burning the ground through layers of soil until the fire met rock.

I remember that fire. I remember seeing it from the boat. I remember the glow on the horizon as I clutched the railing, and Emberfyll fell out of sight.

Maeve did it. She got us here.

"BRIE!" I scream the moment I reach the cliff overlooking the miles long beach that wraps around the northern half of Emberfyll. I've never been far south. That was my uncle's domain. But I know this place. I know the stars and constellations overhead. I know the beach.

I know how to get home.

I scream Brie's name again, yanking on our bond, but I'm spent. I would feel it if she died, though? Right? The bond would have snapped like the moment we rejected each other. I would have felt that same empty desperation.

But would I have felt it if she was left on the other side of the veil?

Soft stumbling footsteps alert me to Maeve's presence nearby. She grips the trees that are nearly as tall as her, snapping them as she tries to brace herself. Her legs shake violently as she shuffles in my direction, breathing hard. Her face is still so pale. I sigh and reach for her, hauling her into my chest to keep her steady so she doesn't fall over the cliff.

"What happened here? These trees are new. This forest is... a baby."

"There was a fire shortly before I left."

"That would have been… a wildfire? This damage is insane, Logan, even for that."

"It was likely more than that," I mumble, scanning the beach and the water beyond for any sign of Brie.

Maeve goes deathly quiet for several seconds before asking, "It was magic, wasn't it? Like my flames?"

"I was too young to know the details, but I've wondered."

She doesn't press for information, which I'm thankful for. My chest aches with each passing minute without knowing where Brie is, and I'm starting to panic. If I was stronger, if my body was more capable after being thrust through space and time with Maeve's magic, I would shift. I wouldn't stop running until I found her.

"I need to–to go down to the beach. I need to find her," I say, my voice like gravel as exhaustion sweeps through me in throbbing waves that are nearly enough to drag me to my knees.

I can feel Maeve looking at me when she replies, "We need to just sit down. I know, Logan, and I'm sorry. We'll find her, okay? But we're both in really bad shape."

"And what kind of shape do you think she's in?" I snap.

Maeve's lips thin, her eyes turning back to the water. She's trying not to cry, that's obvious.

I want to tell her this isn't her fault. But that's not true. Losing her sister wasn't her intention, however, so I can't really be mad at her, despite how I feel right now.

We return to the fire after several minutes spent debating our options. In the end, I can't shift, can't use the mind-link, and Maeve has no power left. She's teetering on the edge of freezing solid, and I can barely keep the fire burning hot enough for her.

"We need to start moving. We need real shelter–and food," I tell her over the crackling embers. "It's nearly morning. We'll have better light to continue our search for Brie, but we have to find her as soon as we can." I close my eyes against the pain of not knowing where she is. "She's likely on land. She has to be. I can feel the bond. She's here, somewhere, and we need to find her."

Maeve is asleep, however, with her forehead resting on her knees as she sits beside the fire.

I consider sleeping, too. I need it, but we're out here alone and exposed. The woods offer no cover. I can see for miles through the thin trees. But I haven't been keeping an eye out like I should have been because the second I look over the top of Maeve's head and into the woods, a shadow catches my attention. I'm up on my feet, leaping over the top of Maeve's head, within a breath.

Maeve yelps when the sole of my boot grazes the top of her head, but the sound is stolen by my body colliding with another man, the two of us hitting the ground with an echoing thump and rolling into the sparse underbrush.

He screeches in pain, but I cut off his breath with a hand clamped around his neck, squeezing hard. He's a thin man. Thin, and maybe just a little shorter than Maeve. I can feel every bone in his body as I press him to the hard, blackened ground.

He looks up at me in terror, his dark brown eyes wide and short blond hair catching the moonlight, which reflects off his slightly pointed ears.

He murmurs something, but his voice is choked, his eyes beginning to bulge. Only when his body relaxes do I let him go, but I stay straddling him, keeping him pressed to the ground. He's probably Maeve's age. A teenager. Gangly but severely malnourished. I glance at the shadowed heap beside us and notice a skinny, diseased rabbit lying limp, all skin and bone. Not enough meat for much more than a few bites of protein.

I look down at the man again, scanning his face. "Who are you? What are you doing out here?"

"Simon," he rasps, struggling to breathe. "I was just hunting."

I tilt my head toward the rabbit. "Having any success?"

He grimaces, his eyes watering, but I slowly rise, feeling down his body for weapons. I take the two knives from his belt and step away, holding them out in warning. Simon rolls over, coughing violently, then fists the rabbit carcass and presses it to his chest. "Who are you?" he asks, glancing at me before trying to look around my body to where Maeve's sitting by the fire, wide-eyed and silent as she watches me and the man.

"Where's the nearest village?" I ask, but my mind is reeling. I didn't know if there would be anyone left here. This fellow would have been an infant when I left Emberfyll with my parents. Someone raised him. His well-made homespun clothing and weapons make me believe he lives with someone–with people who have skills.

"About five miles east," he says, then swallows, unsure whether or not to give me exact directions. I don't blame him for being wary. "Is she hurt?"

"Don't even look at her."

Simon flinches and purposely looks toward the woods instead. He's pale and refuses to meet my eyes as I step toward him, heaving a breath and preparing for his answer to my next, and final, question.

"Who is your king?"

Simon looks slightly taken aback. Finally, he looks up at me, shrugging boyishly. "We don't have a king."

I feel the air leave my lungs in a whoosh, replacing some of the tension in my body with an odd wave of calm.

"But yesterday afternoon Elder Seamus found a lady on the beach who said she was the missing prince's mate–"

"What?" I grab his shoulders. "Did you say Seamus?"

"Who's Seamus?" Maeve quips, but I ignore, hauling Simon to his feet.

"What did the woman he found yesterday look like?"

"I'm not sure. We've just been hearing things in the villages. Some of the older men are out in groups searching for her companions…" His eyes go suddenly wide as he looks up at me, then glances at Maeve. His mouth moves but no sound comes out. "Y-you are–you're Prince Logan, aren't you?"

I let him go. He staggers backward, losing his footing and falling right on his ass. The rabbit slides out of his grip as he kneels forward in a deep bow. "*Alpha King.*"

Maeve claws her way to a standing position using my arm leg, then my arm, for support.

Simon echoes his statement–that I am the Alpha King. The words work through my body like tendrils, like claws, awakening my wolf powers again.

"Where is my mate?" I ask him, my voice low and serious. "Take me to her."

45

THE BETA

I WAKE IN THE EARLY HOURS OF THE MORNING TO SOFT SUNLIGHT brushing over my cheeks. I'm sure I cried myself to sleep last night. I forgot where I was, but only briefly, reality rushing in, reminding me that I made it to Emberfyll alone.

I roll in the furs, letting the warm, morning sunlight play over my face, but then I hear a commotion coming from outside.

Yips and barks dance through the air. I rise, clutching the windowsill for support as I squint into the sun and see a dozen wolves racing through the flattened, charred space that used to be the front garden. Smoke rises in the forest from chimneys, the villagers waking for the day, but I can't see past the trees and their thick summer canopies.

The wolves are racing into the forest.

I whirl to heavy footsteps running into the room I was given to use as my own last night. Seamus braces himself in the doorway, panting like he ran all the way here from the depths of the castle. I

347

wait for him to tell me we're under attack, or something, but when he lifts his head, he's smiling. It's a smile I find so familiar.

My chest tightens as the air leaves my lungs in a whoosh. "You found them?"

He nods, that smile widening, and extends his hand. "Come with me."

I grab his hand, and then we're racing out of the castle. He found me sandals to wear last night but they're slightly too big and hamper my progress as I race after him through the garden.

Just as we reach the tree line, I stop. Logan's mark on my chest tingles as my excitement builds, but my intrusive thoughts steal whatever relief I feel.

What if it's not them? What if they're hurt?

The wolves trickle out of the forest, leaping and hopping, spinning in excited, wolfish circles as their barks and yips cut through the sound of the breeze rustling the trees overhead.

Two shadows move through the forest. My heart quakes when Maeve's face comes into view–pale and gray–but otherwise, she's alive, and leaning on Logan for support. I catch my breath in one smooth inhale and run to them. Logan's expression–stern and serious–shatters into a look of sheer relief as I leap into his arms. His embrace closes around me, tugging me tight, his face buried in my hair.

I flail my arm for Maeve and catch her shoulder, dragging her between us, where our reunion is nothing more than muffled, delirious sobs and the occasional broken laugh of disbelief.

"You did it," I tell my sister, pressing a rough kiss to her forehead. "Oh, my Goddess, Maeve, you did it. You clever witch!"

She's panting weakly, but her watery smile settles in my heart. I can see how weak she is. She's cold to the touch but upright, which is a good sign. It could take days for her powers to return, but we have time.

We made it.

We're in Emberfyll.

Logan is *home.*

I notice he has gone very still, however. I'm aware we're being watched. I'm acutely aware of the dozens of sets of eyes from the people creeping through the woods, everyone watching us, watching him, their king.

But Logan is looking over the top of my head at the man who saved me from the beach, who brought me into his home and fed me, kept me warm.

A man, I realize, that Logan remembers.

Logan's eyes are watering, but he refuses to shed any tears. A very manly thing, I suppose, even in the face of a complete undoing of what he thought to be true.

He told me once that he didn't think there was anyone alive here. That his pack left on boats, having no other options, no other choices. They left to try to save their lives… and he was the only survivor.

Now, we both know that's not true.

I slowly unravel my hands from around his waist, stepping to the side to steady Maeve instead. I watch as Logan takes two cautious steps toward Seamus, like he can't believe he's really there, like all of this is just some dream.

Seamus opens his mouth, but words fail him. Logan just stares, unable to speak. All around us, the remains of the pack watch Logan. I wonder what they're thinking. I wonder if they recognize the boy within the man he is today.

Seamus sees that boy, though. He shakes his head, grunting as he swallows past a sob and nods several times, saying, "It's about damn time you showed up, kid."

The ice shatters, and Logan and Seamus embrace, both of them laughing in disbelief and utter joy, maybe a slice of heartache.

The next several minutes are a whirlwind of activity. Seamus quickly, and without fanfare, ushers us back into the castle, keeping his hand on Logan's arm like he's afraid he will disappear again if they're not touching. Two warriors help me take Maeve into the room I slept in last night, where I tuck her into the furs and sit beside her, encouraging her to drink hot tea laced with fresh, creamy milk until her eyelids begin to flutter, and she falls into a deep sleep. Only when I feel like Maeve can be left alone do I leave the room and pick my way through the castle, trying to imagine what these toppled hallways used to look like before the castle was nearly destroyed, burned, and then taken back over by nature.

I find Logan and Seamus on the bottom floor in a wide room where one of the walls has caved in completely, giving a full view of the sea beyond. The storm that was raging in the distance is gone, replaced by calm, sparkling water and a scattered group of small fishing boats that hug the shore, shadowed figures moving across the decks.

Logan rises from a stool when I enter the room. I take his hand, letting him crush me to his chest. He takes a deep, restorative breath, murmuring into my hair, "Are you all right?"

"I'm fine. Are you?"

"I'm okay."

I nod, holding his gaze as I trace his jawline with my fingertips.

He turns to Seamus. "Thank you for taking care of her in my absence. I'm indebted to you."

"No, you're not," Seamus laughs from his perch on a pile of rubble covered in moss and creeping vines. He sips from a mug of what smells like tea. "She's our Luna. A pile of furs and a plate of food was all we had to offer."

I pull away from Logan, swallowing hard and moving in Seamus's direction, but stop several feet away. "I told you yesterday that my family is sending a fleet of ships here, and that's true. They will not harm you, and in fact, will be able to offer aid. We didn't know what we'd find here. Logan wasn't sure if anything was left, honestly. Do you know your exact numbers?"

Logan sinks back onto the stool in silence while Seamus thinks about my question for a moment. "Roughly eighty. There're a few children in the villages, but no more than four or five. It's hard keeping the young ones alive."

It's like a knife to my heart. I glance at Logan, seeing the guilt flaring behind his eyes. These are his people, and they've been suffering, starving, for two decades.

"Can you gather everyone together tonight for a meeting? Everyone—every man, woman, and child? They need to be aware that in a few weeks, boats will be landing on the shore. Friends, not enemies."

"Your people can't pass through the veil—"

"My sister," I cut in, pointing at the gaping holes in the ceiling, "She's resting now, but with some food and a few days to recover her power, she'll be able to break the veil. Completely, actually. It'll be gone, and Emberfyll will join what we call the Allied Kingdoms. Logan will take his title as Alpha King, and your people will be under the protection and unity of my family." I glance at Logan, hoping that he agrees with what I'm saying. I might be the Luna, but he ranks higher than me, technically. He spent his entire life training just to make it here, not to be the Alpha.

I spent my entire life training to be a Luna.

I know exactly what to do and how to help these people.

I begin to pace, tucking my hands behind my back, but he can't answer the questions I have, not until we know the whole story of what happened here. I look at my mate, sending him a quiet command to ask the questions he has before I bulldoze through the conversation with my own inquiries and start planning how to make this war-torn kingdom our new home.

But Seamus beats him to it. "After you left, the fire burned through everything. I'm sure you remember watching the flames from the south creep closer to our forest." Logan nods solemnly but stays silent, even as Seamus turns his attention to me. "The King of the South wasn't really a king. He'd been feuding with Logan's father long before Logan's birth. When Logan was born, his uncle saw his birth—the birth of a son, a future Alpha King—as a threat—and broke from the royal pack of Emberfyll, starting his own in the south, and immediately declared war. It was bloody and brutal that first year. We had a hard winter, but the battles kept going. Years passed like that—nothing but war. It ruined our farmlands, our forests, our rivers. Bodies polluted the water, and sickness began to spread during the seventh year of what ended up being a twelve year war. It started in the south, killing everything in its path. By the time it reached us, Logan was ten and had only known hardship, chaos." He licks his lips, shaking his head. "The fire was meant to eradicate the sickness in the south. We didn't start it, but after years of draught and dry, hostile winters drying out what was left of the forests and farmlands, it burned through everything, burned uncontrollably, fueled by whatever magic started it."

"It was a spell?" I ask.

Seamus purses his lips. "It was a curse."

He goes on to explain the decision to leave Emberfyll, and my heart sinks with every passing minute as I watch Logan relieve memories I think he would have preferred to forget.

"Some of us stayed behind to make sure they weren't followed, the boats, but there wasn't anyone left to follow them out into open water at that point. About a year after Logan and his parents–our Alpha King and Luna–left, some of us, the strongest, those able to withstand the journey, traveled into the southern lands and didn't find a single survivor. The madman who started the war was dead in his own bed, nothing but mummified skin and bone. He died from the curse he created, we think. And so we... we've done the best we could to survive. The past few years have been bountiful. The animals have been returning, as well as the fish. The forest is waking up, and things are growing again. We took that as a sign that maybe he'd–he'd be returning soon, and we were right." He looks at Logan. "The king has returned at last."

Logan nods, but I can tell something is weighing on him. I know it's guilt, for not returning sooner.

But he couldn't have, not without dying trying to cross the veil.

With the story concluded, I take a deep breath and become the diplomat these people need.

"So," I say to both Logan and Seamus, "you've been leading these people all these years. You are our Beta now, Seamus. Tell us what we can do to help."

46

LUNA RISING

THE CASTLE GLOWS LIKE LIQUID GOLD FROM THE LIGHT OF WHAT MUST be hundreds of tallow candles. The gathered crowd shuffles to find a spot to sit or stand in the wide, toppled ballroom of sorts. I'm not sure what it used to be, but only so many rooms are still fully enclosed. The weather in Emberfyll is mild. I imagine when the forest grows back, it'll be borderline tropical.

A feast of fish is laid out on makeshift tables or on long strips of fabric where people are seated on the floor, passing pewter plates down the line into hungry hands. Others break bread or pour tea and mead into mugs.

I watch from the front of the room where I'm seated against a backdrop of the ocean and the clear, star filled sky.

Maeve's still asleep. She's been sleeping all day, since the moment she arrived, but I imagine that won't change for a while. I'm worried about her–have been checking on her all day while also juggling creating a plan of action with Logan and Seamus for when my father's warriors arrive.

The thought of my family makes my stomach curl. Dad's going to be so mad. Grandpa, too, is probably raging right now. I wonder if Grandma will attempt to come here, breaking the veil down herself, but part of me believes that someone must have put this idea in Maeve's head. She's not normally that reckless. Scheming? Yes. But not irresponsibly so.

The fact that she made it here, alive, with us in one piece is astounding. I've had to pinch myself repeatedly to confirm I'm actually here, and I know Logan is feeling the same way.

He's barely said a word all day, but we're exhausted. His expression is what's killing me the most, however. He just looks broken. *Guilty* and broken.

I wonder if it's too late to fix what's been broken in his heart since he was just a child. I'm not sure even our mate bond can heal that, but I can try.

Seamus waves for the crowd to quiet down, his voice soft and friendly as he smiles. I worried that Seamus might take offense to being called Beta, but he'd been… relieved, I think, to be done with his duties as the de facto leader of these broken, hungry, tired people. But he's been with them since the beginning.

I found out how he's related to Logan. He is his cousin, the eldest and only surviving child of Logan's eldest aunt on his mother's side. They're the last of their family left, the last of the pack that chose to leave. The rest of these people are refugees from other packs that no longer exist, thrown together out of survival.

I rub my temple, closing my eyes against the mental list of things to do, but open them when a very small child taps on my shoulder. She's likely four or five years old, if that. It's hard to tell because the children and teenagers I've seen are all small and skinny, having grown up without enough to eat. She hands me a small, slightly wilted flower, like it's been smooshed in her pocket all day.

I smile at her, and she runs away, giggling, throwing herself in her mother's arms. I meet the woman's eyes and nod, noticing the glint of tears in her eyes. Tears of relief. Tears of someone who finally sees a future for her child, even if that future depends on the witch sleeping off a power-induced coma several stories above our heads.

If Maeve can break the veil, it would mean that once the warriors arrive, the colony could be set up, offering extra food and supplies for the people here. But then a few ships could turn back around and go to the mainland for help—more food, more supplies, a handful of healers who could come to live here and get these people back in shape.

While Seamus begins his speech, my mind reels over what the next couple of months will look like. Logan and I will need to stay here… unless I go back without him to go to Moonrise to gather healers and carpenters, pleading my case as Luna to my grandmother's council of elders to send as much as they can to Emberfyll.

I'm not listening to the speech. I can hear my own heartbeat in my ears as Logan rises, extending his hand to me to help me up. My stomach pitches with nausea I equate to nerves at having a group of eighty people looking at me, watching every step I take as Logan moves to the center of the crowd and stops, heaving a breath.

I shaved his face for him today. It was the only moment we had alone together, and it was spent in silence, both of our minds wandering to what we discovered and what it means for us now.

But he grips my hand, looking down at me with so much love in his eyes that it untangles the knots of worry in my brain, and there's nowhere else I'd rather be than here, with him, fulfilling this purpose.

The Goddess chooses wisely, doesn't She?

She knew I'd be needed here, that he'd need me.

And I'd need him.

Logan licks his lips before turning to the crowd. His mouth parts to say… something, anything, to his people, but a man in the very back of the crowd stands up, tears in his eyes as he starts to clap. Other's stand, following his lead, and soon the entire group is rushing out of their seats and from the floor, cheering and hollering, raising pewter cups in blessings on our name.

"The prince returned! He returned as king, as prophesied!" someone shouts, which is followed by more shouting and clapping.

Logan looks entirely overwhelmed, and for once, at a loss for words. So I do what any good Luna would do and step past him, addressing the crowd. "My name is Brie. I know this is a shock, and there's a lot of confusion about what will happen next, but I believe in the Moon Goddess. I believe that all of us are here for a reason—that every one of you were chosen from the stars by Her hand, knowing you'd be strong enough to withstand what you've been through. I know you look at me—at us—and see strangers. I know the news of a fleet of unfamiliar warriors from an even more unfamiliar land is daunting. But I swear to you—to each and every one of you—that my sole purpose in this life is to serve you as Luna, to care for you and your children, and rebuild the kingdom you loved enough to protect for two decades while our Alpha King found his way home."

The crowd quiets, but a few people whistle, and a few clap and nod.

I continue. "Tomorrow morning, I'll be here in this spot. I want anyone who wishes to talk, who has questions, to do so. Together, we will get through this."

I turn to Seamus, who's smiling at us both, but Logan remains behind me, his expression suddenly steely as he scans the crowd.

I wait for several seconds then step back, feeling a little on edge under the watchful gaze of everyone in the room. Logan clears his throat and starts speaking, but it sounds... strange. I know the words, but the inflection is off. His voice is low and guttural, his vowels rolling in a way I've heard before, but not for a long time. It strikes me then that he's speaking in his native tongue, but I can understand him. I can comprehend the soft echoes of understanding and murmured praise coming from the crowd as well. His words are quiet and laced with what I can only describe as music. I blink, wondering if anything I've just said was understandable to these people. I feel my cheeks going a bright pink, but then the crowd starts clapping, and people start eating again. Logan takes my hand and leads me back to our spot.

Sitting down, I ask, "Did I just make a total fool of myself?"

"No, why?"

"Because you had to translate for me."

"I didn't have to. You were speaking the language, Brie. You have been since you arrived, which is why Seamus thought you were from one of the villages at first."

"What–no, I couldn't have been–"

"Maybe it's our bond, I don't know, but I've been wondering about it all day." He settles beside me, laying a hand on my thigh. "Maybe you have powers after all, Brie."

I look into his eyes, happy to see a flicker of contentment there before he dips his head, scanning the plate of fried fish in front of us.

I GLIDE ON SOFT FEET INTO THE ROOM WHERE I LEFT MAEVE SEVERAL hours ago. The moon is high in the sky, sending silver beams through the windows that cast shadows over her face as she sleeps soundly, curled in the furs.

I sink down beside her, placing my hand over her forehead, and exhale deeply in relief to feel she's no longer freezing cold, but she flinches under my touch. Her eyelashes flutter as she tries to open her eyes.

"Go back to sleep," I whisper, but she groans, rolling onto her back and untangling her arms from the thick furs to rub her eyes.

"How long have I been out?"

"All day. I think it's nearly morning, actually."

She tries to sit up but thinks better of it, grimacing like the smallest movement hurts. "Are we in Emberfyll?"

"We are."

"Logan met someone in the woods, but I couldn't understand a word he was saying."

I roll my lower lip between my teeth. How do I explain that I suddenly have the ability to speak their language? I do my best, and after recounting the massive feast and my speech, Maeve just rolls her eyes, chuckling as she says, "You don't remember, do you?"

"Remember what?"

"That summer you spent in Silverhide. You were six, I think. It was a year after Logan came to live with Ryan and Aviva, and we went to visit. You ended up staying for a few weeks. Logan was learning how to read and write in our language, but you picked up his native tongue. You came home talking in that language."

I narrow my eyes at her. "I don't remember that at all! I feel like I would have remembered spending an entire summer with my own mate, don't you think?"

She shrugs. "The Goddess works in mysterious ways."

"How–how would you have remembered that, anyway? You were like, three years old!"

"I'm a witch, Brie. I remember everything." She smiles sleepily, closing her eyes again, but then frowns like some memory is flickering behind her eyelids.

"What's the matter?" I ask, smoothing her hair away from her face.

"Do you know anyone in the Ghost army that has tattoos of the constellations on their hands?"

What an odd question. "Uh, no, I don't believe so."

"Neither do I," she whispers.

"Are you okay?"

"I'm tired."

"I know." I run my fingers through her silky, dark hair. "Thank you for doing this for us, Maeve."

"It's what sisters do," she replies, and my heart aches as she tries to stretch out but winces in pain. "I'll try to break the veil tomorrow."

"We're not going to rush it, okay? Just rest. We're fine."

"I have to tell you something," she says, blinking blearily up at me.

"What?"

"I should have told you before, but I didn't. I was scared you'd be mad, that it would make things worse when Logan left, harder to say goodbye, but… you're pregnant, Brie."

I stare down at her as she closes her eyes, her words slightly slurred.

"Are you sure?" I ask, wondering how she knows, but… my sister's a witch. She just knows these things, doesn't she?

"Blake confirmed it," she whispers, and then sighs, falling asleep as I run my fingers through her hair again, over and over, while my mind reels.

Maybe the timing isn't great, but… I know someone who will be desperately happy to know we have a baby on the way.

I rise, leaving my sister to sleep, and go looking for my mate.

We were given a small room on the side of the castle that's somehow still standing. He's shirtless, as he looks out the window at the night sky. He turns to look at me, and I have a sudden vision of that time on the ferry, just hours after we rejected each other. When I'd sat back down, not realizing he'd been following me around all morning, and the look he'd given me… it'd been warm, concerned, maybe even a little curious, but I hadn't seen it like that back then.

I close the door behind me with effort since its hinges are bent, but I keep my eyes on him. Words fail me for some reason. It's been a long day. All I want to do right now is lie down with him and close my eyes.

The rest can wait until tomorrow. Maybe even the next day or the day after that.

47

—

UNVEILED

Brie

I wake up the next morning curled in Logan's arms. I doubt we got more than a few hours of sleep, but my mind won't shut off, and I doubt his has either.

We lay there in silence for several minutes. Logan draws lazy circles on my arm while staring up at the ceiling. I want to ask him what he's feeling right now. I've never seen him this quiet, this at a loss for words.

So, I'm the one who talks instead.

"Do you remember me as a kid?" I ask, and he nods, then shrugs one shoulder.

"I suppose. You're seven years younger than me, though. You would have been playing with dolls while I was out hunting or training to be a warrior."

"Maeve mentioned last night, when I told her I could speak your language, that I spent a summer in Silverhide while Aviva was teaching you how to read and write. Apparently, I picked up your language back then, and just… forgot about it."

His fingers stop moving for a moment, but then he chuckles low in his throat, rolling over to face me. "I actually remember that. How does Maeve remember that summer? She was a toddler."

"She's a witch. I have no idea. But I have no memories of it whatsoever."

"You came to stay for a few weeks leading up to the harvest festival, I remember that. It was chaos, actually. I was… thirteen, so you would have been six, I think. Misty brought her kids down too, and Sydney and Sarah were there for a week with all of their kids. Sarah was pregnant with their last kid, but I can't remember his name off the top of my head–"

"Noah." I laugh, trying to dig up the memory of what must have been a large family reunion of some kind.

"Everyone came down to see Nora for the first time," he says, laying his head against the rolled up fur we'd been sharing as a pillow. "Aviva had her about a week prior. That's why you came to visit, but your mom stayed longer than the rest of the family to help Aviva."

"But how did I end up learning the language of Emberfyll?"

"Aviva wouldn't give me a break from my lessons even after having a baby. She threatened to not let me go to the Harvest Festival if I didn't buckle down and focus, and when I balked, she sat you down at the kitchen table to babysit me, essentially. You were a total brat, you know."

I scoff, swatting him on the chest, but he tugs me close.

"Not a brat, really. I don't think there's a word in either language to describe what you were like as a kid. Bossy? Yeah, that works. You were… justice oriented."

"Justice oriented? You mean I was a tattle-tale?"

"You were a snitch, Brie. The second I took my eyes off my textbooks, you'd run and tell Aviva. So, I had to come up with a way to keep you busy. I gave you some paper, a pen, and you'd scribble little pictures and hand them back to me, telling me what they were in your language, and I'd tell you what they were in mine."

"We taught each other how to read and write."

"We did," he breathes, a nostalgic smile touching his lips. "I'm... I'm kind of sad I forgot about that, knowing what I know now."

"That we're mates?"

He nods, but his lips thin, and that heavy silence seeps between us again.

I nestle close, resting my cheek in the crook of his shoulder. "Do you... do you regret coming here?"

"No," he replies. "I think I thought I'd feel differently when I did get here, though. I'm struggling with–with how I feel about being back. I feel guilty that I didn't come back sooner."

"You didn't have a way to get here."

"I know. There's nothing I could have changed, but they suffered for so long, and seeing this place...." He sighs heavily, looking up at the vaulted ceiling and the graying rafters ten or so feet above our heads. "This used to be where I lived. My home. Where I spent my childhood, but when I think back on being a little boy, I think of Silverhide, not here. The only thing I remember is war. I only remember my parents' faces from the boat when we went into the water. I hate to admit it, but part of me wants to just go back to East-onia and pretend this never happened, but we can't. I can't." He takes another heavy breath. "If you want to go–"

"I'm staying here with you. That's final."

"It's going to be a lot of work. Years of work, Brie."

"And those are years we'll have together. We're going to figure this out together."

He briefly squeezes me, closing his eyes as his body presses into mine. He smells like everything I love. All those warm scents heightened by sleep and being in a cozy little nest of furs with him all night.

But he's right. We have work to do. We have a lot of work to do.

For the next week, we find out just how much needs to change, needs to be mended and healed.

Each day passes in startling clarity instead of a hazy rush of time. Maeve recovers–but slowly. A healer from the nearest village just beyond the castle walls comes to stay with her, feeding her tonics and smoothing tingling lotion over her skin to try to speed up the recovery process. Maeve doesn't object to the stranger's touch, but she's quieter than usual. I think she's mentally preparing for what she promised she'd do.

I'll never know what it's like to be her—to have that much power in her body begging to be released on the world. I do know the crushing weight of the responsibility of being a future ruler, however. As I go through the motions of helping my mate find his footing with his born pack, I realize the training and studying I'd put myself through to help Maeve ascend her throne was actually... meant for me. I'll be a queen before her. I'm a queen now, even if that hasn't hit me yet.

And on the eighth day in Emberfyll, the future Queen of Eastonia finally gets out of bed and walks outside. Maeve spends hours walking up and down the beach with me, looking at rocks and shells, sliding some in our pockets to take back to the castle to decorate the window sills with, as silly as it sounds.

And on the ninth day, I miss my monthly cycle. I admit that I wasn't ready to tell Logan until I knew for sure, that I thought Maeve might have been out of her mind when she told me in the middle of a power haze... but she was right.

And on the tenth day, while Maeve walks up and down the beach at sunset in preparation to bring down the veil, I sit with Logan on a large rock just big enough for the two of us to watch the show. In fact, the entire population of Emberfyll is on the beach or perched on the cliff. Small warming fires burn along the coarse, rocky sand and the smell of mead and roasting meat is heavy in the air as Maeve's body fades into the glare of the setting sun.

"She's nervous," Logan says as Maeve turns into nothing but a shadow and slips out of sight. The sun dips below the horizon, painting the sky in strips of gold and crimson.

"She shouldn't be."

He smiles softly to himself. "I know. I've never doubted her powers. Her being able to control them, to wield them... that's another story."

"She'll learn. She has to. She has... she has two more years until she ascends, and that's enough time."

"Do you think she wants to be queen?"

"I do," I say, knitting my fingers in his.

When Maeve doesn't return, the conversation drifts from her to our plans. Logan says, "Once the colony is built, and we have warriors stationed here to help, to start rebuilding, I want to go back to Silverhide for a while. Ryan will be able to help us gather supplies—crops, livestock, whatever we think we'll need to get fields of grain going, a few farms. I think a month is plenty of time to be away. It would give us a chance to see your parents and try to talk ourselves out of whatever punishment your dad has planned for me."

I smirk. "He's not going to punish you, Logan. I think you're the only man he would have been okay with when it comes to me finding my mate. I see it in his eyes. My grandpa, too. They hated what they thought they had to do to us."

He grits his teeth but nods like he's trying to convince himself that's really how they feel. But he says, "We'll come back in early fall with enough supplies to get us through the winter. The winters here aren't bad at all. It's stormy and wet, mostly. Like Maatua, but not nearly as warm. But we'll make it. Come spring, we'll plant crops and try to rebuild. I'll put out a notice, have it sent through Eastonia and Crescent Falls, about territory up for grabs if any Alphas want to move here."

"That worked for Ryan."

"It did, didn't it?"

I smile up at him. He's so much calmer and at ease now. He spends a lot of his time with Seamus lately, catching up, telling him all about the land beyond the veil. At first, we offered the people here a way out, the option to go to Eastonia and set up a new pack, but every single one of them refused. This is their home.

This is my home now.

Several gasps bounce down the beach as a ripple of energy makes the pebbles along the water rattle. The waves retreat, simmering like the water is boiling. Logan and I look down the beach to where we can just make out Maeve. She raises her hands to the sky, her fingertips glowing like embers in the creeping darkness.

"Logan," I say as the first glimmers of her powers streak across the sky like shooting stars.

"Yeah?"

I reach for his hand, lacing my fingers with his, and slowly bring his hand to rest on my stomach. A shockwave rushes down the beach at the same moment he looks down at me, his brows furrowed as he searches my eyes for silent confirmation about what I'm trying to tell him, even if the words seem impossible.

It should be easy to tell him I'm pregnant. I should be able to shout it to the rooftops, but the only thing my mouth manages to do is smile deliriously as tears prick the corners of my eyes. Another shockwave booms across the beach, carrying excited gasps and shouts as the entire island trembles under the wake of Maeve's enormous, unimaginable powers, but Logan's eyes remain locked on mine, glowing like polished, imperfect emeralds.

"Are you pregnant, Brie?"

"I am," I answer tearfully.

"Oh–" He sucks in a breath before dragging me into his lap and kissing me wildly, laughing against my lips. "Oh, my. Thank the Goddess. I love you. I love you–"

I can barely get the words out when I echo, "I love you!"

Crimson shimmers race across the sky over our heads like fireworks, tearing down the ancient veil, cutting through the misty and perpetual storms that lock Emberfyll away from the rest of the world.

Maybe one day I'll wonder why Emberfyll was hidden. Whatever old god who did this was either trying to keep something out or lock something in.

But it doesn't matter now.

I found my Alpha, and he loves me more than life itself.

The shouts of awe abruptly turn to eerie silence as the last of the veil falls like burning pieces of parchment, spiraling toward the water. Logan and I look toward the water at the same time, and his grip on my body goes slack.

Several large boats bob in the distance, distinguishable by their blinking lights. But three in particular zoom ahead of the rest, passing through what used to be the veil, but is now open.

Apparently, Emberfyll was quite close to Tarsian after all. A ten day journey. That's all.

My cheeks burn with a smile as the *Artemis*, *Asteria*, and *Atropos* race into view, their sails stretched wide against the wind, their wooden bodies leaving the fleet of high-tech Ghost naval cruisers in their wake.

4 8

PERFECTLY IMPERFECT

Logan
Several Months Later

MOONRISE IS WASHED IN RAIN AS I PACE THE UPPER HALLWAYS OF THE grand palace. My muscles are impossibly tight as moans echo toward me and away again. I pace in the opposite direction of the cries of agony that cut me to the core.

It's been like this for hours now. We'd arrived in Moonrise last night with plans to visit for a few days before leaving for Veiled Valley for the next month or so, returning to Emberfyll in time for the birth of our child with time to spare, but things went awry.

A nurse–a witch–rushes in my direction, her face pale and washed in concern. "Alpha King Logan? It's time."

"Is she all right?"

"She's okay," she lies, her eyes giving away her worry.

I brush past her, the hallway blurring as my vision hones in on the door behind which my mate is writhing, begging for relief, but also more time.

Our son is months early. Eight weeks early, to be exact. The witches have been trying to stop the labor for hours, but Brie's in so much pain, and the baby is coming whether she's ready or not.

I step back into the room preparing for the worst, and the sight of Brie—pale and sweating on the bed—is my undoing.

I'd been asked an hour ago to leave the room because I was being… I wasn't being very nice to the nurses and midwives trying to tend to her. To put it plainly, I'd threatened to kill all of them, feeling the same kind of gut-wrenching, overwhelming emotional pain Brie was going through like it was my own, and they were hurting her. I removed myself from the room before I did anything I'd regret later.

"Logan," she whimpers as I kneel by her side. Her hand shakes as it wraps around mine. "It's too early. He's coming too early."

"I know," I breathe, fear mingling with the emotional distress threatening to split me into pieces. I've never felt as… worthless as I do right now. I can't help her. I can't stop the pain. I can't stop our son from making his early entrance into the world.

"We wanted him to be born in Emberfyll," she whispers painfully, tears streaming down her flushed cheeks.

"It doesn't matter. He'll be born here, like you were."

"I'm scared."

"I am too," I admit, brushing her sweat-damp hair away from her face.

The door opens with a jerk, and several people rush inside. Misty's pale gold hair comes into view as she reaches up, placing a hand on Brie's thigh. "We're here now, sweetheart. Everything's going to be fine." She looks at one of the nurses as Cole, her mate, and a physician in Crescent Falls, enters the room and takes stock of the situation, but hangs back in the doorway. I meet his eyes, and he gives me a short, knowing nod and smile, but his eyes are dark as Misty says, "Is Kenna still conferring with the other midwives downstairs, in the infirmary?"

The nurse nods.

Misty licks her lips, her eyes distant as she smooths a hand over Brie's stomach, leaving a trail of glimmering blueish white power behind. "Everything's going to be fine, Brie. He'll be okay. You both will."

Brie shakes her head and cries out as another contraction rips through her. They're so intense. Her body bows and trembles as she rides through it, and all I can do is watch, praying that it ends soon.

Cole says, "Everyone needs to leave, except for you and you," he points at the lead midwife and her assistant as he steps into the room.

Everyone obeys, and soon the air feels less stuffy, and the chaos that'd been brewing starts to lessen, but I'm still on edge.

He leans in to whisper something to Misty, who nods, her eyes locked on Brie's face. Misty leaves in a hurry while Brie whimpers, shaking her head and pleading with Cole to stop the labor, but he gently lays a hand on her shoulder then mine.

I don't know Cole all that well. I remember him from his time in Silverhide when I was child. I liked him then. He's an easy-going man, easy to be friends with, but seeing him work as a doctor is like watching him put on a mask. His personality shifts, turning to steel.

"This baby is going to come—and soon. Within the next half hour," he tells her, his eyes not leaving her face. "Misty is going to stay with you for the labor, heal you, and then she's going to take him to be tended to. He's going to be small, Brie." He looks at me to make sure I'm listening. "He's going to be very small, but he's going to be fine. You probably don't remember when Briar and Celeste were born, but they were also very early, and they're okay. Sarah was okay. Your mother was born so early she shouldn't have survived, but she did, and that was without the kind of help we have available here at the castle." He hesitates before asking, "Do you want me to stay?"

She nods, sniffling.

"Do you want me to help your mother deliver him, or do you want me to stay here, by your side?"

"Help her."

"Okay," he says gently, nodding. He squeezes my shoulder. "Are you ready?"

I shake my head, but the tension my chest eases. The door opens, revealing Kenna and Misty.

I feel like I'm watching the scene from the corner of the room, watching myself clutching my mate while she cries through each increasing contraction, watching me pray to the Goddess, willing to give up everything for their safety and welfare.

Brie is... strong and fierce as she brings our son into the world with a roar that shatters the remaining walls I've built around my heart. And he's... small. So small and quiet.

"Take him," Cole rasps, his face cold and serious as he rises with my son in his arms and hands him to Misty, who wraps him in a warm blanket, her fingers glowing as her healing powers set to work.

Brie is exhausted, but she watches them leave the room with tears in her eyes before turning to look up at me. "Is he okay? Logan?"

"He's okay," I lie, and her lower lip trembles.

"Go–go with him. Please go with him!"

"Go," Kenna echoes as she tends to her daughter. "She's okay, Logan. I've got her. Your mate is okay."

My vision blurs as I press a kiss to Brie's forehead, murmuring something akin to a prayer of thanks that comes out as a garbled, "I fucking love you, Brie. You're amazing." I tear myself from the room before I lose my nerve, chasing Misty down a staircase while she rushes to the infirmary.

Her face is pale and set in determination. Neither of us speak until we reach the sweeping, high-tech hospital–even for Moonrise, which keeps to their traditional, magic ways when it comes to healing. We're within the lower levels of the castle. It's the only area with public access, situated along the backside of the palace. It's not ornate. There's no glint of gold in the marble walls here. It's sterile, and thankfully, quiet.

Misty rushes us around a corner, and that quiet stillness snaps. Activity erupts as Misty hands my son to an unfamiliar witch who tenderly carries him to a little crib with warming lights all around it and places him inside.

Misty holds my hand and squeezes as we watch the nurses tend to the baby.

"We named him Kieran," I say, not sure if the words left my tongue.

"That's a beautiful name. A strong name, for a strong boy."

"It was the traveling," I whisper. "I knew it was a bad idea."

"Addy came early, too. Not this early, but still. Some babies are just ready. It's not your fault, nor hers."

We watch the nurses flutter around the baby for what feels like an eternity, but Kieran is… he's fine. He starts to whimper, writhing in the blanket, his tiny fist poking through the folds of fabric, trying to grasp thin air.

My feet move on impulse, cutting through the group of nurses working quietly, taking his vitals, scanning screens and taking notes. I reach into the crib, smoothing my hand over his light brown hair–which he has so much of already. He blinks, wrinkling his nose as he whimpers, his eyes open to slits. It'll be a while before we know for sure what color of eyes he has, but I hope they're Brie's eyes. I hope he takes after her in every way. I feel on the verge of tears all of the sudden. I hate that they're separated, that she didn't even have a chance to hold him.

"Cry," I command. "Clear your lungs. Let us hear you."

He gurgles a soft cry before it erupts, loud and clear as a bell, the same bells ringing through Moonrise to announce the birth of a new royal–the first of his generation.

A prince.

I could fall to my knees right now in thanks.

Eventually, I'm given a chair. A nurse unbuttons my shirt, pulling the fabric to the side before placing Kieran against my bare chest. I sit there with him, absently rocking, my eyes locked on the far side of the room. I'm not sure how long this goes on, but people filter in and out. Misty leaves then returns to check on me some time later, but doesn't say a word. Nurses move around us, checking Kieran, asking if I need anything, but my mind is on Brie, levels above us, alone without her mate and child.

"He'll stay here for a while," Kenna says. I don't remember her even coming into the room. Her voice is hazy and distant as she explains, "Until he gains a little bit of weight and his color gets better. A few weeks, at least. It could be less. It really just depends on him."

A shadow passes over me. I ignore it, still locked on the far wall as my mind wonders, but Ryatt smooths his hand over Kieran's head, his thumb brushes over the baby's cheek, then higher, over his ear, where he stops and drops his hand.

"What is that?" Ryatt asks, and Kenna moves to his side, officially breaking me from the trance I've been stuck in for well over an hour.

"What is what?" I mumble, having to clear my throat between the words.

Kieran winces when Ryatt smooths his thumb over his ear again, letting out a soft, breathy whine.

I look up at them—father and daughter… Great-Grandfather, and Grandmother of my son—and notice the lines of concern and confusion casting shadow's across their faces.

I look down at the baby and notice his pointed ears.

"What is that?" Ryatt asks again with unease wrapping through every syllable.

Kenna's at a loss for words for a moment before saying, "I've never seen that before."

"It's nothing," I tell them testily. "He's not deformed, if that's what you're getting at." I shift my position to try to ease the knot in my back. "It's uncommon, but some people in Emberfyll are born with it–" Ryatt grabs my ear, pinching along the faded, hairline scar on the back of my ears. I yank of his grasp, glaring up at him. "It's also common to have an infant's ears shaved down."

"What the fuck," Ryatt rasps, "Why–"

"I don't know. I never thought that deeply into it. I haven't thought about that custom until now."

But Ryatt looks at Kenna, and Kenna looks at me. "Do you have powers, Logan?"

"No," I answer without hesitation.

"Are you positive?" he asks.

"I'm sure. You had me tested as a child, Ryatt, if you care to remember. Now please, I need to focus on him, my son. My wife." I look at Kenna. "Is she all right?"

"She's going to come down soon. Cole wants her to rest for a bit, but she's–she's dying to meet him."

I'm still watching Ryatt's face, however, as he stares at me and my son. He looks uneasy and slightly confused, like he's remembering something but can't place it, can't find a way to make the memory fit.

He turns abruptly on his heel, asking a nurse if she's seen Misty.

I exhale, watching him go, feeling a ripple of unease pass through me before Kenna places her hand on my shoulder. "Happy birthday, Kieran," she whispers with tears in her eyes as she strokes her knuckle across his perfect cheek.

49

WHAT IS HE?

BRIE

"I can walk, really," I say with a hint of annoyance as Maeve wheels me in a wheelchair down the hallway.

"You just had a *person* exit your body rather violently," my sister quips, obviously enjoying herself at my expense. "I wish I'd seen it."

"I'm glad you weren't in the room," I reply, sniffling dryly as she takes a sharp corner, nearly tipping me over. "It wasn't a fun time."

"It didn't sound fun," she admits, laughing sharply. "You scared me to death!"

"You didn't have to linger outside the door, you know."

"Where else would I have been? You're my sister. You just gave me a nephew. Of course, I was going to be there."

She stops at a seldom used elevator and slams her fist against the button, tapping her foot.

"I can walk–"

"No, this will be faster."

"No one uses these elevators, Maeve. If we get stuck–"

"We're not going to get stuck," she grumbles, pressing the button repeatedly until the doors finally slide open. Then, she wheels me inside, flipping me around to face the doors again.

Kieran was born three hours ago, and I haven't seen his face in person. Mom and Misty took pictures of him and showed me, of course. I tried to mind-link with Logan, but I'm... spent. I couldn't shift right now if my life depended on it. Maeve, however, is buzzing with energy. She taps her foot like a nervous tick, and the moonstone amulet around her neck is brighter than I've ever seen it before, glowing under the pressure of her raging powers.

She was... terrified, wasn't she? When I was fighting for my life and Kieran's? She waited outside the door from what I was told, slumped against the wall or pacing until she left tracks on the carpet. She didn't leave that spot. She stayed there, and when Logan left, she raced in and didn't leave my side again.

The elevator opens to the first level of the palace. Maids run around, elated, stopping to bow and rush out their congratulations. Maeve smirks at each of them as she wheels me to the infirmary built on the back side of the castle, but when we get close to the doors, she asks, "How fast do you think this thing can go?"

"Don't you dare–" The words are stolen from my tongue by a yelp as she sprints, tearing down the hallways with me at her mercy in a wheelchair. "Maeve!"

But I'm... smiling. Tears of happiness slide free, and I don't try to stop them. It feels good to be home with my family. It feels right that Kieran was born here, surrounded by everyone I love, even if this wasn't part of the plan.

But my smile fades into something deeper, something I can't even begin to describe, when Maeve slows to a crawl and wheels me into the room where Kieran has to stay for a few weeks, at least, and I see Logan holding him, his eyes closed and head leaning back in a big armchair with Kieran resting against his chest.

Maeve wheels me beside him, squeezing my shoulder before planting a kiss on the top of my head, and leaves, closing the door behind her.

I'm not sure what to do or think. My hand shakes as I reach out to brush my fingertips over Kieran's skin, into his soft, light brown hair. He's so little and just… perfect. My son. *Our son.*

Logan stirs, grunting softly as he blinks into the bright warming light heating the room. He looks at me, slightly surprised to see me, but gives a sleepy smile that makes fresh tears blur my vision.

Then the dam breaks, and those tears slide free… for both of us.

With great care, he rises and places Kieran in his crib, then helps me into the chair he just exited. He drapes a blanket over my weak legs, tucking me in, but his chest heaves as he unbuttons the hospital gown Mom helped me change into before allowing Maeve to take me down to see my family.

Kieran wakes up as Logan places him on my chest. He looks up at me, blinking into brightness he's not used to.

"Oh, my darling," I whisper, my voice shaking. "Look at you. You're perfect. You were ready to be here, weren't you?"

"He didn't want to miss all the fun." Logan chuckles, kneeling next to my chair, his hand resting on Kieran's back, which makes the baby so much smaller than he actually is. He could fit in Logan's hand perfectly, I bet. Kieran's lower lip trembles before he closes his eyes again and nuzzles against my skin, his mouth suckling as he roots for my breast.

"He's going to be here for a while, they said," Logan says tearfully. "But he's okay. Just little."

I nod, holding back my tears as Logan's hand moves to rest in my lap. He presses his forehead against my cheek, wrapping his arms around us while still kneeling on the cold, hard tiles. And then, I think, he silently lets himself unravel. I lean my head against his, closing my eyes as the world fades away, leaving only the three of us. Safe, warm, and whole.

"I love you," he whispers. "Brie, you did so well."

"I love you, too," I echo, tearfully. "I love you so much."

Logan and I fall to pieces together, our bond pulled tight as we pour all of our love into our son—into the greatest gift we've ever been given.

❀

Aviva smiles down at Kieran as the sun sets over Moonrise. Family has been arriving the past several hours, eager to see me and meet the baby. Ryan and Logan are standing off to the side, and I can tell Ryan is proud even if he's trying to keep cool and composed. He keeps clapping Logan on the shoulder, his eyes brimming with tears as he glances at Aviva holding Kieran, and the sight is just... everything.

That rift between that side of the family has been mended, sewn together with strands of pure love, and it warms my heart to be able to see it in real time.

We were moved to a room outside of the infirmary, in one of the private apartments in the upper levels of the castle. Kieran has everything he needs here–nurses to keep watch over him. The warming lights. Special milk to supplement my breast milk, which hasn't come in yet. In the few hours after his birth, he's proven to be a strong kid already. He'll be fine. He'll be better than fine, I know it. A few years from now, when he's scaling the walls and scaring us to death, I'll think of this quiet time we had with him fondly, even if right now it feels like... everything went wrong.

I'm resting in an armchair picking at a plate of food when my grandpa arrives, looking worn but happy to see everyone gathered in one place after a long time apart.

Maeve shifts her weight in the chair beside mine, however, when Grandpa Ryatt goes to speak to Misty again, and the two of them turn to look at Logan and Kieran.

"What's wrong with Grandpa?" I ask quietly, ensuring I'm not overheard.

"He's been weird all day."

"I haven't seen Grandma in a while, either," I add, picking up my cup of tea and bringing it to my lips.

Maeve breathes. "That's because she's in Veiled Valley, fetching Arthur."

"Arthur?" I gasp. "Why?" I think of the tiny, ancient... *being*, who has been alive since what seems like the dawn of time, who haunts the library in Veiled Valley.

Maeve licks her lips. "Have you seen Kieran's ears? They're pointed. None of us have ever seen anything like that before."

"Some people in Emberfyll have them," I cut in. "Kieran is perfect–"

"I never said he wasn't, but Grandpa is uneasy about it, so Grandma went to fetch Arthur to run a few tests."

"They want to test Kieran for powers?"

"They want to test Kieran *and* Logan for powers," she corrects, swallowing hard. "Ryan and Aviva had him tested years ago as a child. It was inconclusive. But he never developed anything outside of being a wolf."

I have a sudden memory of the night the royal armada of KiloKilo attacked our ship. Logan's eyes... I thought it was just a trick of the mind, a reflection of the sunlight off the water, but his eyes had glowed. I'm sure of it.

"Does anyone in Emberfyll have powers?"

"There aren't many people left, remember? And no, not that I've seen or heard of. And Logan... Logan would have told me if he could do other things than just shift–"

"I don't think..." Maeve tapers off, biting her lip. She shakes her head. "They're just a different kind of wolf, that's all. Like Aviva and the tribes are different from you and the shifters in our family. That's all."

"Sure," I murmur under my breath, but unease prickles through my skin as Grandpa Ryatt approaches Logan and Ryan, dropping into what looks like an easy conversation.

I glance at my parents, who are talking with Sydney and Sarah, and wonder if anyone else is wondering why my son has pointed ears... because now I wonder why he does.

Maeve must have been watching my face, watching the questions bounce behind my eyes, because she leans in, saying, "Logan told Grandpa it was common for a baby's ears to be shaved down shortly after birth. Logan has very faint scars, I don't know if you've noticed."

"I haven't." I swallow the words, blinking as I try to come to terms with what she's describing. "I haven't noticed them at all. He never said anything, and we won't be doing that to Kieran. I refuse."

"It's all right, I know you wouldn't."

"Why would they do that?"

She sighs heavily, her shoulders going slack. "The only thing I can think of is… trying to hide that part of themselves and their children, whatever it is." We both look at Kieran, still tucked in Aviva's arms, at the same time.

"What is he?" I whisper to myself, then glance at my mate. "Logan has no idea, does he? That they're different somehow?"

"Logan doesn't care. He only cares about the two of you. Don't worry about it, Brie. You can refuse the testing."

I chew my lower lip as Maeve rises, mentioning something about getting some fresh air, and leaves me with my tangled thoughts.

It doesn't matter, does it?

In the end, we're all wolves.

Me, my mate, and our son.

My *Alpha King*, and our prince.

Aviva notices me staring at her and brings Kieran over. Sarah moves the food tray from my lap while Aviva rests the tiny bundle of blankets in my arms. The conversation around me fades as I hold my son, smoothing my fingertips over his face, his hair, and those perfect, pointed ears.

I barely register people leaving the room. I don't notice the time going by until Logan sits down beside me, smoothing his hand down my thigh.

I blink up at him, smiling faintly.

"You need to get some rest. I'll take him for a while."

"You need to rest, too."

"We have plenty of help here." He laughs. "Our whole family has made it sound like they're all staying for a while. It's a big reunion. Kieran won't know what it feels like to sleep outside of someone's arms, that's for sure."

"He's a lucky kid, isn't he?"

"He is."

We look down at our son, smiling through sighs of relief.

Weeks from now, when he's fit to travel, we'll return home to Emberfyll. We'll bring a prince back to the island where Logan is working tirelessly to rebuild his homeland, his pack. Alpha Alex and Luna Monica will have their first baby soon, a few months from now, and time will move on, always forward, and never back.

And Logan and I will rule together, as mates, as lovers and friends, while raising this child and all of our children that come after because I want more, and I know he does, too.

I got my Alpha, didn't I?

I smile at the silly thought, leaning my head against Logan's shoulder, and drift to sleep, utterly, and wholly *happy*.

5 0

YOU DON'T HAVE A CHOICE

THE GRAND BALCONY OVERLOOKING THE GLIMMERING CITY OF Moonrise spills soft light into the complex and lovely front garden. Beyond the tall, exterior castle walls, the city stretches under a blanket of stars, lights flickering in tune with my own heartbeat.

What a day it's been. I'm not sure how I feel. Relieved that Brie and Kieran are okay? Yes, I feel that. Happy to be an aunt? Of course. Anxious about the future and what it holds for my sister and her son?

I look down at my hands as they curl around the railing then sink into a nearby chair and hang my head.

Minutes creep by in silence. The entire family is going to be gathering here over the next couple of days to celebrate Brie, Logan, and Kieran, and his safe, but early, arrival into the world. Yet, I feel shockingly alone as I gaze out over the city and the lake, which reflects the stars above like a pool of diamonds.

There will come a time when… I'm alone here. I know Grandpa and Grandma mean to move back to Veiled Valley. That was always the plan. It was their first real home together. They raised my mother

385

there until this city—the city Grandma pulled from the lake using her powers—was ready to be lived in by all, not just the king and queen.

Veiled Valley is the ancestral home of Grandpa Ryatt's people—the Shadowsyngers, and I know it's been calling him back for many years now. They've ruled for over forty years… they deserve to rest, to just be Ella and Ryatt again, after all this time.

But that means the weight of the world they built will fall on my shoulders.

Brie told me once that I wasn't ready to be queen. It broke my heart at the time—sliced me into pieces, actually. I doubt I'll ever recover, but only because she was right.

I turned twenty a few days ago. It was a quiet birthday. For the past year, ever since Brie disappeared and the family dealt with the fallout of me using my powers to break a veil, KiloKilo taking that as an offensive move and promising war if anyone from the Allied Kingdoms ever came near their oceanic territory again, I've been keeping a low profile.

I stay in the castle. If I'm not here in Moonrise, I stay in the castle in Veiled Valley. I haven't been seen in public, at least, according to the news outlets, for a year, and I mean to keep it that way until my coronation.

Footsteps echo nearby, and I turn my head as Blake steps onto the balcony, his violet eyes shining in the starlight. He arches a brow as he comes to stand against the railing, looking down at the city below. "You missed dinner."

"I wasn't hungry," I murmur. "And since when do you show up for family dinners, anyway?"

"I just started to do so tonight," he says. "It wasn't as bad as I thought it would be."

"You act like you're allergic to our own family."

"Maybe. I should probably get that checked out. I'm sure Cole could refer me out to someone."

"Are you being… sarcastic?" I laugh, glancing at him.

He shrugs one shoulder, his eyes still downcast on the city below. I haven't seen Blake in months, not since Brie's elopement.

He kind of just disappeared after that, but through the family grapevine I've learned he's just a busy man. He's an engineer, like his father. He often goes to the northern kingdoms, Celestoria and Lunaria, for work, but... he's also staying out of the public eye–like me.

Yeah, it's smart. Now that Brie's married, and the queen of her own kingdom, the tabloids are betting on who will be next–Me, Blake, or Aris?

But it's not just the royal family who've been quiet lately.

"Is there any news on Hannibal Arachnis?"

He shakes his head, his eyes scanning the lake. "No."

"There haven't been any new assassinations, either. Not a single one in months. Do you think the Blade is dead?"

"The Blade?"

"That's what the news called the assassin. I'm assuming it's a him, not a her?"

"It's a man."

"How do you know?"

He shrugs again. "I may have used my powers to the family's benefit to try to find *him*, but that's about all I could see. Hannibal has powers, but no one is sure what he is exactly. A warlock? A wizard, like the royals in KiloKilo? Something else... like Gabriel of the Draven Coven, and the old kings of Eastonia, or, like Richard of the Arcane Umbra? Using stolen magic?" He licks his lips. "I can't see him. He has shields around himself, which has made it impossible for any warriors from any army to locate him and his lair. His assassin is the same."

"Could Hannibal be his own assassin?"

"No." He answers quickly, sharply, before dropping his voice with a sigh, "No, he's an old man from what we've been told by the cronies we've been able to catch and interrogate, but they're all under his spell. His assassin–Blade, or whatever you want to call him–is young. Healthy and active. A shifter, we believe."

"Well, there's millions of shifters between the Allied Kingdoms alone, so that narrows absolutely nothing down."

"Well," he mimics on a breath, "it doesn't matter anymore, seeing as there hasn't been another murder for almost a year."

"It matters to me. In two years' time, I'll ascend the throne, and therefore, this will be my problem, and I won't be wasting time."

He arches a brow. "What do you mean?"

"I mean… I've given it a lot of thought–how I want things to go when I begin my reign. KiloKilo will bend the knee to me or else," I say, holding up a finger, "I will break their veil and unleash hell on their capitol. Knowing what they did to that Alpha's mate Brie and Logan are so close with, I imagine they're hiding other atrocities behind that veil, and I'm not okay with it. I'll destroy them if I have to."

"Unprovoked?" he laughs, but I don't find anything funny about the situation.

"They provoked me the moment their messengers told my grandparents and your parents they'd invade Maatua again if they felt like it."

He smirks but still isn't looking at me.

I raise a second finger. "Secondly," I begin slowly, drawing out the word, "I'm over this Arachnis business. It's tiring and boring, and I have plans to bring him to slow, torturous justice by any means necessary. I'll sic every mystic on him and his people until they're found, taking them out one by one until he's the only one left, and he can no longer hide." I turn to my cousin. "Anyone in my way will meet a swift end; that's a promise."

He looks at me, stars dancing in his eyes. "You want people to fear you?"

"I have already accepted that I will not be loved." I bite out, the words sinking into my skin, the truth painting me like a tattoo, like a scar. "My reign will not be a merciful one. I will not be known for my kindness. I will be known as the first full-blooded Firestone Queen of the modern era, a Golden era for Eastonia, and I will ensure that, even if my name is written into the history books, naming me as ruthless, merciless, and bloody."

I slowly raise my third finger, holding his gaze without blinking,

"And thirdly," I say in a whisper, "you will be serving as my second, my Beta."

The corner of his mouth lifts into a disbelieving smirk, like he thinks I'm joking. "That's hilarious. I didn't realize you were so funny, Maeve. If this whole queen thing doesn't work out, you could be a comedian—"

"I'm serious, Blake."

He stares at me, his tongue sliding along his lower lip as he processes what I've just said to him—*demanded* of him.

"You're going to abdicate your place in line for the throne of Crescent Falls, giving your spot to Liam. Let him rule. He's a child of Crescent Falls. You are meant for more."

"You forget who you're talking to," he sneers, chuckling darkly.

"I haven't forgotten. I'm reminded every time I look at you and your mystical, all-seeing eyes that you are meant for Eastonia. Just like your mother. Just like what creepy little kids you'll produce in the future. You are *king* of the Mystics," I grind out, arching a brow.

"I am the royal prince of Crescent Falls above all else—"

"Wrong," I demand, crossing my legs and looking up at him.

His jaw clicks as he frowns at me. I can feel that he's on the verge of simply disappearing, going back to his darkened, unstimulating apartment high in the sky overlooking the city where he's never once felt like he belonged.

"You're lying to yourself if you think you're going to grow up to fill your father's shoes. You're delusional if you truly believe you'll marry some basic shifter and have children—heirs to that throne—boys who won't possess your same skillset. You're like me, Blake." I growl, rising slowly from my chair. "Look at the rest of your side of the family and tell me the powers passed from our great-grandmother aren't waning. You are the only one in that entire line, in our generation, who has power. Real, dangerous, power. Power that's only going to grow, not fade, in the next generation, like mine. I will birth Firestone females—women who will eventually outdo me in power. Aris has more Shadowsynger gifts than my grandfather and his father have combined."

His eyes narrow as I continue, "You are meant for more. You are meant for *here*. And you will be my second. I command it of you."

"I will not bend the knee to you, Maeve. You are not my queen–"

"I will be."

Silence settles heavy and thick between us. I silently dare him to challenge me, to try to prove me wrong, but he can't.

"You feel at ease here. It's why you spend so much time in Eastonia." I step toward him, pressing a finger over his heart. "You run from Crescent Falls at any chance you get, and it's not only because of Marianna–"

"Do not bring her into this."

"Serve me as Beta of Eastonia."

"No."

I step away from him and sit back in the chair, gracefully crossing my legs while inspecting my nails. "Then we will go to war against each other. You can't stand here and act like you haven't seen that in your visions because I know you have."

He pales but only slightly. I chuckle at the confirmation.

"See? We're either going to be the greatest rulers Eastonia has ever seen or enemies. You decide, Blake, which tangled path to take. A mundane life spent trying to control your powers to blend in, or a life here, being what you were always meant to be?"

He turns away, resting his elbows on the railing, and sighs.

I smirk, knowing I've won.

Well, that's a weight off my shoulders, another line to cross off the checklist of things I need to do before my coronation day.

"In the meantime," I breathe lazily, closing my eyes. "I want you to do something for me."

"What?"

"Find the assassin and kill him."

"What makes you think he's the bad guy here, Maeve?"

I open one eye. "What do you mean? He's a murder–"

"Every Alpha he killed had a seedy past. Secrets they thought would never live to see the light of day. Yet, in death, all of that information was anonymously released."

"Well, five Alphas are still missing as well–"

"And they are the good ones, with families who then decided to fade into obscurity. Is that not strange to you? That their Lunas and children disappeared from the public eye in the wake of their absence?"

"What are you saying?"

"I believe the assassin is… working to undermine the Spider."

"That's ridiculous. He wouldn't be able to do that by himself. He's only one man."

"How do you know he's only one man? What makes you think he's doing this alone?"

I stare at Blake, unsure what to make of his tone. "What do you know?"

"As much as you. Nothing. It's just a theory."

He turns back into the castle and disappears, leaving me reeling, and wondering, what our futures hold in more ways than one.

BONUS: TO CATCH A THIEF

Soren

Light creeps over the wet cobblestone in the inner city. Moonrise is washed in pale gold as the sun sets, the glowing orbs outside each home, each business, light the narrow, ancient streets as the sun's warmth fades beyond the mountains.

My boots squelch in the puddles left behind from an epic rainstorm that nearly flooded Old Moonrise, but this city is raised above the lake, safe from the high water.

In fact, the pebbled beaches that line the long, turquoise waters are completely submerged now, and rain still patters overhead, pinging off awnings and pouring out of gutters, further soaking the street I'm following uptown.

The castle rises into view, its windows shedding light across the more affluent neighborhoods, parks, and shops that surround its massive gates. Impenetrable gates, they say. It's said that it's impossible to get into the city-sized palace, and on an average day, I'd believe it.

But it's not an average day by any means, even with the storm still passing over the capital of all of Eastonia. Litter coats the street. Confetti in shades of crimson and gold hug the curb, piling into a mass of soggy paper as the rain tries to carry it away. Incense and the smell of food fill the street where a night market is raging, music cutting through the downpour.

An entire month of festivities have been ordered in honor of Princess Maeve. A month from now, this entire section of the city will be full of people clambering for a view of the wide balcony currently casting a shadow across my body while I edge across the street, my chin pressed to my chest in an attempt to shield my skin from the slicing rain.

I hope, for the royal family's sake, the weather is... fairer for the princess's coronation.

Yeah, a month from now, the people of Eastonia will have a new queen. A full-blooded *Firestone* queen.

They've only been waiting... three-thousand years or so.

My footsteps splash as I weave through the market. I side-step through the crowd, ignoring the vendors shouting about their wares. People try to reach out and grab my arms, the leather of my jacket, but my feet are steady and unwavering. I glide over the cobblestone, skirting the outer ring of the tall, white stone wall surrounding the castle grounds.

Wolves rush past me in warrior garb, bearing the royal crest on fabric over their backs. I keep moving, glancing over my shoulder while they disappear into the crowded market square. I take a single breath before tearing down the street, kicking up muck, my boots crashing through puddles of water littered with confetti.

I slide around a sharp corner, and the main gates to the castle rises above me, open to the public for the first time in... well, I don't know how long.

But warriors are everywhere, monitoring the crowd as they explore the royal garden. More music drifts through the hedges towering over the top of my head. Fairy lights dance, casting a twinkling, golden gleam over the white stone pavers leading to the impossibly steep staircase that climbs up to the front doors of the palace.

I look up at the massive fortress. I've never been this close to it before.

"Hey!" A hiss breaks over the music. "Psst! Soren!"

I blink, tearing my gaze away from the two-story high doors inlaid with spiraling stained glass, and turn to the voice as a hand breaches the darkness, pulling me swiftly into the cover of a small outbuilding, a shed, or something of the like.

"You're late!" Beckett snarls, his black hair swept back and fixed in place by thick, sticky hair gel that smells like a spicy–yet sweet–artificial vanilla.

I wrinkle my nose. He shuts us into the shed, hastily snatching a duffle bag off the dusty floor.

"Here, change–and quickly. You're going to be one of the last guests arriving, and that's a bad look, you'll have a target on your back already." He tosses me a jet-black tuxedo.

I shake my head when he tries to shove the white undershirt in my hand, reaching into the inner pocket of my jacket and handing him a sack of coins.

"The shirt I'm wearing is fine," I grumble, snatching the tux jacket and shrugging out of my wet clothes, changing quickly while he counts the coins. "Is that enough?"

"How'd you get all this?"

"You said you wouldn't ask questions."

His dark eyes meet mine, his tongue sweeping over his lower lip, his brow raised as I shrug into the tux jacket. "You sure about this?"

"You're not involved past this," I hiss, motioning to the tuxedo. I fish the invitation to the ball out of its pocket with a short sigh of relief. "Remember?"

He grinds his teeth for a moment. "You're really going to rob the royal family?"

"I am," I admit, meeting his gaze and smoothing the fabric, then brushing my hair out of my face. "Just not tonight. I need to get a feel of the place, find my ins and outs."

"This is probably the riskiest thing you've done so far."

"You don't know the half of the of," I murmur, bending to fetch the dress shoes out of the duffle bag. "Where's the mask?"

Beckett looks around in the dark before reaching for a black mask lying in the dust. He beats it against his thigh before handing it to me. I slip it on, sighing as my eyesight adjusts. It's simple—black silken fabric with eyeholes. It covers about a third of my face, but that's all. I pull my black gloves out of the pocket of my leather jacket before hanging it on a rake, which promptly falls to the ground with a clang under the rain-soaked weight of it.

"Get going," Beckett rushes out.

"We'll talk again soon," I assure him with a nod, but it's a lie.

I think he knows it, too, because he watches me slip on the gloves with a heavy sigh, his gaze locked on the silver bracelet clamped around my forearm, my skin scarred around it from years of wear.

I smooth my sleeve over the bracelet, giving him a quick nod before pulling open the door to the shed and scanning my surroundings.

The garden is still full of public onlookers and explorers getting a taste of the castle grounds for the first time, but I'm not here for the garden party. I'm not here for the masked ball taking place within the castle, either, but it's my in.

I jog up the steps, the invitation clamped in my left hand, and stop at the threshold of the doors where several guards are lingering in watch, checking a group's invitations before letting them pass.

A hand flies over my chest hard enough for my lungs to contract. "Invite only, wolf," the guard sneers. I thrust the invitation against his chest, arching a brow he can't see behind my mask.

He scans my face. "Identification?"

I reach into the tuxedo pocket with a silent prayer that's answered in the form of an identification booklet—a booklet full of lies.

According to its pages, I'm a merchant out of Tarsian with ties to the royals there, and in the Deadlands, where I do most of my trade... legally. Which couldn't be further from the truth.

The man who put this together for me did a fine job because the guard steps aside, handing me back my things, which I tuck away as I stride past him with a smirk.

The doors open wide, revealing a sweeping grand foyer and a twin staircase made of the purest white marble that spirals five stories above my head. Two more stories overlook the foyer, their balconies shadowed against the domed, crystal ceiling. Murals are brushed down every wall as I follow the crowd into the ballroom, which is teeming with people in their finest gowns, jewels, and masks.

Soft, ethereal music wafts through the air, carrying the scent of wine and whiskey. I side-step, moving into the depths of the crowd, until I see it.

See *her*, more like it.

Her gown of crimson illuminates her fair, milky skin. Her face is flawless, like she's been airbrushed after being sculpted by the gods of old–or the Goddess Herself.

Long, thick, dark brown hair falls in loose curls down her back, pinned half-up, half-down with clips glimmering with rubies and diamonds–also flawless.

Her neck is slender, like her shoulders. She's tall but appears dainty, especially as she mingles, occasionally stepping to the side to allow another person to join her conversation. She moves like every step is a rehearsed dance. But I know she's not weak. Her daintiness is a front, a cover for the beast that writhes beneath.

She's wearing a mask, but I'd know those eyes anywhere. I've seen them before–twice now–in person. The first time, she spilled boiling hot tea all over my stomach. The second, she'd been trying to hide herself in that grimy booth in that even grimier diner in Veiled Valley. Each time, those eyes gave her away. They're the purest blue-green, like polished sea-glass plucked from crystalline, sparkling sand on a far off beach.

Princess Maeve–soon to be Queen Maeve of Eastonia–turns her head ever so slightly, revealing the diadem resting on the top of her head, her hair woven through it to keep it place.

That's what I'm here for. I'm here for the diadem, the jewels on her fingers, on her wrists, and her neck.

Diamond earrings the size of one of my knuckles glisten on her earlobes. I want those, too.

And I'll take them, once I know how to get in, and out, of this Goddess forsaken castle without getting caught.

She's an interesting creature. I wouldn't consider her a person, by any means. I doubt any of the people in the room do, either. Most give her a wide berth, but some are... braver. Even those that flank her, leaning in cautiously to speak to their future queen, are careful not to get too close, careful not to touch her, lest she burst into flames.

I haven't seen her in…three years, at least. The diner was the last time, and even then, it had just been a glimpse, a familiar shadow out of the corner of my eye. Since then, she's removed herself from the public eye completely, holed away here in the castle. Only over the past few months leading up to the festival season in Moonrise has she been spotted again–a woman now–no longer the spindly, irresponsible, and hot-tempered teenage girl I remember.

I lift a glass of whiskey from the tray held out by a passing servant, pressing the chilled crystal rim to my lower lip, and inhale, watching her.

I should be... moving through the castle by now, internally mapping the maze of hallways and wings that space the length of what I'm sure is several miles, but I watch her instead, awe-struck and entirely uneasy as her gems catch the light of the grand chandelier hanging precariously over her head.

She turns to me abruptly, her hair swinging gracefully over her shoulder, sliding down her bare arm. Her eyes meet mine, and she tilts her chin ever-so-slightly in hello, like we know each other.

I raise my glass in greeting, a silent toast in her honor, and sip, keeping my eyes locked on hers.

She wants to remember who I am, I believe. That's why she's still staring at me, a look of slight confusion passing behind those beautiful eyes. She turns away, hesitating for a single second before dropping back into conversation with her group, and if she turned again, I wouldn't know it because my feet move, carrying me through the crowd, past the servants so busy keeping everyone's drinks full that they don't notice me slipping through a backdoor into the maze of servants' hallways that run parallel to the main thoroughfares used by the royals and their guests.

I have it on good authority that her personal quarters are on the fifth floor, where two towers split the sky into halves. I also know that the royal vault is a myth, and they're so secure in their powers and highly trained guards that they keep their riches in jewelry boxes and dresser drawers.

At least, the princess does. *I hope she does.* I'll find out for sure in a few days' time.

I slip through another door before I'm spotted by a rush of servants carrying trays of appetizers. The hallway is narrow and dark, but I exit into a main hallway cloaked in shadow, the thick, velvet curtains drawn against the market and festival just beyond the gardens.

Mirrors line the walls. I pass them like a shadow, catching a glimpse of my all black tux, my chestnut brown hair starting to dry in curls around my ears, and a flash of my eyes when I pass a single lit sconce.

I pull my mask down, trying to shadow the colors that are my dead giveaway for anyone who thinks I'm even remotely familiar. My left eye is… so icy blue it's nearly white. The other, well, it's like the Goddess couldn't make up Her mind and made it half brown, half steel gray.

I'm nearly to the far doors on the very end of the long hallway where I know a staircase leads to the private apartments and rooms used by the royal family when a sharp sting erupts through my arm, flaring out from the bracelet fixed against my skin.

I brace a fist against the wall and double over as my skin burns, bubbling and blistering.

I can't take it anymore. This pain. This debt I've spent my entire adult life trying to pay.

The pain rings out again, loud and sharp, until I'm forced against the wall, sliding down, breathless.

It's a summons. The same summons I've been ignoring for a year. The summons that come with a promise of death I can't continue to outrun.

I suck in a shuddering breath, covering the heated silver band with my gloved hand, waiting for the pain to subside.

A flash of white steals my attention. I turn my head as a small, fluffy white cat pads into view, a pink collar fixed around its neck with a shimmering moonstone hanging from it.

"Go away," I hiss. "I'm allergic."

The cat sits down several feet away and begins licking its paw, its snubbed face cast in the shadow of the amber light spilling from the single sconce. It eyes me wearily, purring softly as I rise on unsteady legs.

Blood trickles down my arm and into the glove.

I turn to the doors–the doors granting me an escape from a life of servitude, and sigh, which turns to a violent sneeze everyone in the near vicinity will hear, completely blowing my cover. I glare at the cat, stepping past it, making my way back to the party, then out into the night.

I'll have to do this job blind.

I've had to do worse, I suppose.

Hopefully, Princess Maeve is still that oblivious royal she used to be when I first set my eyes on her all those years ago because she's my ticket out of the grave I've been trying to dig myself out of since childhood.

"I'll be back," I whisper into the night as the festival swallows me whole.

Thank you for reading! Book 14 is now available. Find *Abducted by the Alpha here.*

ALSO BY BELLA MOONDRAGON

The Alpha King's Breeder series:

Bought by the Alpha: The Alpha King's Breeder Book 1

Loved by the Alpha: The Alpha King's Breeder Book 2

Lost by the Alpha: The Alpha King's Breeder Book 3

Luna of the Alpha: The Alpha King's Breeder Book 4

Legacy of the Alpha: The Alpha Kings's Breeder Book 5

Daughter of the Alpha: The Alpha King's Breeder Book 6

Descendants of the Alpha: The Alpha King's Breeder Book 7

Shadow of the Alpha: The Alpha King's Breeder Book 8

Son of the Alpha: The Alpha King's Breeder Book 9

Spare of the Alpha: The Alpha King's Breeder Book 10

Claimed by the Alpha: The Alpha King's Breeder Book 11

Atonement for the Alpha King: The Alpha King's Breeder Book 12

Rejected by the Alpha: The Alpha King's Breeder Book 13

Abducted by the Alpha: The Alpha King's Breeder Book 14

Abandoned by the Alpha: The Alpha King's Breeder Book 15

Wolf Shifter Fairy Tale Retellings series

Beauty and the Alpha Beast

Sleeping Beasty

Tangling With the Alpha

The Luna's Vampire Prince series:

The Culling

The Kingdom

The Conquered

Pregnant With Four Alphas' Babies

Chosen As the Breeder

Mated to Four Alphas

Threats Against the Breeder

At War for the Breeder

The Stolen Breeder

Four Alphas, Four Babies

Becoming the Luna Queen

Descendants of the Breeder

Desired by the Devil series

Whispers of the Devil

Banter of the Devil

Murmurs of the Devil

The Mafia Kings series

Indebted to the Mafia King

<u>Loved by the Mafia King</u>

Claimed by the Mafia King

Secrets of the Mafia King

Burned by the Mafia King

Kidnapped by the Mafia King

Dark Stalker Romance series

Tempted by Sin

Fated to Sin

Secret Billionaires series

Finding the Secret Billionaire by Olivia Bhelle Kildare

Falling for My Secret Billionaire by Bella Moondragon

Driven by the Secret Billionaire by ID Johnson

Wolf Shifter Alpha Kings series

Ravens and Ruins

Sundrops and Shadows

Snowflakes and Sabotage

The Vampire King's Feeder series

Claiming the Alpha's Daughter

Loving the Alpha's Daughter

Finding the Alpha's Daughter

Bewitching the Alpha's Son (coming Sept 2025)

Writing as B. Moon

The Boy Who Died

Sign up for Bella's newsletter here.

Or get a free novella from The Alpha King's Breeder series when you sign up here:
The Beta and the Maid

Follow Bella on Facebook here.

Follow Bella on Bookbub here.